I0653829

The Teacher

An Irish Family in Boston in the 1950s

The Teacher: An Irish Family in Boston in the 1950s

by Robert Crotty
©2024 by William Crotty
All rights reserved.

This is a work of fiction. Names, characters, businesses, places, events and incidents are either the products of the author's imagination or used in a fictitious manner. Any resemblance to actual persons, living or dead, or actual events is purely coincidental.

Published by Piscataqua Press, an imprint of RiverRun Bookstore
142 Fleet St. | Portsmouth, NH | 03801
www.riverrunbookstore.com | info@riverrunbookstore.com

www.piscataquapress.com

ISBN: 978-1-939739-12-4

The Teacher

An Irish Family in Boston in the 1950s

A Novel

Robert Crotty

Introduction

Robert Crotty (1937-2011) was my brother.

We were part of a family of six children. I was the oldest, Bob next in line, then Ed, Frank, Walter, and Mary Regina. Bob and I (to my distress from the constant comparisons, generally unfavorable toward me) were in the same class from third grade up through high school. Bob skipped a grade in grammar school, much against my father's wishes. From that point on, he sat in front of me in every class in every school year until we graduated from high school in 1954.

Our father was a teacher and school administrator who came down with multiple sclerosis in his forties. In time he became incapacitated and bedridden but managed to survive, mostly by will power and a refusal to concede anything to his condition. He lived through a number of heart attacks over another twenty years. My natural mother (Bob's and mine), Rita Connaughton Crotty, died not quite a year after Bob was born. Our new mother (stepmother, although no one ever referred to her as that), Helen Morrison Crotty, had lived across the street from us. She was a teacher (we come from a family of teachers) before she married my father. She returned to teaching after his death. You could not say we were wealthy but we were part of a large and close Boston Irish extended family. Several of my father's sisters and brothers took Bob and I in to live with them for a period after our mother's death (Bob with my Aunt Winifred and our Uncle Walter, although they already had a large family; me with my aunts Kay and Esther and my Uncle Frank, living in my father's family home) until my father could come to grips with our changed circumstances. They were very kind and loving to us all.

In a family of strong individuals, by unanimous agreement Bob was the most talented, most adventuresome and, although there was competition for the title, most idiosyncratic of the bunch.

After high school, where Bob, a muscular, strong guy, had played football even though his vision demanded startlingly thick eyeglasses, we attended separate universities. Bob graduated from the University of New Hampshire, attracted there by its writing program, where he could continue to play football. He spent two years in the army reading novels on a mountaintop in Alaska while monitoring Soviet radio signals. He then attended both the University of Missouri at Columbia School of Journalism and the Iowa Writers Workshop, which made a particular impression on him. He was there during the Raymond Carver years.

Bob eventually ended up living much of his life in Maine, while I headed south for graduate school. I would occasionally bring my family to visit, though we found it hard to adjust to the cold weather and frigid temperatures, both inside and outside the family's home in Kennebunkport. I was a quiet, skinny kid who had played basketball, liked to plan and laid out a career path for myself that I pretty much followed in the years that followed.

Bob, consciously and subconsciously, like many of our generation, was a devotee of Jack Kerouac. He came to believe, although this could be said to be a core part of his personality in general, that a good writer had to experience everything he intended to write about. It was an impossible standard but did lead to an unusually varied and interesting life. Bob was reluctant to stay in any position for a great length of time. There was too much to experience. He was, over time, a university professor, dean of a college in Maine, director of the American Civil Liberties Union of Maine, an actor, an educational consultant, a newspaper reporter, a swimming pool lifeguard and so on. He delighted, perhaps even more so, in his stint as an eyeglass salesman in the optometry department of a Sears store in Maine; giving impressive and popular but factually questionable submarine tours in Portsmouth, New Hampshire while dressed in period costume; selling tickets to musical events (and strongly suggesting ways to improve operations) at the Music Hall in Portsmouth, New Hampshire; working briefly in a post office (too conventional I suspect); and driving his beat-up van around the country while giving motivational talks to salesmen. Bob would periodically drive over the front curb and land in our driveway in Evanston, Illinois, late at night, if he had been on assignment in the Midwest. I always marveled that he got across country and back without serious injury to himself or others. These various career junctures would arise suddenly. One day he was a postman, the next day the Communications Director in Jimmy Carter's Maine presidential campaign (he refused the opportunity to go to Washington). One interest did remain consistent over Bob's life - his writing.

In fact, writing defined his being as he saw it and provided his most prized outlet for his talents. Bob wrote short stories, some published, most not, stage plays and movie scripts (unpublished), newspaper articles and essays. He was not the most assiduous in following up on publishing opportunities. Most regrettably, outside of this novel he gave to me years ago, I have only a copy of a play he wrote and none of his other stories or writings. Most likely, these were lost or misplaced after his death.

The present novel was written on an old, what I would describe as a broken-down typewriter, missing a few keys and with other keys damaged. It was well past what most would consider its useful life. Bob always carried it with him. I came to think of it as part of his anatomy – a precursor to the smart phone people carry much more easily today.

It took some hard work and a sense of commitment by Chris Doucette in particular, a talented graphics specialist, to turn a faded and erratically typed copy of indeterminate age into digital form and a polished final product suitable for publication.

The novel itself was written over a self-imposed one year sabbatical in Greystones, on the southeastern coast of Ireland. I cannot vouch for the models of the characters in the book or the settings. Bob called on his own wonderful imagination, seemingly limitless in its creativity, and let his innate talents take over.

Robert Crotty

Bob married Mary Jane Burbank, whom he met in college. They both became real "Mainers" and raised three boys in a small house on a teacher's budget very near the Bush compound in Kennebunkport. Two talented people who eventually divorced but were tied to each other emotionally. They remained in close contact until her death. Mary Jane, primarily through her tenacity and commitment to their children, saw that their three sons, Sean, Liam and Brendan, attended Yale and other top-ranked schools. Mary Jane and Bob viewed their sons as their greatest treasure.

This novel is a story of an Irish family in Boston in the 1950s. Bob had a keen eye for appreciating the relationships and challenges they faced at that time. This he captures in his book through the eyes of "The Teacher."

The story is told a few decades after "Irish Need Not Apply" signs used to appear in stores.

The family is most pleased to see Bob's novel, which we believe to be a powerful testament to his talent, appearing in published form. My one regret is that it did not appear in print during Bob's lifetime. My hope, and Bob's, was that the novel would be the first of many exceptional works.

Tom Holbrook of Piscataqua Press expertly turned Bob's manuscript into published form.

For the present, and wherever you are, Bob (he was not a religious person so I have to feel heaven is out), I hope you like what my wife Mary and I have done and I am sorry you are not here to enjoy it.

Love,

Bill

Note: More information on Bob is available on his son Liam Crotty's website at: http://www.liamcrotty.com/index.php/obituary-robert-t-crotty-photography-from-his-funeral-somerville-massachusetts/

Vincent Crotty, whose painting appears on the cover of this book, is an internationally acclaimed artist with showings in the United States and Europe. Classically trained, he specializes in cityscapes and landscapes that evoke a sense of mood and presence rare among contemporary artists. http://vincentcrotty.com

1 | The Impostor

If I get up now and pull the buzzer, he'll stop before the bridge. But if I wait til the bridge and there's no traffic in front of him and the light's green, I'll be lucky to get off in time. Get a dirty look too. Why'd they put these stops so close together anyway. It's a railroad bridge. Maybe they make all the riffraff get off this side of the tracks. Royalty—Sir Sean included—live on the other side. Not exactly. Pa would like to think so—Sir Bernard. Better make it Ben. Christ, we're on the bridge. Duffel bag. Run.

Sean Connell pulled his duffel bag roughly down the two narrow steps and jumped from the bus to the curb, eager as always to please strangers such as this bus driver who pulled the lever and closed the door without realizing the kindness done him. The square had changed little. Only the names of the young Catholic hoods who leaned against the ice cream store had changed. As their predecessors, they too sneered charitable disciplined Christian hate, taught by nuns with rulers, at all who passed.

The radio store now sold fish, and the insurance company Italian grinders, meatballs and pizza. There was a Chinese restaurant where there had been only an American one. The movie theatre was still boarded up, ghost of its pre-television grandeur. To Sean it meant *The Yearling*, Donald Duck in South America with a crazy parrot (was it a parrot?), and warm, safe, dark and brave afternoons ending too soon in the loss of courage at the first corner.

Turgot's was still in the square. As Sean crossed the street, a patrol car with two officers pulled up in front. One officer stepped out and went directly into Turgot's while his partner drove the patrol car around the corner. Seconds later, as Sean reached the curb, the policeman came out of the dry goods store, carrying a small, light brown paper bag which could have held two sandwiches and a piece of cake or enough nourishment to sustain the boys in blue and the politicians who protected Turgot's bookie practice for another week.

Only Ma would go in there for socks. Only Ma would go in there to buy anything, always at the last minute. 'I've got to pick up a pair of black socks for your father. Come in with me, Sean.' I never knew why she was nervous until the raid just before election and the high school cafeteria, the whole cafeteria it seemed, laughing: 'Your family buys things there!' 'You're kidding.' 'You can't be serious.' 'It's always been a bookie joint.' 'You sure your mother wasn't backing a horse on the sly.' Old man Turgot likes Ma. Huffing and puffing up his crude manners and rusty salesmanship, he'd hurry around the counter to close a sale which had been decided before we set foot in the shop.

Pete has nothing against Turgot. 'If people want to gamble, they'll gamble. Prohibition didn't work because nobody wanted it to work. When people want to do something, really want to, they do it. The same guy who cries about how terrible it is, is taking his Share on the q.t. Turgot's no worse than a lot and better than some. Far as I know, he's never welshed yet.' Pete would say "yet." I wonder how he's doing.

Children had invaded the upper end of his long street, and the houses were more rundown than Sean remembered them being. There was a fat stump at the beginning of the street where a huge tree had once loomed paternally over the sidewalk. The lawns in front of the houses and between the sidewalk and the street did not show the careful grooming that had once made this part of the street the most attractive. Patches of brown earth showed through the sporadic coverings of September leaves.

Who'll Pa blame this on? The Jews? Doesn't figure. If the street's going to Hell, the Jews are gone. Further out. Concord. Lexington? Don't shoot till you see the color of their money. Who then? The Italians? Mrs. Flanagan's house there, no lawn left to speak of, with those two brats on the porch; must be almost, fifteen now, wise little bastards. It'd be nice to give 'em each a sweet rap in the teeth. Wahp! That's for a snowball five years ago that gave Margaret a headache for two days. Oh, did I forget you. Wahp! That's for anything you like, just because you're ugly. Pa can't blame the Italians for the Flanagan mess. I hope he doesn't cry, and start hugging me, blubbering on my neck. And then—try to kiss me. Oh Christ!

Since he had stepped on the train at New York until this moment, pausing beyond the Flanagans' green-and-white shingled house to shift his duffel bag back to his right shoulder for comfort, Sean Connell had thought only of the reception his father would give him and of his own best way of reacting to it. His parents knew he was coming home, he had written his mother, but they did not know the exact time. He withheld it, writing that he was not sure of the train schedule, so that his father would not go to great lengths and expense to prepare a homecoming.

Please God, I'll believe in you for an hour, a day, maybe even a week. I'll make the sign of the cross three times over my shoulder behind my back and between my legs. Just don't let him get sloppy and pour his tears and tripe all over my uniform. All right. It isn't tripe. He's my father. If I say I love him, because I'm supposed to, if I write him a postcard and say "Dear Daddy, I love you", will that do it? I doubt it. Besides, he'd suspect that. He knows, you can bet your Christly ass he knows, I've called him "Pa" since the first day, irrevocably since that first day, he tried to make me say "Dad."

You were horrible, *Dadd*-dee, when I left, wanting to make last-minute phone calls to the draft board, sure enough the honorable James Michael Curley himself. Then, seeing I wouldn't buy that, the tears, the take-care-of-yourselfs, the I'll-pray-for-yous. Holy Christ, God (you there?), if he did send up prayers, divert them. Use them for someone who believes in them. (If you're not there, forget it.)

'Don't be flip about God with *me!* Is that all you learned in that school, to be flip about God. Must have some fine teachers up there.'

'It's a college and they have professors. They're okay.'

'How the Hell would you know?'

'I'm your son. I ain't stupid, nohow. How could I help knowing about education, and educators especially, when I happen to be the son of the most prominent educator on this whole block, maybe inclusive of the next street over too.'

'You're going to get your face slapped. You know that, don't you? You're really begging for it.'

'Forget it. Try Ma. She's more your speed.'

'Why, you louse, you lousy son-of-a-bitch, you think I'm going to take—'

'I told you—forget it.'

'You low-life bastard. You'd actually hit your own father!'

'If he'd hit his very own son, yeah.'

Then the tears the next day, parading out the gulps and the sobs and the questions: aren't you going to miss us, you will write, you'll have the decency to call your aunt once in a while? Why couldn't I have said "No!" to all that mush? It would have saved the front door scene, the shaking hands and making me feel like an ass because I was finally doing what I had wanted to do for more than a year. I listened to your garbage that year before, Daddy, and believed some of it. There was still the doubt. Fathers know best—perhaps. Finish-your-education-crap and when I finished my freshman year, I was over you and your bullshit. College helped that. So why, why did you pull that at the door, the very last thing before I leave, leaning forward with that hangdog look, the sad clown with his turned-down mouth and his bucket of spilt son.

'What are you doing?'

'Kissing you goodbye. Is that all right with you?'

'On the lips?'

'You too big for that too? Too big for your britches, and too big for God, and now too big even to be kissed by your own father.'

'Not on the lips, Pa. Yeah, I'm too old for that.'

'What's wrong with kissing my own son on the lips, I'd like to know.'

'Oh, Pa.'

'Ahhow, Pa. Is that all you can say?'

Shaking the hand I extended as a poor replacement, shaking his head, too. Never heard of homosexuals or pederasty or anything? Hadn't he ever read the books I had in that last year; never dodge the games I had? Didn't his father ever tell him anything about the birds and the gay bees? Mine didn't.

I hope now, two years to think about it, if he ever thinks about anything more here, he won't be the same sloppy Joe, oozing emotions, spilling tears over the goddamn floor until you can't get a solid footing.

Nice day. Gonna get cold. He'll probably be over talking to Pete: Sean's coming home, ma boy, the boyo, etcetera, etcetera, ad boredomium. Pete must get tired hearing about all the fine Connell kids. You'd think he had no kids himself, the way Pa rambles on. That's not fair. I guess Pa listens to Pete once in a while. Just because I've never caught him at it—maybe he'll be sitting on the steps, can't see yet. Always sitting out on the front steps after bitching for months to get us to put up all the screens and awnings on the porch. No. A lie. He does read the paper on the porch, for about ten minutes, until he's restless again and has to get out from behind those screens and awnings. Talk to anyone who's willing to listen, or, drastic step but sometimes necessary, listen to anyone who's willing to talk. Sometimes, with Pete I guess, a fair amount of both. Politics. Jesus, as if either one of them had ever done *any*thing, even wear a button or pass out one leaflet.

Tonight he'll water the same spot of grass for an hour before putting the hose away for another week, the expert gardener, 'Never water the lawn in direct sunlight,' or else shake the railing and threaten it with a screwdriver long and loud enough to disturb Pete, until he can't stand to hear it anymore and has to come over and put a few screws in the rotten wood to hold it til next month. Unless he asks me to do it tonight. No, he wouldn't. Not right away.

Sean stopped at the corner of the street that intersected his. He was pleased to see two new stop signs where before there had been none, but then he felt slightly cheated, as if life were more dear now than when he had played on these streets. He had an impulse to jump over the metal stump of what had once been a police callbox, but he did not, recalling his ancient fear of ripping and splitting himself. He laid down his duffel bag to study the thin, sturdy tree by the corner house, a tree he remembered especially for the sense of accomplishment he felt the first time he climbed it to join the ranks of all its conquerors, to become one of the big kids. It had taken him long enough. How many times had he tried to shinny up that tree? Sean nicked up his duffel, gave the tree a friendly kick, and started on the last lap home.

Several houses away from his own, Sean realized something was wrong. There was not one awning on the front of the house, unless they had been taken down already, and that was hardly likely. Late November or early December, when the chill had long arrived, was Connell time for removing awnings and putting up storm windows. There was something else beside the lack of awnings. Grass, out over the curbing, leaning down to touch the street. The bushes looked like jungle specimens.

He must have really taken the summer off, or else he's building up a backlog of things to try and keep me at home. Silly bastard. How did Margaret get away with doing nothing? He's up there, sitting on the porch. Got his glasses on in public. Big step in the right direction. The steps! That's what it is. Cement steps, with a fat, solid railing. Must be easier to keep, but they're ugly. Quieter too, or maybe you're getting deaf, old man.

Your hair's whiter, old man, not just grey any more. Are you getting deaf and blind. Do I have to drop my duffel bag on your foot to make you look up. Oh, finally going to grant me a glance? Fold your paper and look up.

Wait a minute! Oh no, you're not my old man, not the old Irish fool I left behind me. My old man, my father, Ben Connell, wouldn't sit there, aiming those two gray stones at me. You're not Pa. Look away, old man. I know better. Who have you been fooling? You won't me.

My old man, the Irish Da I left at home before I went away to peacetime war, wouldn't sit there like a zombie, with nothing on his face, looking like he didn't know me or care to. My old man was young. Get up and out, old man. I don't know you. You're not he. I know my father. He would be on his feet now, off balance and clumsy and grabbing my hand, trying to hug me and kiss me like the rich fool that he is; he's not an old cold fool like you. Where is his foolishness, you? His warm, sloppy, wet, dog-tongued, sentimental foolishness? *You!* You couldn't drown a dry pea in tears. The world was in danger when he let loose.

Get up, old man, run fetch my father; tell him his son is home, home to do him honor, to unsay all said things, to ask forgiveness, to beg his boon, to say, 'Father, I love you,' and 'I am sorry.' Go old man and bring here my sire unto me. Bring me the man who lives and breathes as my sire; offend me not with your sickly satire of a man. I would have audience with my father! I would have—

"You're home."

Move, old man. Insult me not with your nothings. Run tell my father I have been abroad as a man these two years and would have him to understand that I understand more, having dealt in the realm of men, read in the minds of books, fought the fight against myself. Run, tell him so. His son is home a man.

"For how long this time? A week? A day? Or did you just drop by for a meal and five bucks?"

Old man, old, old man, I do wax wroth. Wilt move? Wilt summon m'lord or taste the lash of m'tongue? Wilt—

"Marion's in the kitchen. She'd like to see you. If you have time, that is."

2 | Ben's Boys

"If I should die before I wake, I pray the Lord my soul to take."

God listened.

"And if Joseph should die before he wakes, I pray the Lord his soul to take. And if Thomas should die before he wakes, I pray the Lord his soul to take."

God was amused at Ben Connell's irritation that "wakes" and "take" did not make a perfect rhyme.

"Take Tommy to Heaven first. Don't kill him first—I mean have him die first—don't, but no matter who dies first, he's youngest. He hasn't had a chance to do much. Take him to Heaven first. Then Joey. Then me. Me last."

God was highly amused.

Ben knew that God knew what Ben really meant. No matter how Ben phrased it, in what order or intensity of silent earnestness, Ben Connell was most afraid and pleading most for himself.

For some people, God was in the trees, the animals, the rocks, the earth, the leaves, the wind. Ben Connell had nothing to say to those people. He knew only that God was there, listening at the very end of each day, at the last moment before he gave himself warily up to sleep. A young man, 32, Ben saw himself in God's View as clinging shamelessly to the carcass of life.

Ben urged his mind to focus on the discussion, the problem, and to hurry, while they were alone. Unlike most Catholics, Ben found no Holy Trinity in his sphere—just the two, God and the other forces.

The others rose and shaved and ate with Ben Connell, coveted his children, informed God of Ben's every slip, waited for the infinitesimal pull on the infinite strings, the signal that Ben must ache again for his own eternal sake, that Ben needed a painful nudge forward onto the slippery bridge to Salvation.

"Another housekeeper is better than farming them out." God listened to Ben's small talk, smugly content in His Knowledge.

"I do love them. I'm doing my best for them. For God's Sakes, I'm doing all that a man can!"

God frowned at Ben's emotionalism.

"I know what you're thinking and I know what Catherine said and I know damn well what I promised and that is what I'm going to do."

Ben wasn't sure He had left until he felt familiar breaths chilling his bedroom. He clutched the bedclothes around his throat and shut his eyes quickly.

Ben Connell hit the alarm button, threw himself across the bed and down over its side, his hair brushing the floor, and rummaged for his socks. Blood filled his head as he tugged a reluctant black shoe by the laces out of its dusty resting place.

Wait a minute, bull. Not today, you don't have to escape today. None of your pleading-ranting: up-wash-dress, boys, eat your breakfast, I have to shave, get in the car, get in car, in car, Christ! Get in the car, say hello to Aunt Rose for me, say hello to Nana, say hello to Mrs. Tully, say hello, goodbye, pick you up at five-fifteen—not today. No need to jump the lights, hit the office by eight for thirty minutes of newspaper-coffee-doughnuts to try and start the day without that 'When, Daddy?' look in their eyes blocking vision, spoiling all views. Eyes on the sidewalk waving goodbye-hurryback' When Daddy?'

She's coming today, today, today; she's coming today, today, today, and I very well, may stay, may stay, may stay—iihnn bed. No, get up you lazy bastard, you loveless son of a bitch, poor Bennie Boo. Up up. Up up up up. She's coming today—hoo-ray!

Pleased with his silent song, Ben sat on the edge of the bed leisurely scratching his crotch and anticipating a gradual beginning to the new day. He dismissed his oft-broken rule of brushing his teeth and gargling before smoking, reached for a cigarette and matches on the wicker chair by the head of his bed. With the first smoke he tasted all the rotten night cigarettes of the past months, months spent roaming the rooms, shaking his head at ghosts and smothering the body of hurt his boys bequeathed him each night before they went to sleep. That last night, before he gave in for just one more housekeeper, had seemed the worst, perhaps because of the cumulative effect of the ones that came before it.

Why are they always good during supper? We talk, I guess. Or I listen. To them and the six o'clock news. Nana said Mrs. Tully can have us to visit Hitler next week. Mmm. Mrs. Tully said Aunt Rose can have Prime Minister Chamberlain next week. Oh. President Roosevelt today explained why Prime Minister Chamberlain said Mama can march on Aunt Rose if Mrs. Tully will mind Hitler. Yes.

Always play in their rooms with crayons and coloring books until I finish the dishes. Wipe my hands, dash for the living room, scan the headlines, page two, zip to the sports page, and then—the march. The out-of-seen, soft, terrifying tread of two unhappy, inquisitive boys. Mia bambinos. Joseph leading the inquisition party down the stairs, through the hall, company halt at my chair. His best professional smile.

"Daddy, have you met any nice ladies?"

Then Thomas, his turn, more to the point.

"Dahee, you always gonna be my Dahee and mumma?" "We'll see what happens."

"I doh wanna see." Thomas. "I want my mumma."

"Are you going to try and find us a new mother, Daddy?" Joe. "Aunt Rose said—"

"Now I've told you time and time again, Joseph, that I can't just find a mother for you, and I wish you wouldn't get Thomas all worked up. It isn't that easy."

Put down the newspaper. No use. Get Tommy's pajamas from the dining-room table, Joe's from the coffee table, get them on them, get them out of here.

"Why, Dahee?" Tommy.

"Because it isn't. First of all, Daddy remembers your mother too well to look for another one. But, if someday Daddy should meet a nice lady and she likes Daddy and he likes her, then maybe, someday, she would be your new mother."

"Who, Dahee?"

"THE NICE LADY! I don't know who, Thomas. Now, please, just put your arms up so I can get your jersey off."

Tommy, arms high, serious face to match his serious effort, little belly against my groin, little hands high and wide apart, surrendering to my commands.

"She make biig pilea jelly?"

He remembers that. Or did Joe tell him? A nice lady who made big piles of red and green or yellow gelatin for dessert. For her boys. Sweet Catherine. I'll remember.

Ben rose from the bed and pulled on his pants. For a few seconds, he listened at the door which separated his bedroom from his boys'. They were awake, playing quietly. Ben picked up the dirty black socks, the blue, black, and white shorts, and the faded white undershirts that littered the room, and stuffed them into the bottom drawer of his dresser.

"Joseph, Thomas. Time to get ready for breakfast. Pick up all your toys and put them in the toybox. Miss Hodgkins won't want to stay if she comes into a messy house."

Nice going, Ace. She hasn't even come yet and you're telling them she might not stay. Good psychology. Rose would call it lack of common sense. She's got enough of that to spare. 'Leave the boys with me, Ben, just till you think things out. It'll do you a world of good. Traipsing them back and forth from one house to the next—it's no good. You should be alone for a while, think things out, maybe get out a little and see...'

That's common sense, Rose. Keep it. I'd go right out of my Goddamn head. But I'd be alone and I'd be showing common sense. You're getting fat, Rose, fat in the head too. Or were you always that way? You mean well. Say it again, bull. She means well. 'Another housekeeper won't do it. She won't be good enough for your boys. If your own sister ... well, you just can't go on this way and you...just can't go on ... you just can't...'

But I will. I made a promise. All right, a promise to myself. I'll show Him and them and anyone who cares to look. Joe will be five next year and he'll go to kindergarten and Tommy, Tommy. Well –I'll do something. I'll get by. Something will happen. I'll make it. I'll best it. For you, Catherine, even if you said you didn't want me to, I know you didn't mean it. You really didn't. You were sick and weak and trying to be brave, and you were brave, but no woman means that kind of talk, no man either, that selfless kind of the-boys-need-a-mother bullshit. You weren't a bullshitter, Sweet Catherine, no.

Measuring oatmeal carefully into water that had been boiling for five minutes, Ben Connell asked himself if he had been too finicky about housekeepers. One had stolen a few odds and ends, not valuable, but full of memories for him. There had been a redhead, whose hair color and principal means of relaxation both came from a bottle, who was fond of adjusting straps and belts and soft, rustling garments around corners Ben was sure to walk. She had to go. Others had different things wrong with them, certain objectionable habits or idiosyncrasies which disturbed him greatly at the time, but which he could not remember as he put the cover on the oatmeal and turned the gas to high.

Miss Hodgkins in half an hour? Won't be finicky, will I? Got to feed them. What's taking me so long today? Coming unglued at the seams. Keep it up, lose my greater Boston oatmeal crown. There. Done. Just right of course. What's that?

Ben reluctantly investigated the noises coming from his back hall, opening the door as cautiously as if he were peeling a Band-Aid from a hairy portion of his arm. He had never heard a mouse scratch that loudly before and the thought that he might have a rat in his house terrified him. When he had inched the door open enough to slide his head through, he located the source of the noise and turned to see a little gray-haired woman peering through his back-door window, smiling doubtfully and moving her fingers at him in a poor imitation of a friendly wave. Ben opened the door.

"Oh, Mr. Connell, Mr. Connell? I'm not late, really late, am I?" she burst—"I mean," looking at Ben's bathrobe, "I'm not too early I hope, am I?"

"Yes, no, you're fine, Miss Hodgkins," Ben said. He retreated into the kitchen before her darting, pecking advance. "Come in, come on in. Take off your coat," he said as she laid her heavy black coat across a kitchen chair. "Have a cup of coffee?"

"I couldn't, I couldn't do that," Miss Hodgkins said.

"I just couldn't. I can't sit down, I thank you." She brushed back strands of gray hair and smiled coyly. "My mother always said, 'Never rest til you've earned it,'" Miss Hodgkins said, in a sweetened voice that suggested her mother was still alive and advising, and she, sweet young thing, still following those words of wisdom.

Ben studied Miss Hodgkins as intelligently as if she were an uncooked doughnut dropped on his plate. Her puffy arm was pushed through the loops of a bulging shopping bag. She struggled it into the pantry and onto the washing machine while unwinding a long tan scarf from her pale neck.

"Why didn't you come the front way?" Ben asked.

"I didn't know if you were expecting someone so I thought I'd better slip around back. Oh, gracious. You haven't had breakfast. Look here, let me finish up."

Ben started to protest, changed his mind and sat down. He said nothing when Miss Hodgkins turned the gas on under the cooked oatmeal. He was nurturing his resentment of women who treated men in the kitchen like stray pieces of overstuffed furniture.

"Just call me Thelma, Mr. Connell," she said, as Ben envisioned the oatmeal hardening to the bottom of the pan, 'catching on' his mother called it. "Cooking is women's work so you just set and have yourself a nice cup of coffee," as she began to pour the coffee without removing the insides as Ben always did to avoid grounds, "and let Thelma worry about the food." She poured his cup three-quarters full. Ben decided not to tell her immediately that he drank his coffee black and therefore liked his cup brimful. She was probably used to handling children who were always a danger to tip cups and glasses over. "Will the boys eat eggs?"

"I was just going to cook myself some fried eggs," Ben said. "The boys eat scrambled eggs once in a while, but they're having oatmeal this morning."

"No trouble for me to scramble a few eggs," Thelma said. She pulled a hairpin out of the bun perched on the back of her head, held it in her lips while she pushed the stray strands back into place, jabbed the pin into the bun, and sprinted for the pantry.

Ben picked up his coffee cup and reminded himself to look for hairs in the scrambled eggs. He watched Thelma plow through the pantry cupboard, a prime exhibit in the case against Ben Conner, housekeeper. She came out of the cupboard and the pantry with three plates and a huge, dusty, cracked, yellow mixing bowl, smiling as if she had just decoded a difficult message.

Ben counted the three eggs she broke into the bowl, wondering, 'What will the boys eat?' He watched Thelma pour not enough milk into the bowl and begin to beat what dawned on him was for both him and the boys.

"I think I brought some preserves," she said. Bouncing back into the pantry, she pulled out of her shopping bag an iron, a small bag of flour, an ironing cord, knitting and needles, jumbles of tan yarn, and a jar of purple jam covered with wax paper which was held fast to the rim by a fat elastic band. "Now, there," she said, holding the purple jam up to the light, ready to receive her blue ribbon. "Oh. A knife." As she rattled through the silverware drawer, Joseph and Thomas Connell came down the stairs and into the kitchen.

"Good morning, Boys!" Thelma said, rushing into the kitchen, knife in hand. "I'm Thelma Hodgkins and you must be Tommy. And I'll bet," she aimed the knife towards his Adam's apple, "you're Joey. Sit right down and I'll pour your porridge while it's hot."

"Good morning, Ma'am," Joseph said. He seated himself solemnly.

Tommy climbed up on his chair and tried to pull it forward to the table. His first words to Thelma were: "Push me in." As she gripped his chair, he looked up. "You gonna be my mumma?"

Ben leaned his sternest face forward, but neither his son nor Thelma paid him any attention.

"Let's say," she said, "Thelma is going to be your day mother for a while, Sweetheart."

"You make biig pilea jelly?" Tommy asked.

"He means gelatin," Joseph said.

"Oh, sure. Piles and piles!" Thelma said. "Orange and red and blue and green and any color you want, Dear. As long as you're a good boy and eat up all your food."

"They don't sell blue," Joseph said.

"Guhness sakes," Tommy said. He began spooning his oatmeal with great dramatic sweeps of his arm, checking often to see if his new Jelly-maker was watching the good boy he was being.

Ben felt a little guilty about his habitual breakfast feedings of Tommy and Joseph when he saw them eat most of their oatmeal and all of their scrambled eggs, but he also felt hungry after his meager third of the too-dry eggs had been consumed. He soothed his guilt and hunger by buttering and jamming a third piece of toast, and smiled a satisfied smile as Thelma poured for him another cup of ground coffee. After his meal, he lit a cigarette and decided it was nice to have a woman in the kitchen again, even if she moved a little too quickly to suit his early morning lethargy and had yet to learn his cooking secrets and dining preferences.

To reach the office by eight-thirty, Ben had to lean on the accelerator. It was important to Ben that he be on time, but he usually left himself only seconds leeway. After the first red light, all the traffic signals were green—his color—go. Green grow the 'lectric lilacs ho. Ben was sure it was another sign—all of them signs—of fresh new growth, a new beginning, a happier time for himself and his boys whom he had just left behind in the watchful care of Miss Thelma Hodgkins, shepherdess, Day Mother For A While for his day monsters, big daylight sweetheart to his little dear pains in the arses.

When he parked his green Plymouth outside the monstrous dirty red brick building that housed the finest educational brains in the city, Ben was half in one diagonal parking space and half in another. Leave it, he decided grandly. He was no more going to worry about petty incidentals, fuss over trivial details.

"Never again!" Ben exclaimed to the receptionist as he strode into the outer office. He stopped himself short as Marion Toomey waved appeasingly and pointed to her switchboard to indicate that she had an open jack and was placing a call. Ben nodded and marched purposefully past the cluttered desks of the secretarial pool toward his office, occasionally waving and nodding briskly to the girls who were checking their pale skins in hand mirrors, smoothing out nylons, pulling tissues from pocketbooks, and watching what their peers were doing as they prepared for another safe, fairly predictable day.

A few minutes later Ben returned, gingerly holding, as if it contained wet diapers, a paper bag which held a cardboard container of coffee and a plump jelly doughnut.

"I forgot," Marion said. "That's right. Your new housekeeper started today. Do you think," she asked, smiling the confident smile of a woman who thinks she knows a man because she knows one or two of his weaknesses, "it would ruin your day to have another cup of coffee and one or two bites of a Jelly doughnut?"

"Perhaps not. In fact, NO! Nothing's going to ruin my day. A new era is underway; a new leaf is being turned. I may be off coffee and doughnuts this early in the morning forever. Today I'm going to clean out my desk, answer every letter I owe and to hell with the rest of the almost-oweds. Onward and upward. Fight, fight, fight. Laugh and the world laughs at you; is that it. Ay?"

"Gee, Mr. Connell," she said, "I haven't seen you like this since—"

"What!"

"—for an awfully long time."

Ben searched his hot brain for something cool and crisp to say to pay this female back. Nothing came so he marched back to his office, slammed the door, and threw into the wastebasket the cup of coffee, which was followed shortly by the crumpled-up paper bag. He placed the jelly doughnut on his desk on top of the morning newspaper.

An awfully long time, Ben thought as he paced determinedly about the room. An—awful—long—time. He slowed down, paused, stopped to stare out of his office window at dirt-blackened red brick opposite. Forget for a second and some Goddamn sob sister pokes it down your throat. You poor man, all alone without a wife to screw. You poor unfortunate widower.

You assholes, I'm alive! She's 'poor unfortunately' dead. Bury your own dead. Leave mine to me. No resurrections for ogling and patting and comforting, please. I've dug her up but she won't breathe anymore. The flowers by her bedside were more like her but not strong enough; so many bunched together they cancelled out each other's lovely singularity. One a day would have lasted a year, but that wouldn't have been practical.

For the first of many times, standing at his wife's bedside, Ben Connell explored his religious beliefs. Until then, he had thought infrequently and vaguely of Heaven. It was a place to go, unless you were a really rotten son-of-a-bitch, directly or shortly after you were through living out your time on earth.

Hell didn't really worry Ben. He thought himself easily good enough to escape its fires; but even Hell seemed better than Limbo. At least attention was paid. Warm enough for you, Friend? The thought of little babies, floating around in the unlimited, undefined spaces of Limbo, because they hadn't had water and words sprinkled on them in time, frightened Ben. He had to dismiss Limbo to believe in his Catholic faith; so he did.

Purgatory was the place that really interested him. Though he never admitted it out loud, and tried to exorcise it from his mind, the thought that Purgatory sounded much livelier than Heaven often occurred to Ben. Once you make it there, he reasoned easily, you know you're going to the top eventually. Pick up some gossip, find out how the other half lives, then ride a few prayers and penances and special graces coming up from those you leave behind, ride them up and you're home free. Unconsciously, Ben aimed for Purgatory rather than Heaven. If goodness emanated from him too long a time, he felt a definite debt to himself to get drunk, cut loose, and counterbalance his fund of credits with a few debits. He was good enough, but not too good.

Ben tipped his hat when driving by a church and knelt upright at late Sunday mass until his back felt like a stiffly starched shirt. Only then did he allow his bottom to sink onto the crowded pew with those other bounteous ones of late, but religious, risers. No meat on Fridays was fine with Ben. Fish was good for you; protein was brain food; he did not eat enough. Fast days and days of holy obligation, Ash Wednesday with its charcoal smudge worn proudly on the forehead, all appealed to him as breaks in the year's routine. They were something to remember, to become irritated about when forgotten until the last possible moment, to rush to fulfill the requirements of, and to congratulate oneself about for having such remarkable days in a year too full of calendar numbers exceptionally the same.

The real, the intimate rite of the Catholic religion for Ben Connell was confession. It made him think while offering him a connection with the Almighty. Kneeling in preparatory prayer near the confession box, viewing what he had done to hurt God since the last time, gathering and adding his sins, he was surprised to find always pleasant memories mixed in, words and thoughts and nuances of feelings he might have forgotten if he had not passed them again in his silent search for sin.

If he was honest with God through his emissary the priest, Ben felt newborn holy coming out of the confessional. Ben's penance was always five Our Fathers, five Hail Marys, and five Glory Bes if he went to his usual confessor, Monsignor Conley, the elderly pastor who assigned penances which alleviated his fear that one busy Saturday the church would be chock full of praying, ranting penitents, crowding and spilling over into his quiet, dark confessional.

As he stood by Catherine's bed, the whole concept of religion changed for Ben Connell. He considered, for the first time, a jealous

God, a God who wanted Ben's wife beside him; a scheming God, Who arranged it so that, as people said, "The best die young;" an unfair God. Catherine's eyes had closed. She fell asleep. Ben was startled by a black glove laid on his forearm.

"I know what you're thinking, Ben, and I feel the same," his sister Rose said as she wondered what she could fix as a special supper treat for her husband who had taken time off from the office to drive her and her brother to the hospital. "We should go now. They're all gone. No one's left but you and me. Donald's waiting in the car. And he does have work to do."

In his worst depression after his wife's death, caught in his most intricate self-spun webs, he found temporary relief in the simple Catholic faith of his mother. Revered by all her children, a woman whose only use of the word "troubles" referred to the Irish fight for independence and the civil war that followed, Mary Connell had secretly hoped that her son Ben, third of eight children—quiet, amiable, intelligent Ben—would become a priest.

After his wife's death Ben, always an unquestioning, devout Catholic, came too often to visit his mother, dumping his children in the kitchen to play and, following her from room to room, impatient to hear and savor and perhaps swallow whole words and phrases that she had never before considered special.

"God works in mysterious ways," Mary Connell said in a high, nervous voice, holding back an impulse to shout at her son to stop hanging on her every word. "Every act of God carries its own message." She said only what she had always said, words that carried her through from day to day as she awaited her reward, but to Ben the words were a positive force, a gong ringing through a sea of shifting, tinkling, dying sounds.

If God wasn't guilty, who was? Ben took his mother's words whole and tore at any instance that might pin down his part in the death of the woman he loved. He did love her, he decided; there was no reason for guilt there. Yes, he had been a good husband, perhaps better than most. Was that pride? No, only the truth. Had he been a good father?

A good father? A father?

Mulling that question over every night for two weeks in his parlor led Ben to pronounce himself guilty—in the presence of the oriental rug, the picture of Virgin and child, the comfortable stuffed chairs, and his walnut escritoire, and his old law books—guilty of neglecting his children. What did he really know about his boys: the foods they liked, things they were learning, children they played with in the neighborhood, the dates of their birthdays? Practically alone, Catherine had brought the boys up. She had tried to tell him these things, details she felt he wanted to know, never realizing that he was studying the contour of her mouth or breast as she talked; he was intent and absorbed in his role as lover and not interested in any other. She was the teacher, the disciplinarian, the judge of what was best and worst for the boys.

When the mood struck, he had been the playful teddy bear. As much to win her approval as to please the boys, he hid behind doors while they routed him out riotously, threw and kicked a red beachball in the tall grass and weeds of the backyard, lost himself easily in a boisterous commitment to movement, action, simple fun. A half hour, though, was his limit. He would withdraw over the boys' protests and then avoid his children as best he could. He could switch back to the track of his adult world and ignore, even strongly resent, the two clamoring boys who hated to lose their large, delightful playmate.

God, in His Infinite Wisdom, had devised this punishment, had taken away Ben's stanchion, the woman who was both mother and father substitute for the boys, and left him with the dreary realities of child rearing. That night, before sleep, in the first of their bedside visits, Ben admitted his guilt to God.

"Help me," he asked. "I'll do my best to be a good father from now on."

Pacing his office, grabbing and wolfing the doughnut Marion Toomey had bought him, and wishing he had not thrown the coffee away even though now it would be ice cold, Ben Connell asked himself if he had done his best. He became aware of a light noise at the door.

"Mr. Connell," Marion said in a soft, imploring voice. She opened the door, but made no move to come into Ben's office. "I knocked. I was wondering if you had any letters you might want me to type and send out this morning?"

Shuttling two young boys around to different friends' and relatives' houses each week was not being a good father, Ben decided. He would not do it again. Not if it was humanly possible to avoid. He would hold on to Miss Hodgkins —Thelma.

"You have that meeting at eleven," Marion said. "Lucille will watch the switchboard if you want me to take dictation?"

"No," Ben said. "Thank Lucille for me but, on second thought, I think I'll let the letters go until this afternoon. I'm working on a problem right now."

"Can I help?" Marion asked. "It gets awfully dull in the summer sitting by that switchboard. I'd as soon be doing something."

"No thank you," Ben said. You've been wonderful. Thanks." I've got to hold on to Thelma.

"Well, back to the plugs," Marion said. "I guess I can stand it for a few more months. I'm finishing up my courses this summer for my master's. I'll be teaching again this fall."

"Yes, I'm sure you will," Ben said. "You'll do a fine plug." Got to.

After a pause, Marion asked: "Did I tell you it's definite? I'm going to Europe for three weeks at the end of the summer."

"No," Ben said. "Have a nice trip."

Marion stared at Ben for a few seconds, then glanced at the doughnut crumbs on his blue tie, the still-folded newspaper on his desk and the coffee splashed about his wastebasket before backing out of the room and closing the door.

Must have said something, the way she looked at me. Hope I didn't hurt her feelings. Been damn decent, doing letters and getting coffee, the paper, doughnuts. Maybe that's it. The coffee. Everybody's been so damn decent and I haven't. Christ!

Ben felt huge debts of kindness burying him. How could he repay them, Rose and his mother especially, but all of them, the friends and neighbors who had gone out of their way to help him? Listening in those first desperate months after Catherine's death when he phoned at eleven p.m. and talked so fast no one had a chance to answer. None of them had the answer, but they listened. If he tried all his life, he could not pile up enough kindnesses to equal those mounted on him.

But I'll try. I will try. Things will be different now.

Ben snapped his fingers and reached for the telephone. When Marion answered, he asked for an outside line and dialed his home. He had told Thelma he would call to see how things were going. He had almost forgotten.

"They're darling boys, Mr. Connell," Thelma said. "Sweet as apple cider. I'm just tidying up the pantry a bit and then I'll fix an early lunch. After that, I'll put them up for a nap."

"They haven't been taking—too many naps lately," Ben said. "In fact, Thelma, I guess you could say they've been getting away with murder."

"Don't you worry now," she said. "I've handled enough young boys in my time. They won't give me any trouble. Do you like baked potatoes, Sir?"

"Yeah, I love them, but I don't expect you to cook. Surely you've got enough—"

"Oh, I love to cook," Thelma said, "and I couldn't have you coming home to a cold kitchen. I'll just put a few potatoes and a little piece of meat in the oven and an odd vegetable..."

Shot from his depression, Ben rushed from his office to tell the first person he met that he was going to make it. The other offices were empty so he headed for the secretarial pool. Joe and Tommy could go half days to nursery school. Thelma would be growing old, but she could work half days. He could get the boys off to school. She could come around eleven-thirty to fix lunch. With her help, he was going to make it.

There would be no pressure to find a "nice lady." He could make it up to the boys for all the times he had neglected them. With Thelma to do housework and cooking, he would have the time and energy for trips to the zoo, rides to the ocean, visits to the circus and the park and the playground, and walks, long walks, just the three of them, Ben Connell and his boys, Joe and Tommy.

One of the secretaries, an older girl named Pauline whose idea of sexiness was to let her slip show until a male approached and then tug at her drab skirt girlishly, was trying to cram a stuffed folder into an overflowing file cabinet. Two of the other girls were draining the water cooler. The rest of the secretaries were busy typing and licking envelopes and counting petty cash and daintily blowing noses. Marion, at the switchboard, was the only one available at the moment to hear his wondrous news.

"Marion!" Ben yelled from thirty yards away, causing typewriters to stop clacking and heads to swivel. "I'm in love."

Marion swirled around on her wooden stool and took off her earphones. "Ohh! Congratulations."

"With a woman," Ben said, "who's sixty years old if she's a day and ugly as burnt toast, with my new housekeeper, that demure darling, Miss Thelma Hodgkins."

"You like her?" Marion asked, straining to join in the fun without saying anything upsetting as she had done earlier.

"Like her?" Ben thought of the queer little woman who was spilling motherliness into his empty house. "No. I'm in love with her." In a deep bass voice, occasionally on key through no control of his own, Ben sang:

"I'm in love with a girl named Thelma, Thelma, Thel-uh-ma.

I'm in love with a girl named Thelma,

And I think she's in love with meeeeee.

"Like her? Marion. Your powers of understatement amaze me. She comes this morning in time to cook breakfast," Ben said, aware that he was coloring the truth a little but unwilling to qualify, "and tonight when I get home, she tells me just now, supper-will-be-in-the-oven. And she's going to iron my shirts. She'll probably go ahead and iron everything: the drapes, the curtains, my socks, and the linoleum on the kitchen floor. Then she'll get out her trusty screwdriver and fix the freezer compartment in the icebox and then wash the stove and wring it out to dry. And, she had the audacity to claim that my two darling monsters are going to tippytoe into dreamland for an afternoon nap. Do you think—could you let me use the switchboard a second?"

Ben reached over and plugged a jack into his office connection, twirled the dial and took the earphones from Marion.

"Is it you, Thelma darling? I forgot to tell you I love you. Yes, 1-o-v-e. If you iron my shirts and fry my eggs, we'll live happily ever after. Run away together? Well, Dear, as long as you don't mind the boys tagging along. Oh there'll be plenty of time for that sort of stuff..."

Ben continued his imaginary conversation long after he ceased to think it amusing. He found himself lingering, perhaps loitering, near Marion long after his watch had told him it was time to get ready for his masters' meeting. He could wrap it up early, postpone his correspondence, and take the boys to the zoo.

The front door was locked when Ben pushed against it.

I'll have to tell her it isn't necessary, a good neighborhood, thank God. Where did I put the key? Shhh, Quiet, Hoss. The boys are probably taking a nap.

Ben walked softly into the empty kitchen, turned on the gas under the coffee pot, after lifting it to see if any was left, and lit a cigarette. After a few minutes and no sign of Thelma, he drank the last of his coffee and tiptoed up the stairs. Near the second floor landing, he stopped to listen to the squeak of the rocking chair coming from the boys' bedroom. It sounded threatening in the silence filling the rest of the house.

The boys' door was ajar. Through the opening Ben saw Thelma rocking slowly, a few inches back and forth, and knitting. Her diamond-patterned black-and-green ironing cord hung over the maple arm of the rocker; its sprocket nudged Tommy's bed every time she rocked forward. Ben signaled, shaking his hands and pursing his lips, for her to stop before she woke Tommy up. He stopped signaling when he saw a slight movement from Tommy's bed, a flick of an eyelash directed to the other twin bed where Joe was.

He's awake. And Joseph must be too if Tommy's trying to get his attention. The little devils. Poor Thelma thinks she has to sit there and knit. She can't get a thing done, what with watching those two. I'd better tell her it isn't necessary. If they sleep, fine. If not—

Ben moved to the bedroom door, peering through the opening and waving his hand slowly to catch Thelma's attention. He didn't want to get the boy's up if she didn't think it wise, but Tommy saw his father, pushed the bedclothes off, jumped up and shouted: "Dahee."

Thelma's knitting was on the floor and she was on her feet. "You know the rules," she said. The ironing cord flashed, striking Tommy on the shins. "I told you the rules. Not a peep out of you until I say so. Your daddy won't be home until tonight. Lie down now or the bad cord will hurt you again."

Tommy screamed when the cord struck. Then tears of disbelief mingled with those of pain. He never took his eyes from his father as he sank down and crawled slowly under the bedclothes. His voice was choked and the sound caught and gagged in his throat, but he managed to whimper: "Dahee."

"Are you deliberately defying me?" Thelma asked. "You know what Joseph got for that. Do you want another taste of the cord."

Ben watched, flinched painfully when Tommy was struck, and cried out silently.

No, no. No, Thelma, Miss Hodgkins. Don't. I can't have you hit them. No nap. It's all right. Don't hit them. No. No. They've had enough. No.

Finally, the word broke out.

"No!"

"Oh my sweet Jesus!" Thelma's eyes were wide and white and terror-stricken when she turned. "Oh Mr. Connell, I thought it was the devil himself. Oh, you startled me." She fell into the rocker and put her hand to her heart. "My good God, what a start you gave me. My old heart can't stand such a strain."

Ben walked to Tommy's bed and picked up his son. Tommy's body was convulsing in sobs, and his heart racing. He buried his tears in his father's neck. Joe leaned out of bed and threw his shoulder into the back of his father's knee, and wrapped his arms around his father's legs. From the impact, Ben nearly pitched forward onto Tommy's bed.

Thelma was on her feet again.

"Now, boys, this is naptime," she said. "The way you're acting, a person would think I—Mr. Connell, I ask you, is this for the boys' own good? You comin' in here, scarin' me half out of my wits and getting the boys all upset just when I had them calmed down? Is it?"

"She told us," Joe said, "that she'd come back at night with the bad cord if we told you she strapped us, Daddy."

"I'm just looking out for the boys' own good," Thelma said. "Give 'em an inch and they'll run a mile. I know."

Ben asked: "How do you know—Miss Hodgkins?"

As Ben put Tommy down and bent to pick up the ironing cord from the floor, Thelma backed away, feeling behind her for the doorway. Ben folded the cord and thrust it into her hand.

For the next two hours, Ben played passionately with his boys, building garages and bridges of wooden blocks, moving tons of earth with tiny metal bulldozers, hiding from, and seeking, his slightly hysterical sons until he lost his breath and interest, and begged off.

"Un more time, Dahee," Tommy pleaded.

"I'll be 'it'" Joe offered.

"No, no, that's it," Ben said. "I have a lot of thinking to do and then it'll be time to start getting supper. When it's almost ready. I'll call you and you can help me set the table.

"No!" Tommy said. "I don wan you go." A sullen pout on his face, he held Ben's pant leg with his little hand. "NO!"

"Let go, Tommy," Ben said, fighting the panicky feeling that he was trapped. He could not move without knocking his son down. "You let go right now or I'll give you a good crack."

Joe pulled Tommy away and gently steered him into their bedroom.

"Daddy," Joe said, "doesn't want us with him now, Tommy."

Ben walked down the stairs slowly, heavily. His hot blood and dark mood, unreleased, seemed to cram his head. He knew he had to call

Rose and see if she could take the boys in the morning. He was more concerned with the tough session he faced that night. He gathered his points.

"I couldn't let her stay if she was going to beat them, could I?"

God would probably be doubtful.

"All right, I get mad and maybe I whack them once in a while, but that's different—I'm their father. I know. I know. You're their Father too, but I have to raise them right now. Something will work out."

God would be offended by Ben's presumptuousness.

"You want me to leave the boys with Rose and circulate? If that's enough for you, I'll do it. But I'm not looking for a wife."

God would listen patiently.

"Listen! I know what You're thinking and I know what Catherine said she wanted me to do and I know what Rose thinks I should do—AND—I know what I promised, and that is what I'm going to do—if it's humanly possible."

God, Ben was afraid, would be smugly content.

3 | Beneath God

Old man, old fool, is that why you set here, why you've been sitting here for four hours, knowing he was coming—for the "pleasure" of insulting him? And why him, Old Hoss? To see if you could hurt him? Now you know he cares. So what? You didn't know before? But why does it matter, Bull, why matter so much with this one, this third son Sean?

Ben Connell had eased into his blue chair as slowly as he had come to ease into his mornings, looking this way and that cautiously, before committing himself to a descent. He sat there four hours, refusing lunch, before he heard his son's approach up the thick ugly cement steps. For four hours, he had gone over what he would say to Sean, the greeting he would use to welcome home his third oldest son, his second youngest child.

'Welcome back'?

'Hello, Son, it's good to have you home'? (Since when "Son"?)

'We've missed you, Sean.'

And that missing, that empty spot in the family life, incensed Ben because there had been times when Sean could have eased the emptiness, filled his spot, if only for a week or two.

'What do you mean, you're not coming home for Christmas?'

'I haven't been away that long. It'd really be a waste of leave time. I get paid when I get out for any leave time I don't use, and I could use the money for school.'

'Thanks. Thanks a lot. We wouldn't want you to waste your leave time.'

'That isn't what I meant, Pa!'

What did he mean? That I wasn't paying his way through college? I told him I couldn't. Damn him, he's gotten more than his share out of me. Who in Christ's name does he think he's kidding—" use the money for school." He'll blow it all in a week, if he's got any left now. Didn't come straight home anyway. Must have stopped in New York. For what?

When his son had finally come, no thought was left for a fond homecoming greeting. Instead, Ben Connell had built up all his grievances against soldier Sean—few letters, not one leave taken in two years, unanswered questions, offhand thanks to his Aunt Rose six months after a gift was sent—until Ben thought only of shocking this careless young men into a state which more closely approached one that he, Ben Connell, could accept as worthwhile in a son. It had done, and would do, no good to be emotional; he would have to maintain his distance and affect a neutrality which, as his anger at injustices committed by his son mounted, would be truly difficult.

He had sat down that morning thinking that he must not be too sentimental, must not embarrass this young soldier who was now a man and happened to be his son. But as the day wore, so did Ben Connell's sentimentality. Roughly he refused lunch when his wife offered it, because this was one sure way of letting her know that this day was different. Silently, but none the less self-righteously, Ben congratulated himself for picking out the most effective method of shocking his wife out of her domestic stupor. Since meals were never missed, she had protested.

'But you've got to eat to keen up your strength.' 'I do not intend to eat.'

She would not soon dismiss the matter from her mind. He had accomplished his goal; she would see, would realize that this day was to be different in many ways.

When his son had dropped his duffel bag in anticipation of a greeting, Ben Connell was hungry and angry and determined. "You're home." he said. And startled his son. When Sean had gone into the house to see his mother, Ben did not follow. He had shown Marion, taught Sean a lesson, proved himself capable of self-control; yet he felt as if he had lost a terribly important battle, or perhaps even a whole campaign. The very idea that he should have to fight one in his old age with this, his third son, angered him. What kind of society allowed a man's eldest and next eldest to stray and left a man to wrestle with the youngest male—the least respectful, least promising, least comforting, and most irritating.

Why, Bull, does it matter so much with this one? Happy now that you hurt him? Is that all that's left, to hurt him because he's here and Joseph and Tommy aren't? Where are they, my boys? Gone. Gone and left me with this strange child I can't understand. God knows I've tried. I've given him everything. No one in their right mind could say I've been unfair. It's the other way around; he hasn't been fair with me.

Ben Connell knew he would not have this problem if he were in Ireland. For in Ben Connell's Ireland, family life was as strong and as close as ever. Ben loved Ireland as only the narrowback son of a broadbacked father could. Ireland was Galway Bay and the Rose of Tralee and Casey Who Waltzed With The Strawberry Blonde and I'll Take You Home Again, Kathleen to where your green hills and carts slowly wend their way to Dublin and the market. These, and wandering tinkers, and thatched cottages were more integral parts of Ben Connell's Ireland than what little he had seen in his short stay in the little County Cork town of his ancestors and relatives.

A man with an Irish accent was Ben Connell's friend. The sound of an Irish brogue assured Ben Connell that the speaker was either a poet or a saint. Ireland and the Irish were all things promised: life without strain; a deep simple faith, rock-like in a shallow and complex world; philosophy in every hedge; poets before each turf fire; healthy bicyclists rather than sickly motorists, youth and freshness and gaiety, but never disrespect. Children were obedient and respectful and loving and religious—the Church and the Family together for Christ—and children remembered and cared for their parents when they grew old. The Irish Da was the head of the family, the divine ruler, beneath God but far above child and wife—in Ben Connell's Ireland.

Tommy and Joe would be working the fields now, telling me not to worry, they'd bring in the potato crop. And Marion would be fixing me a cup of tea in my own mug to enjoy by the fire with the paper. Daily paper? Have one mailed from Cork I suppose. And she'd be puttin' on the spuds, b'Jezuz, an' what else. Cabbage. Corned beef. An onion?

'Can I fetch your pipe, Da?'

'Sure now, Thomas.'

'And I your slippers, Da?'

'Right you are, Joe! Do be bringin' the children up so I can spin 'em a yarn. Do, Boys, do.'

'Aye, Da.'

'We'll run fetch them now, Da.'

'Now, Ben, don't be tirin' yerself out with the story-tellin', hear?'

'Ah, sure, Marion love, and why not. Aren't they the sweetest grandchilden a mawn could ha'?'

'Well then, don't be stuffin' them fulla sweets. You'll have Irene and Jane down on me.'

'Down on yeh, is it? Let them say their piece to me. I'll fix that.'

'True for you. They'll smile at you. Ah, Ben, yer a regular gas man.'

Ben Connell resented coming back from his Ireland and his warm fire to his porch where a chill breeze was blowing from the north, stirring the last dead ashes of a stale cigarette. It would be winter soon and if he did not get Sean to put up the storm windows on the house and porch before he got away, it would not be done. Margaret had silently suffered last year, straining to match the poorly-marked windows, straining perhaps too to keep from answering him back. The strain had been too much, not just last year, but all the years she had watched and listened and tried to obey and say nothing, and now Margaret was no longer available for that kind of work.

He mustn't think of her, Ben knew, for she was too far away to bring back by mere thought, and if he dwelt on her, it would be an easy thing to go and join her there, a too easy thing.

But Joe and Tommy, where are they now that they can't honor their father? Chasing fame and a fat young wench? 'I have this opportunity,

Dad, which involves a move to the West Coast. You know I'll miss you and Marion...' How do I know, Joseph? Take your word for it? 'This is Jane, Pa. We eloped.' And how did you do that, Thomas, for surely Hannibal moving his elephants over the Alps had less of a logistical problem than you. 'How do you do, Jane.' You've done me. Cheated me of a wedding, an excuse to be happy. Sweet young darling hippopotamus.

But where are Joe and Tommy? We were so close.

Oh, where have you gone, Tommy-Joe, Tommy Joe.

Oh, where have you gone, darling T-J?

One has gone to conquer life,

T'other to catch a merry wife,

And left their Da to—to—

Shit in his hat, to borrow Marion's favorite phrase. I'm passing the torch to you, Joseph, upward-bound, serious-born, but how can I if you're not here, passing through instead like a stranger, stopping over in motels. 'We didn't want to inconvenience you, Dad, have you go to a lot of bother.' What did you do for twenty-odd years but inconvenience and bother? Motels more comfortable? We were, so close. If your face turns elsewhere, what should I do? Give it to your younger brother, sweet Tom, silly Tom, giggly-wiggly Tom (Hello? Dad? Guess what Tommy Junior did today. He was watching television...) and watch him fall on his face. He's too busy anyway, ballooning out his Janie-blossom.

Must I turn then to him, half-brother, second litter, third-born? And fill the torch with all the wisdom I have gathered and earned, and hand it to him to watch him drop it in disgust, laugh at me, turn away and return to his playthings. I will not. Sweet Margaret's gone. Never to come back? Are Marion and I to spend our last days together, trying to gloss over sharp memories.

Joseph, Joe, Joey, we were so close. You and me and Tommy and that's all there was. Doesn't that mean something, a bond forged that shouldn't be broken, a link too strong to rust, to snap, a love too sharp to fade. Shouldn't that mean something. You and me and Tom and your dead mother's memory and that's all there was. Shouldn't that mean more than a rare visit on holidays, a few letters a year, and now, the privilege and duty of crowing over the grandchildren from afar. We were so close. You and Tommy. And I.

4 | The Cymbals Clang

Ben Connell fought valiantly to keep himself from fully enjoying his second honeymoon. He was enjoying it more than he would admit to anyone, more than he could ever think of hinting to himself. But Ben staunchly defended his memory—a memory that told him he was still madly in love with his first wife—whenever the thought stole into his conscious mind that maybe, perhaps, could it be, it would seem, he was enjoying his second honeymoon more than his first.

Love is lovelier the second time around.

Ben caught the orchestra in a lie.

Volume doesn't make it true, boys. They could turn YOU UP to full tilt, paint you red, white and blue and shoot streams of papaya juice out of your guts and—boys—hear me good boys—it'd still be a lie.

Lovelier! You look at her. My sweet young drab. My toothy, tasteless, twitterbirding thweetheart. 'Oh, Ben, loooook! They're going the hula.' Yes, Marion. 'Oh, Ben, isn't it beautiful?' Yes, Marion, but don't say it is. Puhleeze! Let it ride, let it swing, let it hang, let it be. I got words to tell a story—'Oh, Ben, that's so funny!'— words to squall and hang on a wall, cut people down to size—'How could he do that, Ben?!—and spit in their eyes, but no words to strap in a sunset, girdle a mountain, pull down the moon and wrap it in adjectives and verbs. None, none at all. Let it be. Set it free.

"Ben," Marion whispered, none too softly. "Isn't that woman over there, the one in the white sheath, isn't she beautiful? She must be Hawaiian."

"Marion. Don't point."

"What's the matter?"

"No matter. Just don't point your stubby little finger. Tuck it in your palm, hold it with your thumb, sit on it conveniently hidden away. But don't point your knuckly little pickle at anyone. Impolite. Most improper. Thoroughly shocking, to express an opinion guardedly."

"You're talking funny, Ben. I think, maybe—"

"Perhaps?"

"—you probably—"

"One can never be sure, can one. One?"

"—have had just a little too much—"

"Inched over the line?"

"—to drink. I really think so, Ben."

"Don't be so definite, my darling girl. Sober until proved drunken, disorderly and disshaven. That's the American way."

"Maybe it might be best—"

"Oh God, Oh God, Oh Merciful God, Maker of Heaven and Earth, make her say what she's thinking and re-think what she's saying. Nominus forbiscuits duem dayemm. Ay, ay, ayyy all Ameriicain."

"Ben, people are looking." Marion sank her eyes into the gold-fringed tablecloth in the belief that the elegant people present could not see her if she could not see them. Ben became irritated at the elevating of noses going on around him, as if certain bejeweled personages were daring him to check their close-cropped soot-free, silk-blown nostrils. He countered with, "Choo Choo! Chug-achuga chug chug chug. Choo choo!"

The assistant manager started toward their table, but Ben winked and waved him off. He was quiet for a moment, giving Marion the courage to raise her eyes. She dropped them immediately. Her new groom was freezing his face into a grotesque smile until some understanding person at a nearby table smiled back. As soon as anyone did, Ben dropped the smile, sucked in his cheeks, pooped open his eyes and stared at the trapped soul in startled idiocy. When Ben ran out of victims among the socialites, bored businessmen and their wives, and the few military officers, he turned back to his wife.

"Lift up your eyes, Marion," he coaxed. "You can't be a squirmy little silverfish and crawl away, so lift up your eyes. No longer am I fun-loving and fancy free. From now on I promise to be the respected and honorable Bernard T. Connell.

Lift up your eyes my lovely,
Lift up your eyes right nice,
Or your darling hus-a-band,
Will warm your neck with ice."

Marion looked up quickly, in time to see the orchestra leader—a huge man in a red jacket with black lapels—make his mistake. His face, which looked as if it had been left awake too long, eased into an ugly genuine smile. He was actually amused by Ben's antics, a big and slow and naturally silly elephant grinning at the white hunter who had come for his tusks.

Ben was up from his seat and across the floor, racing a straight line he could not have walked, gathering momentum until he jostled his victim whose arms were raised, but not in time lowered, for the downbeat. Ben smiled at the startled orchestra leader in imitation of that professional's tight, canned smirk.

"Do you by chance, my good man, know 'McNamara's Band'?" Ben thought he had asked the question politely and suavely.

Cursing himself for a fool, the orchestra leader eyed two waiters, then jerked his head toward Ben and raised his arms again for the downbeat. Ben retreated from the advancing waiters to a position between the orchestra leader and his musicians. Ben's head hung sadly; he had just learned of betrayal by a friend.

"Ah, let him sing!" a lone sailor shouted.

"Yes, do. Let's hear him out," the beautiful woman in the white sheath added.

"Let him sing," the patrons chorused.

"Hurray for McNamara!" the same sailor, obstreperously seeking recognition as a wit, shouted.

The orchestra leader nodded to the audience as graciously as if it had been his idea in the first place to invite Ben to perform. He gave the downbeat to his musicians who were saying ugly things back to him with their eyes.

"You're on," he grunted to Ben.

Ben adjusted his tie, buttoned his blue sport coat, and cleared his threat.

"Bruummpph. Haven't had the pleasure of singing for quite a while, but I'll do my best for such a wonderful group of people."

The audience clapped. The orchestra began again

'My name is Ben E. Connell.

I'm the total of a band.

And if you've never heard me-us

We-I'm the finest in the land.

The drums go bang

And the cymbals clang

And the music is something grand,

The finest in old Hawaii is

Ben E. Connell the one-man band."

The patrons clapped loud enough to make it necessary for the orchestra leader to diplomatically shove Ben off the bandstand.

"I could come up with an encore," Ben offered. The orchestra leader didn't seem to hear him, but his disembodied arm was able to reach out and secure the ten-dollar bill Ben proffered.

"Nice people here," Ben told Marion, apparently forgiving all of them for their previous boorishness. A cup of black coffee was waiting when he sat down. He studied it, leaning his head from side to side so the entire shape of the vessel could be checked. Satisfied that it was what it appeared to be, Ben faced his newest bride. "Who—ordered—this?"

"Well, I thought—"

"Who ordered it!"

"I did," Marion said, sighing and hanging her head, ready to accept verbal punishment for her upstart brashness.

"Damn fine idea," Ben said. "In fact, so close to brilliant, who am I to split hairs. Your initiative and intelligence is matched only by your timidity."

He fished an ice cube out of his highball glass and dropped it into his cup. Using a bent straw, he began to sip the coffee. Marion was happy again because Ben wasn't mad. She felt it safe now to leave him and make the trip to the ladies' room she had fought to postpone.

"I'll be right back," she smiled.

Ben smiled lazily in reply. The sweat was cooling in his pores and he felt a chill. His blood was running cooler and his mind slowed down to a trot as he watched the short, shy woman make excuses, unnecessary and ignored, as she wove her way across the dance floor, never bumping into anyone or anything but the shifting shadows of her mind.

Where did I get this one? Where did I find Sweet Marion from Pike? Who crossed the wide prairie with her husband—Ben? 'Oh, Ben, the flowers are gorgeous.' 'Ben, can we really afford this trip?' 'Bennn! This place looks sooo expensive.' How did I miss it? All those times at the office. More, the times I visited her classes. Why did she squint then, examining every little word the kids uttered, if she was going to play the game wide-eyed with me? Same person, same dresses, same hair, same body, and some same body she has. Not like Catherine who, truth to tell Old Dear, you were a little on the slim side for me. An elegant body, long and slender, a body to be draped in smart clothes. Jimmy John would have loved to drape it.

Why Jimmy John? Why now lately always Jimmy James John Johnson with thoughts of Catherine. Grave, cautious Jimmy John who never rushes into a word headlong, censors his thoughts, re-censors them, sends them to committee, and then carefully utters them. 'The way I would approach this situation, Ben...'

Why not Grave James? Wasn't he the first, the one who Catherine was sure she was almost sure about until you, sweet Ben, noble Ben, stealer of hearts not purses. "Keep your gold. I'll take the woman. That one. Tall Blackie," came to the rescue.

Ben Connell could not kid away the sourness that came with the intrusion into his thoughts of James Johnson, his colleague and friend of many years, the man he had stuck with the label, "Jimmy John." Ben could make no sense of, see no reason for, nor ever forget his first wife's attraction to Jimmy John. He could not help asking about that attraction on his honeymoon.

"What did you ever see in Jimmy John, Catherine?" It was the first sharp question he had asked, the first note that cut the soft air around their New Hampshire lakeside cottage, the first words that penetrated the hazy honeymoon days and made Massachusetts and Boston and work and worries not a half day's driving away, but right across the glorified pond they sat by.

"Oh, nothing," she had said, in her meaningful tell-nothing manner that became more and more of an irritation to Ben as their married life continued.

"Nothing. You must have seen something in him. You went out with him for almost a year before we started going out."

"He introduced us, Ben."

"I know that, Dear." (Was that the first time he used Dear, that hated word, instead of Honey or Sweetheart?) "I realize he introduced us. I'm most grateful to my beloved colleague. I just asked: what did you see in him?"

"He's firm," she said. "He has ambition and purpose. I think he'll go a long way. And he's intense. He seems to be forcing everything out of every minute. That's what I liked about you, Ben. You can relax. Could you see Jim now, sitting here, looking at nothing in particular, doing nothing really exciting. It would kill him."

And because he could see "Jim" planning an outing, driving into the mountains, stopping to tear through a shop of hand-woven baskets, talking ceaselessly, charming one and all, because he could see Jim pulling out his wallet, counting out each of the bills he had hoarded dutifully, naturally, because he could see Jim providing more intense fun, more orderly fun, more disciplined fun, Ben Connell had to fight to keep the rage in his gut from escaping in a harsh remark.

"He is firm," Ben said. "In fact, he's so firm that the other masters refer to his pupils as Jimmy John's Jumpers because, like Molloy said last week, those kids are so scared they jump if Jimmy John clears his throat. He's firm, all right."

"I thought Jim was your friend?"

"He is! Been my friend for years, the only reason being I don't trust him as far as I can throw him. He's put the knife into more than one back and he'll do it again. He'd do it to me if I turned my back. That's why we're friends. I don't turn my back."

"Oh, Ben. I think you're imagining things."

Is that why I can't stand to hear Marion say, "Oh, Ben"? Because Catherine dismissed so many proper fears as if they were promoted by childish delusions, monsters under the bed, ghosts clanking chains in a dark cellar. "Oh, Ben. Really!" Not again. Not again.

"You have to pay a dime," Marion said, "to use their toilets."

"Live it up," Ben said, tossing two dimes on the table. "Have an extra on me. You're in The Big-time now, Baby."

"Oh, Ben, don't be foolish. I had a dime. I'm all through. Do you feel better?"

"No. I feel sober."

"That's what I mean."

"Meant."

"All right, Mr. Einstein. I suppose I'm too dumb to even dance with?"

"You're too good-looking not to dance with."

"Gee, you must be sobering up. That's the nicest thing you've said all night."

"Never felt drunker. Let's dance, Sweetbody."

"Ben!"

This one melts, moves with you. Doesn't care how far you go or if you ever get there. Just dance. Not Catherine. But then, dancing was something else for Catherine. Her tight, controlled days unwound, unloosed, twisted, bent and swayed, jumped, set the world on its ear— on a dance floor. But not with Ben the Bungler.

For Catherine's taste, Ben had warmed too slowly to the dance floor, fought too hard for the ease and confidence she knew immediately. He strained to match her light steps for she was leading, she was leading. Sat to watch another man, other men, whirl his

41

rhythmic wife. And decided he didn't like dancing.

"Oh, Ben, what do you mean you don't want to go?" Catherine had asked on their honeymoon.

"I just don't feel like going out."

"You won't have to dance, if that's what's bothering you? And I won't dance. I'll just sit there and tap my foot and watch everyone else dance and I won't say a word."

"I don't think we can afford it."

Catherine was quiet then and Ben proud and guilty since he had pulled one on her, given her a taste of her own medicine, let her hear what he had heard all through their careful, measured, miserly honeymoon.

They had gone out for three years before they married and Catherine, by paying attention, knew more about the state of Ben's finances than he did. She tried to be kind—it was a honeymoon—but was very firm. "Ben, we can't afford it," was her final, fatal word on any doubtful, impulsive proposal.

Ben had wanted to explode, to burst happiness all over the world, to laugh on rooftops and spit across canyons and tell funny stories to cheer up mankind. Instead, he found himself carrying suitcases the length of a sleepy railroad terminal to avoid tipping a could-care-less porter, walking, strolling, and basking in the Goddamn unlively lovely sunshine, drinking coffee in the afternoon instead of champagne in the evening.

And all through his ordeal of quiet restraint, Ben knew exactly how right Catherine was when she said, "No, Ben, really, we can't afford it." He was living on assistant principal's pay, which was money in the Depression, but he would not, could not, have saved enough for a two-mile trip on a bus if it had not been for Catherine. He respected Catherine for her practicality, agreed wholeheartedly with his relatives that she was the best thing that ever happened to him, and, at times, fleeting instances, swift seconds that ran darkly, he adored her not quite as much as he did when she was not playing the cautious banker, the financial analyst, the inescapable reminder of his lowly economic state in the land of milk and-money. At times he wanted to strangle her a bit.

Slowly. Spanish garrote?

"Ben," Marion said, "You've got a faraway, dreamy look in your eyes."

"Do I? Oh yes, well, just dreaming about my island paradise. Didn't tell you about that, did I. Well, one of these days, when my ship comes in, I'm going to run off to an island in the South Seas. Thousands of young maidens wearing sarongs will parade and prance and carry baskets of fruit on their heads, all for Bwana Ben. If you play your cards right, I might, I might just put in a word for you as assistant handmaiden. Have to acquire a bit of a tan though."

"It's lovely out. Can we go out on the balcony?"

Ben watched Marion walk around the perimeter of the balcony, stop to lean on the balustrade and gaze into the darkness.

"It's so beautiful here," she said. "It's gorgeous." "Absolutely."

Marion smiled, happy that her husband shared her appreciation.

"It's really breath-taking," she said.

"That reminds me let's go in and sit down. This fresh air is gagging me."

Ben's cold coffee stared at him as he sat down. "Waiter. Waiter! Take this offensive black liquid away and bring us a magnum of champagne."

"Ben, can we drink all that?" Marion asked.

"If not, we'll donate it to our poor friends here." His sweeping arm embraced the ringside tables where he saw pearls catch the light and emeralds flash their thankful replies.

"A magnum it is, Sir."

Ben watched the waiter stop on his way to the bar to talk to a short, swarthy man.

"Songbird at number five wants a magnum. Shall I shut him off?"

"What the hell," the assistant manager said. "What more can he do. Give it to him. His money's green."

What are you two jawin' about? I'm not drunk. Might be after a few sips of the bubbly. Worried about the money? Don't be. Daddy

Warbucks has made arrangements. Yes, a little deal in Venezuela. Stuffed a cork in a bothersome volcano. Two million for that, and yes, the Nicaraguan caper. Another thousand thousand for training the llamas to lay eggs. Daddy's got the dough, don't you worry.

In preparation for his second honeymoon, Ben had determined not to worry about money. He knew he wasn't greedy, never wanted more than his fair share of the money printed daily in this world, just enough to do what he wanted to do when he wanted to do it. Not a fortune hunter was Ben Connell. Only a man who wanted enough money for a summer vacation when summer came and a new car when he saw a blue De Soto that looked better than his green Plymouth and a new coat of cream paint for the trim of his house when the old coat curdled.

Rose knew he was not hungry. Her brother, whom Donald occasionally referred to as her "borther," wanted enough when he needed enough, and that was all. Rose convinced Donald that $100 would be a more practical gift than a silver tea service. Enough is not too much, she understood.

A few other friends and relatives, including Jack's Uncle Daniel who had disowned most of the family and retreated to the backwoods of western Massachusetts, sent cash because they had become unused, in Depression America, to buying gifts. Their happiness offerings and the ten dollars Jack had set aside every week for six months amounted to almost five hundred dollars. That wasn't enough, despite the fact that his first honeymoon cost less than two hundred dollars. It wasn't enough.

"And what do you intend to do with the five hundred dollars, Mr. Connell?" the credit manager of the Simplicitee Finance Company asked. His casual tone suggested that he was merely interested, implied that he actually had no urgent desire to know.

"Fix the gutters on my house," Ben said.

"Repairs are high these days," the manager said. He tested the taste of his pencil's eraser, found it rubbery, and smacked his lips. "You see—"

"Paint too!" Ben said. "Forgot that."

"Yes?"

"I'm going to paint my house. Myself. Save on labor costs." Ben did not want to elaborate for the benefit of this pencil-pushing loan shark. He knew his credit was good. He considered rolling up his sleeve and offering a vein, but it was not necessary.

"I see." the manager said, and signed his name to the loan form.

Now, nearing the end of his honeymoon and one thousand dollars, Ben wondered how much it would hurt to deduct $69.50 a month from his check and speed it along to Simplicitee. Spending it had not hurt at all. Hula dancers, trinket shop proprietors, waiters, musicians, bartenders and bellhops could attest to the fact that he had enjoyed himself. There were the rare occasions though, such as now, when he had to wait for the concrete evidence of his momentary solvency to arrive, when he had time to consider if it might not be better to cancel the order and save the money, when he felt tempted to order another cup of coffee and forego the champagne.

"Here he comes," Marion said.

Ben grimaced as he watched his wife lean forward to chart the course of the fast-stepping, sleek waiter and his cargo of champagne resting expensively in a silver ice bucket.

Where, oh where, did little Marion come from. I thought she was going to kiss the priest, Monsignor Conley at his merriest, on the lips when he married us. Another glass of champagne at the reception and he would have attacked her.

"Your champagne, Sir."

The waiter advanced the bottle with its imitation gold lettering on a white label for Ben's inspection.

"Mmmm," Ben said.

The waiter poured a sip, waited for Ben's nod of approval, then filled Marion's glass and returned to fill Ben's. Ben finished one glass neatly, waved the waiter away, and poured himself another.

What's he bucking for, ten dollars? Why not. He knows a big-time spender when he sees one. Or does he think I'm a rube who doesn't know the score. Doesn't matter to him if I overtip as par for the course or overtip cause I don't know any better. He still gets his overtip, thin-legged spider that he is. If he dances around Marion one more time, she'll swoon. 'Oh, Ben, isn't he a wonderful waiter?' I've waited on table and he's not that sharp, Dearest. He's better than I was, but look at his shoes. Cheap. Not shined on the back. Heels run down. His belt. Imitation leather. Two for a dime? Shirt collar's wilting. And the way he minces and flits, he must be a little gay. Gay, Dear—no, not happy—gay. Never mind. Why corrupt your simple mind?

I wonder if Jimmy John's gay. It never occurred to me. Work late at the office, always off to a meeting. WHOM is he meeting? When does he poke old Peg? Coffee breaks. He's never in his office when you call him. No, he's too methodical for romantic dashes to his loved one's arms. Probably in a classroom showing off his stuff, drawing slick pictures on the board, adding sums in his head that he figured out before hand, dazzle 'em with chalkwork.

Not fair. He's got a good mind and you know it. Watch that. But the sonovabitch has to show it off. Do ye ken Jim John when he's farr, farr a-way, with his chalk and his Peg in the mooooornin-gg? No. Then why are you always bringing him up? Haven't you got anything else to think about. Of course I have. What? Nona your Goddamn business. Oooh, now we're mad. No, we're all right. We get along, don't we? Well, don't we? Mmm. MMM, yourself.

Jimmy John, Jimmy John, where have you been? I've been to see Catherine, now I'm back again. Is that it? Yeah, I suppose. What in Hell did she see in him? Firm. I can be firm. I won't make that mistake again. Let up a little and a woman runs your life. I'll be firm this time around.

Ben firmly gripped his fifth glass of champagne and downed it as Marion sipped and giggled into her first.

"I feel so lightheaded, Ben. Do you want to dance?"

"No, and that's final." Ben shook his head for emphasis. "That's all there is to it. I don't want to dance. Period!"

"Oh," Marion said. "Okay. Are you mad about something?"

"Of course I'm not mad. What in Hell gave you the idea I'm mad.

Dogs are mad. I'm not even angry."

God, she can be aggravating. What is she so mousey about? What kind of a woman is she if she can't stand on her own two feet. Not like Catherine, solid as a ten-legged two-ton piano, but I do want her to be more independent.

"Don't sit there with that hangdog face. C'mon, let's dance."

'Are you mad about something?' Admit it, Bull. You are. Mad about J.J., not because of what he is, but because you know. You know and you can excuse him. The marching martinet, marching his young troops around the corridors, 'Pencils and books, all pencils and books in the left hand.' Hup. Yrrup. Drawing his pretty pictures on the board, his lovely diagrams, his colored chalk swans.

Why can't you hate him? More? No. Why can't you hate him at all. Because you know what it's like to stand in front of a room, to see the forty faces eager. Well, thirty of them anyway, and the other ten you're going to save. Save 'em, Bull, save 'em. Awaken and arise my children. Go forth in light. Shun darkness. Learn. Live. Love.

Or learn, lie down, and lose. Hey, hey, all the way. Take it on the chin the educated way. Don't let reason bend or sway. Am-bisstch-hun. Ambition! Ambition! Yeay!

It got to you, Bull. Left the law books lie alone. Ugly, musty, museum-piece law books in the hallowed sanctuary of the law library. Eyes and ears and throat and nose choked with dusty print, musty print, cases and torts, logic and hodge-podgic. Bernard T. Connell, Attorney-at-Law. Why, Bully boy, why? Don't you know. It got to you, babygod. Standing in front of the class, a high school ragtag summer class, spouting that goood talk. Listen at me, Chillun. Leave me in those eardrums. The word, I said the word, you want the word, I got it. The word.

But it warn't all that, Bull. It warn't all that by a long fandango. Was it the court cases? Sit in, m'boy, and learn the law. Learn the legalistic lie. 'Have you stopped beating your wife. Answer yes or no.' Twist and crumple and trומple the truth and you'll be a shark, my son. 'Your Honor, my client's name and that most valuable of all his possessions, his reputation, have been ground and stomped upon here in this very courtroom. My worthy colleague, our admired and respected city attorney, has seen fit to leave his principles home this day. We all know he has principles. Should we hold it against him that he chooses...'

Weak stomach, Bull? Insist on finding out if the man is guilty or innocent? Fine lawyer you'd make. The Weeping Willow of Superior Court. Weeps his clients all the way to ruin. But he plays fair. Oh yeah. That means something. Somewhere. Not in the Halls of Justice but, Oh Yeah, that boy plays fair. Get him outa here. Quick!

Is that why you left the men's league, Bull boy? Teach the kiddies to say goo comma goo, instead of plain old unadulterated goo goo. Say it right, say it smart, say it nice for old Softheart. Goo, comma, goo. You comma goo. Goo comma, you comma, gooyou comma. Goo you kid. Bull Softheart, sweetheart of the sixth grade simpletons. And their teacherkins. Waiting now for Daddy Bull. Come home and mend the naughty breaches. Spanky word.

Marion Connell was startled as her husband broke into a polka, pulling her around the dance floor fiercely to the music of a foxtrot, dancing as if his feet were two madmen trying to fit all the puzzling dance steps of a lifetime onto that one small jigsaw floor.

Ben's waiter stopped by the assistant manager.

"That's what more he can do, Lou," the waiter said.

"Yeah," Lou said. "Maybe he'll fall down and pass out."

5 | A Cup of Tea

Sean's first view of his mother in almost two years was from the rear and at an angle. She was stooped over in the back hall, wading through bottles that had to be returned, shoes that no longer fit, newspapers and magazines that were patiently waiting to be read by Ben Connell, rags that would not be used in a year of cleaning, and clothes that were due to be washed soon. It seemed to Sean that his mother had spent half the time he could remember either wondering where she had put something, or, as now, searching for it.

"I'm home. Ma," he said.

"Oh, Tommy, Joe, I mean Sean. How are you?"

"I don't know. Are you sure it's me?"

"I was looking for the shoe polish. I'm supposed to go to a wake with—welcome home!"

He hugged her and kissed her on the cheek, wondering how she had managed to become more disorganized than ever. The shoe polish, at least, had always been kept in the same place, in a box on the cellar landing. It would be all right if she were searching in the back hall for socks or soap or toilet paper, ties, thread, rope, aspirin, or hair tonic— but not the shoe polish. Sean never ceased to be amazed at her unchanging faith that if only the back hall were cleaned up or out, the whole house would be put in order and she could find whatever she was looking for.

"I've got to get to this back hall someday," she said. "As soon as I get a minute."

"I'm glad you're all squared away," Sean said. "Everything as shipshape as usual."

"You sound like you just got out of the Navy, instead of the Army," she said, turning to him again. The sun slanting in through the filmed kitchen window caught her gray hairs showing through the brown. "I suppose you're going to be hard to please now. A place for everything and everything in its place." She turned in her lips and bit them, narrowed her eyes into a firm, calculating expression, then swung by him, counting cadence, to turn on the gas under the tea pot. "Hup, two, thuhree, foah, Hup. Hup."

"Huh, that'll be the day when this place is regimented."

"Why, you shit. You big shit. You just get home—what's the matter with the place. Doesn't it look good?"

"Sure, Ma." Towels off the radiator. Probably thrown in the back hall with the dirty laundry. Coats off the door knobs. Crowded into the hall closet. Floor swept. Top of the stove wiped. Practically spotless. "Don't get upset." "Did you see the new steps?" she asked, trying to reserve her pride in case he didn't show approval.

"Yup."

"Well? Is that all you're going to say?"

"A-yup."

"Don't you like them? They cost a hundred dollars." "I like them, I like them. They look very—practical. They look like—a hundred dollars."

"That's the least you could say. He needs them now." "For what?"

"His legs are gone."

"What does 'gone' mean?"

"He's supposed to go in the hospital for tests to find out what it means, and he's not supposed to be sitting on a cold metal chair half the day. But he wouldn't go."

"Why?"

"Why do you think?" she asked. She began looking in the cabinet for a tea bag.

"Oh, no," Sean said. "Don't give me that. He hasn't been waiting for me. He doesn't give a shit whether I come home or not."

"Don't be vulgar," she said. "You know better than that."

"Do I? It would have killed him just now to shake my hand. He acted like I had the plague, so don't give me that jazz about waiting for me. He may not want to go in the hospital, but he's not postponing it on my account. He's probably scared to death."

"Oh shut up! What do you know."

"Not much," Sean said, "but I know he didn't wear his arm out writing to me for two years. And I wrote once in a while to him, or to you at least."

"Big deal," she said, wishing she hadn't.

Sean turned away and started to bump his duffel bag with his knee up the stairs to the second floor.

"Any clean towels up here," he called back from the first landing, "or are they the same ones as the day I left?"

"Go shit in your hat," she yelled and slammed the door at the foot of the stairs behind him. "You Connells are all alike. Why don't you go visit your aunt?"

"I just might," Sean called from the top of the stairs. "That's a good idea."

"Go ahead! Marion opened the jammed door. "Go ahead! See if I care! Go ahead."

Home again, home again, jiggety—jog. Mother Dear. Ma-Mah. Mater. No. Maaaa. Same as Baaaa. Baaa, Baa, black sheep, have you any wool? Yes sir, yes sir, three dirty laundry bags full. So what. Well, I'll be a son-of-a-bitch. Look at Margaret's room. I've never seen it this clean. Bed doesn't look like she just pulled the covers up. Looks like she's ready to stand white-glove, quarter-bouncing inspection. Nothing on the bureau but a doily. Nothing hanging on the rocking chair.

Sean pulled back the spread on Margaret's bed. He started, as if he had found a thin-pressed corpse under the spread. Staring back at him was the old blue-and-cream-striped mattress and its loose fluffy knobs.

"Ma" he called on his way to the head of the stairs. "Hey, Ma. Where's Margaret?"

"Don't shout!" Marion Connell said. "Come down, if you want to talk to me."

When he got downstairs, his mother was out on the porch. She had left the front door partially open and a few words were filtering through the screen door.

"...tell him..."

"...go ahead...later..."

"...please, Ben...owe it..."

"...alone...alone..."

Not again. No. Not again. Jesus. Home five seconds and the whispering starts. Jesus Christ. I'll throw a brick. Why can't they come out and say what they're thinking. Top security for the shopping list.

Sean stood at the landing, trying to decide whether to go down the three steps into the front hall and intercept his mother or turn down the steps into the kitchen and wait for her. While he was deciding, she rushed into the house and, head down, headed for the kitchen.

"Conspiracy over?"

She didn't answer so he went down the steps into the kitchen and sat down to watch her moving things around on the shelf above the stove in search of a match to light the cigarette hanging from her mouth.

"I've got a match."

She accepted the light, then she drew back, puffing and squinting and blowing the smoke upwards out of the side of her mouth.

"Big Shot, smoking now," she said.

"Ma, I've been smoking for three years and you know it." "Well you shouldn't smoke around here. You know what your father thinks about that."

"I don't have a cigarette hanging out of my mouth." "Don't get wise with me. I never smoked in front of you kids."

Never did. Bathroom was awfully smoky when you got through in there. Never smoked in front of us though. "What about Margaret?"

"...so don't go flashing matches in front of your father. He's no fool you know."

"Ma! Margaret."

"What about her?"

"Oh for Christ's sakes, will you stop it. I would just like to know where my sister is. Is that too much to ask?"

"Don't take the Lord's name in vain."

"Maaa!"

"She's visiting."

"Visiting who?"

"A girlfriend."

"Who?"

"You wouldn't know her."

"How do you know?"

"She just met her. I can't even remember her name."

"When's she coming back?"

"I don't know. In a while. Now don't bother me; I have things on my mind."

"Are you telling me the truth?"

"If you want to take a bath, there's that big blue towel in your father's room on the radiator."

"Does her girlfriend have a phone so I can call her." "No. No phone. Now do you want to take a bath or not?"

"Yeah, I'll take a bath. But you better be telling me the truth."

"Don't you dare talk to me in that tone of voice. Who the hell do you think you are? Just home from the service. Big deal. You think you can—"

"All right, all right. Don't get wound up."

"Wound up. Who's wound up. You're the one who's all wound up. You come in here and you start right in…"

Her words followed him up the stairs and gradually died out. They would tell him when they were ready. His mother did not forget girlfriends' names—mix them up, perhaps, but not forget them. He might as well take a bath. They, despite the whispers, were not ready.

Have to install a shower or have one installed. This is ridiculous. Sitting in your own dirty water. Fill the tub up to soak, hot water runs out. Rinse yourself off with soapy, lukewarm water cause you can't stand one panful of cold water at a time. Not like a shower. Same pan, same leak. Same lousy tiles I put down five years ago. Never finished that last tiny piece in the corner by the tub. Coming up now. Suppose I could fix that if I were staying home for awhile. Can't. Same place I left, only worse. She seems tougher. He seems nowhere. And Margaret?

"Sean!" Marion Connell called. "Shoh-unn!"

"What do you want!"

"When you get through your bath, your father wants to talk with you!"

"I just got in here!"

"Well shake a leg!"

Now they're ready. When I'm through, he'll have changed his mind. Better get down there. What a nuthouse.

Sean started to step out of the tub before realizing there still was no bathmat. He held onto the tub with one hand, put the wet ball of one foot on the floor gingerly and stretched to the radiator for a dirty towel. After wiping up the wet spot his foot had made, he spread the dirty damp towel out and stepped out of the tub. He had left his blue towel hanging on the doorknob. He hopped across the floor on one foot, snatched the towel, and hopped back to his made-do mat.

Ben Connell was easing himself into his chair at the head of the kitchen table when Sean came downstairs dressed in chinos, a sweat shirt and sneakers. He resolved not to say anything to upset his mother since he needed to ask her to do a laundry of socks and underwear. Ben was lowering himself into his chair as slowly and gingerly as a man whose legs were made of flour and would disintegrate if bumped. He did not look at his son, choosing instead to plant his elbow on the table and rub his brow as he studied the kitchen linoleum.

"Pa," Sean said. His father did not answer nor look Up, "Where's Margaret?"

Slowly, Ben Connell turned to face and study his son. "Already you look like a bum," he said. "Can't you wear socks?"

"I haven't got any. I was just going to ask Ma to do my laundry."

"Sure. Bring home your dirty clothes for your mother to do, and instead of thanking her, give her a lot of guff."

54

"Oh, Ben, I was going to do a laundry anyways," Marion said. "I can just throw them in with it."

"You said you weren't going to do one until tomorrow," Ben said. "He can wash his own things out in the sink. It won't kill him."

"Yeah I can," Sean said. "I just thought you might be doing a wash."

"Bring them down and I'll throw them in the machine with the other stuff. I—I have to do a wash anyways. I was thinking I better do it today."

"Never mind. I'll wash them out by hand. I don't want to cause any problems."

"No, bring them down. I'll—"

"You can borrow a pair of my socks," his father said, "if you have to, so you won't look like a beggar. You're not going any place anyways, are you?"

"I don't know," Sean said. "I—where's Margaret?"

"Your mother told you that, didn't she? She's visiting friends."

"Friends? I thought it was one girlfriend?"

"Don't be a smart aleck. You know what I mean."

"Pa, can't you tell me?" Sean asked. "All right. Never mind. Keep another one of your goddamned secrets. The Great Conspirators huddle again."

"Don't you talk like that!" Ben Connell ordered. You ought to wash your mouth out with soap!"

"Oh for Christ's sakes." Sean threw his arms up.

"Now Ben," Marion said. "Don't get upset. You know—"

"He's got no Goddamn right to speak that way!" "For Christ's sakes!" "You listen to me, you, you—"

"Ben, please."

"You shut up. As for you, you BUM, that's all you are, a bum! "

"Okay. I'm a bum. See you later. Not soon I hope."

"Where are you going!"

"Out. O-U-T. Out of this madhouse. Good-bye." "You'll leave this house when I say you'll leave it!"

Ben stood up and tried to rush across the kitchen after the retreating figure of his son.

"Ben!" Marion screamed as she saw her husband's legs fold and his head strike the kitchen stove as he fell to the floor.

Sean turned back into the kitchen when he heard the noise. "What's the matter? Pa!"

"Help me," Marion called, "get him into the dining room. His bed's in there."

"Tell the bum he can leave," Ben said as his son and his wife helped him to his feet.

Sean put his father's arm around his shoulder and, ignoring his father's muttered directions to the contrary, helped his mother ease their heavy burden into the dining room. "What's the bed doing in here?"

"His legs, they fall asleep. The doctor said it would be better."

"You don't have to explain anything to him," Ben said in a firmer voice. "He doesn't care about anyone but himself."

Desperately, Marion signaled her son to say nothing. Sean grimaced but kept his mouth shut. He eased his father down on the bed and stood back. Marion untied Ben's shoes, took them off and swung his legs gently onto the bed. She fussed with his pillow until he waved her away.

"I'm all right. I'm all right," Ben said. "Not that it makes any difference to anyone."

Sean watched his mother squint her eyes and clench her fists. She inhaled and exhaled deeply before saying anything. "We'll leave you alone, Ben. So you can get some rest."

"Sure. Sure. Leave me alone. No one listens to me anyways."

Sean preceded his mother out of the dining room and into the kitchen, wondering if he had ever seen his father like this before. Those rare times when Ben Connell had been sick, he had endured real pain quietly and then had exulted in his convalescence. Sean remembered him glorying in his enforced bed rest—ordering special magazines to be purchased from the drug store, relishing his meals served on a makeshift tray, enjoying a few chapters of books he would not otherwise find time for, and booming out orders to his family of nurses like a wounded general on a battlefield who expected his soldiers to accomplish what he had failed to do. "Did you cut the grass, Joe?" "Tommy, I want those screens cleaned thoroughly and painted before you put them up." "Now, Margaret, you haven't been helping your mother much. See if you can't darn some socks and give her a hand." "Sean, I want to talk to you." "Marion, let's see if we can't get that back hall in shape. I'll paint it as soon as I get on my feet." It was as if his father expected his world to mend as he did.

Sean could never remember his father whining or feeling sorry for himself. His mother said his legs were gone. Perhaps they were, but something else was gone too.

"I'm going for a walk, Ma. I'll be back for supper."

"Get a quart of milk. Do you have money?"

"Do you really need it?"

"Yes, it won't kill you. Here's a dollar. You can get some doughnuts if you have enough change."

"Might as well take a shopping list."

"I'm glad to see the Army hasn't cured you of being lazy."

"It isn't that. I'd just like to take a walk some time without worrying about taking something with me or bringing something back."

"I hope it doesn't hurt your mind to remember two little things."

Marion Connell ignored her son's brief snide smile and toyed with the tea bag in her forgotten cup of tea on the stove until she heard the front door close. Then she carried the dripping tea bag to the pantry and threw it on top of a brown paper bag full of trash. She sat down, sipped her cold cup of tea, took a cigarette from the broken green teapot that served as a bill file, got up and hunted for a match. She found a half-used book of matches among the crumbs under the toaster on top of the refrigerator. She lit her cigarette, squinting at the sharp smell of sulphur, put the matches on the stove and sat down; then she got up and searched for an ashtray. She settled for a dirty saucer by the pantry sink, dropped the burnt match in it, and carried it back to her seat. She was sure now that she was ready to relax. The tea was cold but that was nothing unusual. It was better than no tea at all.

"Marion!"

She ground out her cigarette, pushed herself up and walked to the dining room, opened the door gently and stuck her head around the corner.

"What do you want, Ben?"

"Come in, come in."

"What is it?"

"Did he leave?"

"Yes."

"Oh."

"Is that all?"

"Isn't that enough? Isn't it all right if I ask what my family is doing?"

"He went for a walk and he'll be back for supper and he's going to pick up something at the store."

"What?"

"A quart of milk and maybe some doughnuts." "We have doughnuts."

"There was only one left and it was three days old and looked soggy, I figured no one would want to eat it."

"So you threw it out. Still think I'm made of money, don't you."

"Did you want anything else?"

"No. I'm sorry I bothered you. I know you have so many important things to do."

"Do you want your supper served in here?"

"No, I don't want my supper served in here. I'll come to the table. You seem pretty anxious to keep me out of the way."

"I'll call you when supper's ready."

"Thanks a lot."

Marion returned to the kitchen table, sat down, and took another cigarette from the teapot. She got up and searched under the toaster for the matches until she remembered she had left them on the stove. She lit her cigarette, sat down, dropped the burnt match in the saucer and the matchbook on the table.

He won't stay, why should he, I'll have to call Winifred O'Leary and say I can't go, but if I do, she'll tell someone in the school and they'll call and Ben'll be mad, he'll bitch about it for days, I better say Sean's home. She'll understand that. She talks about her own kid as if he was God's gift to this earth, he could never do anything wrong, not him. I'll just say Sean's home and—and that'll be enough for her. Why the hell should I go to a woman's wake I don't even know. Winifred doesn't know her either. You'd think she was running for office, maybe she is, she's no fool, she's always looking out for her own, at least she sees them once in a while. If Margaret calls I don't know what I'll do, they wouldn't let her call, places like that shouldn't let—people call, maybe they should, I don't know, just don't God let her call when he's here. That would be it. We'd never see him again, he'd call us sonsofbitches and walk out and we might never see him again, he's as stubborn as his father, more stubborn now, I wish Ben would tell him, he always wants me to do anything hard, he'll smile but I deliver the bad news. When did it start, all this stubbornness and—hate, no, not hate, nobody hates their father, but he sounds awful close sometimes. 'Conspiracy over?' he asked, he heard us whispering and he hates it now as much as ever, it's like he never went away for two years, it's all the same as if he went to the park for a walk and all the bullshit and the fighting starts again as soon as he's inside the door, but Ben's to blame too and I shouldn't have said big deal, that was rotten. He wrote and Ben grumped through all his letters as I read them but he listened. It's so hard to write to people. You can't explain what you want to tell them in a letter and it makes them seem like foreigners or something, writing instead of talking to them. If Ben has to go in the hospital his insurance won't cover it all, I don't want to take out any more loans, God no, we're just getting out of that and I've been working eight years, nothing to show for it but a washer and a dryer and receipt slips for loans he took out ten, fifteen years ago, we'll just have to cut down, if I stopped smoking, but Margaret's bills too, two hundred dollars a week. My God. How much will the insurance handle, you pay in all the time, then when you need something, it won't pay enough, another racket and they can make you feel like a beggar if you keep after them, but what are you going to do, you need it, some kind of protection, we'd be lost without it. Ben says let him take over his insurance payments, if he's such a big shot, let him see what it's like to pay through the nose, but he knows what will happen. He'll let the payments go and they'll cancel the policy and twelve years of paying will go out the window. Ben wants me to explain it, but I don't know what to tell him. He should tell him. He'll do it finally, but he'll get angry and he'll try to force it down his throat and then he'll get mad and they'll wind up yelling at each other, and it's still twelve years gone. Why can't he just talk to him. That time down cellar when he nearly killed him with his belt and he still wouldn't cry out loud. Before that. Why can't we all talk to each other. It seems like it's been here forever. I'd like to tell the truth. Once, I'm sick of this whole mess. Sick and tired of it all. Get a divorce?

Like Mrs. Percell? That does a lot of good, change one mess for another, maybe he is a better man, I don't think so, but I never knew him, and now her daughter's turning into a tramp. And I have the Church to think about. That's crazy. I don't want a divorce. At least Ben still gets angry. Winifred O'Leary and Jack haven't even got that. What would I do, go to the hairdresser and try to pretend I'm not getting old. Money? He's never told me the truth about money. I hope to God no more bills come in he hasn't mentioned. I never asked until too late. It couldn't have been just money.

6 | The Closet

There was silence in the back seat of the taxicab carrying Ben Connell and his new bride home to his house. Irritated by the incessant necessity to dip into his pocket for tips, Ben was figuring out how much he should give the taxi driver. Marion was worrying because no stores in Ben's neighborhood would be open on Sunday evening to get something for supper.

Without resolving his gratuity problem, Ben gradually became aware that, already, he missed the oranges and yellows and reds, the blatant, boisterous colors of Hawaii that Medlen had never worn.

To come back at all had not been in Ben's mind. He hated the first sight of the city he lived and worked in. The streets were filled with cars darting across each other's path in a continual test of nerves, with children and mothers chasing balls and each other from sidewalk to sidewalk, and with other children camped in the middle of side streets, resentfully giving way to cars that cut through their playground. Soot, dying trees, stumps, fading paint that announced the Negro section, worn-out houses, scarred lampposts, railroad tracks that faced his section—he saw them all before coming to the quiet lawns and well-shorn shrubs of his street, lawns that paused at the sidewalk, then leaped over to jut another ten feet to the curb.

Memories and guilt overtook him as the taxi pulled up in front of the brown and cream building that would now house his second rife and possibly a second family. He could not feel a second man. Despite the honeymoon, he was the Ben Connell that had married Catherine Rourke yesterday five years ago; he was not the newly wealthy, cheerful, honeymoon Ben Connell who shed dollars like bath water; he was a man who had debts and burdens and new bills to go with his old bull. Ben Connell shrank during the passage from the back seat of the taxi to the curb in front of his house.

The driver lifted the bags out of the trunk and laid them on the grass. He closed the trunk and bent to pick up a few bags.

"That's all right," Ben said. He looked over his shoulder at Marion who was staring wistfully up at the house she was about to enter. For the first time in weeks, Ben asked: "How much?"

"Two-fifty-five."

Ben gave the driver three dollars, held out his left hand for change and searched with his right for fifteen cents at the bottom of his pocket.

"Thanks, Sport," the driver said. He climbed into his cab and turned again for a last sneer before pulling out into the street, swinging in and out of William Bradshaw's driveway, and returning past Ben who stood waving and calling: "Anytime, Friend."

Marion turned from her survey of the house. "Don't tell me you gave him a big tip too? What did he do to earn it?"

"Well..."

"I'm glad all this tipping and spending is over. At least for food and all that. I'm not used to it and I was beginning to get worried. Did we spend too much?"

"Don't worry about that," Ben said. He felt the crumpled five-dollar bill in his pocket that was the remains of his $1000 pile. "Shall we go in?"

Marion stood shyly behind Ben as he unlocked the front door. He turned to her, considered picking her up and carrying her across the threshold, but subdued the impulse. He bowed his head and swept his arm out.

"Mahdahm."

Disappointed, Marion walked into the front hall. A note was wedged between the mirror and the molding over the false fireplace. Ben took it down and read it, smiling, nodding his head, looking serious, smiling again.

"Rose thinks of everything," he said.

When Marion smiled weakly in reply, he expanded. "She wants us to spend the first night here alone. She'll have Donald bring the boys up tomorrow. There's lobster in the icebox. I'm hungry. How about you?"

Without waiting for an answer, Ben led the way into the kitchen and awkwardly pulled the string for the ceiling light with his teeth. Then he dropped the suitcases by the kitchen table and headed for the refrigerator. The damp bag he pulled out barely contained two black and orange lobsters which had wooden pegs clamping their jaws shut.

"They're alive!" Marion said.

"Course they're alive. That's the only way to eat them. Drop them in boiling water, melt some butter—"

"You drop them in alive?"

"Yes. Haven't you ever had lobster?"

"In a restaurant. And sometimes my father brought some home, but they weren't for us kids."

"Glad to see your father had good taste in something."

"What do you mean?"

"There must have been a few times when he was tempted to drop your mother in with the lobsters."

"Oh, Ben."

"Maybe just once in a long while?"

"He used to bring it home in a bag too. My mother wouldn't touch it. She wouldn't cook it, she wouldn't eat it; she wouldn't even look at it. He used to wait until we went to bed and then he'd fix it for himself."

"Are you trying to tell me something, suggesting perhaps that I should be like your father? Is that it? And you play the queen like your mother?"

"Not I was just trying to tell you why I didn't know they were cooked alive. That's all, Ben."

"Mmmm. Well, I'll show you how to do it once, but pay attention cause you'll be lobster chef from now on. All right? Any objections."

"Yes." "No!"

Ben filled a huge pot from the cupboard under the pantry sideboard with cold water, carried it to the stove, and turned the gas on high. He measured out two teaspoons of salt and dropped them in, twisting his wrist quickly for each spoonful and nodding smugly to Marion.

"Juuuuust so," he said in a poor imitation of a French accent.

Marion was glad for the chance to smile.

He dumped the lobsters out of the bag onto the kitchen table. They sluggishly wound their claws in the air and casually tested their cold tails.

"I better get the rest of those bags. If the water starts to boil, you drop em in."

He was out the door while Marion nervously studied the lobsters, hoping and praying that the water would not boil before her husband came back. She knew it shouldn't boil in that short a time, but she was not sure that it wouldn't.

"We don't have any beer," Ben announced as he returned with the rest of the bags. "I'll run up to the Square and get some."

"Ben?"

"Damn! My keys are upstairs somewhere. I suppose I could walk. It'll take me ten minutes. You drop them in as soon as the water boils."

"Ben!"

"What! I'm in a hurry."

"How do you pick them up?"

"Just grab them by the body. Like this." Marion shrank back as Ben lifted a lobster and dropped it back onto the table. "Don't be silly now," he said. "They can't hurt you if you're careful. See. They're pegged. Just watch out for the tail if they wake up."

"Ben. I don't want any beer. I don't need any. Really."

"I like beer with my lobster." He stopped speaking and let his breath out slowly, deliberately. "If you're afraid to do it, I can do it when I come back, but they take twenty minutes to cook."

"Oh I'll do it. I just haven't done it before."

"And get a pan, a little one," Ben called back as he headed out the door, "and melt some butter. I'll be back in no time flat."

As soon as Ben left, as if they were awaiting the slam of the front door as their signal to go into action, the lobsters crawled toward opposite ends of the kitchen table. Marion watched them, a motionless, terrified little girl in an aquarium of escaped octopuses. One gained the edge of the table, leaped to the floor, and lay there on its back, testing its feet and tailsnap. Marion was working up courage to kick it when the front doorbell rang. She ran to answer, ready to embrace Ben and plead for mercy.

Through the glass in the front door she saw a mild-looking man with graying, receding, hair and a jut-jawed woman waiting on the porch.

"Mrs. Connell," the man said, smiling, "my name is Pete Langley and this is my wife, Jenny. Jenny says we shouldn't come barging in like this—"

"Never mind that now," Jenny Langley said. "We're here now. We just wanted to welcome you and give you this." With the air of a woman who is perpetually prepared to have doors slammed in her face she presented a basket overflowing with fruit and covered with yellow cellophane. When Marion did not respond immediately, Jenny Langley sucked in her cheeks and nodded once to remind herself she was a fool for ever having listened to her husband. "It isn't much, but we thought you might not have any—"

"Oh, but it's beautiful," Marion said. "That's the nicest thing..."

"We won't stay," Jenny said, partly because she could think of nothing else to say at the moment and her dumb husband wasn't helping any; partly because she wished to remind this young woman that it would have been polite to have at least invited them into the front hall, but mostly because she couldn't stand the idea of having a weeping woman on her hands. Feminine frailty did not appeal to Jenny's instincts. Any woman that resorted to it was immediately suspect.

"I'm awful," Marion said. "Please come in. Won't you have a cup of tea?"

"I suppose we could find time for that," Pete Langley said.

"No, no, now you know better than that, Peter. You haven't done your union books for the meeting. You said they had to be done before—"

"I know what I said, Dear. Don't get your motor all heated up. I'll get them done. Maybe, if you're good, I'll let you do them." He smiled at his wife who showed little appreciation or even recognition of his sense of humor. "I guess we'll be going along, Mrs. Connell, but we did want to say hello. And please call me Pete. Since your husband's a Democrat, I suppose you're one too?"

"Here we go again," Jenny said.

"I guess I am," Marion said. "Ben is and my family are—is. Is that bad?"

"Figured as much," Pete said. "I suppose it'll have to be all right. But I'm glad you'll be busy with the boys and the housework. I have my hands full arguing with your husband. He can be as stubborn as a Missouri mule when it comes to politics. I hope I don't have to take on the two of you."

"I'm afraid I don't know much about it."

"Politics is people, Mrs. Connell. That's why—"

"Peter!" Jenny said.

"Honestly, Mrs. Connell, I'm—I mean we're—all of us in the neighborhood, even that sonofabitch next door, if you'll pardon my language, but you'll see what I mean, we're glad Ben's found himself a good woman and we hope you like it here." Marion blushed. "If there's anything at all my wife or I can do to help, you let us—"

"Come on, Peter. You're making another speech."

"No, Dear. I was—"

"You could do something," Marion said.

Jenny stopped pulling on her husband's arm to scrutinize Marion. She had become used to her husband's helping out neighbors and friends, especially Ben Connell who was sinfully stupid about mechanical things and household repairs, but she did not want to believe that the new mistress of the house next door would have the gall to put Peter to work the day she arrived. Still, she was puzzled by

Marion's shy manner. Was she always that apologetic or was that part of the act?

"You want Peter to come over tomorrow?"

"No." Marion said. "I feel stupid, but—"

"You want him to do something now." Don't feel stupid. I feel stupid for coming over here. And my stupid husband's falling for the helpless act again. "Well, he's all yours."

"It won't take a minute," Marion called after her new neighbor, but the woman was gone. "I feel so stupid. I hope your wife isn't mad?"

"Jenny? Don't mind her. She's a little strong-minded, but she's a good girl. What seems to be the trouble?"

"Could you come into the kitchen for a second?"

Marion closed the front door, debating a second whether she should or not, put the basket of fruit on a hall chair, and followed Pete into the kitchen. He walked slowly in, glancing about him to make sure everything was in place and working. He stopped for a moment to stare at the Swiss clock on the hall mantelpiece.

The lobster on the kitchen floor had found his feet and was almost under the stove. The other lobster had paused at the edge of the table.

"That," Marion said, pointing at the lobster near Pete's feet. "And that. I'm supposed to put them in the pot. And I don't dare to."

Pete smiled broadly but did not laugh as he bent to pick up the lobster on the floor and then took the other one from the table. He carried them into the pantry, laid them in the sink, and turned the cold water on.

"They do look pretty mean. I'll just rinse them off a little. Ben's pretty fussy about his lobster. Once he..." Pete was putting the cover on the pot when Ben walked in.

"What's the matter, Marion? Is something wrong? Pete?"

"Hi, Ben. Nothing wrong. Jenny and I just dropped by to meet your missus, and wish her good luck, and I smelled your lobster cooking and I just had to have a looksee, see if they looked any good or if you got stung again."

"What do you mean 'stung?' I only got stung once. Why don't you stay and have some?"

"No, Ben, no thanks. Jenny's after me to catch up on my union homework. I'll see you later. It was a pleasure meeting you, Mrs. Connell. If you ever need anything, just ring our bell."

"Thank you," Marion said. "Thank you very much."

"Hope you like the neighborhood. It had to figure, Ben, that she'd be a Democrat."

"At least she isn't a union man who votes straight Republican. You sure you won't have any lobster?"

"No thanks, Ben. Really, I appreciate it but I've got the union books yet. I see your clock in the front hall isn't working."

"No, I've been meaning to take that in."

"Maybe I should take it over to the basement and see if... "

Marion was setting the table when Ben returned from the front door.

"He's a tremendous guy. Getting pretty nosey though. Hey, what are you doing?"

"Setting the table?" Marion stopped arranging the mismatched crockery and silverware. "Did I do something wrong?"

"We ought to eat in the dining room," Ben said, "From the good china. After all, it is our first night in the old house. And it'll be a long time before we get a chance to eat alone again."

Ben poked at the steaming lobsters while Marion took the fragile china from the dining room cupboard and carefully rinsed the dust from the blue and yellow patterns.

"Ben, do we have a tablecloth to put down."

"What's wrong with the one on there? It's hand-crocheted lace."

"For lobster? Don't you want to save it for when company comes or special occasions."

"This is a special occasion. What better time than now. I'm here. You're here. Pretty glistening company, I'd say. Do you want to wait until we're 85? Let's enjoy what we have now."

Wondering how you remove butter stains from lace, Marion sat down to a steaming lobster on a steak platter, melted butter in a fragile tea cup, and beer in a gold-rimmed glass.

"This is living," Ben said. He thrust a linen napkin into his loosened collar then raised his glass. "To us. And the boys." While Marion sipped hesitantly, he swigged half his beer, then put his glass down hard. "Damn! The bowls. I forgot the bowls for the shells. Always something."

"I'll get them," Marion said and pushed back her chair. "I'm sorry. I didn't know what we'd need."

"Don't get up. It's not your fault. I should have told you. I didn't think of it. You might check with me from now on, though, if you're in doubt."

"I'll get them. Really, I don't mind."

"No. I hate to see people get up from the table once they've sat down. We'll just do without. How can you enjoy a meal if you have to jump up and down every two seconds. That's no way to live. We'll be all right. I hate to see people not enjoying a meal and you can't enjoy yourself if you have to leap around like a kangaroo. Eat up and enjoy your meal. We really should have bowls though."

Marion, under orders to have a good time, smiled as she picked meat from a claw, dipped it in the butter, and tried to get it into her mouth instead of on the tablecloth and her dress, but she could not help noticing the water that squirted onto the tablecloth out of the neck Ben was assaulting with metal nut crackers.

Almost through with his lobster, Ben noticed that Marion was still dabbing at hers. He took over cracking her shells and showed her how to pick the meat out of the body. Grateful, but still less than enthusiastic about the fare, Marion was happy to have her gift of body and legs accepted by Ben.

"Best meat there is. Mmmm," Ben said. "That hit the spot. Want another beer? I'll get it. You haven't touched yours. What's the matter?"

"I don't really like beer. But I'd love a cup of tea. Do you have any in the house?"

"Tea." Ben rid his mouth of a word that tasted weak and full of leaves. "I've got coffee around, but you won't find tea on my account. I'll just go in the parlor and read the paper until you're through. If that's all right with you."

"Sure," Marion said, before realizing that an answer was not expected. Alone, she tried to finish her first meal in her new house. Seeing that Ben was absorbed in his paper, she cracked the remaining shells and, without removing the meat, pushed them into the pile of discards. It was a shame to waste the meat, especially since it was so expensive, but she did not like it.

Ben jumped up, threw the newspaper on the floor, and strode into the dining room as she raised her napkin from her lap and wiped her hands and mouth.

"All done? I'll show you my dishwashing system." He stopped and stared at her pile of shells. "Marion! Look at this!" He waved one of the cracked full shells in front of her face, a priest with a chewed and mutilated host. "It's full of meat. What are you throwing that away for? That's one of the best pieces." He pulled her platter to his place, sat down and rummaged through it. Tearing apart each full piece with his teeth and fingers, he lectured her with disparaging sighs and grunts and stern looks. Thoroughly finished, he was still dissatisfied. "Didn't you know there was meat in those shells?"

"Yes," she answered, her eyes on her lap.

"Why—why that's—that's—DECEITFUL! If there's anything I hate, it's deceit. Are you listening to me, Marion?" He waited until she raised her glance, briefly, then dropped it to the table top. "I want everything above board. If you don't like something, just say so. Do you understand?"

"I really don't like lobster, Ben. I—"

"How do you know you don't like it? Have you ever tried it? That's no way to be—condemn something before you even taste it. What if we all did that. Where would we be now? Drinking milk and eating bread. What if the Earl of Sandwich decided he didn't like sandwiches before he even tried them? What would he be eating for dinner today? Soup? Crackers...?"

Marion knew her husband was right, at least about deceit. It was no way to build a marriage. Her own father and mother had concealed so much from each other that they had established two separate worlds in one house. When Ben finished his lecture, led her into the pantry, fitted the metal stopper in the drain, and began filling the sink, she touched his elbow lightly. He started as if she had bumped into him while carrying a sizzling frying pan.

"What! What's the matter?"

"Ben—I asked Pete to come in. He wasn't being nosey or anything. I asked him in."

Ben finished rolling up his sleeves, turned to his wife, and put his hands on his hips. "Why? Anything wrong?"

"No, no, it was just, I was—afraid to pick the lobsters up, and one got onto the floor—"

"On the floor!"

"It's all right. Pete washed it off."

"Pete washed it off. Nice going. My next-door neighbor has to come into my kitchen to pick up lobsters off my floor, wash them off and put them in my pot while my wife watches like an idiot. Nice going. He must think I've married an imbecile. That's great. Just great. I can imagine what Jenny's doing now. Probably calling up the neighborhood to tell them about my stupid wife."

"I didn't mean to do all that. I was just afraid. I've always been afraid of them. My mother wouldn't let us near them. She used to leave the kitchen whenever she saw my father come in with a damp bag. Sometimes, hah, he brought home a wet towel in a double bag just to get her goat."

"Am I supposed to take the hint? Are you veiling a few threats? I don't give a damn what your mother did. My wife will have to know how to cook lobster and that's all there is to it. You leave the kitchen when I bring a lobster home and I'll throw it after you!"

"Ben! I was just telling you about my mother because I thought it was funny. I didn't mean anything. You're awfully touchy."

"Touchy! I just don't like dirty lobster dropped in a pot by my neighbor who goes out of his way to help and has plenty of other things to do. I don't want it to happen again. Jenny's probably having a field day."

Scattering soap flakes into the water with one hand, Ben dumped the garbage into a bag on the floor and plunged the fragile dishes into the sink with the other. "Maybe you can learn to do this right. Maybe you won't be afraid of hot water and soap."

Marion watched, wondering when the first dish would break and wondering if Ben was also used to rinsing mops in the same sink. It looked like it.

"Now. You completely submerge dishes and utensils and let them stay that way for five minutes. Then. All you have to do is softly wipe them with the dishrag. Saves a lot of scrubbing. Then you drain the sink. Adjust the water faucets to just slightly more than lukewarm. Rinse quickly. Fill the sink and then you take each piece out separately and dry it and put it away. Obviously you can't fit everything into the sink at once so you do them in sets. Two sets is normal. Which means filling the sink up twice for wash and twice for rinse. Using the least amount of water possible. Do you have any questions? Does your mother have another way?"

"Don't you have a drainboard or a drainer?"

"Do I look like I have a drainer?"

"Do you use that sink for mops?"

"Of course, but sinks can be cleaned."

"Wouldn't it be cheaper to fill some kind of a basin instead of the whole sink?"

"You—just—fill—it—enough—to cover—the dishes," Ben said, letting his words and breath out slowly.

"Don't you use a lot of towels that way? Wiping them right away?"

"Now listen, if you're just going to criticize—I don't like dishes lying around a drainboard attracting flies. Now if you don't want to do it my way, forget it. Just forget it. I'm sorry I took all this time and trouble to show you. I'm sure your mother has a lot to say on the subject."

"My mother—," Marion stopped herself. It wasn't the time to tell Ben that her mother hadn't washed a dish in years, that the children had taken turns and done them as best they could. "I'll do it your way, Ben," she promised.

When her husband, satisfied that he had set things on the right course, had returned to the parlor and his paper, she finished the first set of dishes according to his method, but she could not bring herself to refill the sink which, despite its soaking in soap and rinse water, still looked grimy. She half closed the pantry door that led to the dining room and parlor, shook a little soap on the dishcloth for every dish and pan and piece of silverware, washed and rinsed each separately under trickling hot water and laid them on a dishtowel which covered the metal top of the tub sink.

Ben Connell had difficulty concentrating on his newspaper. He had not read one in two weeks and felt out of touch, but even the war news from Europe and the Yankees, whom he openly hated and secretly cherished for their winning ways, could not take his mind from the impending return to a schedule. He would have to go back for the masters' meetings in two weeks and now there would be the tests for the kids who went to summer school and then last-minute interviews and reviewing the records of those teachers hired while he was away and then, school.

Two weeks to get used to her around the house. Christ, I hope I don't have to show her how to make the beds. Now you pull the sheet up. Don't forget to tuck the flaps in. What's she been doing for the last twenty-nine years. Being waited on? What'll she do with the boys? Two weeks for them to get used to her and then Joey's off to school. Tommy will have time. This was to be the big summer. Rides, picnics, games, the beach. We did go half a dozen times, but then the marriage, the honeymoon, school soon. "Marion!"

"Yes, Ben."

"What do you say if I go down and get the boys?"

"Oh. Sure. If you want to, Ben."

"Not if you don't want me to. Make up your mind, yes or no. I just thought it seemed too quiet around here. And we did have two weeks alone. What do you say?"

"Yes."

"You don't sound too enthusiastic."

Her husband gone, Marion Connell hurried upstairs to investigate the rest of the house. She found notes from Rose scattered around the rooms, dealing with every aspect of her husband's and stepsons' lives. At first she welcomed the helpful, friendly notes—"Extra towels in bathroom hamper, Dear"—but soon resented the instructive ones—"Joseph trained to pick up clothes. Good idea to continue. Thomas should be taught as soon as possible." Marion began to have second thoughts about the helpfulness of her newly-inherited relations.

In the master bedroom, she enjoyed rummaging through her husband's effects in the vanity and bureau, but the room's wall paper doubly depressed her: because of its drab brown color and its good condition which lent no excuse for early replacement. The mahogany-stained bed did not look wide enough for two people to sleep comfortably. Marion sat on the edge of the bed and pressed her hands into the mattress before submitting to whim and bouncing once. There wasn't much support there.

Marion skipped downstairs and brought up her lightest suitcase. She laid out her pink nightie on the bed and unpacked a few dresses. When she opened the door of the tall walk-in closet, she had an urge to run and find her husband and hug him. At least a half dozen dresses hung from the pole that ran eight feet to the back of the closet. Ben had said nothing about buying her a new wardrobe. He had not even dropped a hint. She swept the hangers into her arms and rushed the dresses to the bed to line them up for examination. It was not until the bed was covered with dresses and she had turned the ceiling light on to supplement the rays of the bedside lamp that she noticed the note pinned to the hem of a soft blue cocktail dress: "All fairly new or in pretty excellent condition. Shame to waste these. Fit? If not, alterations should. If you can't sew, give me a ring—Rose."

She was sitting alone on the bed, the dresses pushed away into a pile, when the phone rang.

"Well?" her mother asked.

"Hi, Ma. How are things."

"Never mind about that. You know how things are here. They never change. How are things with you is the question. Was I right or was I right?"

"Ma, don't start that again. I don't feel up to it." Marion realized instantly that she had said the wrong thing.

"Something wrong already, is that it?"

"No, nothing's wrong, Ma. Everything's fine."

"You certainly don't sound like a blushing bride. Looks to me as if I wasn't far off—"

"Ma, I'm just tired. Can I call you tomorrow? Please?

"When you're too tired to talk, things can't be hunky-dory. Well, I'll wait for your call."

Marion wondered, as she trudged back up to the bedroom to hang the dresses up, if her father had ever really loved her mother. He had stopped showing it in front of the children as long as she could remember. Every night, he came home from work with the newspaper tucked under his arm, said "Hello, Mary," and without ever coming close enough to his wife to know if she smelled of cabbage or perfume, nodded his head gravely and went into the bedroom to read the paper until his wife and children had had supper and his was ready.

Ma never said she cared, but she couldn't have been that cross with us all the time, she couldn't have turned down her mouth so often without a temptation to smile, she couldn't have harangued so much about everything we did bad and pooh-poohed everything we did good without some reason. We had to go to Pa for love, at least for the first open show of it. She held back and tried to look stern and cold and forbidding. But eventually, when the scolding and the cross looks and the nagging and the gumbeating, when they were all done, she would give in, break down, soften up and give us a hug. If it was worth waiting for through all that. And now she lives with her opinions.

"He doesn't want a wife. He wants a maid."

"Ma, we're in love. There are plenty of women he could have had if he wanted to. And long before this."

"He doesn't think, I hope, God knows what the man thinks, that any daughter of mine is being taken in by his pussyfooting around and his flowers. Is he going to get rid of the furnishings or not? Answer me that, Marion!"

"Why make a big thing about furnishings, Ma? He hasn't got money to burn."

"Who's going to Hawaii? Who's playing the Shah of Persia? That man has money for anything he wants money for. It's the principle of the thing. Mark my words, if you don't put your foot down now, you'll be praying to God to have mercy and take you out of all that."

She could never tell her mother about the dresses, for, nosey and irritating as she could be, it was nothing compared to her moments of vindictive triumph. Marion would never hear the end of it if she ever breathed a word of it to anyone in her family. She hung the dresses up, pushed them along the pole to the back of the closet, and hung Ben's loose, floppy scotch plaid bathrobe in front of them.

"Marion, hey Marion, come on down here," Ben called from the backyard. She went into the bathroom, leaned over the tub, and watched through the small, dirty window as Ben and his sons began a game of dodge ball. The boys were yelling ecstatically for their father to try and hit them with the soft, red ball and Ben, for the moment, seemed as young and carefree as they, as full of fun as he had been before bringing his wife back to his home.

They stopped playing when Marion came out on the back porch. She had met the boys before, they had all gone on outings, but then she had been a nice lady.

"Say hello, boys," Ben bullied, "say hello to your new mother."

Marion nodded to Joseph as solemnly as he had said, "Hello, Ma'am," but she could not help smiling when Tommy came up on the porch, frowning and concerned to ask: "Do you like my house?"

"Yes, Tommy, it's very nice."

"D'you see evey bit?"

"I guess so."

"In the attic 'n the cellar?"

"I've seen enough for today. Maybe tomorrow."

"All right, boys," Ben said. "Bedtime."

"I wanta play," Tommy said.

"You haven't played with us for a long time," Joseph said.

"You get ready right away and I'll tell you a story."

"What story?" they asked.

"An animal story?" Tommy asked. "I want a animal story like the kangroo with four feet."

"An airplane story, Daddy?" Joseph pleaded gently.

"I'll tell you the story about—maybe I told you that one. Did I tell you the story about the elephant who thought he was an airplane."

"No, daddy."

"No, you didn't."

Ben came downstairs triumphant after a successful exhibition of his story-telling prowess.

"They really liked it. That should hold them for awhile."

"Do you tell them one every night."

"Almost every night." He picked the newspaper out of his chair and sat down. "Sometimes I don't feel up to it."

"I think I'll get ready for bed, Ben."

"Already! It's only eight o'clock. The night's young. Oh, I see. You're all sexed up and dying to lure me to bed."

"No, I don't feel like that, Ben."

"Oh? What do you feel like?"

"Ben." Marion paused.

She finally received an answering grunt: "Mmm."

"The closet has dresses in it that were Catherine's and there's a note from Rose on one of them."

"Yeah?"

"She thinks I should alter them."

"Yeah."

"And wear them."

77

"Yeah, well it's all right with me. At first, I—I wasn't in favor of the idea, but Rose convinced me that it would be an awful waste since most of them are pretty new. It's fine with me. Go ahead and do what you want with them. Fix them how you like."

"I couldn't wear them, Ben."

"You don't like them? I picked out some of them myself. Catherine thought I had pretty good taste."

"That's just it, Ben. They're Catherine's."

"Aw, come on now. You're not jealous. I'll get you some when I can afford it."

"No, I'm not jealous, but I couldn't wear Catherine's clothes. No matter what."

"Well don't get uppity with me. If you don't want to wear them, you don't. It's your decision. You don't have to climb on your high horse with me. It doesn't matter if it's a Hell of a waste of money. Do you know anyone who'd appreciate them? Since you don't want them."

"Couldn't we just—get rid of them?"

"What! Throw them out! Throw out good dresses."

"I didn't mean—maybe we could give them to the Salvation Army?"

"Just like that. And have any slut of a whore wearing them on her back. Bring in the new and sweep out the old. You don't like them, so out they go. I'm not made of money you know. It cost me a Hell of a lot to take you to Hawaii and now I'm flat broke and I owe a shitload of money and you want to throw things away right off the bat."

"But you said you'd saved—I thought—could I just put them away some place, down in the cellar or maybe in the attic?"

"And have them rot! I'd rather throw them out then that. Just leave them where you found them. I'll take care of them. I'm sure there are plenty of women who would appreciate a new wardrobe."

Marion folded her clothes and hung them over the straight-backed chair beside the bed. She put on her pink negligee because she didn't want to go downstairs for the other suitcase. She felt as if she were advertising false goods.

When Ben came upstairs a few hours later, he was mumbling to himself. He undressed noisily and climbed heavily into bed. Moving restlessly, he occasionally articulated a comment.

"Big night." "Sex unlimited." "Hoo-hah."

Suddenly, determinedly, he turned on his side and thrust his hand up under Marion's negligée and clasped her breast. "Oh, Ben."

He was surprised that she was awake, then startled when she turned to him. The remembrance of Catherine's irritation when aroused from sleep flashed through his mind.

Marion Connell sleepily clung to her husband after glancing quickly at the closet door.

7 | Some Friends

When Sean returned with the milk and doughnuts, he was surprised to see his mother march directly to the front door in response to his knock. She didn't ease into the dining-room first, sneak into the parlor and peer through the curtains to see if it was a salesman or a policeman or a rapist.

"Gettin' pretty brave in your old age."

"Anyone who slit my throat now would be doing me a favor."

"Speak, Great Cynic. I've got a couple of friends who'd be willing to oblige you for a fee. Say, two bottles of beer."

"Knowing your friends, I don't doubt it. Now be quiet. Your father's resting."

"I'm not asleep," Ben grumbled as they walked past the dining room door, "and his friends would slit their own mother's throat for half a glass of near beer."

"Sounds like Sweet Daddy's recovering," Sean said as he placed his bundle on the kitchen table.

"Just leave him alone. Ignore him. He's not up to your wisecracks. And I'm not either. Why don't you go up and smile at yourself in the bathroom mirror. You seem to get along famously."

"Mother, you've been sharpening your wits. And here I come home, full of peace and love, from a short communion with nature. Alas."

"There's another kind of communion you might be thinking about."

"Oh, Christ. Wrong word. Wrong name too."

"It isn't funny. I don't know what happened to you. We brought you up like a good Catholic. And you used to be so religious. What's the matter, you too lazy to go to Mass once a week?"

"No, Ma. It's just that Latin was always my weak subject, pretty dry, and I gag on incense. Guess I'm allergic to it."

"He's allergic to God, that's what he is," Ben called from the dining-room. "Thinks he's bigger than God. Sean Almighty."

"Eavesdropped by my own Da. I'm allergic to God the Catholic, if you really want to know, Pa. Who the Christ are we to pity the poor Protestants and curse those scum, the Infidel Jews. If you want to go to Catholic Heaven, go to it, but leave me out!"

"You are out! And you'd be damned glad to get rid of me wouldn't you. Smart ass. Read one book and think you know all the answers."

"You taught me all the Catholic answers and they weren't enough. You think—"

"Stop it!" Marion cut in. "You want the neighbors to think we're a bunch of Hungarian gypsies yelling at each other."

"You and that infidel crew you run around with. Go ahead. Laugh at God. You'll see. You'll see."

"Can you see in Heaven, Pa?"

"You wise shit. You won't even see the door to Heaven."

"Knock, knock. Who's there?"

"Go upstairs," Marion said, "and stop taunting your father and let me get supper, Why did you bother to even come home if you're just going to cause trouble."

"He's broke," Ben called. "That's why. He's a free-loader, a bum."

"I didn't start this God Almighty conversation, Ma."

"A bum."

Sean was lying on the couch with his back to the den door, watching the Three Stooges on television, when his mother came into the room softly. He pretended not to notice her. She stood behind him, fidgeting with a button on her sweater as she gathered her thoughts.

"Seanie?"

He grunted in response to his childhood nickname. "Supper's ready. I fixed a roast beef, and baked potatoes, and cauliflower because I know you love it."

"Fell out of love with it in the service, Ma. Now I'm mad about brussel sprouts. Got any?"

"Do you have to be so disagreeable? Can't you just come down and, for your father's sake, not for mine, keep your mouth shut and eat. He doesn't feel well. And I'm—I'M AT THE END OF MY NERVES!"

"Take it easy, Ma."

"How can I take it easy? How? You tell me. He sits like a simp on the porch waiting for you all day and he won't eat and now you're home and he's too upset to even talk. Is that any way to treat your father?"

"No. If that's what I did, no. It's no way to treat my mother either. But why don't you just lay off religion and my friends. I'll be down in a couple of minutes, after this is over."

"Supper's going to get cold."

"I'll be right there, Ma."

When Bean came downstairs, supper was on the table and his father was still sulking in his dining-room bed. Sean went to the door.

"Pa."

"Come in, come in. Don't stand there shouting at me."

"I'm sorry, Pa, if I upset you."

"If?"

"I'm sorry. Will you come and eat supper now. I won't say another word. All right?"

"I don't want you to bust a gut trying to keep that promise."

Sean smiled. "All right. I'll say one word and that'll be all. Supper."

"Give me a hand here," Ben ordered, gruffly allowing his son to help him. "Don't go too fast now, I'm not on roller skates."

Marion was trying hard to serve everything at the same time. Her husband had tried hard all their married life—by threat, plea, and imprecation—to teach her proper timing in the preparation of food. In his last few years of high school, her son had taken up the cause from his weary father. Marion did not want any tempers to flare, so she hurried to drain the water from the cauliflower, dump it into a soup bowl, and place it on the table next to the platter of roast beef her husband had begun to carve. She took the fork from her place at the table, opened the oven door, and pierced the nearest potato.

"That damn oven," she said. Turning to her men, "The potatoes aren't done."

"Ma, you've used that excuse—" Sean said. "Marion, If I hear that once more—" Ben said.

Father and son stopped, turned to face each other across the length of the table, and smiled.

"I see you've finally got her trained, Pa."

"Mmm," Ben said, unsuccessful in suppressing his smile. "I'll get her trained when they train elephants to fly."

Marion wanted to get her two cents worth in but, afraid the wrong word would destroy the mood, she sat down silently at her place. Immediately she got up to fill the tea kettle and put it on to boil.

"Sit down, Ma."

"You know I hate this Jack-in-the-box jumping up and down. Can't you sit still for one meal."

"I'm just putting the water on," she said, finishing her task and returning to her place.

The meat and cauliflower had been devoured and they were still waiting for the potatoes. Ben looked at his wife, then at his plate, and spoke to his son.

"You're not twenty-one yet."

"No, Pa, I'm not twenty-one til next year."

"Well, if you don't say anything about it, I don't think it would hurt too much if you had a little glass of sherry, do you Marion?"

"No. Ben, of course not."

"I don't like sherry. Got any beer?"

"How do you know you don't like—no, I haven't got any beer. What are you, some kind of alcoholic or something."

"No, Pa. And I never tasted sherry and I never swilled three-point-two percent beer at the PX and I never was served at a minors joint."

"Never mind. I can imagine what you've been up to. I never took a drink of alcohol until I was twenty-five and that's the God's Honest

Truth. And I don't think—"

"I think the potatoes are done," Marion said.

"Why don't you serve them with the ice cream," Sean suggested.

"How did you know I bought ice cream?" she asked.

When they had eaten the baked potatoes, still a little hard and served with cold gravy Ben told Marion not to bother heating up, the ice cream and mince pie. Ben lit up a cigarette, pretending not to notice as Sean followed suit. Marion, braving her husband's ire, did likewise. She hoped Ben would take the occasion to talk to Sean about his insurance and school and other things that were on her mind but that she could not recall at the moment. Instead, her husband began reminiscing.

"Do you remember, Sean, the time you released the handbrake on the car and it rolled into Bradshaw's fence. When I came out, you were as white as a sheet."

"And that old grouch Bradshaw threatened to sue you," Marion added.

"He never did," Ben said. "and you know it. He was just a little upset. He wasn't used to six-year-olds driving cars into his fence. In fact, he fixed it himself. I think I offered to, but for some reason he did it himself and never said another word about it. He wasn't a bad old coot. He was a Republican, but maybe I would have been too if I had his money. He was a lot better than that Italian trash we've got next door now."

"Now Ben, you like the old man and you're always talking with Angelo."

"They're all right, but that other one, that hussy, that—"

"Don't get upset, Ben."

"She's not worth getting upset about."

Sean did not express his view that a divorced woman with a boyfriend is not necessarily a hussy. He had no hopes of changing his father's mind about that.

"I see the drugstore's closed," he said. "Since when?"

"Last year," Marion said. "The old man retired."

Robert Crotty

"Do you remember the time you ran away," Ben said, "and you got as far as the corner and the Old Man Tsiatsios called me and lured you into the drugstore with a candy bar until I came. The old miser made me pay for it too. Well, he didn't make me, but he kept saying, 'I gave him one of the big ones, the big ones.' So I gave him a dime and thanked him and when we got home and took your jacket off, there was the candy wrapper still in your pocket and it looked an awful lot like one of the little ones, the little ones. Maybe the other nickel was for the phone. He was pretty decent though..."

As Ben rambled on, Sean became less and less enchanted with his childhood actions and the reactions of the neighborhood. Most of the incidents he could remember little about, except that his father had usually chosen to tell his stories in front of company. Bored with the cute child he had been, Sean nevertheless listened. He fixed another cup of tea for himself and his mother and smoked cigarettes, ignoring his father's cautions against them, especially since his father usually had a cigarette burning in his hand as he issued his warnings. Sean listened, and sipped, and smoked, and waited for the phone to ring.

"... and then Joe and Tommy admitted that they had done it and I had already given you the spanking for it so I took you out to Anchors Aweigh, you remember that big restaurant with all the animals in back and the shiphouse, and Tommy and Joe were drooling when we got back—"

The smile disappeared from Ben Connell's face when he heard the phone and saw his son leap to answer it.

"Yeah, Hi." "No." "Nothin'"

Ben winced. Marion stubbed out her cigarette, squinting against the last trails of smoke.

"Really!" "Sure sounds great." "Yeah, yeah I'm sure." "Okay." "No." "Yep." "Yep." "Just honk." "Yes." "I'll see ya."

"Who was that?" Ben asked grimly.

"Just a friend."

"Does he have a name or are you ashamed to mention it."

"Roger."

86

"Oh."

"You remember him, Pa. Remember? The little guy with blond hair and the big ears. He came up on the porch that night before we went to the game and he was talking to you about the Red Sox and—"

"Yes, yes. What did he want?"

"In fact, he just asked me if you'd be home so he could say hello, but I told him I figured you were pretty tired and probably didn't want to talk tonight."

"You told him all that?"

"Well, no, I just said no, but I figured that. You look kind of tired."

"What did he want?"

"He just wanted to know if I wanted to go out."

"Tonight?"

"You just got home," Marion said. She stood up and quickly began clearing the table. "You could spend one night at home."

"Tonight?"

"Yeah, Pa. Tonight."

"How did he know you were home?"

"Well, I gave him a call when I was out for a walk."

"That's pretty sneaky," Marion called from the pantry, "going behind our backs."

"I didn't go behind anyone's back, Ma."

"If you ever want to call anyone, you can call from here," Ben said.

"I just happened to pass a telephone booth and—"

"I'll bet!" Marion said.

"Oh, Ma. Come off it, will you. I'm not one of the Great Conspirators around here. In fact, I can't even get a straight answer to a question."

"Don't start that again," she said, looking to her husband for support.

Ben Connell's head was down and he was fidgeting with his tie. Sean lit another cigarette in preparation for the final word. Marion stopped rattling dishes in the sink.

"Where does Roger want to go?"

"Just down to Revere."

"Revere Beach! Where all the hoods hang out? That's one Hell of a place to go."

"We're just going down to the Dodgems and maybe have a pizza."

Ben Connell retired to his room without further comment, leaving both his wife and son perplexed since the head of the household usually insisted on the last word.

Since the circulation had just painfully returned to his legs, he hated to lie down but he was exhausted.

He's going. He's gone. Back to his friends and his old ways. What are you doin'? Nothin'. My stupid old man is telling stories about when I was a kid and that's nothin.' Let him go if he feels that way. Then it'll be just Marion and me. Can we get along with nothing to argue about? She doesn't seem to care. But she must. Too many bills. Too many problems. She's getting harder. There was a time when she'd plead with him, maybe even cry. She hasn't cried for a long time. He's going to ruin his life. He doesn't take anything seriously. He doesn't take anything seriously. He'll play the fool until it's too late.

Sean was in the den turning the television switch from one station to another, Marion was pacing the kitchen, and Ben was brooding in his new downstairs bedroom when a car horn sounded. Sean turned off the television, picked up his overcoat from the chaise lounge and ran down the stairs. His mother trudged up to the lower landing and met him with a frown.

"Don't stay out late now."

"All right, Ma."

"And don't spend your money foolishly."

"Yep."

She lowered her voice to an intense whisper as he went down the stairs into the front hall, "And don't come home stinking of alcohol, for God's sakes!"

"Sean!"

"Yessss, Pa." Sean stood inside the open front door, studying his friend's car, trying to make out who was in it besides Roger.

"Just a minute."

"What do you want?"

"I want to talk to you about your insurance for a minute."

"Now?"

"Right now. This is important."

"Oh, Pa, for Chrissakes, Roger's waiting for me. Can't we—Where'd you get the cane?"

Ben hobbled into the front hall as his son stared at him.

"Never mind that. Don't try to change the subject. I want you to take over the payments of your insurance. Do you understand? Now this is important. If you don't pay it on time, it'll lapse and—"

"Pa, can I talk to you tomorrow. They're waitin' for me."

"Maybe it would be better, Ben," Marion offered from her perch on the landing.

"You keep out of this! Now listen to me, young man, if you don't—"

"I'll pay the insurance, Pa. Okay? I'll see you tomorrow. I'm gonna go now. Goodbye."

"Just one minute!"

Sean stopped on the porch, chafing as his father hobbled to him.

"What do you intend to do for tuition money?"

"Pa, are you crazy. Do we have to discuss this now. I'll see you tomorrow. We'll talk about it then. All right? Please!"

"We'll talk about it right this Goddamn minute! Do you understand me. Here you go running around spending all your money the first night you get home. You think you can blow it all? Who do you think You are? Do you think I'm made of money. I can't support your foolishness."

"I didn't ask you to, Pa."

"Oh, no, but you'll be whining around, asking me for some as soon as you throw away whatever you have left. How much do you intend to spend tonight?"

"This is ridiculous."

"Oh it is, is it? I consider it ridiculous to go out and blow twenty or thirty dollars on an evening of fun when you've got books and things to buy."

"I haven't got thirty dollars and I'm not going to spend twenty."

"You haven't? You haven't! What happened to all that money you were going to get for not taking leaves. You should have five hundred dollars."

"It wasn't anywhere near that, Pa. Don't worry about it. I'm gonna get a loan. Can I go now?"

"A loan! Did you hear that, Marion. Mr. Bigshot hasn't any money. He couldn't come home for leave because he was saving money. But it disappeared. And now Mr. Bigshot says, 'Don't worry. I'm gonna get a loan.'"

"Oh, Sean," Marion said. Shaking her head, she walked slowly down the steps into the kitchen.

Roger called from the car, "Come on, Sean. What's keepin' you?"

Someone in the back seat added, "Yeah. Let's get outa here."

"YOU MIND YOUR OWN BUSINESS!" Ben shouted from the porch. He saw a mustache on one of the young men. "Sure, go on, get out of here, you bunch of bums and take this bum with you. I don't want you stinking up the neighborhood!"

Sean retreated down the steps, head down, saying, almost to himself, "Please, Pa."

"Who's the nut?" came from the car.

"Sh. That's Sean's father. I never seen him like this."

"Ben? Come in, Ben," Marion asked, wondering which of the neighbors were watching and listening.

"Go on! Take him. Go spend your money on sluts and hussies." Ben was banging his cane on the porch floor. "You're all a bunch of no-goods. There isn't one of you that'll amount to a hill of beans. Get out of here or I'll call the cops. BUMS!" he yelled after the speeding car. "Bums—bums."

No one in the car spoke until they were out of the neighborhood.

"What got your father going?" Roger asked.

"I don't know. He—he gets like that sometimes."

"I never saw him that mad."

"No, nobody ever does, except his family. Let's forget it."

"You know Eddie."

"Yeah. Hi, Eddie," Sean said, turning to face the back seat. Eddie nodded.

"And this is Billy Dunn. He works over at the hospital. Sean Connell."

"Hi," Sean said. He shook hands with a slim young man with a bushy mustache and blood-shot eyes.

"Pretty rough night, huh?" Billy said. "Sluts and hussies. Zow-ee. I didn't know that's what you called a pig. You wanta slug of whiskey?"

"No," Sean said, sure that he was going to hate Billy Dunn. Then he changed his mind, deciding that one way of getting even with him would be to drink his whiskey. "Yeah, I do." He tilted the bottle until he was about to gag, coughed, felt the whiskey come up to his nose, took a deep breath and handed the bottle back. "Thank you." He wiped his mouth with the back of his hand.

"Jezuz!" Billy said. He held the bottle up. "Roger told me you could drink, but Christ. I believe ya. You don't have to prove it anymore. Jeezuz."

Sean kept a straight face, but Billy was funny. A loudmouth, an asshole, but harmless. Gee whillikers! Can you drink! Goshamighty. He'd have to explain about the money. Could he tell the truth, that most of it had gone in the last month to stay semi-drunk, to get through his short time. That had been wild. Sean gradually smiled.

"Good to have you back," Roger said:

"I don't give a damn," Ben Connell told his wife, "what the neighbors think." He stood inside the closed front door and looked out at his neighborhood, wondering what the neighbors would think. It's all his fault anyway. Why can't he be reasonable?"

"That's it. Stick up for him. Take his part. He blows five hundred dollars and you make excuses for him. The two of you make quite a team. A vaudeville act—Sean the Bum and Marion the Excuser. You oughto go on Broadway."

91

"Do you want to come in the kitchen and sit down?"

"I'll sit down when I'm damn good and ready. I'm not a cripple, you know."

"I'll be in the kitchen."

Every time. Every time he talks to him like that. At the worst possible moment. He could have done it calmly and reasonably after supper, but no. Goes on with his gab for two hours and never mentions it til now. I hope to Christ Sean doesn't stay too long this time. But, I hope he doesn't leave right away. I don't care if the storm windows never get up and the grass grows over the house. I can't stand much more of this.

Ben Connell seated himself awkwardly at his escritoire. He opened the lid with the small key he kept hidden in his secret change pocket and began sorting through bills. He was sure, if only he could find it, that there was one bill in there that was incorrect or unjustified. Once found, it would lead to a rebate of hundreds, maybe thousands of dollars and he would not have to worry about money again. He would be able to put his son through three more years of college if he found enough mistakes. Idly he thumbed through a little black account book he had once started back in the days when he had insisted on instituting a budget. Every penny was to be accounted for. The plan had been abandoned when he had discovered that listing his expenses could be a very cramping practice.

"Marion! Marion, come here. Take a look at this."

Marion Connell was having none of it. She slipped into the back hall and closed the door, pretending not to have heard and to be searching for something. She hoped her husband would give it up. Minutes later, when she heard her husband's cane and his shuffle across the kitchen floor she bent over and made a show of rummaging through the piles of odds and ends. The door to the back hall opened.

"Marion, didn't you hear me? What are you doing?"

"I was looking—"

"Never mind. I want you to look at something. See this." Ben handed her the little black notebook and pointed his finger at some figures. Before she could focus on them, he thrust an oil bill, dated from the year before, in front of her. "And now see this! We're spending 50 percent more on oil than we did fifteen years ago when I put the storm windows up. These kids don't give a damn. They just throw them up any which way. Drafts don't mean a thing to them. Well, by God, they're going to be put up right this year or I'll know the reason why. If I have to—"

"Ben."

He scowled at his wife for interrupting him and was impatient to go on with his speech. He had never appreciated students who interrupted him in class with questions just when he was getting up a full head of steam.

"Yes."

"The oil costs a lot more than it did fifteen years ago and the house is a lot older now."

"You never did understand the first thing about economics. You wouldn't know a column of figures from a bunch of watermelon seeds. If you knew how to shop for bargains, you could save five hundred dollars a year. You don't even know the first thing about—"

"Well at least," Marion said, having moved out of swinging range of his cane, "I didn't put myself in hook with loan sharks so I could play the great man with my relatives, like some people I know."

"You'd begrudge a piece of bread to a starving beggar, I never in my life threw money away. Everything I've ever given anyone, they've given me back ten times over, but you wouldn't understand that."

"Like the two hundred dollars you gave your nephew for his wedding?"

"Have you been in my desk? YOU'VE BEEN READING MY PAPERS! Who the Hell do you think you are, going through my personal papers!"

"I'll tell you who I am," Marion said, retreating into the front hall ahead of her frustrated husband who banged his hand on the kitchen doorknob and swore as he tried to catch up with her. "I'm the one who has to go out and work for years to pay off bills you won't even tell me about. I'm the one who has to worry every month that I get checks in the mail on time to ten different loan companies so they won't be knocking on my door."

"Your door!"

"And I'm the one who gets most of your loans paid up only to find you've taken out another one so your nephew can say what a great uncle you are. That's who I am. And I'm fed up with your guff!"

"You bitch. If I had two good legs, I'd—"

"You'd beat me. And that would solve everything, wouldn't it. You can't even face the truth. And you better get used to the idea that you're never going to lay a hand on me again or, so help me God, I'll cut your legs out from under you."

Ben Connell watched his wife run up the three stairs from the front hall to the first landing, turn, and go upstairs. He thought she had tears in her eyes. He shuffled into the parlor, staring blankly ahead. Pushing the piles of paper on the escritoire lid back into a corner, he closed the lid but did not lock it. He sat down heavily in the overstuffed chair.

She can't talk to me like that. I'll kill her. That's what I'll do. I'll—I'll kill her. I'll sit here and I won't say a word until she comes downstairs. If it takes hours. I'll sit here and wait. She'll think it's all over. Then I'll calmly ask her for a glass of water and when she brings it to me, I'll throw it in her face and beat her over the head until she's dead. She can't talk to me like that. I'll kill her.

Seconds later, he got up and walked to the foot of the stairs. He waited a moment, trying to translate his anger into his voice, but when he spoke, his tone was nearly normal. "If you talk to me like that again, I'll kill you. If I have to buy a gun, I'll do it. Don't you ever talk to me like that again."

"Go ahead and kill me," Marion called. "You couldn't do much more to me than you've already done. And when I'm gone they'll be no one to put up with you, no one to wait on you, no one to listen to your bullshit. No Margaret. No Sean. No precious Tommy and Joe. And no Goddamn punching bag. Go ahead and kill me." Marion's voice broke. She was crying openly. "You big bag of wind. Go ahead. I don't care.

Go ahead. I don't care. You'd be doing me the greatest favor you ever did me."

8 | Settling Issues

No amount of bullets could stop this mad American. One of the enemy recognized the charging demon. "It's Old Rough and Ready!" The cry went up and the stampede was on. Most of the enemy dropped their rusty flintlocks and fled. Others tried desperately—bowing and crawling, scraping the earth—to surrender to the bloodthirsty attacker's allies. They were cut down. New-mown men.

Two quivering enemy were left in the nest. Shaking hands chattering away on the machine-gun. Frozen by fear to the metal trigger. Ben leaped forward. Legs straddling the barrel of the machine-gun. Ripped the helmet off the first enemy. Tore the pin from a grenade with his teeth. Dropped it in the helmet. Replaced the headpiece. The enemy waiting wide-eyed for his fate. Fingers in his ears to avoid the noise. Ben glimpsed the face, Mr. Milton. "You!" Ben said. The enemy exploded on, over, and around him and the Dublin Post Office.

Old and fat the second enemy. Jumping out of the nest and running. Wearing a skirt. Running with gross wiggle-waddle. Ben flicked the pin from a grenade. Bowled it forward. Under the skirt. Hits a rock and bounces up inside skirt. Enemy stops to fish out enemy within. Ben recognizes Mrs. Toomey. She spreads jarringly over the misty field.

Ben's lieutenant Little Jimmy John arrives.

"Hear! Hear!" Little Jimmy John checks himself. "Or should I say, here, here, we can't have this sort of thing Ben. We need a prisoner or two, Ben. If you're going to Ben decorate the Ben landscape with pyrotechnical Ben Ben!"

Ben turned to find himself facing a horde of beautiful women who gave way to his wife Marion.

"I think it's time, Ben," she said, easing her heavy body out of bed. She turned the light on and dressed quickly.

"Be with you in a minute," Ben said, turning over and diving under the pillow to prepare a stinging battlefield rebuke to his once trusted lieutenant.

"Ben! Come on. You don't want me to have the baby here, do you?"

"The baby? No! Yes. Come on! I won't dress. We'll take the car."

Ben jumped out of bed, frantically pulled on his slippers and bathrobe and started for the top of the stairs.

"Get dressed, Ben. We've got enough time for that. I'll call the hospital."

When Ben reached the driveway, the car was idling with the heater going full blast. Marion was tucked under an afghan on the passenger side of the front seat. Ben jumped in and slammed the door. He stalled the car driving it in reverse with the emergency hand brake on.

"It's okay. It's all right. Everything's okay," Ben said. He ground the starter as he forced the car to life again. "Don't worry. Old Rough and Re—I'll see you through."

"Take it easy, Ben," Marion said. There seemed to be a smile in her voice.

Neither spoke again until they were almost to the hospital which was located at the top of a hill. Ben slowed down and inclined his head toward his wife.

"Which entrance?" he asked.

"Take me around the back, the ambulance entrance, I guess."

"You guess! That's a hell of a way to do things!"

The car coughed, as Ben sputtered, and died five hundred yards from the hospital. Ben tried twice to start it, but the car rolled further back down the hill. He guided it to rest against the curb.

"We can walk from here."

"You could start it with the handbrake."

"Don't tell me how to drive. You don't even know what door you're supposed to go in. Come on. A little walk will do you good."

The cool air woke Ben and cooled his temper. Feeling guilty, he lagged behind Marion. In case she started to slip to the sidewalk, he could dive forward and break her fall. Marion put her head down against the night breeze and trudged forward solidly. Ben followed her, disappointed, through the front entrance which was nearest and found a nurse waiting for them.

"Mrs. Connell?"

Marion nodded and let the nurse take her arm and-guide her off. Ben followed closely and resentfully. The woman had not even spoken to him. He was framing a complaint about this to Doctor Powers when they reached the end of the corridor and the nurse hesitated momentarily to point out a room to him.

"In there, Mr. Connell," she said, and turned down another corridor with his wife who just had time for an over-the-shoulder glance.

Ben opened the swinging door to the waiting room, full of grumbling thoughts about precise, masculine, lesbian women. He was happy to find a male ally to talk to. A young man in a dark gabardine suit with a loose red tie hung across it was sunk in one of the hell dozen brown leather chairs, his yellow-stockinged ankles crossed, a worn magazine face down on his face, Ben knew that he had been there quite some time.

"Been here long?" Ben asked.

The young man rushed his huge hand over his dark, uncombed, curly hair and scratched his broad belly as he turned to focus on Ben. He worked his full, sensual lips out and in to wet them before speaking.

"Who wants to know?"

"My name's Connell. Ben Connell. My wife just came in to have a baby." Ben offered his hand.

"If ya kin believe it," the man said. He took no notice of Ben's proffered hand.

"Yeah," Ben said. "I've been through this before but every time seems like the first."

There was no answer.

Ben hung up his navy blue lightweight summer coat and sat down, leaned back in the too comfortable chair and tapped his feet as he studied the opaque, beaded-glass door, wondering what was going on the other side of it. His one stay in a hospital had not made him eager to return. Regular meals were served at the same time, the same lukewarm temperature, and the same taste. The nurses had no time for a joke. Expecting a ghoul, he was even more depressed by the lady who came to take his blood, a woman so professionally cheerful, so quick with superior quips, that he felt emasculated by the time she bricked off with his blood for her collection. The only thing anyone who worked for the hospital was interested in was the chart at the foot of his bed. He had nightmares about blood running over the floors of his ward and doctors chopping off patients' limbs as they slept while nurses efficiently filled garbage pails with hands, and arms, and legs—his legs. But the shooting pains in his legs went away and he was released after a few days of pills and shots and observation. And none of the unknown faces that stopped to study his chart misread it, on purpose or not, or gave him the wrong medicine.

"I slit fish."

"What!"

"I slit fish for a living. Whuhdyou do?"

"What?"

"You deaf. Nevamind."

"Oh. I teach. That is—"

"One a them."

"—I'm really an administrator now. I sort of teach teachers to teach. I—"

"Sounds cushy."

"I wouldn't say that."

"I did."

"What I mean is—"

"Sure, you work hard and you're underpaid. Try slittin a few barrels of fish, keepin up with the damn production line." The man clipped the magazine in front of him as if it were a foot-long fish. "Chop." He clipped the head off and whirled the fish in his lap. "Chop." The tail detached, he flipped the fish over on its back. "Slit." He reached inside the fish's belly and pulled out a handful of guts. "Plop," the intestines echoed as they hit the pile in the waste barrel. "That's work."

"Teaching can be hard work."

"Whuuuut. Turnin the pages of a book."

"No, not that. Teachers, real teachers, are always working hard to learn new ways of reaching children. A good teacher is always open to new experiences, he's constantly learning about the world around him, and about people, so he can enlarge the world of his students. He—"

"What good did it do me to go to school. I work on the waterfront slittin—"

"You work down in the harbor where the ships come in?"

"I work down in the basement where the fish come in."

"It must be exciting to see the ships from different nations."

"Who looks at boats. I get an hour for lunch, I go over to Skipper Jack's and have a couplea beers and three or four ham sandwiches. I—"

The nurse who had greeted Marion pushed open the door and stepped in, holding it ajar; "Mr. Donatelli, your wife—" Ben noticed that she had a nice figure and if she let her hair down and did something with her face to color it, she would be more than all right.

"Don't tell me, I know. She should be goin in the delivery room any minute. Three different nurses told me that now in the last twenty hours. Is this some kinda game you made up?"

"If you feel that way, Mr. Donatelli," the nurse said precisely, "maybe it's time for you to go home and get some rest. You're not—"

"Maybe it's time for me to go up on the roof and jump off, but I ain't gonna."

The nurse tried to enlist Ben's understanding with a glance, but he pretended to have missed it. She turned and left quickly.

"What a grunt," Donatelli said.

"A what?" Ben asked. He liked the appropriateness of the word.

"A grunt, a grunt. She sounds like the slicin machine at work. I'd like to stick—"

The door swung open and the nurse, without stepping in at all, raised her nose in the direction of Donatelli.

"I was instructed by the head nurse to ask you if you were interested in watching the birth of your child. I would have if you—"

"Whattayou talkin about?" For the first time, Donatelli's voice had some life in it. "You keep a guy here all day and all night and then you wanna torcher him. No thanks. Just tell me Lois's all right and show me the kid some time. That'll do me fine. Watch him? Not me, Lady!"

"It's fairly obvious that you need some sleep," the nurse said cuttingly, and started to back away.

"Hold it, Sweetheart!" Donatelli said. "My friend here ain't been asked."

The nurse turned her reddening face to Ben with a killing look that accused him of conspiracy.

"He likes to learn all about new things. He wants to go in and learn about his wife's blood, see if it's red and all that, don't ya, Teach?"

"If that's so, Mr. Connell," the nurse said, "I'll see if it can be arranged when the time comes."

"Course that's so," Donatelli said. "He's gonna learn about reachin kids."

"Mr. Connell?" the nurse asked.

"Huh-oh—sure," Ben said. "Yes, that would be fine—if it can be arranged. I don't want to put you to any trouble."

"I'll see what I can do," the nurse said and left.

"I gotta hand it to yuh," Donatelli said, rising from his chair and lifting Ben's hand to shake it. "Ya practice what yuh preach. You wouldn't catch me dead in there, watching some hack pulla tongful of bloody kid out Lois for all the gold in Fort Knox. Sweet Jesus! All that puss and mucus and shit, not me. I don't mind rippin the livin shit outa a fish, guts and puke and intestines and all that crap, but I don't wanta watch em doin it to Lois. I ain't—"

"I think I'll—" Ben said slowly. "I think I'll—go see—if my doctor came," and rushed out of the room, down the corridor, and out the front door.

After gulping in fresh air, shivering, twitching his shoulders involuntarily, and shaking his head, Ben turned to face the hospital again. His feet would not move through the front door. He studied it for a few minutes, sure that his nostrils could detect the acid smell leaking through the door cracks, before he turned down the stairs to the sidewalk.

Forty-five minutes later, Doctor Powers pulled up to the curb and found his patient's husband pacing up and down the sidewalk without even a jacket on, hands in his pockets and shoulders hunched forward.

"You'll catch your death, Ben," Doctor Powers voice boomed out.

"Oh. I'm glad to see you, Doctor Powers," Ben said, jumping into step with the doctor and starting up the stairs before halting suddenly. "There's something I have to ask you."

"Can't we talk inside? I haven't even seen Marion yet."

"It's not Marion. Uh—the nurse said that—that it might be arranged for me to—watch the delivery—uh—"

"Why?"

"Well, just to—you know, to—is it usual for a father nowadays to do that, I mean with modern medicine and all—"

"Let's look at it this way, Ben," Doctor Powers said, stroking his chin as he studied the man for whom he had delivered three children and was about to attempt a fourth. "There are some doctors who feel that this—" He studied Ben's eyes. "I have to be honest with you, Ben. We've known each other too long to begin lying to each other. I don't like it at all. I don't see any sense in it and it makes me nervous to have someone watching me. But if you think I'm getting a little too old for this sort of thing and that your presence might help—"

"Oh no! No! Nothing like that. I just thought it might be a—learning experience."

"Damn it Ben!" Doctor Powers seemed to be getting mad. "I've delivered three of your kids and if you've got something to say about me, I wish you'd say it."

"P—please, Doctor Powers, don't get mad."

"Then stay out of my way and let me do the job you're paying me to do!"

"Yes sir. Certainly. I didn't mean—"

"Go on into the waiting room and I'll let you know—"

"I don't want to go in—I think I'll get a little fresh air for a minute."

"Have you got a screw loose. It's cold out here. Now listen to me. You go downstairs to the cafeteria and tell that dope of a janitor to give you a cup of black coffee. That's doctor's orders. Now march."

"Yes sir. And thank you, thank you very much. I guess it is chilly. Thanks again, Doctor. For the coffee."

Ben Connell was wrestling with a letter to a book salesman. He had never mastered the art of saying no decisively and gracefully. The proper phrase, sounding regretful but not heartbroken, always eluded him. It was his own fault for writing a warm letter to the salesman before. The hangover he had earned celebrating the birth of his daughter was not helping him. His usual guilt feelings about his inattendance to paperwork were intensified and mixed with flashes of heartburn, nausea, dizziness, gas, and fear for the consequences of the night before. He had invited two policemen who followed him home to come in for a celebration nightcap. They had left their drinks unfinished when Ben began to try to explain that he didn't really begrudge them a little graft needed to supplement their salaries.

When the phone rang, he grabbed it and rasped, "Assistant Superintendent's Office." To anyone sensitive to Ben Connell's moods, this was a signal that he was not in the mood for frivolity or long-winded conversations.

"There's a Mrs. Toomey on the line for you, Mr. Connell," the switchboard operator said apologetically.

"Now what in Hell's name does she want?" The switchboard girl did not attempt an answer. "Tell her I'm not here! No, no. Put the old bag on. Please."

"Is that you, Bernard," Mrs. Toomey shouted out of her deafness.

"No!"

"Hello? Hello, Operator? You gave me the wrong man. Operator?"

"Who's dis?" Ben grunted. "Who da Hell you want! Huh?"

"Don't get fresh with me, Young Man. I won't stand for it, and I don't have—"

"Then siddown Lady!"

"You listen to me! I am Mrs. Connell's mother and I intend to speak to Mr. Connell immediately—if you don't mind."

"Hol on! Hey Ben, wake up. Some old bag on the phone for ya!" Holding his hand over the phone for a few seconds, Ben rocked up and down in his swivel chair, trying desperately not to break out laughing. When he had some control, he caressed the phone with a smooth, soft voice. "Hell-loo. To whom do I have the pleasure of speaking? Hmmmm?"

"Bernard? This is Mrs. Toomey."

"Why, hell-loo Mother."

There was a silence. Ben realized he had overdone. In the few years he had known her and during the few contacts they could not avoid, he had never addressed his mother-in-law as anything but Mrs. Toomey.

"Bernard, just what is going on at your office? Some fresh young man used profane language to me. Does he work with you? Is your office always like this? Are you having a party there? Who was that young man?"

"In a manner of speaking to answer your first question, no to your second, no to your third, and that was Sam. The janitor."

"The janitor answers the phone? Have you been drinking? That's not much of an example to set for young boys and girls."

"What do you want?" Ben asked. He stopped smiling and resumed his normal voice. "I have work to do. You know, this is my office."

"Well it's a funny way to run an office, that's all I can say. If I had that young man working for me, I'd fire him. So help me God, I would. I wouldn't stand—"

"Hold on for a minute. Sam! Sam, you'll have to turn in your broom. You're fired. Yes, yes, I know, ten children and all that but—you don't know how to answer a telephone. Better luck next time.

There." Ben took a deep breath and put the phone up to his mouth. "Anything else?"

"I didn't mean for you—" Mrs. Toomey's voice trailed away.

"Is there anything else?"

"I was going to talk to you about naming the baby. I think Marion's right, but you don't seem—"

"Marion's right about what?"

"Naming the baby. I'm not wild about Michele but—"

"Naming my daughter, Michele. Where'd you get that screwy idea?"

"She's been talking about it for two months. I said—"

"Oh. Yeah."

"—that since you named the three boys after your relatives, I should think she'd get out of that rut. Personally, I favor calling her Marion, but Marion likes Michele and if she feels—"

"Mrs. Toomey? Personally. I'm not thinking of naming the baby Michele. So don't spend a lot of money engraving that name on a christening present. Besides, Marion tells me you don't have much to spare."

"I can see there's no use talking to you in your present condition. Of course, Marion—I hear from different sources that you're pretty close to that condition nearly every night. I'll hang up now."

"Yeh. Hang up!" The phone clicked in Ben's ear. "Hang up and dry up! You old bat! You dumb, deaf, stupid bitch! You meddling, interfering, penny-pinching—"

Ben looked at the phone and decided to hang it up. He seized the letter he had been working on and wrote: "Definitely cannot use your book." He bounded his desk once, then changed the last period in his letter to a comma and added: "at this time." He got up and circled his office, sat down quickly and added, "Sorry." He signed the letter, but was too upset to bring it out to the secretarial pool so he put it on top of a pile at the back of his desk, stood up and resumed his pacing.

The gall of that woman! How do you like that! The nerve of her! She's going to tell me what to name my kid.

At his wedding reception, Mrs. Toomey had a chance to say only one thing to Ben Connell and he would never forget it. She had whispered in his ear, as he bent smiling to take her empty punch cup, "You look as cool as a cucumber. A person'd think you'd been through all this rigamarole before." Ben snatched her cup and turned away so his mother-in-law would not see the red hate in his eyes. He did not see her face relax into a kindly grin. He decided then and there that he would avoid this withered old vixen. She would never be welcome in his home. When he did not return with her punch cup, Mrs. Toomey put her son-in-law down as a man with no sense of humor, a dry, conceited ass looking for a woman to mount, and the woman he found was her daughter.

My kid! She wants to name my kid. I'd like to boot her right in her fat ass.

As Ben enjoyed visions of planting his toe in his mother-in-law, Marion Connell was pulling the bedclothes up around her eyes and sinking into her pillow to feign sleep. She had heard Rose ask the day nurse who had just left her room, "Is Mrs. Connell asleep, Dearie?" There was no answer for a few seconds; then Marion heard the day nurse's cool voice, "I'm sure I don't know. You may, if you wish, go in quietly and find out. My name is Miss Altry and I am supervisor of this ward. Hang your coat over there. Pleeze."

After a few seconds of complete silence, Rose came into Marion's room anything but quietly. She was clenching a huge bunch of chrysanthemums and a box of chocolates.

"I'm not sure I appreciate that woman at all." Rose said. "Who is she? Marion!"

Marion did not dare to keep her eyes closed. "That's Miss Altry. She—"

"I know who she is! But I want to know who she thinks she is. For two cents, I'd—oh, hello Young Mother. Rose galomphed over to the bed and bent her huge body so she could kiss Marion. The edge of the box of chocolates pierced Marion's ribs and the chrysanthemums and the fur collar on Rose's coat cut off her breathing as Rose's heavy pocketbook rested on her stomach.

"Rose," Marion gasped , immersed in waves of perfume and flowers.

Rose swung back to her full height. "Congratulations! What's the matter, Dear. Still weak? Aren't you comfortable? Want me to roll up your bed?"

"No," Marion said, gulping air. "Please. Thanks."

"Do you have a bell? Oh there it is." Rose yanked it vigorously. "I'll get the nurse to put these in water."

"Oh, don't bother—"

"No bother at all," Rose said. "You just rest. Here we are."

A young pale nurse's aide came timidly into the room. She was intercepted from behind by Miss Altry's hand.

"I'll handle this. You take care of that bath in 41B." Miss Altry watched the girl leave, then wheeled about. "It isn't necessary—"

"Put these in water for Mrs. Connell like a good girl," Rose said, pressing the chrysanthemums on Miss Altry. "Now Marion, you tell me all about everything. Don't skip a thing. I want to hear every word. Wasn't this easier than the last one like I told you. Are they treating you right here? I hope you're getting..."

Trying to nod answers to Rose's questions, Marion was also watching Miss Altry's Adam's apple bobbing and her neck muscles tightening.

"Mrs. Connell, it isn't necessary to push the bell through the wall when you ring. None of us are deaf. And," Miss Altry said, looking at Rose who was slowly draping her coat over the foot of the bed, "would you please ask your visitors to hang their coats in the hall for sanitary reasons?"

"Mrs. Connell did not ring that bell," Rose said, blocking Miss Altry's approach to the foot of the bed where the offending coat lay. "And if you worried less about my coat and more about those flowers you're crushing in your hot little hands, we'd appreciate it." Rose put her fists on her hips. "Now are you going to put those in a vase of water or do I have to see the President of this hospital to find out why not."

"I—"

"And we can do without your lectures on bell-ringing. You may not be deaf, but you look awfully dumb right now. Close your mouth or you'll catch flies."

As Miss Altry searched for words, Marion cringed in her bed. She imagined Miss Altry would put cold water in her daily baths, take away her morning and afternoon juices, and completely ignore the bell from now on.

"This is a hospital, Madam," Miss Altry finally managed to say, "and there are patients who wish to sleep."

"I don't want to wake up the patients," Rose said. "Only the nurses."

"Ohhh!" Miss Altry exhaled as she strode out of the room.

"Make sure it's cold water, Dearie," Rose called after her. "Or did you know that?"

Rose stared out the door for a few moments before turning to charge at the bell.

"Rose, I think—"

"Let me handle this, Marion."

"Rose, look."

A tall, tanned orderly came into the room smiling and carrying the vase of flowers. He nodded to Rose and put them down on the bedside table. As he was leaving, he winked at Rose. She beckoned him back with her finger, found only a five dollar bill in her pocketbook and pressed it into his hand with her own broad version of a wink.

"You look like a good Irish boy," she said. "God bless you."

Marion wondered if all of the hospital employees would now expect her to tip them.

"That takes care of that!" Rose said. "Don't let that woman bully you, Marion. If she does, you let me know and I'll put her in her place. You've got to stand up for your rights in this world. If people think they can push you around, they'll walk all over you."

Rose walked around the bed, straightening the sheets and adjusting the pillows. She stopped fussing, loomed over Marion, and smiled.

"I'm glad that's over because I wanted to talk to you. About Margaret."

"Who?" Marion asked.

"The baby. Isn't it a beautiful name? I was thinking and thinking and then I thought of Grandma, you know, she came over from Ireland on a boat, Ben must have talked about her, he was her favorite, and her name was Margaret. Isn't it a beautiful name."

Rose beamed down at the little mother.

Ben had not made up his mind by fight day. Joe Louis had been his hero for years, a credit to his race, the American who tore apart Max Schmeling, served notice on Hitler that America-was still strong, fought fairly and lived cleanly, and was as humble in victory as he was fierce in battle. If America did go to war with Germany, Ben would be proud to have Joe Louis on his side.

But Billy Conn had given up his light-heavyweight crown to fight the big men. He was giving away twenty-five pounds to Louis, he was totally outclassed according to the experts, he was a three-to-one underdog with the bookies, and he was acting as if all he had to do was show up to become the next heavyweight champion. He was brash and boyish and cocky and Irish. To Ben, he was Ireland fighting an impossible 750-year war against England. And winning twenty-six out of thirty-two rounds.

Joseph and Tommy had made up their minds. They both wanted to be Joe Louis. They heard their father call him the best in the world, a fine man and a fierce animal, and that was good enough for them. But Joe beat Tommy to the punch by shouting out that he chose the Brown Bomber. By the time Tommy recovered from this blow, he realized there wasn't any choice left. He had to be Billy Conn. This frustrated him so that he tried out a left jab on Joseph's ear when he wasn't looking, and ran to safety behind his father before Joe could demonstrate his uppercut.

"No fighting," Ben said. "I don't want any fighting at all if you want to stay up and hear the fight. Is that understood? Now your mother and your new baby sister are coming home tomorrow. You go upstairs and clean up your room, pick up everything. And hang up your clothes. I don't want this place looking messy when they get here. Go ahead."

Joseph gave Tommy a shove as they started upstairs.

"I said—no fighting. And get your pajamas on and wash up. If you play quietly in your room, I'll call you down when the fight starts. Be good boys and maybe—just maybe—"

"What Daddy?" Tommy asked.

Joseph affected disinterest, but paused to listen. "We just—maybe—might make some popcorn."

"Can I make it Daddy? Joey's Joe Louis. Can I make it?"

"All right. We'll see. Now let's go, let's get this place cleaned up."

Ben did not feel like doing any cleaning himself at the moment. He had done enough while Marion was in the hospital, taking care of Joseph and Tommy every night, cooking their supper, getting them up in the morning and off to school. He had even told them a new bedtime story every night, something he had not done in a long time.

Of course he did nothing that was not immediately necessary. Dirty clothes decorated every corner and chair back and the dust mop gathered dust in the corner of the back hall. All the dishes and pans and silverware were used up in two days so he rinsed three plates and three spoons and one pan before each meal. And took the boys out to eat once or twice. He hauled batches of dirty clothes to the laundry because he did not want to foul up Marion's washing machine trying to make it work. When the bundles of clean clothes came back, he tore them open on the dining room table and let the boys find what they wanted. There was no sense in putting things away in the wrong bureau drawers.

Rose had wanted to do everything, keep the boys overnight every night "to give you a little rest," send up home-cooked meals that just needed warming, throw all the clothes in with her laundry, and fix Ben and his boys a nice breakfast each morning. Ben allowed her to keep Sean at her house, and Joseph and Tommy visited a few times, but he strongly reminded her that he and the boys knew how to take care of themselves. They had run a bachelor household before.

Ben considered getting the dishrag from the pantry sink and wiping the soup stains off the stove, but it was too close to fight-time to be piddling around. Marion could have everything back to normal, which wasn't that clean in the first place, in no time if she really wanted to.

When the boys came down in their pajamas, Ben washed out the frying pan and melted bacon fat in it. He wanted to use butter but he only had enough to melt and pour over the popcorn when it was done. Tommy poured the kernels into the sizzling grease. Fat splattered out and caught him on the back of his hand. Ben ran upstairs for the Vaseline. He spread globs on Tommy's hand, turned on the radio for the pre-fight predictions, and ran up to the bathroom again for a gauze bandage which he wrapped around Tommy's hand and tied with a piece of string.

The bell rang for round one as Ben remembered he had not called his bookie. But then it wasn't his bookie, it was Pete's, and Pete had placed the bets for him, five dollars on Louis and five on Conn. If Conn won, Ben would collect more money, but that wasn't important.

"Come on, Joe, hit him!" Ben smashed his right fist into his left palm.

When Louis followed these instructions, Joseph gave Tommy a superior look.

"Dance Billy, duck, jab," Ben called. "That's It."

With this second exhortation to Conn, Tommy started shifting his shoulders cockily. But as Ben switched his advice from one fighter to the other, Joseph and Tommy ignored each other to watch their father conduct the fight.

At the end of the second round Ben burned the popcorn and swore at Billy Conn. "Are you stupid! Huh! What'd I tell you. Dance, jab, jab, move. You can't slug it out with him, you dumb Mick."

Ben danced from his corner by the refrigerator for the fifth round, ducked a jab, slipped under a right cross and landed his own jab to the jaw. He hooked and jabbed with his left as Tommy and Joe waited to hear who was taking this punishment.

"Try that on for size. Joe," Ben grunted. He danced away.

Joseph was leaning far back in his chair, cringing from the punishment. He looked to his father for a counterattack. Ben threw a long looping left to the jaw, followed by rights and lefts to the body.

"How's that feel, Dancing Man?"

Tommy rocked back and forth on his seat. Ben banged his hip on the kitchen stove, whirled to meet this sneak punch, and dropped his gloves as the bell rang for the end of the fifth round.

Joseph and Tommy scooped up the blackened popcorn which had been neglected during the stress of the round. Ben walked slowly into the pantry, conserving his strength, drank a swig of water from the faucet and spit it into the sink. He grabbed the red, white and green dishtowel from the top of the old washing machine and swiped at his hot forehead. He stuck out his lower lip and puffed gusts of air to blow his hair away from his eyes. He shook his shoulders to keep them from tightening up between rounds and worked his head up and down to keep the neck muscles loose.

"Why is Mr. Louis the Brown Bomber, Daddy?" Joseph asked.

"Huh. Oh, he's a Negro. But that makes no difference. He's a fine man and a great fighter. One of the greatest of all time."

Joseph chewed his popcorn thoughtfully.

During the next few rounds, Ben fought poorly. He was trying to figure out who he wanted to win. Joe Louis and he were two of a kind, men who could destroy if challenged, but men who had more love than hate for their fellow man. But Billy Conn—Billy Conn was ahead by points at the end of the ninth round. A cocky little Irishman fighting his heart out.

Halfway through the tenth round, when Ben was just about to commit himself to the Irishman, Billy Conn lost his balance. He slipped in his corner and was wide open for a knockout punch, but Joe Louis stepped back and permitted Conn to regain his balance while 60,000 fans cheered. How could Ben desert a man like that? How could he forget all the post-fight interviews when Joe Louis proved there was still decency and humility in the world? Every time he said the same thing just about—it was a rough fight, his opponent was a good man, his family shouldn't worry—but Ben listened more closely than he listened to the referee counting the seconds over Louis' knockout victims.

Still, without admitting it to himself, Ben was dancing in the eleventh round. Where he had been a good boxer and a strong slugger in previous fights, Ben was now an artist, a rough-and-tumble ballerina, a man of style and shrewd calculations, dancing, jabbing, hooking, and ducking. And piling up the points.

Joseph and Tommy didn't seem to notice. They were each fighting now to stay awake. Tommy had wasted his energy most in the early rounds and was visibly weakening. His head slumped to rest on his bandaged hand in the twelfth round. "What in Hell are you doing?"

Tommy's head jerked up. His father had stopped boxing and was shouting at the radio.

"Get back, you idiot! Get away! Move away!"

Despite the warnings of his kitchenside manager, Billy Conn stopped jabbing and moving and decided to slug it out with Joe Louis. Ben shouted again, trying desperately to pull his wild Irish strongboy back, to keep him away from the knockout dynamite in Louis' fists. Then the frenzy of Conn's manly desire to punish his man, to win the world championship by outfighting and outhurting his man, caught Ben and stirred a deep fierce warmth in his guts.

"All right, Billy, all right!" Ben gave his fighter the green light. "Hit him then! Give him everything you've got. Hit him! Hit him! Hit that black bastard! Hit him!"

The bell saved Joe Louis. Ben blinked until the sweat cleared from his eyes. His two boys were staring at him.

"I don't want to be Joe Louis," Joseph said.

"No, no, yes you do. Don't—"

"What's bastid, Daddy?" Tommy asked.

"It's a bad name Daddy used. Daddy shouldn't have said it. He didn't mean it. He was just excited. I didn't mean it. Sometimes..."

Ben was still explaining in the thirteenth round when Joe Louis knocked Billy Conn to the canvas. Ben turned the radio off before the post-fight interview. Without a word from his father, Joseph got up and started for the stairs. Passing his brother's chair, he punched him sharply in the ribs. "I won," Joseph said and ran up the stairs.

"You black bastid!" Tommy cried and shouted. "You black bastid!"

"Stop that Thomas!" Ben said. "Don't you ever say that again. That's no way to talk. Joseph? JOSEPH! Come down here! I'll teach you to hit your brother."

9 | Pulling Together

"I just called, Ben, to see, that is to inquire, into the state of your health; to see how things are progressing, you might say."

"There's nothing wrong with me, Jim, that a little rest won't cure, and I've been resting all summer. I'm looking forward to the start of school."

"Is that so! Well, that is good news. It's obvious that what I heard about you consulting a specialist is—a—fabrication."

"Where did you hear that, Jim?"

"I can't say that I remember—exx-zactly, Ben, but it doesn't matter now, since the report is an obvious falsification of the actual conditions. It's good to hear that your legs are in tip-top condition."

"Oh, they might be a little bit better, Jim. But nothing serious." Winifred O'Leary running off at the mouth.

"Nothing at all serious. It was good of you to call though."

"Fine! Fine! You don't know how happy I am to hear that, Ben. I didn't want to ask you until I was sure, but would you consider dropping over for a cocktail tonight. I realize this doesn't provide much notice, but you know how it is when we slip back into our routines. Neither one of us has that much opportunity for social life."

The bastard. There must be twenty steps to his front porch. "That's a great idea, Jim. But why don't we meet down at that new Italian place, Famarelli's, in Temple Square. I've been wanting to see what the place looked like. And that way we won't be disturbing Peg."

"There would be no problem there, Ben. Peg would be happy to see you, of course, but if you have a preference for Famarelli's, I'm sure that I could arrange to meet you there."

"No preference, Jim. I was just curious. I thought this might be a good opportunity. As you said, once school starts, we don't get out much."

"Yes. Certainly. Let me see—shall we say in half an hour?"

"That'll be fine, Jim. See you there."

"Auf weidersein."

That sonovabitching prick. "Marion! I need a clean shirt right away. I have to be in Temple Square in twenty minutes."

"What! Why? What's the matter?"

"That was Johnson, nosing around to see what kind of condition I'm in. See if I'm ready to roll over and play dead yet, the sonovabitch."

"Ben, you shouldn't go. You don't have to go. Call him back and tell him you're busy. You shouldn't be driving in your condition, should you?"

"What the Hell are you talking about— my condition. Of course I can drive. You can bury me when I can't drive anymore. And yes, I have to go. I told him I'd go and I'm going. And I have to get there in twenty minutes so he isn't sitting there watching me drag in. He'd just love to commiserate with me and then spread it all around about 'Poor Ben' who can't walk two steps without a cane. He'd be superintendent tomorrow if I let him get away with that. Now get me a shirt. And bring my razor down. I'll shave in the pantry."

"What about Sean, Ben?"

"Will you get me a shirt and my razor! Or do I have to get them myself!"

What's he got up his sleeve? The job? He's ahead and he knows it. Or does he? What's he up to? Not socializing. We haven't relaxed with each other for ten years. Maybe it is to check on me. But he heard about my falling at the Bledsoe School. He knows. Maybe he's afraid I've improved. I haven't, Jimmy John. The doctor's very nice. They've all been nice. But it hasn't helped. A little rest in the country. and observation will locate the difficulty. They don't know a damn thing. But wouldn't it ruin your plans if I was better. There'd be a real contest when the school board meets Tuesday. And I have a few years on you, Friend. Cousin Randolph's influence with the board wouldn't mean that much. I can count on Dinny O'Donnell. Maybe I could get two other votes if they knew I was healthy. I want that job. Even if I only have it for a week, I want it. If I have to lie on my back and sign just one paper as superintendent, that'd be enough.

Marion wanted to remind her husband that she was mad at him, but she didn't think this was the time for it. She found his last clean white shirt in the top drawer of the dresser they shared.

He can wear this tomorrow if he doesn't stay out too late. But he'll raise hell about it. 'Don't I even deserve one clean shirt a day.' As if he was going to meet the Queen of Sheba. I'll have to take some shirts down in the morning and tell them I want fast service. Maybe Sean will take them down if I can get him up out of bed in the morning. I hate to go in there. Marshatti's so oily. Then as soon as you leave the shop, he forgets what you told him. He shouldn't be going out with his legs like that. He has to see the doctor in the morning. "Ben!"

"Do you have to shout wherever you go! Can't you wait till you come down and talk like a civilized person?"

"You have to see the doctor in the morning, don't forget. You've got that appointment at ten-thirty."

"Let me worry about that. Just get my stuff down here. Did I ever forget anything important? Hurry up."

Marion remembered what her husband had forgotten, that that question—'Did I ever forget anything important?"— had begun as a joke. Ben first said it the night he had forgotten her birthday and rushed out to an all-night drug store to buy her a present. Since then, he had said it so often that, despite repeated proofs of his terrible memory, it was no longer a joke and he believed it.

Marion laid the shirt on the kitchen table and brought the razor, lather and mug into the pantry where her husband had stripped to his undershirt and was washing his face. She put them on the drainboard and handed her husband the towel he was groping for. He wiped his face and looked at the towel he was holding.

"This is filthy."

"I'll get you a clean one."

"Never mind. If you're happy living in a pigsty, why should I expect more. Where's my brush?"

"I'll get it."

"That would be nice. I can't shave without it. And I've only got fifteen minutes left."

Marion slowly climbed the stairs again, telling herself she ought to hurry but unable to do so.

This is worse than getting him off to work in the morning. At least then he's got time. Twenty minutes, he's crazy. He never went anywhere in his life in twenty minutes. Not and shave too. And he knows it's stupid, and he knows Johnson is up to something, and he knows he shouldn't go, and he's still got to go. He better be back when Sean gets home. I'm not going to take any of his lip. I've had enough.

Bending over the sink, Ben splashed warm water on his face and neck. He squeezed the crumpled tube of shaving cream to get the last of the lather out of it, enough to spread a thin white coat over his cheeks and chin and neck with his fingers. He was half-shaved and had cut his neck only once when his wife returned with his shaving brush.

"Here," she said.

"Never mind now," he said, "I had to make do without it. Did you bring my shaving stick? I cut myself."

Marion narrowed her eyes and worked her jaw as she started to pace the kitchen. She stopped, slamming the shaving brush onto the table. "Stick the shaving stick up your ass!" she shouted, heading for the stairs. "And I hope to hell you have a lovely time!"

"That's what I'd expect of you," Ben said, forcing his legs across the kitchen linoleum to the foot of the stairs where he dabbed the towel at his wet, red cheeks before continuing. "That's Just what I'd expect from you, with your upbringing. Your mouth is in the gutter. You wouldn't understand. You'd never understand."

But Marion did not answer. She stayed upstairs until her husband left, attempting to watch television while trying to ignore and hear what

Ben was muttering loudly. The ridiculous domestic problems of a television family caught her eye for a moment, but then her husband and son and daughter intruded again. After watching for almost half an hour and after a happy ending that pleased her momentarily, then irritated her greatly, she went downstairs for a cup of tea. She tried reading a magazine, but film idols and fancy recipes could not fill her mind. She thought of calling her mother, but was afraid she would be asleep. She considered calling Winifred O'Leary, but couldn't stand, at the moment, to hear about her child. She made a second cup of tea and squinted at the pale yellow wall before her.

There was a waitress in Famarelli's with a forty-inch bust and a twenty-eight-inch waist and thirty-seven-inch hips and Ben, puffing and sweating, looked and didn't care. James Johnson was smiling at the waitress and Ben realized then that James Johnson was a good man, a good political man, because his smile never changed. Ben decided too that he himself was not a good political man. When he was a little amused or pleased, he smiled a little. When he was very amused, he smiled very much. And when he was extremely amused, he laughed and opened his mouth and made noises. James Johnson wore the same smile when he told a student, "Your version of the incident is most amusing, but I'm afraid I'll have to suspend you," when he listened to a joke, told rarely by Mr. Milton, which he found abominably unfunny, when he lusted after a healthy, hefty young waitress. He never laughed, but he smiled an awfully consistent smile.

"Why Ben, Ben. So good of you to come." And Famarelli's was suddenly James Johnson's bailiwick, his parlor, his best crystal, and his liveried servants at the ready. "Sit down right over here and make yourself comfortable. This young lady will be happy to take your order. Won't you, Miss—Miss—ah?"

"Jerry. Just Jerry." She turned to Ben and frowned when she saw his drawn face and clenched teeth as he moved forward clumsily and gripped the back of the booth. "What's the matter, Mister? Are you all right? Can I help?"

James Johnson was on his feet. "Ben, you seem to be having

difficulty. Are you ill?"

"NO!" Ben said, and blushed because he had shouted. He lurched into the seat of the booth. "Just got a cramp in my leg, you know. I guess I've been sitting too long."

"Ohhh, I know how painful that can be, when your leg goes to sleep. It's just as if you were being prodded with pins and needles."

"Yeah, that's it. My leg went to sleep."

"Would you prefer to take a little stroll. Our drinks, I'm sure, will be ready when we come back."

"No. I'm fine now."

"Good, good. What's your pleasure? You're keeping Jerry in suspense."

"Rum and coke. Please."

"You want some lime in that?" she asked.

"No. No lime. Thanks."

"And I'll have a Manhattan," James Johnson said. He turned the smile he used to dismiss the waitress to Ben. "Isn't it a pleasure, Ben, to escape, momentarily of course, the usual atmospheric reminders of duty and care."

"Yeh, Jim. It's nice to get out."

"And how is Marion?"

"Fine."

"And the boys? Why Joseph and Thomas must be on their own now, of course they are, you told me that didn't you, it's been some time since we had a really good talk, but of course, I remember. And Sean? Why he must be nearing his release date from the service."

"He came home today. They're fine."

"Ben!" He began to rise. "I feel terrible, calling you out of your home the night Sean arrives. I'll understand if you wish to cut the evening short?"

"No need for that, Jim. Sit down. Relax. He went out with some friends."

"Oh." The smile was replaced by a look of concern. "Young people nowadays. Why, even Greg neglects to come home some weekends."

Even Greg. Even Christ the Son.

"But he has been around all summer, so we won't miss him as much this fall. Last summer, you remember, he was away in Washington on his political internship. Quite a remarkable experience."

You've mentioned it a few thousand times. "How's Jimmy Junior?" Chew on that, old friend.

"Wonderful! You wouldn't recognize him, Ben. One can't believe the difference a year at Farmsworth has effected. Although he has not quite yet decided on a college, he has a fund of enthusiasm for his studies that..."

Dancing a little? A little chink in the armor? Defective product of the loins? Jimmy John raise a hellion? Never! Just a high-spirited lad. Now, with a year of prep school, he's a new person. But if he's doing so well, Jim, why hasn't he 'not quite yet decided on a college'? They tell me school starts in a few weeks.

"...but then we never have been able to spend much time with each other's families, have we Ben. I would guess that the primary reason we have remained friends all these years is that we both recognize in each other a mutual concern for affording the best educational facilities and opportunities that can be afforded, that we can aff—safely maintain within our budgetal limits. The way I see it, Ben, of course stop me if you don't agree, is that we have reached a high watermark in our educational system where we must elect to tread slowly or go forward over the dam with the flow of pure education in search of new directions. That is to say, we have to be now prepared to offer suggestions which, although disturbing to some, will steer us..."

Ben Connell was aware that his associate and sometime friend of almost thirty years was about to say something, but he stopped listening to the preliminaries which James Johnson always offered, the qualifications which would provide escape clauses, ways out of direct statements that could possibly be refuted. He thought instead of another time when new directions were to be explored.

Ben Connell was mad when he read Superintendent Milton's bulletin announcing a special masters' meeting for May, 1947, a meeting entitled "New Directions." Ben was definitely in favor of new directions. He had been since he was first appointed assistant-superintendent during the war. But the new directions sketchily mentioned in the bulletin seemed to him more of the same penny-pinching, nearsighted policies Superintendent Milton had always espoused.

William John Milton had been Medlen's superintendent of schools as long as anyone but the city hall janitor could remember and he could not remember the first name of the man who had preceded Mr. Milton. An old, secretive man, Mr. Milton hid away in his dim office, forcing himself to stay there until the last secretary had left at night so he could maintain his perfect record of having spent more time on the job than any other employee.

"These young people don't know what devotion to the job really is," Mr. Milton told any young person who wanted to listen or could not escape. "I'm sixty-one, but I've never left this office before anyone who's ever worked for me, and I never will."

Although there was this performance pledge to keep, it was enjoyment, not duty, that kept Mr. Milton in his office and in no hurry to go home at night. He sat in the fading light reading historical romances which could easily be passed off to anyone with the temerity to inquire as "research into textbooks, background probing, you know. You can never learn too much." No one had ever entered Mr. Milton's office without knocking so his precaution of slipping the book jacket from a civics book over the latest expose of Andrew Jackson's love life was not really necessary except for his added enjoyment, his sense of illicit achievement.

Everyone within his sphere lived in awe and dread of the superintendent of schools. His frugal habits, "no lights on in my office until dusk," his work record, "never missed a day that I wasn't in a hospital," his late hours of devoted duty, and his lined face made more austere by thin, pale eyebrows—all marked him as a martyr to education.

There were times when Mr. Milton had to go public. A city-wide speaking contest would be held and he would have to pin a medal to the quaking dress of a third-grader, the unlucky winner who instinctively knew that the man before her with sharp pin in hand despised all children. Forever after, the girl would spend her schooldays in dread that a bit of misbehavior might send her through the echelon of command to the office of this man who pursed his pale lips open over yellowed teeth and pretended to smile. Mr. Milton felt that he had a winning way with children, at least he was sure of their respect, but they annoyed him because they were one more reason that he had to leave his office and his books and his budgets.

The most important public appearance each year for Mr. Milton was his presentation of the school budget to the board of aldermen and the mayor. After distributing a thick collection of data sheets well in advance of the meeting, he delivered his long, lifeless speech like a stern Pope with throat cancer. He did not plead for appropriations nor defend requests. He spent three months of each year pruning every possible expense in every school to the extent of limiting each building to one key which had to be picked up at the janitor's home if anyone, especially the Parent-Teachers Association, wanted to use the school for a night function.

With his work behind him, Mr. Milton stood confidently before the mayor and aldermen and told them exactly how many students were enrolled, teachers employed, classrooms available, and soft lead pencils on order. He always threw them a bone: "I don't know what you gentlemen think of the suggested expansion of the milk program. That is for you, of course, to decide since..." before he concluded: "If you wish me to educate your children, that is the necessary figure."

His words earned him a round of applause that the mayor urged on until Mr. Milton had left the council room. The aldermen were then free to decide whether or not to add cookies to the milk program before passing the budget intact. Dinny O'Donnell, who had built his career on personal favors and had backed men, not ideas, could never resist a comment after Mr. Milton's appearances. "As soon as you gentlemen are through with the cookie question, perhaps one of you will run over and tell the Protestant Pope that, all by ourself, we've decided to add vanilla wafers. I'd go myself, but I'm afraid he'd give me his blessing."

The thorough attacking and resolving of a limited number of problems and the distance he consciously maintained, perhaps even with his wife, earned Mr. Milton the reputation of an efficient administrator who could not and should not be bothered with petty considerations. Ben Connell was promoted to assistant superintendent to insure Mr. Milton's tranquility. He was to be the young, energetic, affable workhorse, the contact man who shielded Mr. Milton from the gripes of teachers and parents, and the antics of students.

The previous assistant, Sam Carroll, had grown old and tired of the daily rounds of schools, the climbing up innumerable stairs to have his brain assaulted with the unimaginative whinings of would-be women, marginal scholars, and comfortable radicals who seemed to make up the teaching ranks. Sam Carroll, learning from Mr. Milton, eventually became a long-distance administrator and resolved many questions by avoiding them until they died of old age or by shifting them to another branch of the city's administration. He was indirectly responsible early in his tenure for the heated board of aldermen's meeting which considered and narrowly passed a controversial bill allotting fifteen minutes for morning recess rather than twelve. After that Sam Carroll had blended into the background.

Ben Connell's elevation to assistant appealed to Mr. Milton as the establishment of a solid buffer zone might appeal to a military commander. It was a surprise to Mr. Milton and a bit of a shock when Ben Connell, not content with the work before him, sought out problems and brought them to the superintendent's door. It took six months for Mr. Milton to get across the message that "It's a good idea, Ben, to write out a memo, to get your ideas down on paper," the message that he did not wish to be visited in his office two or three times a week, he did not want to be involved in the rashness of immediacy.

Gradually Mr. Milton sensed that he was going to have to curb this foolhardy, ambitious young man or he was going to cost the system money. Mr. Milton thought of it in terms of costing himself money since he had advanced to the stage where he no longer considered himself chief administrator of a public school system, but rather fancied himself the sole owner of Medlen's thirty-one schools. Anything that cost the system money was as unthinkable as opening a joint bank account with his wife.

"Can't afford it," was Mr. Milton's cryptic notation on the first score of requests Ben submitted for new equipment in the schools. He did not believe his eyes when a subsequent memo from his supervisor of elementary schools read:

"Dear Mr. Milton,

After serious thought and reflection, I have decided you are absolutely right. We cannot afford a new globe for the Hiller School's sixth grade. Therefore, with your permission of course, I will ask the children to each bring in one of the free maps distributed by gas stations and travel bureaus. I am sure we can find someone who will donate a round boulder to which we can paste the maps. The result will, naturally, be a rough facsimile of a globe, in fact the process of accumulating forty-eight states may not entirely succeed (it is understood that we will have to dismiss foreign countries for a few years), but I feel the resulting product will be an improvement over the present Hiller School's sixth grade globe which has huge holes in place of Africa and Spain and enough pinholes to make the names of all other countries undecipherable. Our class globe project should save the Medlen school system a vast amount of money and we can then move on with the idea to the forty-two classrooms which seem to have globes in similar condition.

Sincerely,

Ben Connell

Mr. Milton never forgave Ben Connell for loosening up the purse strings of his school system. But it was a choice between that and being a laughing stock, and Mr. Milton had never been laughed at since childhood. He relented somewhat, but continued to haggle over every penny in his own way by ignoring all of Ben's memos until they were at least a month old. The memos made excellent book markers as long as he did not read them, and this temptation never proved strong for him. Each day that he used a memo for a book marker, Mr. Milton told himself, another day had passed without a useless appropriation. Occasionally he would come across one that should have been dealt with sooner since it was not a request for money.

The first of these was a brief mention that Ben Connell had finished his annual evaluation of teachers. Mr. Milton was furious that Ben had included this information in an ordinary memo that could easily be mistaken as another request for money. He seized his telephone and ordered the switchboard girl to contact Mr. Connell immediately and have him report at once to the superintendent's office. Ten minutes later the girl called back to say that Mr. Connell was attending an administrator's conference in Albany, New York.

"What! Albany!"

"There's a note on his desk. It says if you should want the details, Mr. Milton, to refer you to Memo 42."

"Memo 42." Mr. Milton ground the words.

"Yes Sir. The note's dated two days ago."

"Two days—thank you."

Mr. Milton also never forgave Ben for forcing him to read the memos as they came in, complete with their little numbers in the upper right hand corner. Despite the irritations of reading memos and doling out money, Mr. Milton learned to live with his new assistant and even respected his energy and idealism, qualities which he himself had before he learned painfully that people were looking for a bargain in education, as in everything else, and deified anyone who could give them one.

The cementing quality in Mr. Milton's relationship with Ben Connell was lack of fear. As long as Ben was brash and impulsive, as long as he spoke freely on all subjects without reflection, as long as he offered suggestions without first securing the support of other masters, Mr. Milton could handle him and had little reason to fear him. It was with particular interest that Mr. Milton noted, on his way into the meeting room where he was sure his "New Directions" policies would be approved, that James Johnson, newly appointed principal of the high school, was engaged in a serious conversation with Ben Connell.

"I ... I agree with you, Ben, that change is in the offing. Think of what the word actually means. The direct and indirect connotations of such a word. Change. It means a host of things to a multitude of persons—people. We each have our own interpretation of the word, our own way of viewing its nebulous qualities and, I might add, qualifications. To some, change means—"

"What change, Jim? Just what changes do you suggest?"

"Improvement! That's the key word. Improvement! We must forge ahead to new goals. Improvement! The key phrase—"

"Could you give me a for-instance, Jim?"

"That is exx-actly what I had in mind, Ben. I had hoped we could meet before this to discuss proposals which we both felt were for the mutual benefit of the system; that we could arrive at a consensus of support which would strengthen our cohesive position. Which brings us down to the hard fact. Do you have any specific proposals, Ben?"

"Yes. Several."

"Feel free to adumbrate one. I'd be most interested in hearing whichever one you care to discuss."

"I'm not sure I want to discuss anything, Jim. I have certain ideas which I intend to suggest, but I'm not sure discussion now will help. We only have a few minutes."

"Of course, Ben. We all have certain definite ideas that we feel must be instituted as policies immediately—"

"I didn't realize you felt that strongly."

"—or the system will suffer; but, we must realize that multiple viewpoints and approaches can offer a wealth of divergent but useful thought. We must consider—"

"All right, Jim, all right. For openers, I want to have informal teachers' meetings to replace that Godawful summer methods course that's required now."

"Informal. That strikes me as the key word. What meaning, Ben, do you place on 'informal.'"

"I mean—informal. Discussion groups of teachers, probably those that teach the same grade, who can discuss practical problems without worrying about credits or the administration—"

"I—think—I—see—a problem, Ben. Format. Wouldn't the format for such a meeting have to be worked out carefully."

"Format? No. This is an informal discussion group I'm proposing."

"You are proposing? Do you have a proposal written up that I might glance at?"

"No, it's in my head."

"I see. Well, do you have anything—"

"We'd better go in. All the masters seem to be here."

The first hour and a half of the meeting was filled with inanities, which pleased Mr. Milton greatly. He had intentionally called first on those masters who had no new ideas and many less than startling proposals to offer.

"...so we might look for a new room for a lounge in the Conway. It seems to be pretty crowded. I don't get in there much, but every time I do..."

"...maybe we could resolve this problem by giving each teacher a printed handout that tells them exactly what their retirement benefits are..."

"...and I think Superintendent Milton's proposal to amend the procedural bylaws is most important. Perhaps we could approach the subject..."

Most of the problems discussed, Mr. Milton knew, could be handled before or after the meeting, but he had always found it useful to drag out petty business so that his own programs would be wearily and briefly discussed and passed, and any subsequent new business, any late afternoon proposals that involved thinking, would sound foolhardy or radical to the tired masters.

Mr. Milton surveyed his men. They still looked a little too fresh, too full of juice, not quite docile enough. James Johnson raised his hand. "Mr. Milton, may I please say a few words?" Mr. Milton hesitated, then nodded. Perhaps it was time to lift the manhole cover and see what came out of the sewer. Ben Connell had yet to speak, but he was fidgeting busily in his chair, biting his thumb because there were no ash trays, shifting positions every few minutes.

"Thank you, Mr. Milton." James Johnson stood up, carefully pushed in his chair and strode purposefully to the end of the table where a portable blackboard was supported shakily by three thin wooden legs. "If I may, I'd like to draw a diagram?" Mr. Milton nodded, secretly pleased. Another half hour was about to be used up in a presentation that definitely bore no imprint of Ben Connell's haphazard style. Perhaps Ben Connell did not have James Johnson's support or the support of any of the other masters for whatever upsetting proposal he was contemplating.

"This," James Johnson said, drawing a horizontal line across the middle of the blackboard, "is where our present level of inter-teacher problem communication and solution co-ordination is. And this," drawing an arrow upward and a line across the top of the board, "is where it should be." Mr. Milton smiled, settled back in his chair, and nodded encouragement. The masters would be in proper shape after this presentation. "Now I've been talking with Ben Connell about this—" Mr. Milton sat up in his chair and leaned forward, his eyes scuttling from Ben Connell to James Johnson and back. "—and we seemed to agree that the summer methods course might possible be beneficially replaced by a biweekly seminar dealing with the hard and real problems encountered by teachers in the field. We could entitle the sessions 'Chalk Talks'. Guest speakers, of course, could be scheduled each second and fourth meeting. Naturally, an administrator would be in attendance to lend his..."

Mr. Milton scrutinized Ben Connell's tortured facial expressions as he reacted more intensely to each new item detailed by James Johnson.

"Excuse me, Mr. Johnson," Mr. Milton said. "I don't mean to be rude, but Mr. Connell seems to have a qualifying statement to add at this point." He turned his attempt at a sweet smile to Ben. "Or could I have misread your intention, Mr. Connell?"

"Qualifying statement," Ben said, jumping to his feet, "isn't the word for it. The idea I mentioned to Jim Johnson had little resemblance to the program that has just been 'adumbrated'. I had something else in mind altogether. I had hoped that teachers, and teachers alone, could get together and discuss some of the practical problems they run into every day. I didn't plan on speakers giving out the same old hash or administrators looking over the teachers' shoulders and stifling real conversation.

"Well, Ben," Mr. Milton said, adopting his disappointed-and-hurt look, "it seems you have a limited view of the administrative function. Stifling conversation is not one of our duties or aims."

"Of course not," James Johnson protested, measuring strokes in the air with his piece of chalk. "My proposals were merely intended to create a firm foundation, to place a solid substructure under a vague suggestion."

"You haven't heard the whole suggestion yet!" Ben Connell said. "And I have several more to make that I hope don't get structured before they're even heard."

"It seems," Mr. Milton said, studying the papers before him to hide his relief, "that we have intense feelings about this subject, and since the hour is getting late and we're all a bit tired, it might be best to submit these proposals to my office in written form and those that have merit will be discussed at our next masters' meeting. We really must go on now to our main item of business, our 'New Directions' problem."

Ben had learned that the hour was late only when Mr. Milton decided it was. Some masters' meetings, at which the superintendent wanted his ideas adopted then and there, had lasted until 9 p.m.

"This particular proposal isn't that important," Ben said, "but I have something to say before I sit down. Merely this. I've been attending these meetings for years because I thought solving the little problems would lead to solutions for the big ones. I don't think that way anymore. We haven't built a new school in thirty years. We haven't made a major change in the elementary curriculum in twenty. Our equipment is going to Hell. Replaced at the last minute before it crumbles, usually. What could possibly be wrong then? Only the books and the teachers. Our book budget puts us in a price bracket just above the ludicrous text and just below the worthwhile one. We buy thousands of mediocre books. 'See Jane run. See Dick run. See Jane and Dick run.' See Medlen's kids run—not slow, not fast—mediocre."

Mr. Milton studied the papers before him as the masters squirmed in their seats, waiting for the tongue-lashing their colleague was sure to receive. They bowed their heads and stole glances at Ben Connell.

"How many times can a teacher see Jane run and feel she hasn't been over the course before. For what? A less than mediocre salary and no educational improvements in sight. All the good young teachers get two years experience and leave. The old good ones are eccentrics. They make the kids stand up and recite nursery rhymes during arithmetic period so they won't fall asleep wide awake. They—"

"B—Ben," James Johnson ventured, not raising his eyes, "don't you think you're a bit—out of line. We're maintaining a middle position relative to other Massachusetts schools."

"If you check the figures, Jim, if you really check them, you'll find that we're at the very bottom of that middle position. And what if we were at the top of the middle schools? With our tax base, it would mean we were still catering to the average slob who wants to save fifteen cents a week on education. And we're helping make average slobs of their kids with our average slob of a school system."

A few masters choked, James Johnson gasped softly, but Mr. Milton did not move, did not twitch.

"All we have to do to make this a good school system is ask for more money, demand more money, investigate ways to raise monies and—spend more money. 'We do the best with what we have.' That's great, isn't it. We can have more. We should have more. It's no service to the taxpayers to hold down the cost of education by holding back their kids. A cheap education is a good education. That kind of thinking went out with our grandfathers. If industry used that kind of thinking we'd all still be wearing detachable collars on our shirts and buying one suit every ten years from the local tailor. That kind of thinking is what has made our system—"

Ben stopped. The masters were murmuring softly and stealing glances at the head of the table. Ben looked at Mr. Milton. He sat there, gazing steadfastly at the table in front of his papers where he had placed his white detachable shirt collar.

"...and now seems the time to strive forward, to strike for change," James Johnson was saying as he kept one eye on Jerry the waitress who was leaning over to serve drinks at another booth. "Now is the time—"

"It strikes me, Jim, that the time for change was a dozen years ago."

"Well, Ben, we've got to look ahead. There's no sense in looking backward, is there. No, of course not. The system isn't perfect, but—"

"Perfect? No, I guess not. No, now that you mention It, I guess it isn't quite perfect."

"Feigning sarcasm isn't going to help us develop new ideas, Ben." He glanced sharply at Ben Connell's fifth highball. "I thought we—"

"All right. I'll stop being cynical and start being honest, if you'll be honest with me. As honest as you can. What in Hell's name did you drag me out for tonight? You know my legs are in tough shape. Just what is the purpose of this meeting?"

"I didn't realize—"

"Don't give me that bullshit, Jim. Let's cut the crap. You know it as well as I do. Now what do you want?"

"I just thought, since Mr. Milton is retiring, this—"

"Now we're getting close to the truth. Milton's out and either you or I are going to get the job. So what?"

"Don't get so upset, Ben. If we could present a united front on the important issues, if we could discuss the important considerations in advance of the selection date—"

"That's next Tuesday, Jim." And I've only got Dinny O'Donnell in my corner. And only because he owes me a favor. So what are you worried about?"

"Yes. But do you see, Ben, if we reached an accord, then it really wouldn't matter whom was chosen, would it? The system would benefit from our mutual experience and whomever didn't happen to be chosen would feel that he had vitally contributed to shaping the direction of the future."

"Let me get this straight, Jim. You think we should present a united platform to the school board's selection committee, our ideas should agree. What would be the basis of selection then? Our good looks? The way we dress? Physical condition, perhaps?"

"It wouldn't really matter, would it, Ben? The system would progress and that's the important thing to bear in mind. Isn't it?"

"Sounds awfully good, but I've got a few doubts. For instance, how do we reach an agreement on discipline? We seem to have slightly different ideas on that."

"That's a minor point of divergency I should say."

"I shouldn't say that. It's never been my view that martinets make the best teachers."

"That's just a bit unfair, Ben. Merely because I believe instruction cannot take place in a chaotic atmosphere—"

"And merely because I believe learning can't occur in an oppressive atmosphere. Seems to be a difference of opinion. Spare the rod and spoil the discipline versus wield the rod and bury the student. Minor difference."

"Yes, and we wouldn't have to include that in our joint presentation."

"Forget it, Jim. I've had enough of this. I'll see you later."

Clumsily, Ben got to his feet. He felt no circulation in his legs. They were two unwilling joints of meat that he had to take with him everywhere.

"Ben. I'm sorry you feel this way. I had hoped—"

"Good night, Jim, and good luck."

Pain shot through Ben's legs as he pushed one after the other towards the door. Outside, he aimed for the narrow strip of brick just beyond sight of Famarelli's window, closed his eyes, and collapsed against it. A minute later he headed for his car. He hoped there was enough feeling in his legs to work the pedals.

10 | Setting the Record

Sean cried himself into the house.

"He is so, he is so!"

"There's no need for that, young man," his uncle Donald, following quickly and closely, admonished. "I have no cause to lie to you."

Crying, shaking his head back and forth, pushing his arms out to the side, a swimmer pushing the sea behind him, Sean raced ahead of his uncle through the living room and dining room and into the kitchen of the farm house.

"What is it?" Rose Phelan asked, alarmed, catching her nephew before he ran blindly into the sideboard. "What's the matter, Sean? Did my Tommy hit you? If he did, he'll catch it from me. Here. Here now."

"There's no sense in making a fuss about nothing," Donald said. "No one hit him. There was just a little argument and I had to set him straight about—relationships."

Reverting to his usual shyness, Donald Phelan turned away from his wife to search for cigars in the cupboard, ignoring the two fat ones in his shirt pocket. "You know what I mean, Rosie. It's about time someone told him." He shut the cupboard door and washed his hands at the old porcelain sink, making sure he turned the yellowing faucet off tightly.

Ben Connell came up the back steps. He had been lying on a chaise lounge in the backyard, sunning himself and reading the sports pages when he heard the commotion. He found his sister in the kitchen wiping his son's face with a washcloth and pressing a tootsie roll into his hand. Donald was pacing nervously.

"Here now, Sean," Rose was saying, "you take this out in the backyard by yourself and eat it all up."

"What's the matter?" Ben asked.

"Nothing, nothing," Donald said, dismissing the matter with a nervous shaking of his hand.

"Uncle Donald said a lie," Sean said, contorting his face to that of a sad clown's and beginning to cry again. "He said a bad lie and it's a sin."

"Wait a minute now, Sean," Ben said, stooping down to face his son evenly. "Uncle Donald doesn't tell lies."

Rose ran the water in the sink, rinsing out the face cloth thoroughly. Donald took the black shoe polish from the kit behind the door and began to coat his shoes.

Unused to his father's huge face so close to his, Sean hung his head, shaking it slowly but positively up and down. Finally: "He did, Daddy. He did."

"Donald?" Ben asked. "What's this all about?"

"I didn't tell him any lies," Donald said. He brushed vigorously at his shoes.

"I know you didn't," Ben said, "but—"

"He said Tommy n' Joe aren't my brothers! He said it. He did, and it's a sin." Sean hung his head again, fully aware of the monstrous import of accusing an adult.

Ben Connell dropped his eyes from his son's face. Slowly, his complexion reddened. He clicked his teeth shut and opened his lips only enough to say, "Go outside and play, Sean."

"I can't," Sean argued. "No one will play with me. Tommy and Joe won't play with me 'cause Aunt Rose's Tommy said I'm not a whole brother."

"Go outside, Sean!" Ben said, standing up, breathing audibly through his nose.

"I'll take him outside, Ben—Donald. Come on, Seanie, with Aunt Rose. We'll see if the hens have any eggs. Come on now."

Rose and Sean were not down the backstairs when Ben turned savagely. "WHO THE HELL DO YOU THINK YOU ARE, tellin' my kid that! What business is it of yours what he is? What are you doing! Poisoning your kids minds' so they tell tales out of school to my kids. It's none of your Goddamned business. I thought you learned that once. I'm his father, not you."

"That's it, Ben," Donald said, jerking his head quickly in positive affirmation. "That's just it. You haven't told him, and it was bound to come out sooner or later."

Enraged at the bald truth, Ben clenched his fist.

"Why, you son-of-a-bitch, I'll punch you right in the—"

Ben stopped, not knowing where he would punch his brother-in-law, never having considered it before. He watched Donald stand up, fold his tortoise shell reading glasses and place them carefully on the kitchen table, unbutton his cuffs and roll up his sleeves. "Oh, for Christ's sakes, Donald. Roll your sleeves down. I'm not going to punch you. But I'm still pissed off at you. You had no right to tell him that." Ben slammed his hand down on the sideboard counter. "No right at all."

Donald re-buttoned his sleeves, perched his glasses low on his nose, and looked over them at his excited brother-in-law. Lovingly unwrapping a cigar, Donald tasted the end of it, bit and spit.

"Now, Ben—"

"No right in the world."

"It was bound to happen sooner or later. It's probably just as well that we get this straightened out now. My Tommy remembers your wife too well. I can't lie to him when he asks me about—relationships. And I won't. There's no sense in hiding this, the way I see it. Children are bound to ask questions. It's natural at that age. And I make it a point to answer every question I'm asked as honestly as I can. I remember well, as if it were yesterday, that your wife did the same thing. And I'm sure she'd approve."

Ben sat down humbly, his passion draining from him. He was sure Donald was wrong to tell his son so that he would tell his sons, but now Donald was saying Catherine would approve, but he was sure Catherine wouldn't approve of Sean crying, didn't she say the boys need a mother, she would have wanted her boys, his boys, to play with his boy, Marion's boy, of course she would, what was Donald saying?

"It's pretty rough on Sean," Ben offered weakly.

"Oh he'll get over it. Children have wonderful recuperative powers. He's probably forgotten it by now. They'll all be playing together, having a wonderful time, in ten minutes."

Sean sat on the chaise lounge beside his Aunt Rose, dutifully chewing the tootsie roll, hating and devouring it, realizing his aunt was trying to be kind. He was tensely waiting. Waiting for his father to get through telling Uncle Donald how bad he had been and to come out into the yard and tell him that he was a whole brother, that he was not a Nazi or a nip or some freak not to be played with.

"Doesn't that taste good," Aunt Rose said. "Now you go out front and play and have a nice time."

"No."

"Seanie! You never said no to your aunt before. I don't want you to start now. We're just a little upset. Do you want Aunt Rose to walk out front with you and tell the boys not to tease you?"

"No."

"Well, we can't sit here moping half the afternoon away."

Sean did not answer. He heard ice dropping in glasses in the kitchen. His father was quiet.

Before supper, Ben took Joe and Tommy and Tommy Phelan for a walk. Sean watched from behind a shiny green bush as the four of them walked away, Ben talking quietly. At supper Sean was not fooled by Tommy's and Joe's consideration. He knew they were passing him the potatoes and peas first, instead of last, because they felt sorry for him. They knew he had a disease but they were conspiring with his father to never mention it again. Sean would not talk to his cousin, not even to answer when asked if he would like to check the pigs after supper. Tommy Phelan was not his friend.

"Come on, Sean," Joe said. He pushed back his chair and came around to Sean's place, his usually serious face smiling foolishly. "I know where the rooster is." Sean looked down at his lap.

"Come on, Seanie," Tommy said. "Let's find the rooster."

Sean mumbled something.

Joe and Tommy leaned toward him. "What? Whadj say?"

"Is he coming?"

Joe and Tommy looked at their cousin who looked at his father who looked at his wife who looked at Ben. Ben frowned.

"I'm goin' down to the orchard," Tommy Phelan said and left the room.

"Come on, Sean," Tommy and Joe said.

Ben knew what he had to face. Driving home with Sean half asleep in the front seat beside him, and Joe and Tommy in back arguing sluggishly about which of them was really Tommy Phelan's best friend, Ben knew exactly what he had to face. Marion would be waiting. Miffed at being left alone all day but proud that she had refused to accompany him, she would be waiting to see if her children were returned to her unharmed, uninfested. And Ben could not deliver them that way. Sean would tell her. There would be a scene. There had to be a scene.

Ben wondered briefly why he visited Donald and Rose at their summer farm. But he knew. If only vaguely, Ben knew. Perversely opinionated, insistent on telling the truth to everyone but himself, Donald was still his friend. Donald was headstrong and foolish at times, but he was Ben's friend. Most of the time at the farm, he talked with Ben, listened to Ben, gave sound advice, and occasionally said something fairly original or at least striking. He made no demands on Ben and only rarely, unfortunately in intimate matters, did Donald show his streak of stubborn insistency by telling the truth, the whole truth, and nothing but the truth, so help whomever was the victim of this truth.

And Rose. She had helped her mother raise Ben, had helped him dress for school, had supervised his homework told him whom to play with and whom to avoid, had been his big sister. And the habit had stuck. She passed along all her secrets of childrearing, especially since the older children had married or left home. Ben never thought of himself as being babied at his sister's house, but he did know that he was special people there. There was a warm feeling to driving up to their house and seeing Donald rise quickly from his porch rocking-chair to announce proudly, "Ben's here, Rosie." And his large sister pushing open the screen door before the kids were out of the car to meet him with a hug and a wet kiss at the top of the stairs, "Ben, I'm glad you could come." Her turning then, as always, to find that Donald had slipped inside the house, not to return until the children had been disposed of and she had gone back to her kitchen where she was preparing something special—lobster, venison, roast lamb—because her brother had come to visit. Then Donald would return with tall green water glasses full of ice and whiskey and ginger ale. "Drink this, Ben. It'll calm your nerves." He served the same drink and said the same thing always. And Ben loved him for his dependability.

How could he explain this to Marion? Why should he have to explain that he loved to sit and do nothing and watch the busy hens pecking their lives away. He had been fair. He had invited her, but she had only come once and ever since, when he said, "You know you're more than welcome," she answered, "I know where I'm welcome." Marion had her own ideas about Rose. Donald seemed all right to Marion, a thin, bespectacled figure in the background puffing a cigar, but he too seemed to ask too many questions that sounded just like Rose's. Marion's opinions and suspicions had been confirmed when Donald had taken it upon himself, at Rose's instigation, to explain to Tommy his relationship to the present Mrs. Bernard E. Connell.

Ben knew what he had to face. It was only a few years since he had brought Tommy home crying after a visit to the farm. That too had been an idyllic weekend. Rose took the children to Mass Sunday morning and Ben, much as he hated the inactivity of the sport, agreed to accompany Donald on a fishing trip. They came back with nothing but a mild glow from the flask of apricot brandy Donald always took fishing with him.

Joe and Tommy Phelan were in the parlor looking at photographs when they returned. They closed the book and ran outside when Ben and Donald entered. Before Ben could check the photograph album they had been studying, Rose came out with a towel for him and told him to go upstairs and wash for lunch. Ben had soap on his face when Tommy Connell came running into the downstairs area, crying because the hen had nipped at his fingers.

"I want my Momma," Tommy cried.

Rose did not, as Ben expected, try to console Tommy. He heard footsteps hurrying away from the kitchen, the front porch screen door, then Donald's voice.

"I don't think it's right," Donald said. "Tell, them a lie and they grow up liars."

The footsteps approached the kitchen.

"Do you want me to tell him?" Rose asked.

Tommy, to regain their attention, cried out again: "I want my Momma."

"Just stop that now," Donald said, chiding Tommy for interrupting an important conversation.

"I'll be right down," Ben called and grabbed for a towel. His declaration served the function of suppressing all conversation except for Donald's insistent repetition, "I just don't think it's right."

"What is it, Donald?" Ben asked, wiping his face as he descended into the kitchen. "What isn't right?"

"I want my Momma." Tommy said, holding his sore fingers up for proof.

"Shush, Tommy," Donald said. "Shhh. Don't be a baby. Shush now. Ben, Rose and I don't think you're playing fair with the boy about—relationships. You tell them a lie and they'll grow up liars. That's what this war is about, isn't it?"

"Well, Donald," Ben said. "It's not exactly a lie. We just haven't discussed it."

"A lie is a lie, whether it's one of commission or omission," Donald said. He stuck his cigar back into his mouth with finality, in absolute agreement with himself.

"Donald, please," Rose said. "Don't get self-righteous."

"Who's being self-righteous?" Donald said. "I'm not being self-

143

righteous." He shook his head once, twice. "Not at all. Not at all."

"Please Donald," Rose said. She turned her attention to her brother. "But it is the crucial age you know, Ben."

Ben tried quickly to recall which age Rose did not consider a crucial one. It seemed her children had gone through them once a week. "You're making a big thing of it," he said, "aren't you?"

"I want my Momma," Tommy softly reminded.

"Shush now," Donald said, aiming his cigar like a night stick.

"You can't just shush him," Rose said. "This is a real problem and it should be solved now. Really, Ben."

Tommy, tired of no response, changed his demand: "I wanta go home."

"Yes," Ben said. "We'll go home." He looked relieved as he started for the stairs.

"You've got suitcases up there I haven't even started to pack," Rose said, "and running away never solved a problem."

"It'll work out," Ben threw back. "'He's too young to understand."

"He's five years old," Donald called up the stairs before turning to Tommy. "It's now or never, Ben."

Tommy was frightened by his uncle's cold tone and more frightened when his uncle reached for his hand. It was the first time Tommy's uncle had approached him physically. A few times Tommy had pecked at his uncle's quickly proffered, bony cheek, but Tommy never felt that this was his uncle's idea of fun. And when Uncle Donald laughed, it seemed like he was breaking a rule. Tommy pulled his hand away as his uncle stooped down.

"Thomas, you're a big boy, Tommy, so you listen to me—"

"Donald! What are you doing!"

"Damn it, Rose, I'm doing what we all know has to be done. Now, Tommy, you listen to me," he said unaware that he was using the same tone of voice he had used on his wife.

Tommy cried again and tried to get away from his uncle's blotchy nose and harsh breath. Donald grabbed him by the seat of his pants.

"Daddeee," Tommy cried.

"Donald," Ben called from the stairs. "Please Don, let's forget it for now." Ben reached the bottom of the stairs. "He's scared! Let's—just—forget—it."

Donald released Tommy's pants, stood up quickly, picked up his cigar from the ash tray and bit into it fiercely as he left the room. He came back into the doorway, unnoticed by his wife or brother-in-law but stared at by his nephew, and glared and swelled a moment before speaking. "Your mother is dead, Tommy," he said, turned and disappeared.

"Oh, that man," Rose said.

Ben did not comment at first, but hugged his son who was mounting sobs that would not come out of his chest, and shaking his head. "It's all right, Tommy," Ben said. "It's all right now. Uncle Donald was just playing. He was just playing pretend. It's all right."

"No!" Tommy shouted into the shoulder of his father's blue shirt. "He wasn't. He really wasn't. I want my Momma. I want her. She's not dead. She isn't. She's not. She's not dead."

"That man," Rose said. "He just did that to spite me."

"She's not dead, no, no, Tommy she isn't," Ben said. "We'll go home now and you'll see Momma. She's fine. You'll see she's fine. Shhh, now, it's okay."

The shushing sound, the same one his uncle had used, set Tommy off again. "Yes she is," he sobbed. "Uncle Donald said she's dead. She's dead like the kitten Mr. Bradshaw ran over. Uncle Donald said so."

"Nooo, no, he didn't mean that," Ben said. He tried to keep his voice soothing and calm while he was building up a tremendous resentment against his brother-in-law. Turning his head momentarily to his sister, he asked: "What in Hell did he do that for, Rose?"

"Just to spite me," she said. "Just out of pure spite. He's like that sometimes. I'll ask him to do something and he'll do the opposite just to spite me. Or I'll ask him definitely not to do something and he'll—"

"Oh shut up, Rose," Ben said.

"Well I like that," Rose said. "You men are just alike. You can't listen to reason. All right. I will shut up," she said, in concert with Tommy's bawling. "I won't call or drop you a line or ever bother you again. See if I try and do something for someone again. If that's how I'm going to be treated. I get my husband upset and work myself up to a fever pitch to help my own brother out and he turns on me. I never thought I'd see the day."

"I'm sorry Rose!" Ben shouted. He continued in a lowered voice. "I'm really sorry, but can't you see Tommy's—"

Ben stopped to look at his son. Tommy had stopped crying to witness fearfully the first quarrel he had ever seen between his father and aunt. His mother and father quarreled all the time and that was not so frightening anymore, but his aunt and father were supposed to always like each other.

"It's all right, Tommy," Ben said. "We're just talking."

"No." He shook his head and resumed crying.

"Oh, God!" Ben said.

"The poor child," Rose said. "He's all mixed up. Here, let me hold him, Ben."

Ben knew that it was now Sean's turn to bring back a tale of horror to Marion's receptive ears. She would be horribly, indignantly, triumphant. All the things that had bothered her that she hadn't complained about for the past six months, would now be focused on this. She would be relentlessly, terribly in the right. At least Sean was being quiet. On that other three-hour trip home, Tommy had to be reassured every five minutes that his mother was not dead. Ben had been hurt by the distrustful look in his son's eyes, a look that showed Tommy's first wavering of faith in the absolute truthfulness of his father. Joe had known enough to remain absolutely quiet in the back seat.

"Will Momma be home when we come home?" Tommy had asked again and again.

"Of course," Ben said. "Momma will have a nice supper ready for us. Just like always. Maybe baked potatoes and some meat and—"

"She can't cook supper if she's dead."

"Tommy! She is not dead."

By the time they reached Medlen, Ben had succeeded in diverting Tommy into talk of the next Sunday when he would bring him, Ben promised again and again, to see the roller coaster and ride on the Ferris wheel at Revere Beach. Ben wanted to tell Tommy that Momma might be a little upset if they mentioned anything about her being dead or alive, because she certainly was alive, but he decided this would only refresh the incident in Tommy's mind just when he seemed to be getting over it. "When Ben pulled into his driveway and parked, he did not have time, although he remembered at the last second, to wipe away any trace of tears from Tommy's eyes. As he was reaching for the emergency brake, Tommy bolted out of the car, leaving the door wide open, ran around the house and up the front steps. His panicked, plaintive cry, like that of a child escaping a fiend, could be heard piercingly by Ben as he stepped from the car.

"Momma! Momma! Mom! Mom!"

Marion opened the door, petrified. She stooped to hug Tommy and feel and look for broken bones and blood before glancing up at her approaching husband. "Don't tell me Ben—"

"I haven't told you anything."

"You didn't spank him in front of the neighborhood? What will the neighbors think?"

"I didn't touch him. Why don't you find out what you're barking about before you start in on me?"

Joe, trying to slip into the house past the three figures at the door, was almost trampled by his father. Ben had paused by his wife and son, thought better of it, started forward again. In the kitchen he threw his jacket on a chair and went immediately upstairs to his den. As the door slammed him into his private room, Tommy stopped crying.

"You're not dead, Momma?"

"What! What are you talking about, Tommy? Joseph, come here."

But Joe had slipped out into the back yard.

"You're not dead. You're not!"

"Of course not. Don't be silly. What's the matter with you? Oh,

147

don't cry, Sweetheart. No, I'm not dead. See." She stood up. "Watch Momma do a dance. Can you do a dance?" Marion held Tommy's hand and moved back and forth in a quick jig-step that was intentionally clumsy. "Ooop. Momma's not very good. I'll bet you can do it better. Let me see. Come on. Show me what you learned in Kindergarten. Let me see if you can dance."

Tommy looked at his mother closely, pouted, then resumed crying. "Noooo. I don't want to."

"Sweetheart, what's the matter with you. Didn't you have a nice time with your Aunt Rose and your Uncle Donald and Cousin Tommy. Didn't you see all the animals?"

"They said you were dead. Uncle Donald said it. He wasn't playing. Daddy said he was playing pretend. He wasn't playing. He wasn't."

Marion went grimly about the business of getting Tommy fed and ready for bed. Joseph gulped his meal and retreated to his bedroom. Marion's only words were to soothe Tommy, to say his prayers with him, to assure him of her existence as she tucked him in for the night. She went down to the kitchen as soon as he settled down. With a cup of tea and a cigarette, she sat at the kitchen table, staring at the wall, her fingernails, the floor.

At half past nine, she heard her husband in the bathroom. She waited until he was in bed before she walked up the stairs, paused at the top landing, listening, then walked softly to their bedroom door and opened it. Ben's head was in the middle of the pillow, he was lying on his back, stiff and log-like and his eyes were closed. He apparently thought he looked extremely asleep.

"What happened?"

"Huh? Wha? Hmmm, oh. Did you say something."

"What happened?"

"Do you really want to know? You might have asked me my version when I came in."

"I didn't have a chance to ask you anything."

"You didn't seem to want a chance."

There was a pause as Marion's cigarette glowed in the night. Her arms were folded across her chest, her eyes squinting from the smoke.

"I've asked you not to smoke. What if one of the kids woke up?"

"What happened?"

"I'll tell you when you're in a better frame of mind." Ben turned on his side away from her.

"You'll tell me now."

"Who the Hell do you think you are? All of a sudden."

"I think I'm your wife, you married me, and the official mother of two of your children."

Ben shifted in bed, turning his head partially toward the half open door. "Donald was a little direct in telling Tommy about Catherine. That's all. He didn't mean anything by it."

"Why should he tell Tommy?"

"He thought it would be best."

"And what did you think?"

"Listen. I have to work tomorrow morning, and I'm not going to play twenty questions with you."

"All right. Just tell me what happened."

"I told you."

"You didn't tell me a goddamned thing. Who in Hell is Donald? Where does he get his Christly nerve to tell Tommy about his mother? If anyone should do it, it's you and you damn well know it. And what did Rose have to say about all this? 'Donald's right, Ben.'"

"None of your Goddamned business."

"Oh, I see. This is Connell business and I'm the outsider. Is that it?"

"You said it; I didn't."

"But that's what you mean, isn't it? Donald, whether you realize it or not, is not a Connell, and if you want me to take care of your kids and be your wife, he better not ever stick his nose into my business again."

"Your business? Who the Christ are you."

Marion stood silent for several seconds.

"Nobody! Nobody that matters to the goddamn high-and mighty royal Connells and their big-nosed adopted brother. You're all the same under the skin—louses. Rotten filthy louses. And I don't want anything to do with any of you."

That time Marion had slept in Tommy's bed for a week. Ben had the whole business to do over again: not even a hello in the morning, lousy breakfasts, snide comments, and a month of grudging sex, if any. The funny part of it was that Marion agreed with Rose and Donald. From the first she wanted the boys to call her Marion. Ben didn't consider that proper at all.

Why did everyone think they knew better than he did? Come to think of it, Marion agreed with Rose and Donald about Santa Claus. None of them appreciated the lengths he went to—hiding packages in different houses, creating special stories, patiently answering questions, alerting Coughlin the mailman to save letters to the North Pole—to keep the boys' belief alive.

And now Tommy and Joe whispering in the back seat and Sean sleeping fitfully. Was this better? He would have to wake him up soon and face the music.

Marion opened the door to a sleepy but frantic Sean. "Momma, Uncle Donald said—"

"Your supper's ready."

"Momma! Uncle Donald said—"

"Go in and eat now. Don't let your food get cold."

"He said—"

"You can tell me all about it after supper. Ben, will you take him up to wash his hands."

"You better let him speak, Marion."

"He said—"

"Why should I? Don't I know it by heart."

"—Tommy and Joe aren't my brothers."

"Yes. Don't you worry about that now Sean. You go up with Daddy and wash your hands. And don't get the towel filthy. Use some soap."

Marion swallowed during supper. She ate little but her throat kept working. At no time would she let Sean discuss what was upsetting him. She brushed it away as if he were objecting to having a splinter taken out of his finger.

Marion fussed with Margaret, mildly scolding her for the few green peas she had knocked onto the floor with her spoon. Ben studied his wife, for the first time not sure of who she was.

Before she chased Sean and Margaret up to get ready for bed, she turned to ask sweetly: "And did you have a nice time visiting your relatives?"

11 | Breaking the News

Sean washed the blood off in the men's room and rode home with Roger. It had been a brief fight. Billy Dunn turned out to be a malicious drunk. When he finished tearing Roger's weaknesses apart, making fun of his big ears and short height, he started in on Sean. "Why don't you dance with that hussy, Connell? Afraid we'd tell your Daddy?" Sean got his hands around Billy's throat before catching a fist in the mouth. Roger and Eddie separated them.

During the ride home Roger and Sean made their plans. Roger drove off as Sean's mother let him in.

"I thought you were your father."

"Look again. Did he go out?"

"Yes. He shouldn't have, but he did. Mr. Johnson called."

"Good."

"No it isn't. He's gone drinking and he can hardly drive a car sober. What happened to your lip?"

"Maybe not, but it's good for me. I won't have to say goodbye to him."

"Goodbye!"

"Yeh. Goodbye Ma. In case I forget when I get my bag packed. I'm gone."

"You can't leave."

"No? You gonna stop me, Tiger?"

"Don't be like that! Do you have to be such a wiseguy? Did you get that fat lip from being a wiseguy?"

"No, I got that from having a father with a loud mouth, that's how I got that. Do you have any of my clothes in the wash? I don't care if they're dirty. I'll take them with me. I don't intend to be dropping in here every weekend for a touching family reunion."

"Sean, you can't go."

"Give me one reason."

"Your father—"

"My father go to hell. If you think I'm going to stick around here for a repeat performance of his ranting and raving and foaming at the mouth, you're crazy."

"Well what about me?"

"What about you? You answer me one question and I'll answer you that. Where is my sister?"

Marion slumped into a chair and rested her temples on her fists.

"Silence? Did you take a blood oath to secrecy? Going to be quiet for a while? Good. I want to call Aunt Rose and—"

"What!" Marion's head shot up. Her eyes were bulging. "You're going to do what?"

"I'm going to make a few phone calls, Aunt Rose and Grandma and—any objections?"

"You're damned right I have!" Marion twisted her mouth into an ugly smirk and jerked her head from side to side. 'I'm going to call Aunt Rose.' Tommy and Joseph spend every weekend of their life down there, eating ice cream and lobster and listening to lies, and now you're going to call Aunt Rose."

"She wrote to me in the service, Ma. She didn't have to. And don't you think it's a little ridiculous to keep this up year after year? You're both getting to be old ladies you know. What are you gonna do, sit in rocking chairs in the old ladies' home and throw darts at each other?"

"Are you stupid? Haven't you learned your lesson about the Phelans yet? What right have you to come into my house and tell me you're going to use my phone to call those people."

"Pardon me. I thought it was my house too. And I thought your husband said something about using this phone to call anyone I want. And I thought you said something about phone calls made outside this house being sneaky. But I must have been wrong. So you go to hell too.

I'm going up the Square to phone. I'll give Rose your love."

"Do you know what she did last month?"

"I don't want to hear it, Ma," Sean said, but he turned back from the front door and began pushing at his hair with the clogged hairbrush on the hall mantelpiece.

"She called me up and said she was thinking of giving a homecoming party for you. She hasn't given you or—she hasn't given you the time of day for years, but now you must be pretty thick because she wrote to you in the service. Big deal. Nosing around to find out from you what's going on here."

"That's strange. She hardly even mentioned you in her letters."

"I can believe that. She calls up last month and asks me, would I be able to come to the party she's giving for you. Would I be able to come? I haven't set foot in her house in fifteen years but I'm invited to my own son's party. The only reason I didn't get to be an invited guest was your father didn't feel up to it."

"Sounds like a nice idea to me, and she was probably just trying to be friendly."

"Friendly. Huh! I know what she thinks of me."

"You're really a looney-bird, you know that? You're a fruit-cake, a nut. You think she's down there planning and plotting how to get your goat. She's got a big chart on the wall, 'Let's see, how can I ruin Marion's day today? Hmmm. Maybe I'll use Plan 9 and call her up, disguise my voice, and tell her she just won the Betty Crocker award for outstanding cooking. Hee hee!"

"You didn't lose any weight on my cooking."

"That's the final test, isn't it? Whether or not you lose any weight? I guess that makes the Army cooks pretty good. I gained five pounds in basic."

"All in your head."

Sean's quick smile before he left did not ease the bitter gall that her own son could be drawn into the Phelans' net by a few nice letters. She wanted to call Rose up and tell her to keep out of her life forever. But Sean was right, they were both getting to be old ladies, and there didn't seem to be much sense in picking at old wounds. She would remember, but she did not have to aggravate the situation. The old ladies' home, is that where he would send her?

Sean hesitated before putting the dime in the pay phone. He owed his Aunt Rose a call but he hated to cause his mother further grief. If she wasn't so narrow-minded, she would have made up with Rose years ago. He dialed the number.

"Hello."

"Aunt Rose, it's me, Sean. I wanted to—"

"Sean! Welcome home! When did you get home? How was the service? How are you? Do you feel all right? It's good to hear your voice. Are you coming down to visit? I'd love to see you. And Donald would too."

"I don't think I can."

"Ohhh."

"I have to get up to school early and clear up some things—registration and things like that—you know."

"Ohhh, that's too bad. Your father was looking forward so much to having you home for awhile. Is everything all right at home? You're not leaving because of—conditions, are you?"

"What do you mean?"

"I don't like to talk about—things, but I can put two and two together. It can't be very easy for you around that house. You don't have to say anything, and I know it's none of my business, but your father's said a few things, nothing special, but I can read between the lines. It must be—"

"What are you talking about, Aunt Rose?"

"Your mother. I can understand why you wouldn't get along with her, what with—

"We don't get along?"

"That's what I thought. Donald says, 'How could anyone get along in a place like that.' And he's right. You can't relax in a pigpen. You should have seen that house when Catherine was alive. There wasn't a speck of dirt anywhere. The curtains were always—"

"Aunt Rose."

"—starched and ironed. The rugs—"

"Aunt Rose, if my father's first wife hadn't died, I wouldn't be here, would I?"

"That's no way to talk. I consider that fresh, talking about the dead that way. That woman was a saint, I'll have you know, a saint."

"Yeah, well my mother's no saint, so I guess there's no comparison and—"

"You bet your life there's no comparison!"

"—no sense in talking about it anymore. Goodbye."

Walking home in the dark, Sean remembered all the night fears he had had instilled in him. His mother never walked on the sidewalk at night, not even on her own street, but chose instead the middle of the road, hurrying from one street light to another, living in dread between the pools of light. Sean laughed to himself as he recalled her fearful, alert scurrying but found himself anticipating trees and bushes and dark spots ahead on the sidewalk, and wondering whether there might be less chance of tripping on the uneven cement sidewalk if he took to the street.

Surprised that the front door was unlocked, Sean let himself in and walked quietly into the kitchen where his mother was squinting at a newspaper. He knew she was not reading it since she hadn't put her glasses on. He put his hand on her shoulder and spoke softly to her.

"Can't you tell me now, Ma. Please."

"Don't ask me Sean."

He gritted his teeth, clenched his fist, slammed the table, which caused her to jump, and shouted: "You're makin it worse Ma!" He stopped. "I keep imagining things." He lowered his voice. "Is she—dead?"

"No! Of course she isn't. Don't be foolish," Marion said. She did not consider it a foolish question. The idea appealed to her momentarily: It might be better if Margaret were dead. But she dismissed it quickly, jumping up from her chair and walking the length of the kitchen to, for no reason, shut the door that led into the front

157

rooms, frightened that she could think such a thing.

"Then what is it?" Sean asked.

"Your father will tell you," she said. She was determined that this time Ben would tell him, that she would not be pressured into delivering bad news as she had been since Sean was an infant. She wheeled about and walked past Sean to open the door to the back hall. "Did you leave anything out here?"

"Sure. My father will tell me. In about a hundred and fifty years. When I've had five kids and three wives, he'll decide it's about time to tell me about the birds and bees."

"Don't talk like that. What are you—a heathen? First you don't go to church and now you're thinking of divorce before you've even married."

"I'm sorry. I forgot. God comes down, or is it the Holy Ghost, old devil that he is, and blesses every marriage. Did he stay for your reception?"

"You're not funny. What are you going to do for the next two weeks?"

"Ooooo, well, I thought I might make a novena, then get all my books and read them so I won't have to go to class, then shine a few shoes, then—"

"So help me God, if you don't give me a straight answer, I'll brain you with this kettle."

"Simmer down, Ma. I don't know what I'm going to do. I just know I'm getting out of here."

"Just run out because things aren't going the way you like them."

"Things aren't going, period. I didn't plan to 'run away from home' so soon, but I'm too old to put up with Pa's guff."

"How long do you think I've been putting up with it? And it gets worse every year."

"That's your problem. You married him."

"You bastard! He wasn't like this when I married him."

Ben Connell had his key in the lock before he discovered that the door was unlocked. It seemed a tremendous effort to push the door open. He came into the hall and headed for the parlor, ready to collapse into a chair, when he heard his wife's and son's voices. He shuffled across the rug and stopped outside the kitchen door.

"Just what do you want me to do?" Sean asked. "Stay around and argue with him every chance I get? Laugh at his jokes and listen to his lectures every time I want to go out?"

"No. Just stay around."

"Why?"

"For my sake."

"Where's Margaret?"

The door to the kitchen opened and Ben Connell's head came into view. "Margaret's in the nuthouse," he said. "Are you happy now?" The door to the kitchen closed.

"What did he say?" Sean asked. "Ma, what did he say?"

Marion did not answer. She sat down and covered her face with her hands and rocked back and forth slowly.

"Ma! What did he say?" Receiving no answer, Sean turned from his mother, strode to the kitchen door, pulled it open and went into the hallway to face the darkness of the dining-room. "Pa? Pa!"

"I don't want to talk about it," Ben Connell said. "Go away."

Sean stood in the hallway, shaking his upturned hands, his mouth open, turning from his father to his mother to his father and back to his mother. "Ma. Ma. You gotta tell me. Is she really in a nuthouse?"

Marion Connell took her hands away from her face and looked up at her son. "No—oh no—no, she isn't—no, no."

"Then what's he talking about?"

"She had to go—to a rest home—for a while. A rest home for a while."

"She's in the BOOBY HATCH!" Ben Connell yelled from his bed in the dining-room.

"Stop it Ben," Marion said softly. "Stop it. That's no way to talk." Marion lowered her voice. "She's in a rest home. For awhile. She'll be home soon. She'll be all right." She'll be all right. They won't need those things on her head. He said, only if she doesn't respond. She'll be all right.

"What happened? Where is she?"

"She's at a very nice rest home in Somerset. She has her own room and she gets very good treatment and it's pleasant and—and—she'll be all right, it's very nice there—good people—good—"

"Why? Why, Ma?"

"Everything happens at once," Marion said, staring at a hole in the oilcloth on the kitchen table. She pressed the material around the hole trying to make it smaller. "Look at this. I'll have to get another one as soon as I get a chance. Your father's legs start to go—I'll bet the price has gone up—and Margaret gets—nervous and, I'm not going to get a white one this time, they always fade—"

"Ma! You're not making sense. What's wrong with her?"

"Nothing: What makes you think there's something wrong with her! She's nervous, that's all, she's—"

"They don't lock people up for being nervous."

"Who said they locked her up! Who told you that! She has her own room. There are no bars on the door. They just have the ward door—shut because some people in there are—and the windows were like that when she came. They explained all that."

"Maa. She is in the nuthouse."

"DON'T SAY THAT!"

"All right. A mental institution. What's wrong with her?"

"It's not even that. It's a rest home. You can call the doctor, he'll tell you, he knows what it—"

"Do you have his number?"

"He isn't there now. Leave me alone. Just leave me alone." That's what she said. Leave me alone, leave me alone, leave me alone, said it and said it. She's nervous. It's just a case of nerves.

"Can I see her? Can I visit her?"

"What? Oh no! No, the doctor said it would be better if she didn't have any visitors for—awhile. No, you can't visit her. No." She doesn't want us—there. She's gone to strangers. We upset her. We're her family, and we upset her. I'm her mother.

"Do you want a cup of tea, Ma?"

Marion nodded her head.

Ben Connell lay with his eyes closed, half-listening to his wife and son and remembering Margaret the day he came home after his fall at the Bledsoe School, Margaret helping him up the old wooden stairs.

Daddy Daddy Daddy Daddy! Stop it Margaret, stop it! I'm all right. I just have to rest for awhile. Her face white. Tears. Lurking around me for days, watching watching watching. Stop it Margaret. Stop lurking. You're making me nervous. Leave me alone. Don't you have anything to do? Yes, Daddy. Then do it. Yes, Daddy. And leave me alone. Yes, Daddy. Yes, Daddy, Yes Daddy, yes daddy, yes daddy.

"What did the doctor want to know?" Sean asked.

"A lot of gibberish," Marion said. "About the family—stupid things—gibberish about your brothers and you. And Ben. And me."

"What do you mean—gibberish?"

Marion sighed. She picked up her tea cup and warmed her hand around it. "Foolish things! 'Did she have a happy childhood?' 'Does she have many friends?' 'Would you say your relationship is close?' Give me a cigarette Sean."

Marion, doesn't she ever go out? It seems like she's been around this house for months. Where are her girlfriends? Why don't they come around anymore. She says she doesn't want to go out, Ben. She told me all her girlfriends are gone away for the summer. But I saw Mary Anne up the market. Well, she's driving me crazy, moping around the house. She's always moped around the house, Ben. Not like this. No, but I can't get her to go out, even to a movie.

"She's always moped around the house," Marion said. "You know that."

"Yeah," Sean said, "but she went out sometimes. With Mary Anne or what's-her-name, Judy, didn't she?"

"Yes, but she didn't want to go anywhere."

Margaret, it's not good for you, moping around the house. You're driving me crazy and you're getting on your mother's nerves too. Margaret, are you listening to me. Yes, Daddy. STOP SAYING THAT!

161

Can't you say something besides that! Can't you—I'm sorry, sorry, Margaret. Don't cry, for God's sakes! I'm sorry. Will you forgive me? Yes, Da—what do you me to say? Nothing! Nothing. I just want you to go out and get some fresh air. Take a walk. It's a lovely day out. Look at it. Do you want something at the store? No! I—yes, would you go up and get me a carton of cigarettes. Yes, Da—I'll go up.

"He made me feel guilty," Marion said. "As if we were criminals or something, all trying to ruin Margaret's life. He made me feel as if everything I'd done since she was a baby was wrong. He made me feel—rotten."

The paper didn't come. All day long I waited and the paper didn't come. I was going to give the paperboy Hell, not tip him, or not tip him as much. Ben! Something's wrong. You've got to talk to Margaret. You've got to come and talk to her. What's she up to now. Ben. Please. Marion, I don't want to move. I don't feel up to fooling with Margaret. Ben. Something's wrong. My legs are killing me Marion. Have her come down and I'll talk to her. I'm trying to get a breath of air. Please, Ben, please. Stop that whining. What is it. She's acting crazy. I heard this noise and I thought she was slamming drawers so I called up and she didn't answer, so I went up and she was slamming her bedroom door and I told her to stop and she wouldn't. She kept slamming it. She still is. She looks out and slams the door. And she opens it. And looks out, you can only see one eye. And slams it. I told her to stop. I yelled at her. She wouldn't. She won't. I went in and shook her and she mumbled all this crazy stuff and

"She was saying all this crazy stuff."

"What was she saying, Ma?"

"Just crazy, crazy stuff."

I wanted to slap her, but I was scared. And when I came down to get you, she started slamming the door again. You've got to talk to her Ben. You've got to. All right.   All right, take it easy. Go in the kitchen and sit down. I'll see what's the matter. Don't yell at her, Ben. She looks—awful. Will you let me handle this? Will you please let me handle this. Margaret! Margaret, I want to talk to you. Margaret, I'm coming up to talk to you. Stop that now. Stop it.

"I don't know. Your father talked to her. He heard it. It didn't do any good. We called Doctor Powers and he was sick but he came, and your father was wobbling all over the place and we, he and I, had to hold her so he could give her a shot, a sedative or something, and she pushed Doctor Powers and the needle stuck in your father's shirt and we finally did it. And they came."

Margaret, please stop slamming that door. Margaret? Margaret! What is it? What is it, Margaret? Not going to be nice when he gets back cheap girls aren't nice to leave me alone Daddy won't play with me Aunt Rose wants to know I won't tell anyone leave me alone he doesn't really like me don't say a word leave me alone. LEAVE ME ALONE! Leave me alone shhh she doesn't know Uncle Tim goes out at night can I come what she doesn't know leave me alone, leave me alone Margaret! Stop that! Marion! MARION! Call Doctor Powers! Why don't you lie down and rest Margaret?

I'll play with you Margaret. They don't bore holes in heads. They have good treatment. Uncle Tim loves you. Shock treatments don't hurt, they don't hurt much. Aunt Rose loves you. You get used to them. Your mother loves you. And Joseph and Tommy. Sean loves you. And I love you, Margaret. They won't even use shock treatments Margaret, because you'll respond to drugs. You'll respond.

12 | Haymarket Man

"A dozen big ripe ears thirty-nine cents! Where you gonna get a dozen like that? Where! Beutifool. Delicious. Last chance. How many you want lady? Gimme two big bags, Al. This lady knows a bargain."

"Three pounds thirty cents. Twelve cents a pound. Feel 'em, squeeze 'em. pinch 'em and taste 'em. You ain't gonna find any better down there mister. Cheapest place in the market. His stuff is all rotten!"

"Your face is rotten! Yes, Sir! Three pounds right away."

"Baanaanaass."

"Oriental delights. Figs and dates like ya never tasted. Specialties of the far east."

Sean Connell listened and watched as the Saturday night peddler's market came alive in Boston's Haymarket Square.

The horses stood patiently in their harnesses, oblivious to the hawking cries of their masters. Having backed their loaded wagons to the curb hours before, they had time to sniff the variety of turds on the cobblestone street and shake their heads and neigh loud comments on the medley of colors coming within range of their blinders. They chose to ignore the drab figures furtively circling the wagons, slipping squashed grapefruits from the gutter and street into shopping bags.

Pushcarts and dollies were forced through the crowds strolling the middle of the street. Every inch of curb space was coveted by the peddlers who jostled and jockeyed and argued for position. Empty crates were posted under each end of pushcarts and scales were hung. Small boys ran to get coffee for their fathers. Tissue paper was unwrapped from rows of pears, and apples were rubbed with strips of old bedsheets.

Somewhere ahead, on the sidewalk or in the street, bartering with a peddler or directing a fellow shopper to a bargain, was Sean's father. Burdened with a shopping bag full of figs and dates and oranges in one hand and a bag of apples in his other, Sean had lost sight of his father.

"Hey, Da Seanie, hey Da Seanie boy," Ben Connell called. He was about fifty feet away, standing beside a peddler and waving his arm. "Get upa here. Get upa here."

As he approached his father, Sean avoided looking at people who were trying to understand why a well-dressed Irish-looking man spoke such broken English, like an Italian just off the boat. Sean waited until his father paid the peddler and they moved on.

"You promised on the way in tonight," Sean said, "that you wouldn't call me that."

"That's right," Ben Connell said. He had dropped his role of Italian immigrant and was watching a young boy toting a heavy bunch of bananas. "And I always keep my promises. Here, why don't you make a trip to the car with these things."

"Daddy!" Sean said. Twelve years old, Sean felt a little foolish calling his father, "Daddy," but it always caught his attention, which "Pa" did not. "You're not listening to me. You said you wouldn't call me 'Da Seanie! "

"Oh. Okay," Ben Connell said. "Take these to the car and I'll be right around here when you get back."

Sean was about thirty feet away from his father, on his way to their car, when he heard the familiar voice, this time with a Chinese accent.

"Hey, La Seanlie," Ben Connell called. "Hully, please, hully, hully black. Chop chop."

An hour later, Sean and his father went down into a basement meat store, stepping around little puddles on the cement stairs, and dodging weighty balloons and hoops and logs of meat to listen to a sales pitch. A huge meat man with a black-banded straw hat was telling a doubting Italian matron that his side of beef was so fresh he had to "watch out it don't pinch the lady customers."

Sean watched his father smile as the man rambled on. He was

afraid, if they listened too long, his father would feel compelled to buy the huge piece of meat. They had no place at home to keep something that large and Sean could imagine his mother's reaction. He and his father had already bought and locked in their car more vegetables and fruits than their family of four, temporarily reduced from six, could eat in three weeks. His mother would be mad enough. The side of meat would be the crowning blow. Sean was relieved and embarrassed as he saw a familiar liveliness in his father's eyes.

"That meat sounds wonderful," Ben Connell said to the fat meat man who had lost his lady customer, "but we want to look at your tomatoes."

"What tomatoes?" the meat man asked. He unfolded his hands from the aproned expanse of his belly and took his pencil from behind his ear to help him figure this one out.

"That fellow with the pushcart at the top of the stairs said you had some ripe tomatoes."

"Who says so?" The fat man was bellowing. "What guy? We don't carry tomatoes."

Ben Connell led the way across the sawdusted floor to the foot of the stairs. A tall, broad-shouldered man with a slight paunch, he seemed thin compared to the hulking, red-faced meat man marching close behind him through the lanes and avenues of sausage and bologna.

"He seems to have gone," Ben said. He stood on tiptoe though he could easily see over the shallow stairwell. "He was parked right there a minute ago and I was looking at his tomatoes. I told him I wanted riper ones. He said to come down here, that you had a lot of fat ripe fruits down here."

"He did," the fat man said. Hatred was in his narrowed eyes. "Was he a tall skinny guy with a Army jacket and no rings on?"

"No," Ben said. "He was short with long black hair; He had a ring on the middle finger of his right hand and he was wearing a stylish hat, something like the one you have on."

Touching the brim of his straw hat, the meat man bent to study his reflection in a glass jar holding pickled pigs' feet.

"There's a guy down the end of the block," he said, "sells the best tomatoes in the market. I know. He's married to a friend of my wife's sister. Tell him Mort sent you. He'll give you a good deal. He don't, he knows my wife's sister'll give him an earful."

"I don't know how to thank you, Mort," Sean's father said. He held his right hand out. "My name's Ben—Ben Connell. This is my boy, Da Seanie."

"Pleased to meetchous," Mort said, "Dashony." His huge hand engulfed Ben Connell's, then patted Sean firmly on the head. "Don't forget—Mort sent ya. You'll be okay."

Up the stairs and out into the rush of street smells, Sean's father led the way. Sean knew his father was proud of himself. He had not gone into the meat market to buy tomatoes. There had been no peddler directing him there. His father had made the story up on the spot.

"Why do you do that, Pa?" Sean asked. "Every time we come into the market, you tell some story like that. Why?"

"Why," Ben Connell said to his son. "Sean, I am surprised at you. What if I hadn't told that story. Just think. We never would have met Mort and found out that his wife's sister's friend's husband has that vegetable cart on the corner, now would we?"

"No," Sean said, "but what—"

Smiling again, Ben Connell strode into the crowd, eager to hear the shouts and haggling that rang out just ahead, smell the sweet and sour airs of sidewalk stalls and gutter, join the give and take of market night. Sean followed.

"If you knew how to manage a house," Ben Connell said to his wife Marion, "they wouldn't spoil."

"If I knew how to manage you," Sean's mother said, "I'd be a lot better off."

The tired argument dragged on in the Connell kitchen as Sean, a few feet away in the pantry, filled the vegetable bin with potatoes, apples, oranges and onions. He felt guilty because his mother got up and came downstairs after he had carelessly placed the bag of apples on the edge of the kitchen table and they spilled out and bounced across the kitchen. The argument was inevitable, but it might have been postponed until morning if he had been more careful.

Sean went out to the driveway, unloaded the bushel basket of peaches from the trunk and looked the car. On the way in, he stopped in the front hall to put his father's keys on the white mantelpiece over the false fireplace. Then he tried to sneak through the parlor and dining room to leave the bushel of peaches outside the pantry door.

"What's that?" Sean's mother asked. She picked up her glasses from the scratched and faded oilcloth covering the kitchen table and came into the pantry. A small but sturdy woman with stooped shoulders, Marion Connell, when aroused, seemed to add at least six inches to her height.

"That," Ben Connell said as he strode right behind his wife, "is enough fruit so we won't be running out every few days."

"That's wonderful," she said. "As soon as you and Sean and Margaret get tired of this bargain, we'll be running out to the garbage pail with it. I hope we have room."

"I suppose you don't eat anything I buy. Do you have all your meals sent in or do you dine out?"

"Ben, when I get through school and come home and do the housework and the cooking, I don't feel like eating much and you know it."

"Maybe if you ate more, you'd have a little more strength for housework, because it looks like you get through that before you even start."

"That sounds like your sister Rose talking. Or did Donald say that?"

"It's no secret."

"How could it be, with Tommy and Joe down there every weekend all summer. To top it all off, they get their big chance to visit Aunt Rose's farm this fall and attend a country school. 'Just what they need.' Maybe if they were 'visiting' their own home for a change, cleaning the bathroom and cutting the grass, they wouldn't have so many tales to tell their precious aunt and uncle."

"Maybe if you had ten women to help you, the place would be just as filthy."

"Oh, Ben. You're talking Chinese again."

Sean knew his mother was ready to stop arguing, but his father was heated now and before the night was through, they would run the cycle, arguing housecleaning, money, clothes, relatives, and back again to the enthusiastic purchases of the irrepressible head of the household. They would sit across from each other at the kitchen table after the heat of their quarrel had subsided. In low insistent tones, punctuated only by pauses to drink from their highball glasses, they would each urge their view hopelessly on the other. Too tired to talk or drink further, they would wearily climb to their bedroom around 2 a.m.

Up the winding stairs from the second floor to his attic bedroom Sean carried an apple, a handful of figs, the Saturday night tabloid, and a glass of ginger ale. His hands were so full when he started up that he had to use his little finger to stick through the empty lockhole and pull the door open. For more than a year now, his father had sworn he was going to install a new lock, but he had never gotten around to it.

Sean decided not to take his usual Saturday night bath because he did not want to hear the voices from below—his mother urging moderation in all things upon his father, and his father answering, accusing his wife of taking all the joy out of living, of not thinking and acting big. It would, Sean knew, be a long and futile night for his parents. Neither one of them, since Sean was old enough to remember, had changed their ways.

In his spacious pale-papered room on the third floor, Sean had a narrow bunk bed his father had bought, a bargain from an Army and Navy store. The springs were loose so the bed offered only as much back support as a hammock. Leaning over the low end of the wooden bed, which still wore its institutional gray coat, Sean pulled out the double drawer on the left side of his desk and reached up for an album he kept hidden below the top drawer. Since the drawer was broken and couldn't be opened, no one ever disturbed his album. He lay on his side, resting his weight on his elbow, and slowly turned the black construction paper pages and ate his apple. Familiarly he studied the small breasts of the Folies-Bergère dancers in an old program his father had brought back from Europe when he was a single man.

The cool detached look of the women had repelled Sean when he first found the program among his father's papers in the back room of the attic. Now, increasingly, they attracted him with their promise of reserve and cool sophistication. They all seemed waiting, poised in the ready position caught by the camera, for Sean to turn the page so they could break into fleshy, arduous dances. Even then, they would not sweat. Sean fell asleep with his clothes and the ceiling light on and the album open beside him. The apple core fell to the floor.

Some time in the night he awoke to a brightly lit room and wide awake voices. Before he broke the thin tissue of consciousness, eyes contracting from the light, he dreamed he was being pursued. A man and woman were taking turns chasing him in and out of two rooms, one poorly lit, the other ablaze with light. "Stop. Get back in there," they shouted. "Where do you think you're going? No, you're not. Yes you are." Sean's T-shirt was wringing wet when he sat up in bed and rubbed his eyes.

He shook his head to clear the voices out, but voices persisted. As events of the evening took shape in his conscious mind, he realized the voices were coming up the stairs from the second floor bedroom of his parents. They were shouting, and pushing and pulling furniture around.

At the foot of the stairs Sean stopped behind the closed door and bent to peer through the empty lockhole. Moonlight came through the two curtained windows in his parents' room, revealing a grotesque ballet. His father in pajama bottoms was straddling the bed, leaping unsteadily first to one side, then the other, his feet sinking into the soft springs. Behind the tall bureau which had been pushed up against the foot of the bed, his mother in her faded white flannel nightgown danced and ducked to the side opposite his father. Like a groggy fullback, his father was having little luck feinting one way and going the other. He tripped himself up, fell to a knee and cursed.

"Get back in this bed, Marion. Now!" Ben Connell shouted. "So help me God if you don't get into this bed in two seconds—"

"No," Sean's mother said.

"—I'll punch you black and blue."

"If you touch me again," she said, "I'll have you arrested."

"You bitch," he shouted, "you Godawful bitch. I'll kill you."

"Go ahead. I'd rather you did than spit in my face and kick me and punch me and then think I'm going to climb into bed with you, you drunken—Sean!"

Ben Connell turned. His eyes were red and fierce. Spit was rolling from his mouth to his chin. He stood up.

"What are you doing up? Get up to your room. Get up to bed."

Running into the room and stopping beneath the towering wavering figure of his father, Sean called out for the man he went with on market nights: "Daddy."

Ben Connell cocked his arm as if to give his son a backhand slap. "What are you butting in for? Get back up to bed."

Sean backed away as the door from Margaret's room opened and she ran into the room and the flannelled warmth of her mother's stomach. "Momma, what's the matter?" she asked. "What's wrong?"

Marion did not answer but asked her husband almost triumphantly: "Are you proud of yourself now?"

Stepping off the bed heavily, Ben lost his balance, banged into the radiator and lurched to the foot of the bed where his wife and children stood together. Holding his pajama bottoms up with one hand, he shook his fist in his wife's face. Spit came off his lips as he yelled.

"You bitch! Trying to turn them against me now. You'd like that, wouldn't you."

He took hold of Sean's arm. "Go up to bed now, Sean. You don't understand."

Sean pulled his arm away.

Minutes later, he was on his way to bed, leaving his mother in Margaret's room where she had gone to spend the night. His father was sitting in the churned debris of bedclothes on the double bed, his legs crossed under him, elbows resting on his knees and his head in his hands, fast asleep.

When he woke at ten o'clock, Sean was dying of thirst. His throat was clogged as if his tonsils had swelled during the night. He was drinking his fourth glass of water in the bathroom when his mother came in and said, in a voice just above a whisper: "Margaret and I are going to Grandma's. We want you to come."

Sean was sure then that he hated his father—hated the animal he had seen stalking his wife with rum on his breath. Unable to drive the dismal terror-filled scene of the night before from his mind, Sean drank another glass of water and went in to see his sister. Margaret was puttering—putting clothes, books and trinkets in a suitcase, then taking some out and placing them back in their bureau and dresser drawers. She asked Sean what she should take, but having no idea how long she would be gone, he could not help her.

As Sunday morning wore on, neither Sean nor Margaret made a move to go to church and their mother never mentioned it. Marion Connell had gone to early Mass and was now cleaning the house with a startling energy, welling from the conviction that her husband's relatives were sure to visit and commiserate with him. Stopping only to unskillfully steal a puff from a poorly-hidden cigarette, she walked nervously from room to room, surveying the disorder of daily living. Then she went to work, picking up dirty socks, making beds, closing half-open drawers, dusting in seldom-disturbed corners and restoring a surface look of cleanliness and order.

Despite all the unusual activity, Sean did not truly believe there would be a separation until he went downstairs and saw the kitchen stove. Its white enamel was shining and the tea kettle and the frying pan, one of which was always roosting above a gas jet, were scrubbed clean, lying upside down on the drainboard by the pantry sink.

Sean walked past the stove and turned into the pantry. He filled a bowl with cornflakes, put the box back in the cupboard and took a bottle of milk from the refrigerator. When he was seated at the kitchen table, putting sugar and milk on the flakes, his father came downstairs.

Neither of them spoke as Ben Connell began a production of cooking bacon, eggs, toast and coffee for his breakfast. Everything he had lectured his wife on in vain—she said she didn't have time—such as breaking eggs into a bowl rather than the pan, putting a dash of salt and half an eggshell in with the coffee grounds, buttering the toast immediately after it popped—he now took time to do for himself with a flourish and barely suppressed enjoyment.

Sean knew that his father had trouble any morning to keep from singing. No matter how turbulent life had been the night before, Ben Connell's world—to his son's continuing amazement—became as light and full of promise as the new day. Seven hours of sleep worked like an undercurrent to pull back from the shore of his consciousness all troubles, anger and hurt. Sean remembered his mother chiding his father another Sunday morning a few months before.

"Ben! How can you whistle?"

"What do you mean?"

"Your own mother taken to the hospital yesterday after a bad fall and you come down here whistling."

"Oh, yeah," his father had said, and assumed a mask of gravity behind which he had trouble restraining muscles used to smiling at nothing more than the thick Sunday paper waiting face up on the porch for him.

It was the same now. Sean's father acted as if he had not only done nothing wrong, but as if he were the one who had been abused. He tried to sulk through three eggs fried sunny side up with the yokes unbroken, six slices of crisp bacon, four pieces of heavily buttered toast and several cups of extra strong coffee. The effectiveness of his sulking was decreased by intervals of burping.

Marion Connell had come downstairs during her husband's meal. Avoiding the kitchen, she was moving furniture and dusting in the front hall, parlor and dining room, stopping now and then to listen to anything that might be going on. She became very quiet upon hearing her husband's voice.

"Sliced peaches are good on cereal."

"I don't feel like peaches," Sean said. He paused. "It's too much trouble to peel the skin."

"The skin is the best part," Ben Connell said, "but if you get me a knife, I'll peel you a few."

"No," Sean said. "No, thank you."

He finished his cereal, put the bowl and spoon in the sink, and went upstairs to get his things together.

The hours passed as Sean roamed from room to room, turned over his books without doing his homework, called a friend on the phone, read and re-read the sports pages of the paper. Nothing helped. Night would come and his family would part. His mother and sister were definitely going to Grandma's and he would go with them. They were going to accept the old lady's cantankerous ways, irritating demands for attention, repeated shoutings because of deafness, and last and probably least, her hospitality.

They would eat regular meals—plain and filling—the diet of the die-hard Irish-American: corn, boiled potatoes, corned beef, cabbage, baked potatoes, corn chowder, spare ribs, mashed potatoes, ham, potato salad. Each day would pass unobtrusively. Routine would succeed routine. Treats would be the exception and to the old lady's liking—a hot fudge sundae from Baker's ice cream parlor or a ride on Sunday afternoon to the beach, listening to the old woman scold her 40-year-old son for driving at the reckless speed of thirty-five miles per hour, and telling how she used to take an excursion boat from Revere Beach to Nahant.

What would his father do? Stay in the empty house? Wait for Tommy and Joe to come home? Visit friends until he, not they, wearied of his sparkling wit and fund of stories with which he paid for his meals? Eat out, generously overtipping waiters and waitresses, all the while reprimanding himself for the money he was spending? Cook his gourmet dinners until not a clean dish or pan was left, wearying him of his self-prepared delights?

They would all eat. No one would starve. But how would the time be passed between the supper table and bed? When his father had read the paper, the house would still be empty. There would be no Margaret blushing and pushing back her straight brown hair, calling her father a fibber. When his mother had corrected her class's homework, the old lady gone to bed, he and Margaret done their homework—what would they do? Who would supply the blarney he, his mother and sister had come to depend on? Who would send them out to the world thinking they were special people, chosen to excel? On whom would his father lavish overstatements, sumptuous praise—the secretaries at his office, the men he worked with? Who would garnish life and serve it up to the Connells with brilliant reds, softer-than-air blues and Irish greens, if not Ben Connell himself?

It was hard for Sean, because he was wrong, to look at his father as the day grew short. It was different this time. His father could not sing or laugh or talk his way out of the wretchedness that was creeping into his being, silencing him and turning his thoughts and soul inward.

Five o'clock came and a strange silence reigned in the kitchen, empty of the usual bustle that meant supper was being prepared. The family wandered into the downstairs rooms. Margaret knelt on the kitchen linoleum, looking for an earring under the kitchen stove. Her eyes were red. Ignoring the fact that her daughter was dirtying her new cream-colored wool suit, Marion Connell walked from kitchen to pantry, emptying and refilling the tea kettle with tap water, biting what little lipstick remained on her dry lips.

Ben Connell sat in front of his escritoire in the corner of the parlor. Heaps of personal papers were stacked on the open walnut lid. An attempt had been made and abandoned to divide the papers into two piles. He sat running his hand through his shock of hair. A cowlick that he had never conquered rose up on the back of his skull like a shredded horn.

Sean stood at the dining room table. He tried to stuff a paper bag full of socks and underwear into another paper bag of the same size. The first bag had burst at the bottom and would not fit into the second.

Sean's mother made the move they all awaited. She picked up her suitcase and handbag, carried them to the front door and set them down on the edge of the oriental rug. Margaret gathered up her things quickly and put them beside her mother's. Sean swooped down on his brown paper bags on the dining room floor and hurried them through the parlor to put them with the others. His father stood up as he passed, looking like a man who has been startled out of a nightmared sleep. Sean felt then that he, his mother and sister were rushing through a conspiracy, expediting an act of which they were ashamed.

Ben Connell moved slowly into the front hall and stood watching his wife and children put on their coats.

"Goodbye, Ben," Marion Connell said. She grabbed her suitcase and handbag, opened the door and went out on the porch before her husband could speak or touch her.

Margaret started to follow, holding a large suitcase in one hand, a hat bag in the other. She turned and ran to her father, banging his knee with her suitcase and kissing him on the cheek at the same time. "Oh, Daddy." She ran out the door crying.

Sean, head down, moved his bags from one arm to the other, wedging them against his body so one hand would be free for the shopping bag. He postponed looking at his father until he was almost sure he would not cry. When he raised his head, he did not see the sorrow or despair he expected. Instead, his father looked stunned, like a wild animal shot with a sedative, being carried into captivity. To Sean, the desertion of his father seemed as cruel suddenly as the relegating of a lion to the flea-ridden cages of the zoo they—his family—had often visited in Winchester.

Sean put his bags down and went out to the porch. His mother and sister were waiting below on the sidewalk.

"I think I better stay," Sean said, "and see if I can help Pa."

His mother started to say something, but changed her mind. She motioned to Margaret to start walking.

"I'll come to visit you at Grandma's," Sean said.

"Bring your washing when you come," his mother said, "and his too."

177

13 | Echoes

"I'll come home next weekend. All right?"

"Why do you have to leave? What are you going to do?"

"Six weeks?"

"He said six weeks, or maybe two months, before she can have any visitors."

"I'll come home this weekend. I promise. And I'll help you—do things around here."

"I don't want you to go. Your father doesn't want you to go. Really, he doesn't. You don't have to do anything. Just be here."

"I have to. I have to get away for a few days. I was just gonna go because I was mad, but I'm not mad, Ma, but I still have to go. I promise. I swear to Goh—od. I'll come home this weekend."

Sean kissed his mother drily on the forehead. She did not seem to notice. He carried his cracked, faded blue suitcase into the front hall and returned to the dining-room door.

"Pa?"

Ben Connell opened his eyes, considered the ceiling, and turned his head slowly to look at his son.

"Roger's due any minute. I just wanted to say goodbye —so long, and I'll be back in a few days. This weekend probably, this weekend."

"Sure. Sure."

Sean turned to go: A car horn sounded outside. "Come in a minute," Ben said.

Sean knew what was coming, but he did not now object to it. Always before, when his father had pressed money on him at the last moment as he was leaving on a date or going out or back to school, he had protested. "I don't need that much Pa," had become a standard parting line. "Just put it away," his father always replied, as if greatly irritated. "And don't say anything to your mother." And Sean had closed his fist over the ten or twenty dollars reluctantly, guiltily. The money, a bonus, had rarely been spent wisely. Now, as he walked to his father's bedside, he knew that it was necessary to accept and he hoped to do it graciously.

"Yes, Pa?"

"There's an envelope in the buffet drawer. Take it with you. The top drawer. Over to your right."

"I've got it. Thank you."

"What? Oh—you're welcome."

Ben awkwardly extended his hand. When Sean shook hands gently, Ben restrained an impulse to pull his son close. He had an image of Sean when he was first learning to walk, his chubby face lowered, proud of himself, tottering, falling. Ben held on.

"Have you been drinking?"

"I had a beer, Pa. I better go now."

Ben watched his son stride away.

"Goodbye, Pa. Goodbye, Ma. I'll see you soon."

Marion went past the open dining-room door on her way to the front door window to watch her son climb into his friend's car. Ben heard no sound in his house for a few moments, then Marion's feet heavily ascending the stairs. When the sound of the departing car died, Ben eased his head into his pillows, closed his eyes, and after a short period of numbness, roamed the rooms and environs of his home.

In the kitchen Marion was smiling her cautious smile as he came in and took his hat off. She turned to him and opened her arms to welcome him, but she was not relaxing until he had his arms around her. Still then her body was somewhat tense, afraid that he would spot something that would irritate or even incense him.

"I'm glad you're home," she said.

"Whose sweetheart are you," he said.

She relaxed fully then, hugged him around the waist, laid her cheek on his chest, raised her mouth to kiss, her heels planted on the floor.

"Do you have to act like that in front of us?" Sean asked, indicating his sister who sat a little away from the table, smiling mildly, waiting her turn to welcome her father. "Do you have to act so mushy?"

Ben turned the embrace into a joke for the benefit of his 14-year-old son. He slapped his wife on the bottom. "Ben!" she said. "Get atta here Sean."

"You're getting to be a stout wench," Ben said.

Arriving home from the drugstore, Ben stopped at the end of his driveway to watch Sean soaping the new blue Dodge. He smiled at the serious, intent look on Sean's face. It was obvious his 10-year-old son was trying to make up for being bad at supper, for kicking Margaret under the table, for taking a piece of meat off her plate that he did not really want, putting it in his mouth, taking it out and asking her, "Do you want it back?"

Ben felt ashamed, as he watched Sean scrub the fenders of the car, that he had whacked him so hard with the back of his hand. Joseph had left the table immediately, Tommy finished his meal without another word, Margaret lost her appetite and squirmed in her chair, and Marion made a production of bringing ice upstairs in a towel to put on Sean's face. He had hit him too hard.

As he started up the driveway to compliment Sean on the fine job he was doing, Ben noticed the can of scouring powder beside the pail of water.

"NAAAAAGHH! STOP! What are you doing! That'll RUIN the car. Stop it!"

Sean had dropped his rag and was cowering before his father's advance.

"Are you crazy! A brand new car and you're using that stuff on it. That'll ruin the finish!" Ben seized the green hose and attacked the grey film on the fender. "Oh my God! Look! Look! Look at what you've done. It isn't coming off. It's dull. It's scratched! It's ruined!"

Marion ran out the front door, down the steps and around to the driveway. She thought one of her children had been killed. She found her son backing slowly away from her husband who stood looking at the ground, shaking his head, holding a limp, dripping hose. Marion looked at the fender and the scouring powder.

"He was only trying to help, Ben."

Ben nodded his head morosely.

In the parlor Margaret was fussing around Ben's chair, waiting for him to finish reading the sports section and the editorial page. He peered at her over the top of his paper. "What are you up to, Margaret?" he asked, in a deep voice and with a mock serious look on his face.

"Daddy?"

"What have you got to say for yourself?"

"I thought—"

"Just as I suspected—gibberish."

"I thought you might want to—"

"Speak up. Speak up." Ben tossed his paper aside, assumed a stern face and shook his arm and hand and index finger as if they were palsied. "You must get to the point, Young Lady."

Margaret looked at the rug and was quiet.

Ben studied her a moment, smiled, and lunged up and out of his chair to tickle her skinny ribs. "Ah ha! Ticklish, ay? Take that. And that. And that and that and that." "Daddy, daddy," Margaret was twisting and screeching and laughing, "stop, stop it Daddy, stop!"

"Now. That's taken care of. What did you want, you little tinker."

"Would you—tell me a story?"

"A story, is it? Well then—did I tell you the one-no, I probably told you that one—maybe I better—"

"Which one, Daddy?" Margaret rose from a sitting to a kneeling position on the rug.

"Oh, I was going to tell you the one about—Dinty O'Dooley—the Irishman who—who—gave up potatoes for life, but you probably—"

"You didn't tell me that one, Daddy. Please. Tell me."

"Wellll, all right, if you-promise not to blow your nose on the rug when I'm not looking. Do you promise?"

"Oh. Daddy, you're silly."

"Is that so? Well! All right then. Now, let me see. Once upon a time there was an Irishman named Dinny O'Dooley who—"

"You said Dinty, Daddy."

"Of course, of course, Dinty O'Dooley, how could I ever make that mistake. Once upon a time, Dinty O'Dooley, an Irishman of low tastes, decided to give up potatoes forever. He was tired of potatoes, potato pancakes for breakfast, potato salad for lunch, potatoes baked and boiled and filleted for supper. He was definitely tired of potatoes. In fact, he couldn't stand the sight of them, so he went to the market to find a substitute, to buy something else but potatoes, and when he got there..."

Sean came through the dining-room and stopped at the entryway to the parlor. He leaned on the jamb and listened a minute before speaking. "his name was Dinny Dunnigan when I heard it and he's allergic to everything but potatoes. He got boils."

"DAMN YOU!" Ben exploded out of his chair and bumped into Margaret as he chased after Sean who ran through the dining-room and kitchen and out the back door. "Come back here! Damn you! I'll kill you!"

"Daddy," Margaret called as she tried to catch up to her father, "I don't care. I want to hear the rest of it. Please."

"No! No more stories. Where did that son-of-a-bitch go!"

Marion stopped at the landing and bent over to see her husband as he sat with his cup of coffee at the kitchen table.

"Ben, you'd better come upstairs. Something funny happened to the wallpaper in the den."

"If the wallpaper wants to curl up, fall on the floor, and roll away, I could care less. I'm tired. I want to finish my coffee."

"But Ben" "I want to finish" "you should see the wallpaper," "my coffee, I've had a hard day and" "There's a big hole in it," "I'm not up to any foolishness, What?"

"There's a hole in it and brown stains and scratches all around."

Ben followed his wife upstairs. "I can't get a moment's peace here after a hard day's work. Christ, there's no sense in coming home. You're supposed to be able to relax at home. It turns out I do more relaxing at work, though God knows I work hard enough there."

Marion led the way into the den silently, pointed at the wall and stepped back. Ben examined the jagged edges of light brown wallpaper surrounding the exposed plaster, and the dark brown stains on both. He rubbed his finger against one of the stains and lifted it to his nose. "Where are they?"

"What is it, Ben? They're in their bedroom."

Ben stopped outside the bedroom door, listening for a moment to the whispering, then quickly opened the door. Joseph and Tommy had their back to the door as they huddled over their night table. They slammed the drawer shut and wheeled around, both looking surprised and fearful.

"Joseph and Thomas. What is the meaning of this?"

"We were playing Daddy," Joseph said hastily. "Playing with the ambulance," Tommy said. "We were just running it up and down the wall" My little brown Army ambulance" "to see if it worked right." "with the rubber wheels that are skinny."

"Just a minute. Just one minute. You mean to tell me you were running an ambulance up and down the wall? Is that it?"

"Yes, Daddy," they said.

"And this ambulance, this ambulance with rubber wheels, jumped out of your hands when you weren't looking and bit out a piece of wallpaper? Is that how it happened?"

Joseph and Tommy looked at each other desperately. They started to shake their heads and turned back to their father to form an answer.

"Never mind. Don't answer that question. Take yourself down to the kitchen, both of you, and wait for me there."

Marion edged into the bedroom as the boys raced down the stairs. She watched her husband open and quickly shut the single drawer of the night table, and turn to her, his cheeks puffed and his lips pressed in in an effort to restrain a guffaw.

"What's so funny?" Marion asked as her husband sat on the bed and made churning noises. He pointed to the drawer. Marion opened it and gasped. Arranged neatly by size was a layer of turds individually wrapped in toilet paper. "BEN!"

Ben Connell broke out laughing. "Heeheeaaahaaasshhheeeee!" He rolled back on the bed, pumped his feet high in the air and slammed them down on the floor, laughing uncontrollably.

"Ben, that's awful! It's disgusting! Do you know what this means? They've been saving them! Ben! Do you want them to hear you!"

Ben shook his head up and down and then back and forth as tears came from his eyes and he continued to laugh.

Catherine answered the door and hurried back to the pantry, tossing a greeting to her husband over her shoulder. Ben followed her into the pantry and, knowing it would not please her but unable to resist, hugged her and kissed the back of her neck as she vigorously stirred something pale yellow in a bowl.

"Not now, Ben. I don't feel like it. I have to finish this cake and get supper started."

Catherine's squirming aroused Ben. He held onto her waist and kissed her behind the ear.

"Ben! I'm hot and tired and I have to change Tommy and get supper. Stop it! Please!"

Ben tore off his undershirt and threw it in the corner of his bedroom. He was angry because it was a hot May day and he wanted to take a quick shower but he had never had one installed so he had to settle for a soak in the bathtub which was now slowly filling. He untied his shoes quickly and pushed them off using his feet, pulled off his pants and threw them on the bed and sat down heavily to puff a cigarette and contemplate the problems involved in the installation of a shower. Hearing a noise behind him, he turned to see the closet door opening and Catherine's broad-brimmed straw hat with the false flowers and her pale blue dress floating low across the floor toward him. He leaped up, his heart tightening. "Oh my God," he whispered.

"Hi, Daddy," Margaret said, raising the brim of the hat to expose her smiling face. "It's me. I'm playing house."

"Mahgget." Ben choked on the word. "Margaret. Margaret, don't you ever do that again. Take those clothes off and stay out of that closet. Take them off! I don't want you to set foot in that closet as long as you live!"

Margaret took the clothes off, crying silently.

Ben sat straight in his chair at the head of the dining-room table, expertly carving the roast beef in sure search of medium rare. A dish of vari-colored mints replaced the usual ash tray in front of his plate. At the other end of the table Marion smiled appreciatively at her husband's skill, relaxed and confident in the knowledge that everything necessary to the full enjoyment of the meal was at hand. Sean courteously was helping Margaret to boiled onions. Joey, smiling, asked a serious-faced Thomas to please pass the gravy. After serving the roast beef Ben cracked and distributed the lobster tails and requested an ear of corn from his eldest who relayed the message down the table. Marion lovingly chided Margaret for using her salad fork during the meat course. Ben sliced the venison and lamb and gently announced that those who desired turkey stuffing could nod once. The ringing telephone and knocks at the door and the radio which, untouched, had begun to play, were ignored by the close-knit family group as the children listened respectfully in silence as their father and mother discussed their philosophy of life and cooed endearments for each's contribution to the Golden Mean. In turn then, beginning with Joseph the eldest, the children presented a three-minute report on the day's activities, ending always with a summary of what they had learned to better equip them in service to God and Man. Ben's post-meal grace was short but dignified. He stood up, rolled up his sleeves, and with fork and knife directed his melodious clan in a medley of hymns, chants, and lively Irish ditties before the group adjourned to the living-room for Ben's reading of carefully selected related passages of the Bible.

In the den Marion was throwing an ambulance-shaped turd at Catherine who was pouring a bowl of cement over Margaret as Sean chased Joseph in the bathtub where Marion hugged Ben's blue Dodge

Catherine slapped Ben's blue bottom Margaret took Sean out of her mouth 'Do you want it back?' Sean poured scouring powder on Ben's limpdrip hose Catherine hugged Marion bit her neck 'Now! Now!' Tommy threw potato pancake turds down Sean's smiling throat Ben hugged Margaret aroused.

Ben Connell sat up in bed sweating and gasping, forcing his eyes open and shaking his head to disrupt the shifting, changing, ballooning feathery logs in his skull. Slowly, frighteningly, his mind drained and left his body in a cold empty sweat.

There was no noise in the house. Marion was upstairs sleeping in one of the rooms on one of the beds. Sean had left with his friend. Margaret was locked away. Joseph and Tommy were married. Catherine was dead.

Ben wanted to get up and fix himself a drink but his legs were unsteady and the house was dark and he did not want to drink alone. Unwedging the broken-hinged yellow door to the back pantry cupboard where he kept his rum out of harm's way would require too great an effort. He was not that thirsty.

14 | Waking the Dead

Margaret was waiting.

Her father had asked Joseph if he wanted to go with him, but Joseph said that he had a history paper to write. Without asking the destination, Tommy wanted to know, "Can I come."

"I'm going to a wake. To pay my last respects to a dead man."

"Oh," Tommy said. "That's no fun."

"No. Do you still want to come?"

"I don't think so, Dad."

Margaret wondered why her father never asked Tommy to go anywhere with him. He always said that Tommy was the best behaved boy he had, but he never really wanted to take him anyplace alone. Instead, it was Sean, the worst behaved of the children, who went most places with her father. Margaret had heard her father say to her mother that Sean "was enough to try the patience of a saint," but again and again he had asked him to go with him, after Joseph had said no and Tommy wasn't asked. Margaret was asked only when Sean did not want to go.

"Where the Hell is he?" her father asked.

"I don't know," her mother said. "He should have been home half an hour ago. He has his—"

"I haven't got all day you know."

"—good pants on. I know, I know. I told him to come right home and change them before he did anything."

"Well I'll give him five more minutes and that's all."

Margaret looked at the clock. She figured Sean had twenty minutes before her father lost all patience and turned to her. She would have time to wash up and comb her hair and put her coat on a chair in the front hall. She said a little prayer to the Virgin Mary that Sean, if he got home in time, would not want to go.

Tommy was right. A wake did not sound like fun. She had never seen a dead person. But she would be with her father and she would not have to do anything except maybe say a few prayers. It would not be like going down to Tiffin's bakery on Saturday nights to buy the leftovers. Sean was good at that. He would stand there, after the man had finished putting cakes and bread and pastry in the shopping bag, and shake it so the things would fall down inside and not look like so much and sometimes the man would add another loaf of bread or half a dozen coffee rolls. She could not do that. She would hold the bag open, blushing and looking down, not even seeing what the man put in the bag, and when he was done, give him the quarter. Her father was often unhappy when she came out to him waiting in the car and he saw that the bag was not very full.

"That man's a cheat. He plays favorites. I wish Sean were here."

Sean had done it for almost a year, but now he said he was too big to beg and he would only go shopping with his father when it was the first of the month and he had been paid. So Margaret went back to the loading platform in back of the bakery, building up her courage as she waited for the trucks to come in and unload their leftovers. She was determined to be as bold as Sean was, because it was the end of the month and they were charging food and they did need all they could get for a quarter, but Margaret could not help noticing how poorly dressed the old women and the other children were and she thought that maybe the man was right in giving her a little less. When her turn came, she jumped off the table and ran up and hung her head and blushed and failed.

Going to a wake would not be like that. She might have to talk to people though if there were people there her father knew. She never knew what to say to people. Her father could talk and talk and Joseph could too if he wanted to. Joseph even asked people questions. And Tommy was friendly and everyone liked him. And Sean didn't care what people thought, he said whatever he wanted to say. But she never knew what to say when her father took her to the office on Saturday morning or met someone he knew when they were out shopping and smiled and said, "This is Margaret, my favorite daughter." If Sean was there, he would say, "You've only got one daughter," and this would give Margaret a chance to back away, but if he wasn't there, she would have to try and answer questions—"How old are you?" "What grade are you in?" "Do you like school?"—and since her father was a school man, she could not tell the nice ladies and men she met that she hated school, that she hated the teachers who went out of their way to be nice to her, that she hated the children who treated her as someone special or whispered about her or said right to her face that she was the teacher's pet because her father was a big shot. If any boy said something like that to Sean, he'd laugh or, if he didn't like the boy, punch him in the mouth. She couldn't do that. Her mother had explained to her what was ladylike.

Margaret was combing her hair in the mirror over the mantelpiece in the front hall when Sean came in. Another five minutes and she would have been gone with her father. Sean's 'face was flushed and his hair was mussed. He looked very nice.

"Marry me, Margaret!" Sean grabbed her around the waist, hugged her, and hooked her shoulder with his chin. "You're beautiful, the most beautiful girl in the world! Marry me! I'm madly in love with you!"

Margaret was mad with Sean because he came on time to go with her father and he only said nice things to her when he was kidding and he was always grabbing her and tickling her and trying to wrestle with her and she didn't think a brother should act that way. "Let go, Stupid! Let go! You're messing my hair. Let go! Sean!" She didn't mean to smile when she yelled at him but she couldn't help it.

"Leave your sister alone," Margaret's mother said as she came into the front hall. "Where have you been? LOOK at your, pants! YOUR NEW PANTS! I told you—"

"I just shot a few baskets."

"—to come home and change right away. Basketball? Ben. Ben?"

She walked into the kitchen. "Ben, where are you! It'll take me two dry cleanings to get those clean. Brand new pants."

Margaret heard her father coming down the stairs. Sean waited in the hall until his father went down into the kitchen and then hurried up the three stairs from the front hall to the first landing.

"Did he finally get home?"

"Yes, and you should see—come back here you! Where do you think you're going! You come down here and show your father what—"

"I have to change my pants."

"I haven't got all day, Marion. It's almost four now."

"But his pants, Ben, his new pants. He's ruined them. Take a look. Just take a look at them. Come down here, Sean."

"C'mon, Ma, they're not ruined. You're always exaggerating."

"I was going to ask you to come with me, Young Man, but if this is how you obey your mother, I don't think I will."

"Where you going, Pa?"

"Don't tell him, Ben."

"I'm going to a wake, and don't call me 'Pa.'"

"You mean I can't go with you now?"

"That's right. Next time you'll listen to your mother and be a little more careful. Margaret, do you want to come with me?"

"Yes, Daddy."

"All right. Get ready, I can't waste any more time."

"Oh, that's not fair," Sean called back as he went upstairs.

"That'll teach you a lesson. C'mon, Margaret." Margaret knew from Sean's tone of voice that he was not really disappointed. She wondered if her father knew too. "Is that all you're going to say to him?" Margaret's mother asked.

"What do you want me to say to him? I'm not letting him come with me."

"But those pants are brand new, Ben. They cost six dollars."

"Don't keep it up, Marion. Margaret, are you ready?"

"Yes, Daddy."

"You let him get away with murder."

"I don't have time to discuss it now. Marion." Margaret went down the front steps and toward the driveway. Her mother followed her father out to the porch.

"You didn't even ask me about taking Margaret. She's a little young to be going to a wake. Do you have to take her?"

"It won't hurt her. It's about time she realized that none of us is going to last forever."

"Are you coming home for supper?"

"If we ever get there."

"Well, we don't have much money to be eating out."

"I—said—I'd—be—home. Now go in the house. You're making a spectacle of yourself. Margaret, I think we'll walk. I need the exercise."

"I want you to talk to Sean after supper."

"We'll see. Goodbye, Lovey."

Margaret's mother smiled when her husband called her the silly name, but she stopped right away and went back in the house.

Even though the funeral home wasn't very far away, just up past the Square, Margaret was sorry they weren't taking the car. It meant that her father would not take her out to a special place for supper and he wouldn't take her for a ride or even to get an ice cream cone at Dairyland. Besides, it was too close to supper. But she might be able to talk with her father during the walk up or back. He might tell her one of his special stories about Ireland or what it was like when he was a boy or what his ancestors found when they came to this country.

Today Margaret had to hurry to keep up with her father. Sometimes he moped along, as if he had no special place to go, but today he was taking giant steps and humming to himself. "Nice to walk for a change, isn't it?"

"Yes, Daddy."

"I should walk more often. I'm always riding or sitting. That doesn't keep you in very good shape." He took his pack of cigarettes out of his pocket and tapped a cigarette into his hand. "And these things don't help any. I should give them up."

193

He held his cigarette in his hand until they had almost reached the Square. Then he stopped and lit it and turned to Margaret. "I'm going to stop at Donovan's."

She nodded.

"You don't have to mention this to your mother," he said as they continued on to the package store.

She shook her head. She knew he would not have to say that to Sean or Joseph, or even Tommy, if they were with him. She wasn't a tattletale. It was just that she spent so much time with her mother that things had slipped out, things she didn't even know she was not supposed to talk about. She was going to try to be very careful to never say anything about stopping at the liquor store. Her father did not take her out often. She did not want him to get mad and never take her out. She was not a tattletale.

Nervously, Margaret watched through the glass window in the door of the liquor store as her father talked to the man behind the counter. He had said he was in a hurry, but he must have forgot and she was afraid they would be late for the wake and it would be all over and the body would be buried and he couldn't see the man he wanted to see.

Her father was always like that in a store. Even in a store where he didn't know the people, he couldn't just go in and buy something and come right out again. He had to stop and talk and smile and ask about things and sometimes buy things that he never really wanted. Whenever Mrs. Klein at Klein's Klothes Factory showed him a suit for Sean or Tommy or Joseph or a sweater for her or her mother, Margaret's father would say that she had very good taste and that's why he always brought his business there. Her mother didn't think that the Klein's second floor in a big building in the east end was really a factory. She called it a hole-in-the-wall and said you could get better buys on clothes in Boston any day of the week. But Sean and Tommy and Joseph didn't like to go intown with her mother and Margaret didn't either, even though she went more often, because her mother wanted to buy as much as she could for her money, always things that were on sale, and you had to fight people in the basements of the big stores or they took things right out of your hands and you had to try to try on everything before you bought it and you only had time for a little snack in a coffee shop before you hurried to other stores and took the subway home too tired to talk and dragging packages.

It was much easier with her father. He never seemed in a hurry once he got inside a store and he'd talk and talk with someone like Mr. Klein who would tell him what it was like in Russia and Mrs. Klein had everyone's measurements and she'd pick out a suit and show it to her father and he'd say it was gorgeous and Mrs. Klein would say yes, it was beautiful material.

"But I can't afford that. That looks too rich for my blood."

"For you," Mr. Klein said, "a beautiful sixty-dollar suit, only twenty-nine ninety-five."

"I couldn't take it at that price. You couldn't possibly make any profit. I'd be arrested for theft."

"You should let me worry. Mamie, you mark down on the slip alterations included. Twenty-nine ninety-five. Total!"

"Oh no! You shouldn't. Tommy, did you hear that? Isn't that a beautiful suit?"

"I guess so."

"What! Mr. Klein's giving us this sixty-dollar suit for twenty-nine ninety-five, alterations included, and you guess so. That's no way to be."

"I like it. It's nice."

"That's better. While we're here, Mr. Klein, you wouldn't have another one like that for Tommy and maybe one for Sean?"

No one listened to their mother when they came home and she objected that they did not have enough money to pay for all the clothes in one month and asked why Tommy had to have two suits at one time and Sean none. Her father explained that they didn't have any real buys in Sean's sizes but he would take him back next month, but he wouldn't. It would be a long time before he went shopping for clothes again. And no one mentioned that they had driven out to Anchors Aweigh for fried clams after they bought Tommy's suits.

Robert Crotty

Margaret's father came out of Donovan's liquor store with a small bottle in a brown bag which he put in his overcoat pocket. He was smiling.

"That didn't take too long, did it?"

"No, Daddy."

"He was going on and on about Florida. He keeps talking about opening a nightclub down there. The closest he's been to Florida in the twenty years I've known him is the travel section of the Sunday paper. But he's a good man. He means well. Even if his prices are no bargain."

Her father's ideas about bargains were funny. Sometimes he would read an ad in a newspaper and drive miles and miles to find the little store where the bargain wasn't really a bargain, it was just something to make you come in and buy other things, and her father would buy the bargain and another thing and leave, saying, "That's the last time I ever come here." And other times he would find real bargains but he would buy so much that it went bad like the flashlight batteries that were no good because they got lost in the cellar so long and then he would get mad. But he went to many stores, like Mr. Asoorian's the butcher's, when he knew he wouldn't find bargains and he would buy lots of stuff and go back again. Margaret heard him call Mr. Asoorian a thief once, not to his face but to her mother, and he also said Mr. Asoorian sold horse meat, but whenever he got tired of her mother's cooking or wanted something different he would say, "I think I'll go see what Assroarin's trying to peddle today." And he would go in and Mr. Asoorian would be happy to see him and they would smile and talk about their families and Mr. Asoorian would show him a piece of meat.

"It—looks—pretty fatty to me."

"Fat! Fat! Whatdyou talkin fat! That skinny liddle piecea white's faflava.. Faflaava! I cut the fat myself. No fat. It's deliciousannutritious. No fat."

"Well, maybe, but it looks a little old."

"Old! Last week it was walkin around sayin Moomoo. He's a beautiful piecea meat."

"In that ease, it can't have been aged properly. I can't eat raw meat."

196

"Age! I nevuh sell meat she doesn have age. It's aged fresh. Fresh aged! Delicious. A dollar nine a pound. I should get more."

"Fresh aged? I don't believe I've tried that. Ever. You'd better give me a few pounds."

And sometimes the meat would be good and sometimes it wouldn't be and Margaret's mother would say it should be good at a dollar nine a pound and her father would say you should thank God we can afford it and her mother would say I'm not sure we can, Ben. But it is nice for a change.

The doughnut shop was full when they passed. Margaret knew that boys and girls went in there in the afternoon after school and at night but her mother said the only girls that hung around there were cheap girls. Margaret wanted to look in and see what cheap girls looked like and why they were cheap which would help her to know what cheap girls were, but she didn't dare so she only glanced out of the corner of her eye and she saw very little.

"When we go in, Margaret, you can stay in the front room if you want to. I'll only be a minute. I want to say hello to the family and say a prayer or two. Unless you want to come in?"

"I'll wait." Margaret summoned her courage. "Daddy, who died?"

"Didn't I tell you? Old man Brady the undertaker. This is his son's first funeral, burying the old man. Half the people'll be there to see how Brian Junior makes out. He's not exactly the spitting image of his old man. Old Brady was a divil of a man." Her father was smiling. "A terrible, terrible man."

Margaret was sure she did not want to go in and see that man, even though she knew she should because God in His Infinite Mercy spent more time making sinners well than with saints, but she secretly agreed with her mother when her mother said about someone she didn't really like, "God have mercy on her soul, I can't."

The funeral home was a big light brown house that looked like the other houses on the street but it was a little bigger and had a long porch in front and very wide steps and green awnings over the windows with a fancy letter B on them and a green awning over the sidewalk. Her father jumped up the stairs two at a time, pulled open the screen door, pushed open the inside door, folded his arm over his belly and bowed his head. "After you, Sweet Princess." Margaret felt foolish and happy as she ducked her head and smiled and blushed and clumsily stumbled up the stairs and into the front hallway of the funeral home. She was glad she had come.

A fat man came down the hallway to say hello to them. He was wearing a long black coat with tails in the back and grey striped trousers and a white shirt and a black tie. He didn't have a lot of hair like her father but it was combed neatly. His cheeks were red but the rest of his face was very pale. He looked like he had a bad cold and he had just come back from a walk but his cheeks were the only things that felt better.

"Mr. Connell." His voice was low and sad. He could not have used it to tell funny stories. "It was very good of you to come."

"Junior." Margaret looked at her father. The man he-called Junior looked as old as he was. But he wasn't kidding. But she couldn't always tell. "I'm sorry to hear about your father. He was a fine man."

"We've been expecting it for some time. His life was full. The Good Lord will understand if—"

"Yes, yes. There's a place in Heaven saved for your father. I have to use the bathroom. I thought it would be all right for Margaret to wait in the front room, Junior?"

Mr. Junior Brady didn't answer right away. He looked like he wanted to say something. "Uh—certainly. Certainly! I'll show her in myself."

Margaret followed Mr. Brady into the front room. He walked very slow and she almost stepped on his heels when he stopped. He pointed to a chair and Margaret sat down. He walked over to the drapes and pulled a cord and the drapes opened a little more and let a little more light in. Mr. Brady walked up and down with his hands together behind his back.

"How old are you?" Mr. Brady asked Margaret.

"I'm—" Margaret started to tell Mr. Brady that she was twelve but she was interrupted by a loud noise from the doorway.

"Huh! Don't believe a word of it, Junior. She's fifty-one if she's a day," Margaret's Uncle Tim said as he walked into the room and threw his arms open to hug her. She stood up. "She's a midget, Junior, a tall midget, would you believe it? And you'd better look out, she's fond of bachelors with rosy cheeks."

Mr. Brady slipped along the wall and out of the room. He tried to nod and smile as he went but it looked like it hurt him.

"How are you Margaret darling?" Uncle Tim hugged her very hard. He wasn't a big man, not nearly as tall as her father, but he had strong arms and bushy eyebrows and a big chest and his breath smelt funny. Margaret's mother thought it was funny that her mother, Grandma, thought Uncle Tim had something wrong with his nose or his throat because he always caught colds and had to stay home from work lots of mornings but he didn't really have anything wrong with him, he liked to drink a lot sometimes.

"Fine."

"What do you mean—fine?" Uncle Tim pushed her away and held her at arms' length. "You're a knockout, that's how you are. Every boy in Medlen will be knockin on your door. If they aren't already. How's your mother?"

"Fine."

"Is that so? You're a great one with words, aren't ya? If the Blarney Stone fell on ya, it wouldn't help any. Where's your old man?"

"I'm right here, Tim," her father said, "listening to your guff." He came into the room and held out his hand.

"Ben!" Uncle Tim said. He jumped across the room and shook her father's arm. "How goes it? How goes the battle?"

"Fair to middling, Tim. A lot better than Old Man Brady in there."

"Oh, it's a terrible thing, Ben, a terrible thing. That dear old man, torn from his loved ones at the tender age of seventy-five. Ripped asunder from the bosom of his family with thousands of widows left unrobbed and millions of social security checks uncashed. Oh, he was a dear darling man. May God have mercy on his soul; He's the only one I can think of at the moment who might."

"I was going to ask you to come up to the bathroom and gargle your throat, but it looks like you've beat me to it."

"I did fortify myself a bit, Ben-O, but you know me. I'm not the one to pass up a chance to wet my whistle, what with the sadness upon me and all. Lead on MacDuff."

"Ahh, yer past the mark already. Is it MacDuff, ya say. I told ya me name was MacConnell."

"I give a damn if yer name's MacScagg. Lead on ya worthless lump of—coal."

Margaret liked to hear her uncle talking like an Irish man but he didn't always. Sometimes when she went to her grandmother's in the morning or on a Saturday he wouldn't say anything. He just walked around in his bathrobe and looked for cigarettes and ignored her grandmother's deaf shouts. And if her Uncle John turned the radio on or even rustled the newspaper, he got very upset.

Margaret sat down in the chair again and looked at the rack of pamphlets along the wall. There were some from the Sacred Heart and the Holy Trinity Society and one from Sodality about marriage. She wondered if the cheap girls in the doughnut shop ever went to novenas and heard the priest say that boys and girls should not kiss unless they were engaged to be married. Cheap girls must be girls who did kiss. But maybe they just didn't go to the novenas, or the right ones. Or they were all Protestants. If she was a Protestant and didn't really have a good chance to go to Heaven, why shouldn't she kiss and be cheap? It was a bad thought. She had to push it away and say an act of contrition. O my God I am heartily sorry for having offended thee and I detest all my sins because I dread—

"Has your father gone in?" Mr. Brady asked.

"I think he went upstairs for a minute."

"Ohhh?" Mr. Brady's voice didn't sound sad and low. "I thought he came down." Margaret didn't know what she was supposed to say. He pinched the skin around his chin and jaw which made his cheeks look fatter. "Tell him I'd like to speak —no—yes, you'd better say—never mind. I'll see him myself."

Mr. Brady turned quickly and walked away. Margaret got up and softly walked to the door and looked after him. At the end of the hall he opened a door and went into another part of the house. Her father and Uncle Tim came down the stairs. Margaret backed into the front room.

"It's a grim business all around," her Uncle Tim was saying. "Particularly for the Missus. She didn't give two hoots in hell for him, which was only fair. He didn't care a rat's ass for her. Never did. The boys at O'Brien's say she spent her honeymoon in a graveyard cause Brady couldn't pass up the opportunity to make a buck. I wish we could find her. She's a good girl."

There was a pause.

"No, she's not in there, at least she wasn't. She'd appreciate a belt of that about now I'm thinkin. That I am."

"That you are, Tim lad."

"That I am. Well, let's us go in Ben-O and send up a fairvent prayer. He's gonna need all he can get, the darlin digger is."

"Righto."

Margaret liked to see her father happy and with her Uncle Tim because he was the only one in her mother's family that her father really liked. And she was glad that she was sitting in the front room so she wouldn't have to answer all of her mother's questions. She couldn't answer them if she couldn't hear anything. But her mother would ask if Uncle Tim had been drinking. And about her father too.

Her mother always knew the right questions to ask and Margaret didn't want to lie. But she couldn't keep saying she didn't know to all the questions. Her mother would get angry and wouldn't talk to her for a day. But if she said anything her father would be disappointed in her. She was glad she was in the front room by herself even though there was nothing to do because her father didn't seem to be in a hurry now and they would probably miss supper, but she really didn't know what went on and she wouldn't be telling lies.

Once when they were out and missed supper her father said to her mother when they came home, "May God strike me dead if I'm lying," and he was. Margaret worried about him for weeks, but nothing happened. Still, it could have. Her father didn't mind telling lies to her mother sometimes if it kept her mother from pestering him. It seemed like a smart thing to do because it saved a lot of trouble, but Margaret knew it was wrong and she hated to tell a lie. She wished she could. She wished she had told a lie the time her father had taken her to Aunt Rose's to visit. Aunt Rose was better at asking questions even than her mother. She asked about all the children and her mother and even her father who was in the kitchen with Uncle Donald and she asked if there was anything the family needed and Margaret should have lied but she didn't think Aunt Rose really meant it, she thought she was just making polite conversation, so she said her mother was looking for a washing machine. Aunt Rose told her father that she was getting rid of her old washing machine because Uncle Donald had given her a new automatic one for Christmas but the old one worked perfectly even if you had to fill it and empty it and put the clothes through the wringer. But her mother didn't appreciate it.

"What the hell are we Ben, the poor relations! She gets a new machine so I get her hand-me-down one! Did it ever enter your mind to buy me a new one? Did it?"

"That's gratitude! What do you want, life handed to you on a silver platter? Would you be happy then? Is that what you want?"

"I want your nosy relations to stop butting into our business, and I'd like something of my own for a change!"

"I'll give you something of your own if you keep shrieking like that."

Margaret was scared but her father did not hit her mother that time. Every time after when Margaret was around and her mother used Aunt Rose's old machine to do her washing, her mother said, "I could kill you for opening your big mouth! Don't you ever, ever, tell that woman anything again. Nothing! Does she tell you what she's doing or anything about her family? You bet your damn life she doesn't. So don't ever let me catch you telling her anything—ever again!"

Margaret was glad she didn't go very often to see Aunt Rose. Tommy and Joseph went most of the time and sometimes Sean, once in a long while, or her father went alone. Whenever he wanted to go someplace alone, he put on his coat and walked out the door and her mother had to run to ask him where he was going but sometimes she didn't dare because he would yell about something, bills or kids who always wanted to tag along and never gave him any peace, and then he'd walk out quickly putting his coat on and he was gone. Whenever he hung around the house and talked about a place he had to go then Margaret knew she had a chance of going with him.

"Come in, Margaret darling, come in!" Uncle Tim said. "We want you to meet the Missus."

"My father said to wait here."

"Sure and isn't it your father who sent me for you. Come along now, me darling."

Uncle Tim took hold of her wrist and elbow and pulled her to her feet. He slapped her bottom. Margaret blushed and smiled and let Uncle Tim pull her down the hall and through a door into the private part of the house. They went through a dining room which was very neat and into a kitchen where her father was standing up leaning against the sink and nodding to an old woman who was sitting with her elbows resting on a metal-topped table. Her face was resting against her fists and she was talking and nodding and sighing and looking at a glass of liquor in front of her. Margaret's father had a glass in his hand. His empty bottle was on the table and a bigger half-full one was beside it.

"Oh Margaret," her father said, putting his drink glass down on the sink. "Missus Brady, this is my daughter Margaret. Margaret, say hello to Mrs. Brady."

"Hello Mrs. Brady," Margaret said. She knew she should say something else. "I—I'm sorry."

"Yes Child. I thank you. Ben, see if there's a glass of milk in the icebox for the child."

"I'll get it, Ben," Uncle Tim said. "I wouldn't want to slow you down."

Her father smiled and leaned back against the sink and picked up his drink glass. Uncle Tim went to the refrigerator and pulled it open and moved his head back and forth as he looked for the milk. He had a bald circle on the top of his head in the back. Margaret didn't want any milk but she was standing in front of the stove and had nothing to do with her hands and the woman was trying to be nice even though she hadn't looked up at Margaret.

"They'll all be going home for supper now," Mrs. Brady said. "One good thing about Old Brady, he never did eat much. He was as skinny yesterday as the day I married him. If that's any consolation."

"Shame. Shame on you, Bridey," Uncle Tim said as he pulled a bottle of milk out of the refrigerator. He knocked some butter off a shelf and had to grab it.

"Ah, go on with ya, Tim. Everyone in the parish knows what kind of marriage we had. No matter what the good Monsignor, God bless him, said last Sunday, this one wasn't made in Heaven."

"Did he say that?" Uncle Tim asked as he poured the milk into a glass cream pitcher. Her father nodded. "I hadn't noticed."

"Joke about it now," Mrs. Brady said, "but when you get to my age, what else is there to do but listen and hope all the Christly words you've been hearin all your life amount to more than just a bag of wind."

Margaret was embarrassed and afraid. Mrs. Brady's talk sounded sinful. At Confirmation she had heard about people who lost their faith. Her Uncle Tim stopped smiling and frowned toward her father who looked upset and put down his drink glass.

"We should be going now, Bridey," her father said.

"Do you have to?" Mrs. Brady asked.

"I'm afraid so. Come on Margaret, your mother will be looking for us. I'll just stop in and pay my last respects."

"Save your breath," Mrs. Brady said and drank from her glass.

Her father didn't say anything but he looked at Uncle Tim and raised his eyebrows and his eyes and opened his mouth and clenched his teeth and his neck was tight. He tipped his head toward the hallway.

"I'll be right along Ben," Uncle Tim said. "Now Bridey, if there's anything at all you need…"

Her father led Margaret through the dining room and across the hall into a room that was dark except for candles around the coffin which was at the end of the room up on a platform and the wallpaper was red and gold and there were flowers around the coffin and seats for people but no one was there and there was a little piece of wood covered with something soft to kneel on like in church in front of the casket and a rail around it.

"You might as well come and have a look," her father said. "It won't kill you."

The door opened behind them and Uncle Tim came in.

"Thank God they've all gone," Uncle Tim said. "I took the liberty of refilling your little peashooter here from the good widow's bottle so we could properly toast Old Brady."

"How is she, Tim?"

"She's gonna be fine. Her problem's the same as mine in the morning when you pull up a shade in a dark room and it takes a while to get used to the light. I convinced her she's had enough to drink so actually we're doing her a favor drinking her whiskey."

Margaret followed closely behind her father and Uncle Tim. She didn't want to go near the coffin but it was better than standing alone in the back part of the room.

"Here's to ya, you old son-of-a-bitch, you hard-hearted pillar of the CYO," Uncle Tim said and waved the bottle at the coffin and drank from it and passed it to her father.

Margaret looked at the body. She was surprised. He wasn't a terrible-looking man. He looked old and waxy but he was almost smiling.

Her father lowered the bottle from his lips. "Here's to you and yours and the other brave Knights of Columbus." He passed the bottle to Uncle Tim, who drank quickly.

"To the Robin Hood of Medlen. He robbed the rich, but he was a fair man. He stole from the poor too."

"May your soul rest in peace and your conscience trouble you till the end of time."

"May the road rise with you and lead straight to Hell."

"May the souls of the dearly departed dance on your grave."

The little bottle was empty. Uncle Tim took it and leaned over the railing and put it in the dead man's hand. The door to the room opened and Mr. Brady gasped.

"Mr. Toomey."

"What is it now, Junior?" Uncle Tim said as he turned around. "Oh that. I was just buttonin his vest so he wouldn't catch his death o'cold. May the saints prezairve us."

"Mr. Toomey, and you Mr. Connell, you know better than doing a thing like that."

"Oh that we do," her father said. "That we do, Junior. But it's a terrible thing to send a man off with his button open. A terrible thing."

"It's indaycent, Junior," Uncle Tim said, "that's what it is."

"I've been meaning to ask you," Mr. Brady said, "not to call me that."

"Call you what, Junior? Call you what?"

"You've a terrible mouth, Tim."

"Have you been lettin fly with the swear words again, Ben-O. What did he call ya, Junior? I'll wash his mouth with soap."

"Please gentlemen. Have you no respect."

"Respect is it!" Uncle Tim said and began waving his arms and walking toward Mr. Brady who started to back out of the room into the hallway. "What kind of respectable place do ya run here? Call this a pub? Me lad-o and meself stop in for a pint of Guinness and what do we find? What!"

"A dead. man in the parlor," Margaret's father said and shook his finger at Mr. Brady who looked very scared. "Have ye no shame!"

"Is this a way to run a business! Do the daycent thing!"

"Bury the corpse!"

"Hide the body!"

"Boil the potatoes!"

"Clean the cabbage!"

"Brush your teeth!"

"Blow your nose!"

Mr. Brady backed into the hangers and coats that were hung on a pole in the hallway. He was surrounded by her father and Uncle Tim.

"Please," Mr. Brady said in a squeaky voice.

"What in God's good and gracious holy name are you doin there?" Uncle Tim asked. "What in hell are ya doin?"

"He's pickin pockets."

"Thief!" Uncle Tim said and ran down the hallway. "Thief! Oh Lord's mercy! Villain! Thief! Oh Lord, oh—oh to hell with it." He came back.

Margaret's father was smiling at Uncle Tim and turning his head back to Mr. Brady to frown.

"Look Ben-O! I come out here nice as pie, if it please ya, to get my hat and what do I find?"

"Junior himself standin on it."

"Stand—," Mr. Brady said and looked behind him and saw that his shoe heel was on the brim of a wide soft brown hat. "But—it's on the floor."

"Mind yer own manners. His father was a terrible man Ben-O, but there's one thing I'll say fer him."

"He wasn't the one to run up and down under clothes racks stompin on hats."

"Never to me knowledge."

"Not a bit of it."

"Good day to ya, Surh," Uncle Tim said as he slammed his hat on his head and took her father's arm and marched down the hall with him.

Margaret ducked her head and hurried past Mr. Brady.

"A grand workout, a marvelous time," Uncle Tim said when they were outside on the sidewalk, "but it works up a terrible thirst. Where's your car, Ben? We'll drop Margaret home and I'll show you a little pub I found."

"I didn't bring it, Tim. I—we walked."

"What! I've never seen you naked without a car. And I didn't bring mine cause it's in the repair shop. This is a fine how-do-you-do. Well, we'll have to stop in at O'Brien's, that's all there is to it. Margaret, you'll have to run on home and tell your mother that your Uncle Tim had some important business to discuss with your father. I'm sure Marion will understand. Only too well."

Margaret looked up at her father. He was looking down at the sidewalk and rubbing his lower teeth against his upper lip.

"Would you mind Margaret?" Her father looked at her. Margaret wanted to say no, Daddy, but it seemed like an awfully long walk home in the dark and there were boys on the corner by the ice cream store who said things to girls when they went by. She wanted to say I don't mind Daddy. "Why should she mind? Uncle Tim asked. "It's only a hop and a skip to your house."

"Well, maybe not this time, Tim."

"What! Margaret, you don't mind, do you? Margaret, look at me when I'm talking to you."

"Leave her alone, Tim. She's not used to being out alone after dark."

"For God's sakes, Ben, she's nearly a grown woman."

"I told Marion I'd be home."

"Since when did you mean it?"

"I'm going home, Tim."

"I'd never have believed it."

Her father and Uncle Tim didn't say anything as they walked on and came into the lights from the stores in the Square. Margaret wanted to apologize so they would be friends again.

"You haven't told me yet about your trip to Ireland," her father said. Margaret thought his voice sounded funny.

"There's a time and place for everything," Uncle Tim said.

"The west of Ireland is beautiful. And I've been to County Cork.

But what's Dublin like, Tim? Are the people as friendly as they are in the country?"

"The people in Dublin," Uncle Tim said, "are about like the people here, good and bad and indifferent. And henpecked and otherwise."

"Isn't it a beautiful city?"

"Boston. With new history and old dirt."

They stopped in front of O'Brien's Cafe.

"Well here we are," her father said. "I'll see you later, Tim."

"Sure," Uncle Tim said and opened the door and went inside.

Her father hurried away and Margaret had to strain to keep up with him.

"I don't want a word of what went on repeated to your mother."

"Yes, Daddy."

"Not one word. Do you understand?"

"Yes, Daddy."

"You'd better."

Margaret felt awful. She wanted to cry. Her father never hardly spoke to her like that. And he was mad at her and had the awful look on his face that he got when he was very mad and he wouldn't talk to her.

When they got home, her father pushed open the door and rushed into the kitchen.

"Where's Sean?"

"He's upstairs," her mother said. "I finally got him to start his homework. He—"

"Tell him to get down here."

"What's the matter, Ben? Did—"

"I said, tell him to get down here."

Her mother looked at her father and went to the foot of the stairs. "Sean," she called softly. "Come down here Sean, right away."

"Aww, Ma, I'm doin my homework."

"GET DOWN HERE!"

"Take it easy now, Ben, don't get yourself worked up." Margaret heard her brother's chair scrape the floor upstairs.

"What do you mean, don't get myself worked up. You said you wanted me to speak to him, didn't you. Who are you to tell me not to get myself worked up! Who are you to tell me anything! You wanted me to talk to him. Now get out of my way!"

Margaret's mother came over to her and whispered, "What happened?" Her father heard it.

"Nothing happened! None-ah your Goddamn business what happened. Don't pick at Margaret!"

"I just—"

"Just shut your mouth!"

Margaret saw Sean peek around the corner.

"Come down here, Young Man."

"What's the matter, Pa?"

"Don't you Pa me. I'll tell you what's the matter. You ruined your good pants today."

"Oh Pa, I didn't ruin them."

"I said, don't call me Pa. And don't you ever contradict me."

Her father's face was all red and his fists were tight. Sean looked annoyed and scared.

"I'm sorry," Sean said. "I won't call you Pa."

"I can fix his pants, Ben," her mother said. "They're not as bad as I thought."

"YOU SHUT UP!" Her father slammed the table and the two plates and the silverware jumped. "Get down cellar Sean."

"Come on Pa, I'm too old for—"

"What did you say?"

Sean started to say something, then let his breath out. He looked at her father in a way that scared Margaret and opened the cellar door and walked down. Her father started after him. Her mother grabbed his arm.

"Please Ben, take it easy. This isn't good for—"

"If you interfere Marion, so help me God, I'll kill you."

Her father charged down the stairs and her mother followed him and Margaret carefully followed her. When she got down to the bottom steps she stopped. Her father had his belt out and his shoulders were heaving up and down. Her mother was standing behind him, moving her hands but not touching him. Sean was looking the awful look at her father.

"I'll teach you to ruin good pants."

Her father swung his arm back. Her mother lunged for the belt and missed. Sean jerked his arm away when the belt hit and grabbed the belt with his other hand.

"Let go. Let go of that. LET GO!"

"You're drunk, Pa," Sean said. He did not let go of the belt. "You're crazy."

"You son-of-a-bitch! You'll apologize for that. You'll apologize!"

Her father let go of the belt, pushed her mother back and reached up on the top shelf on the wall and took down a shillelagh and shook it at Sean.

"Oh don't Ben!" her mother said. "Oh my God! You'll kill him!"

"My father used this," her father said and spit flew out of his mouth, "to teach me to keep away from his horse-cart and my grandfather used it to teach him to get wood and his father used it to teach him to clean milk and by God I'm going to use it to teach you obedience."

"Oh no, please no." her mother said as her father hit Sean with the stick across the leg. Sean jerked his leg. Tears were coming down his cheek and his mouth was open and his face was shaking and looked like it would fall apart and he didn't cry out.

"Don't you ever call me, Pa! EVER! Do you understand?"

Sean did not answer. He just looked. Her father swung the stick and hit his other leg. Her mother was crying.

"Do you understand? Damn you! Answer me! DO YOU UNDERSTAND!"

Margaret was watching.

15 | Getting Ahead

Margaret was waiting.

She used to hide around corners, waiting for His Coming. The Great One. Blow ye trumpets. Hark ye heralds. Strew ye roses. The Great One—Is Here. A little trouble? Mmmm. Few thousand bills coming in. Kids want to go for a ride with their Da-Da. Called you a what? A bloodsucking vulture draining the juice from his guts? Mustn't mind The Great One talking through his rum. Here. A little pat on the ass. A great jolly Bear hug. Smooth honeyed Blarney. There. World all better?

The Queen has balled the Bear. The King died and then the Queen died. Of dust? Treats him like her mother. I'll call you later, Ma. And later and later and later.

"Sean, slow down, willya?"

The Mad Old King and his daughter one. One half? Three fiddling sons. Distinction. Distinction called for. Two sons. One court jester. He's gone, he's fled, he's flyin out, catch the next plane out of hell, vroomm. Wings on fire? How you talk.

"If you're not going to slow down, Sean, I want to drive."

"Girls be there?"

"Yeah," Roger said. "Ten for every guy. That's what Angie says, but you know him. We'll be lucky if there's two decent ones there. Angie doesn't seem to mind dogs barking around his place. I hope his old lady isn't home. She's living death on..."

Honeysucker'll fix that. Big, wild, whammin whoppin Honeysucker's acomin. Mothers and maids, dogs and drabs. EEeeeyaahooo! Since when? Wellll. Little mild-mannered tepid-tasting court jester? How do you do my partner, how are you too day, would you like to, hoo-whoo, I will show you the way. Er, that is, unless of course, you want to show me the way.

The road rose up, a sheer firm film of black and blue and purple with a white rail in the middle. Sean steered the automobile onto the rail and wished his foot down to drive upwards.

"You CRAZY bastard! Get over! Are you tryin to kill me. Get the hell over and slow down!" Roger was gripping the dashboard. "Give me that bottle—asshole."

"All right. Allll's right."

"What's all right? What are you doing? Watch the road! Put that bottle down. Gimme that!"

Roger grabbed for the bottle but Sean thrust it back between his legs, sloshing whiskey on his chinos.

"You're drunk. You are drunk. Do you understand? If you don't let me drive, I'm going to jump out of the car, I don't care how fast it's going. Do you hear me! We're not even going to make it to Goff's place, never mind Angie's, unless you let me drive. Sean?"

"Can't give it to you. Crotch warm."

Roger edged back into the seat, his small, tough body intense, his facial expression working from fear to doubt to anger to cunning. Sean lifted his hand to reach over and pat Roger's neatly combed blond hair, but the effort seemed too much; instead, he patted his own knee.

Don't sweat it, Roger-Dodger. There, there. We're all in this together. We'll pull through. I'm lucky. Ride my coattails. Never had an accident yet. Incidentals. Didn't get my license til just before the service? Haven't driven much? So what! It's the thought that counts, and I'm thinking, Roger, all the time. You better believe it. Did you know that Alaska has a mosquito problem in the summertime? See! You didn't. Gotta know about these things if you want to be a good driver, keep to the straight and narrow. Right? Right. Never look a man in the eye if he's on the straight and narrow. Never pinch a girl if—

"Look, Sean, there's a liquor store up ahead."

—she deserves to be patted. A bird in nine is worth two in the bush.

"Why don't you pull over and we'll get another bottle. You've almost finished that one. You don't want to drive all the way up to New Hampshire dry. Pull over."

Easy now. Whoa, boy. Easy now. Whoa, boy. No bucking, you want your oats. Ghost rider's got you, tall in the saddle.

Sean fondled the labels in the window with his eyes: Old Crow, Virginia Gentleman, White Horse Scotch, he hated it but the horse was nice, Black Horse ale. He resented the thick glass keeping him from touching his bottles.

"Let's go." Roger's voice came from somewhere behind Sean.

"Inside."

"It's closed, Stupid. Now let's go."

Sean pulled at the door and then kicked it. It was closed and it wasn't fair. He had to drive to New Hampshire.

"I saw a cop car back there. You want to get picked up for breaking and entering, keep it up."

"Cop" made Sean turn and swivel his head slowly to study the area. He saw no lights and heard no sirens. But Roger was sitting behind the wheel. "Hey."

"That's right, I'm driving. Now are you coming or aren't you."

Sean walked past the headlights of the car with his chin high and started up the highway. It was cold. A trailer truck roared behind him, forcing him off the road, nearly knocking him down with its blast of air as it rushed past. The driver honked his horn. Sean raised a threatening fist and tripped on a bush.

Roger had the door open on the rider's side of the front seat. Sean ducked his head to climb in, still attempting to hold his chin high.

"You through with your little tantrum? Got any more games left?"

"Bastard."

"Sure. I'm a bastard because I want to live. I won't let you drive me into a tree. That makes me a bastard. Good thinking. Why don't you get some sleep or you won't be any use at all."

That's all right. I never forget a friend. Stop for gas. Why don't you stop for gas. You get out of this car for one second and I'll leave you in greasemonkeyland for the rest of your life. You won't even see my smoke. But you've got gas, probably a full tank. Foresighted bastard. That's a clever plan. Stop for a bottle. You knew it was closed. I've got a plan. The radiator's going to blow up. You get out and lift up the hood to look at it and —AAACK. Goodbye Roger. I won't sleep. You think I'm going to sleep. I'll close my eyes and pretend I'm going to sleep—to fool you. But I won't be asleep. I'll be waiting right here for my big chance to…

Jimmy Goff came down the driveway and across his lawn, talking to Roger. "…and if you and Connell help me roll it out to the street, you can give me a push. It'll start right away.

"Why don't you just come with us?"

"What if I want to leave early? Or take off with a honey? I hate to go anywhere without my wheels. It won't take long."

"Okay, but Connell's out of it. He's smashed. We can do it ourself."

"Let me get my coat and my toothbrush and I'll meet you at the garage."

Jimmy trotted to his front door and Roger walked up the driveway. Sean felt loose as he got out of the car. He was not mad at anybody but it did seem impolite that no one asked him if he wanted a glass of water. He did. His head was free and floating and his groin was warm and stirring but his mouth was bitter and sticky and his tongue was taking up too much room.

Through the screen door Sean saw a lovely pair of hips and buttocks waiting for him. He eased into the room, closing the screen door silently behind him. His glass of water no longer seemed necessary. His hands closed on the hips as his groin pressed against the buttocks.

"AAAHHHaaahhhHHHH!"

The lovely hips and rump jerked away from him and disappeared. In their place, Sean faced an old, terrified woman. "Get out! GET AWAY! Get away from meeee. JIMMY! HENRY! Help, help me."

Jimmy came running down the stairs with a toothbrush in his hand as Roger burst through the front door.

"Oh no," Roger said.

"What is it Mom!" Jimmie asked, looking menacingly at Sean who was studying the ceiling and Roger who had stopped inside the door and was shaking his head.

"He grabbed me. That one. HIM. He came up behind me and tried to—he GRABBED me!"

"Let us not fabricate. I was on my way to a glass of water when your friend here—"

"That's my mother!"

"—seemingly improves by bending over. I can assure all who know that not for nothing was I known as a hip man and never would venture to friendly pat anyone who didn't deserve it, no matter her age, rank or—it was a lovely rump—"

"Get outa here, Connell."

"Come on Sean. Get in the car."

"—but I had no idea what was connected with it. The attachments do not do justice—"

"Gertrude! What is it, Gertrude, what is it? I'm coming."

"Jeesus! It's my father."

Sean heard loud, threatening noises coming down the stairs. He allowed Roger to pull him through the door and down the walk. In the back seat of the car, before he lay down, he saw an angry, stocky, white-haired man shaking his fists and shouting from the doorway of the house.

"...so I think it's important to have a goal in life. Daddy keeps laughing at me and saying, 'Don't worry, Sweetheart, it'll all work out,' but I don't want to approach life that way. I think a girl shouldn't think about getting married until she knows who she is, really knows who she is. My mother..."

The little girl's mouth was working faster and faster. Sean shrank back into the chair Roger had deposited him in. He was afraid, if she leaned closer, the girl would nip him with her teeth.

Perhaps I should bite first. Roger's doing me a big favor, sending this scrawny little bitch over, tiny talker. I want something big and bountiful, none of your piss-assed peewees for me. Dugs unfit for a butterfly. If she'd only shut up, I've got something to tell her. What? Something very important. I'm sure. Why doesn't she shut up. What's she saying? I don't know. Can't be as important as me.

"...and the whole thing with Daddy is, you can't have one of these EEdapuss things going, but he doesn't see that, he thinks I'm just his little girl and I'll always be his little girl, but I'm a grown woman, a fully developed, grown, mature, woman."

Sean wanted to wave the little girl back but he was afraid, if he lifted his arm, he could not avoid hitting her in the stomach.

"Move back."

"What? Have you been listening to me?"

"Move your sack of bones, back to Daddy, if he wants you. I don't. Things to say. Get away or I'll huff, puff, blow you to yesterday. Boo."

"You can't talk to me that way," the little girl said, stepping backwards. "If my fath—if my friends were here, they'd teach you a lesson. You're the rudest, most despicable person I've ever spoken to."

"Thank you."

She wheeled about and marched away.

"Come again when you grow up. Eat spinach. Lot of spinach. You'll look like Popeye stead of Olive Oyl."

Sean put his drink down on the floor, gripped the sides of the chair and pushed himself to his feet.

Everyone's being rude. No one's listening. Angie's laughing at one of his own jokes again. Poor Roger. Trying to climb a tall honey. Why doesn't he pick on someone his own size. Maybe I should introduce him to Daddy's Girl, at least she wouldn't be able to knock him down in a fight. Maybe I should smash the record player. Everyone would stop dancing. But that would be rude too. It wouldn't be polite. Whose girl are you? Daddy's girl. I don't believe you Margaret. You're nothing but a tinker. I am not a tinker. She is not a tinker. "She isn't a tinker, Margaret, my sister, isn't really a tinker, you see, my father—"

No one seemed to be listening. They were dancing and talking and shouting and kissing in dark corners and going in and out of the kitchen with drink glasses, but they weren't really listening. Sean picked up his nearly full drink and swallowed it. He stepped up on the cushioned chair, fighting for his balance.

"My father called her that but he—she didn't really like it, at first she did, it was a game, a game they played, father and daughter, oh, believe you me, he had lots of games. Some of them were—fun—I guess, but suppose you found out what tinkers were, gypsies, wandering about Ireland in these carts and not washing, not washing, that was the thing, you can't blame Margaret, and putting invisible marks on gates. He—he said it sometimes if they were something special, free, not tied down in one spot, but if they didn't wash and you were Margaret and they came to your house—you're not listening to me."

No one seemed to be. A couple on a sofa near Sean got up and walked away smiling.

"SHE ISN'T A TINKER!"

That's better. Now you're listening. I don't think he meant any harm by it, it was "Just the way he said things sometimes. You didn't feel comfortable. He—seemed—sour. She—"

"What the hell are you doing now?" Roger asked. "Get down offa there. Jimmy Goff's looking for an excuse to belt you in the mouth, you've insulted half the girls here already, and Angie's pissed off at me for bringing you, and now you gotta climb up on a chair and try to wreck the party. Get down."

"Connell," Angie said, pushing Roger out of the way, "Why don't you grow up."

"What—you—you—"

"Growww up. And get off my chair."

Sean did not leap from the chair. He fell forward, with his fist clenched, into Angie's jaw. His stomach landed on Angie's head as they hit the floor. Sean heard a T-shirt rip as something squirmed beneath him. He wedged his forearm into a throat.

"I'll kill you! Get up! Get offa me! I'll kill you!"

"You're not being polite. That's very—rude."

Sean felt hands lifting him up, but he did not see anyone. Angie's face bobbed up. Sean noticed that he had a lot of hair, black hair, some even coming out of his nostrils. Angie made a rasping sound in his throat and opened his mouth. Sean's nose felt wet.

"That's what I think of you. Let go of me! I'm gonna kick the living shit out of him. LET GO!"

Sean counted three hands on one of Angie's arms. He felt very tired. The back of Roger's head partially blocked his view. But it was a good tired, the first time he felt relaxed since he had come home. He should explain to Angie.

"See? If you let me explain. She didn't really mind, but—" Roger's face stopped in front of Sean.

"Shut up! C'mon on, Angie, take a drink. I'll keep him out of your way. If he gives you any more trouble, I'll take him out of here. He's drunk. Forget it. It's a great party. C'mon Angie C'mon Angie, C'mon Angie, C'mon Angie….

Sean did not like sitting in the corner. It reminded him of the bad row in the first grade. Miss Halstein roped off the last row by the window, Roger had taken his shoes, and called it the bad row. The only day he ever sat there his father came to visit the classroom. He had to sit on his feet so no one would see the hole in his sock.

"You look like Buddha."

"Did your father ever embarrass you in front of all your friends and say you must have done something ferocious to have to sit in the bad row?"

She pressed her back against the wall and slid down beside Sean. Her hair was straight but soft-looking. Her left eye twitched.

"No."

"Did he ever make a speech telling everyone how good it was to be in the good rows and bad in the bad rows?"

"No. But he told me I shouldn't drink."

"What's so hot about that?" Sean did not want to offend her. She was willing to sit in the bad row with him and her eye wasn't twitching. Actually, it was winking at him. "I didn't mean to offend your father. He seems like a nice man. From what I've heard of him."

"No. He told me I shouldn't drink because he didn't drink until he was twenty-one, and I told him he sure made up for it since then."

It was the funniest thing Sean had ever heard. He laughed and laughed until he was bent over almost touching the floor, his stomach and his head hurt, and his holy sock was showing. Grimly, he tucked it back under his leg.

"I don't care if you have a hole in your sock. Why don't you stretch your legs out. You don't look very comfortable."

"Thank you. That's the nicest thing anyone ever said to me."

"If you want to thank me, you could get me a drink."

"I can't. Roger has my shoes."

"You can't walk on your socks?"

"If I cause any trouble, he said I'd walk all the way to school. Don't 'want to wear them out."

"I'll get you another pair."

"You're the nicest person I ever met."

'My name is Sheila."

Sean pushed against the wall and climbed to his feet.

"Don't you want to take my glass."

"Shhh!" Roger was nowhere in sight. Angie had his back turned. Craftily, Sean eased across the room and into the kitchen. He ran to the cabinets and pulled open all the doors. A few beers were in the icebox. The vodka was in the oven. He pushed the bottle inside his shirt, put a loaf of bread in the bag and put it back in the oven.

"Shhhh."

"What have you got?"

Sean eased down beside her, his back to the room, pulled a throw rug over his back and head and motioned to Sheila to peek behind it.

"A bottle of vodka. Nice going. Did you get any ice?"

"Too much noise."

"I don't know if I can hack it warm. I suppose I can. I need something after that animal tried to rip my clothes off upstairs."

The thought appealed to Sean but it seemed to call for a tremendous effort. She looked light and fast. "You look nice with your clothes off."

"I take my clothes off for the right person. Give me some vodka."

She didn't say please, but it sounds polite. We have some animals. Would you take your clothes off for me, Sheila? Would you? Would you take your clothes off? I'll bet you're beautiful with your clothes off. I'm—we have a Bear and a rabbit. But the bear became a rabbit and the tinker's gone away. She wasn't an animal. The rabbit became—a cougar? Panther? Lion? "What's that word for a female lion?"

"Sheila, Honey, Sheila." She laughed softly. "More, and try for the glass this time."

Sean carefully poured her vodka and drank from the bottle. It hit his stomach hard and hot and started back up. He coughed.

"Take it easy, Honey." She slapped his back. "You all right?"

"Fine. Fine."

"If you don't swill it, this stuff isn't bad. You done good."

Sheila's slaps and words were soothing. "If you go up the stairs, those stairs, right there, and I go out the back right through the kitchen and climb the pipe, I could meet you—we could—would you take off your clothes upstairs for me. Please."

"It's crowded upstairs. But I've got a car out back. And I know a cabin that nobody's using. You can do all your climbing there, Tiger."

Sheila put her hand on Sean's thigh. He looked at it, knowing it was supposed to arouse him, but it seemed distant, far away, five bony hooks digging into a stranger's chinos. It seemed silly.

"Give me the keys."

"The keys are in my coat, Honey, and I better drive."

"You think I'm drunk." Sean picked up the vodka bottle and moved it another two inches away from him.

"We're both on the way, but that doesn't bother me. You see, I don't have any registration...if we got stopped...better...know the cops...if we got caught in the cabin..."

It isn't her cabin. Can't rest there. We'll have to watch out the window for the cops. We'll—can't touch the bottles for breaking and entering. Roger's waiting. Lied. It isn't her cabin. Skinny hips.

"You don't love me."

"You wait here and we'll settle that in a few minutes, Honey Tiger."

Sean watched her walk to the closet, take out her coat, remove her purse from a pocket, lay the coat on a chair and walk into the bathroom. He forced himself to rise and, whistling drily, nonchalantly walked to the chair, picked the coat up, and folded it across his forearm. Watching to see if he was being watched, he strolled through the kitchen and out the back door, dug frantically in the pockets for the keys, found them, and dropped the coat on the ground. He ran from car to car, bypassing those he knew, looking inside and smelling each car. He knew the pink convertible with the electric-eyed monkey on the back windowsill was Sheila's. It had her smell too. He tried all the keys until one fit and the motor woke.

Goodbye, Sheila.

Sean's foot circled around, searching for the clutch pedal. Realizing the transmission was automatic, he jammed the stick all the way to the right, then eased it back a notch until the arrow pointed to drive. He stepped on the gas, slammed on the brakes, and hit his head on the windshield.

No registration. Roger's got one. No matter what anyone says, he's a good shit. A really good shit. A hot shit, no, but a good shit, yesss.

Sean lifted his foot from the brake and the car started forward. He stepped on the brake and pushed the arrow to park.

Roger's glove compartment was full of papers. Sean sat on the front right seat, sorting the maps, letters and receipts into piles. The fresh cool night air reached inside him.

I can't put up with this. My head hurts. He has to have a registration here.

"Has anyone seen my coat? Or that tall guy with the brown leather jacket?"

Yes. Yes, Ben, I'll look. Maybe you left it in your other pants. Well, hurry up, Goddamnit. I've seen him.

Sean gathered the pile of papers to his chest, ran across the yard and threw them into Sheila's car.

"I don't even know his name. What'sis name?"

"Sean. What did he do now?"

"Hey! Hey, Tiger!"

"Sean!"

"Oowwwhooo! They're off! Comin down the thunder road!" Bailln the jack, Rabbit. See you in Sonora, Sheila. Forgive me, Roger, for I have sinned, but you ain't seen nothin yet. High-rollin, jack-hammin, motherhumpin, pedalpushin son of a free-wheelin bitch.

"Shaaaawnnn!"

You drive too fast, Ben. I want to get there. I wanta get there. I wanta get there. I wanta—

Sean swerved the car onto the highway just before it charged over the embankment directly across the dirt road he thundered out of.

Cool now. Cool as ice. Hands of steel. Nerves of ice. There are mice in those walls. I can hear them running around. What do you want me to do, crawl in and bite their tails. Doesn't it bother you. They don't bother me and I don't bother them. There's enough food to go around. We can afford a few crumbs. Monsignor, my husband sent me down here. He's too ashamed to come himself. I could kill him for this. That's no way to talk, Mrs. Connell. I could. Who's this you've got with you, Joseph or Tommy. You call me Joseph or Tommy again and I'll bite your fat ass. Give us the food. There's enough to go around. I'll drive Sheila's car up your aisle and up your ass—Doremus Dominoies, Aaah-men! They'll have to pump you full of wine to float the fender free.

Sean tilted his head to the right so he could watch the road to steer around a curve with one hand as he drank from the bottle. He liked the automatic transmission which eliminated the necessity to shift gears. The road ran on to possibilities.

If you were here, Tommy, you'd advise me to slow down. With your serious fat-cheeked advice face. Might be better to slow down, Sean.

Diplomatic. Chuckle, chuckle. But serious for fat, free, advice. Not Joseph. He didn't care. He lives in Joseph World. He can be hated and goodbyed. Not looming Tommy. Want to help out? Set everyone straight. Margaret circulate more. Whisper Ma about it. Joseph lower voice, but he didn't whisper. And Sean, man-to-man, heart-heart, face face, good-old-fashioned, down-earth talk with Sean Problem. After whispers. Psssssssssst. You don't understand Dad. He's been through a lot. Don't Dad me, fat fearful wind-blown ass. If Butterball Jr. here, his sister-wife, I'd strap them to wheel, listen tuh advice remove the squish. You don't know Dad I understand.

I don wanna go upsairs, Margret. Pleece. Aweright. Margaret was scared. She held Sean's hand as she pulled him into their parents' bedroom and pushed him ahead of her to the closet. Don't push, Margaret. I really saw her. Really I did. You're full of it. I did. Where? Right down the hole. The boards in the back of the closet were torn up. Mr. Langley could work on the insulation only on weekends. Don't fall in. You can let go now; I'm not going to disappear. Be careful, Sean, please. She's down there. You're nuts. I saw her, sitting up and lying down and she has a white gown on and she's going to look up this way and try to come up when we're not looking. You're crazy. There's nothing there. Just a pile of sawdust. She's hiding in it and she's going to float up and take her dresses and—You're crazy, Margaret, you're crazy, Margaret, you're crazy, Margaret, Margaret

No you're not. You're not. Right there. I see her Margaret, sitting up and lying down, sitting up and lying down, I'll sit her up and lie her down. I'll fix her.

The car caromed off the side of a parked truck and lurched toward the other side of the road and a stop sign.

Won't stop me. Little belt won't stop me. Comin at you. No stops. I'll fix her, Marg.

The car hit the stop sign, bent it, and slid past into a field.

Can't hide out there. Gonna get you. Gonna find you. Gonna stomp you.

The car bumped through the field and plowed into rows of corn stalks. Sean charged the gas pedal, mowing down the corn as he hunched over the steering wheel, searching ahead. Somewhere there were voices.

The corn disappeared. The sky vas red. Except at the bottom. It was grey.

Like a wall. Like a wall. A wall.

Sean slammed the brake. The car skidded and smashed into the barn's foundation. Sean lurched forward, bumped his head and stared out the window at the barn, wondering why he had come this way.

He slowly, drowsily, eased his head around. People were running, smiling, waving their hands, running toward him. Sean jerked open the door and jumped out. He pushed his hands out from his chest and pulled his arms back in. "Hellooo," he called. He smiled. Then he waved again.

"You fool! You blamed fool! You could have killed yourself."

They weren't smiling.

"Are you all right?"

"What the hell's the matter with you!"

"Are you crazy!"

"...so we have to have your name. Would you like to tell, us now?"

The policeman seemed friendly enough, but his partner was definitely rude.

"I tole you, John L. Slulivan, Irish strong boy, thas me. Who'r, you?"

"Patrolman Dolan."

"Yer Irish!"

"Half and half. And don't change the subject."

"S'long's you gut wee bita the Irish in ya, yerrawrighht. Whus he?"

"What are you, Fournier?"

"I'll tell ya what I am. I'm tired a playin pattycake with this wiseass screwball. Now you just drive to the station, Dolan, and you, wise guy, shut up and sit back."

"Take it easy, Fournier."

"I'll take it easy when we get him behind bars."

"Don be shamed. French's Fournier. Frogs aweright."

"Don't call me that."

"Dolan's halffrog. He's aweright Buh! Yoh gotta have wee bita the Irish in ya, righ Dolan?"

"If you say so, Kid." Dolan did not turn his head. His eyes were on the road.

Although he could not maneuver into position so he could check it in the mirror, Sean was sure he heard Dolan's voice smiling. Patrolman Fournier was another matter. He didn't seem to be enjoying himself at all.

The squad car crossed a bridge. Must be Owl Creek. Sean was tempted to leap out of the back seat, dive over the railing, and swim down river where they would never catch him. But if he did, Dolan would be disappointed, the water would be freezing and he would probably catch a cold, and Fournier would be grumpier than ever. He needed cheering up.

Patrolman Dolan interrupted Sean's thoughts, for which he was grateful since he was having a difficult time recalling an anecdote that would prove it was necessary to have a wee bit of the Irish in him. "Where'd you get the booze?"

"Store."

"Did you buy it?"

"Roger."

"Roger Littlefield?"

"You know'm?"

"That was his car you were driving, wasn't it?"

"Didn say that."

"Where did he get the license plates?"

"Uhdonno. Store?"

"You wiseass PUNK!" Patrolman Fournier's large head swung around to face Sean who studied the thick eyebrows, wide, flat nose, and pockmarked skin. "Answer the question! He's asking you why you were driving a car with Massachusetts registration and New Hampshire plates."

"Ah didn."

"I'm gonna cream him."

"Take it easy, Fournier. Let me handle this."

"Right Led Dolan hannle this. S'nod Frog bizniz."

"I said, don't—call—Me—that! I'm gonna cream him. Pull over, Dolan. I'm gettin in back."

"Sit tight, Fourn. You'd better lay off the officer, Son."

"How'd yuh know my name?"

"Sonny?"

"Sean. Mispernounced id. Evybuddy does."

"Can you answer Officer Fournier's question, Sean. About the car?"

"Well. The steps were new. Margreh's gone. Fahhhway. Roger's good-shit—balled the Bear—skinny liddle girl—nice ass—too ole. Gotta have a wee bit. There wuz these two Micks—no—one Mick, an' one Frog, thah's iht. Walkin' down streed. Frog says—"

"Dolan! Tell him to shut up!"

"Thah's rood. Frog upbringin."

"I'm gonna-pistolwhip him when we get to the station."

"Syas, why duh Irish dring so much? Patty. Why d'Irish dring so much, Patty? Uuuhhmmm."

The squad car was almost to the station. Patrolman Dolan eased his foot off the accelerator.

"Uuuhhhh? Mick sez—Patty—Patty siz, Sose we don have tuh smell worl's bad breath. Frog sez, You talkin—"

"I'll take him in. You get some gas."

"—bouh me? Mick sez, If a leg fids—"

"I got plenty of gas. I'm going in with you, Fourn."

"If a leg—well, th wuz pree funny way my father tells id."

16 | Oversight

Margaret was waiting.

Mrs. Marjorie "Marjie" Hulitt walked briskly into her sixth-grade classroom. Her lesson plan was ready, had been ready for years, and had only needed slight revisions twice when the textbooks had been changed. She had read it over the night before and was satisfied with its precision.

Mrs. Hulitt turned to the class without raising her eyes. There was no need to. Every student, she was confident, was watching her intently.

"Good morning now we'll begin where we left off in our history page 229 after the Civil War began the period known as Reconstruct—"

"Teacher."

Mrs. Hulitt jumped. A strange voice in her classroom had interrupted the flow of education.

"Who said that!"

She looked up fiercely to find Ben Connell smiling brightly at her from the back of the room where he had squeezed into a desk seat and desk designed for twelve-year-olds.

"Teacher, can we do geography today?"

The children, although they recognized Mr. Connell, were uneasy. As long as no one whispered or passed messages or spoke out of turn in Mrs. Hulitt's room, the day went smoothly enough. But if someone angered Mrs. Hulitt, the whole class suffered. They might all have to stay after school or write an extra paper on the function of verbs in a verb phrase. The children wished Mr. Connell would act like a grown-up, get up, and go away.

"Look children," Mrs. Hulitt directed. The children looked obediently but shyly at the large man bulging out into the aisles. "Mr. Connell has come to hear our history lesson. We're all happy to—"

"Can't we do history and geography, Teacher?" Ben asked. "For instance, Japan."

"Well, Mr. Connell, we're right in the middle—"

"In fact, Teacher," Ben said, squeezing himself out of his chair, "I'll be glad to incorporate history and geography and social studies and hari kari into one lecture, brilliant of course, on Japan." Ben smiled.

Mrs. Hulitt hesitated. She didn't know if she should go immediately to find Mr. Molloy, her principal, or try to steer Mr. Connell out of her classroom. Obviously he had been drinking, but he was walking a very straight line to the front of the class—the front of her class! And he suddenly looked very grim. If she didn't do something, he was going to—take over. She reached for her lesson plan and held it up.

"You see, Mr. Connell, we have to cover—"

"Thank you, Mrs. Hulitt. Now children," Ben said, turning to face the class, working toward a smile as he spoke, "Japan, as you all know, was our enemy in World War II. But now we are working to help the Japanese people rebuild cities that were ravaged by the atomic bomb. Why should we? Shouldn't we make them pay..."

The children, before committing their full attention to Mr. Connell, watched Mrs. Hulitt. They were afraid she would take her pointer out of its tray beneath the blackboard and rap Mr. Connell on the wrist. They watched her walk back and forth behind Mr. Connell—who paid no attention to her—start for the door, stop, come back again, and, finally, slump down at her desk where she began reading her lesson plan to herself. The children relaxed slightly.

"...so we can see that a vindictive policy would be foolish. Now who knows anything about Japan? Anything?"

The children felt threatened.

"Anything at all that you know about Japan? How about you?" Ben asked a boy in the middle of the class who looked less cowed than the others.

"They torture babies," the boy said. "They throw them up in the air and stick them with bayonets."

"A lot of babies," Ben said softly, "and innocent people were killed by both sides in the war. When we dropped the atomic bombs, a lot of babies died or suffered. Let's try and forget the war a moment and talk about the people and the country. Let's..."

Mrs. Hulitt stopped fuming at her lesson plan and opened her desk drawer to secure paper and pencil. This type of talk would provide evidence for a formal complaint. To someone. Mr. Molloy? No. Those two were thick as thieves.

"...For instance, do they have sixth grades in Japan? Are boys and girls your age going to school right now? What do they do after school? I wonder if they..."

"Are you drunk?" Donald asked. He was standing barefoot in the darkened hallway, holding the phone in one hand and trying to tie the cord of his bathrobe with the other. "This is a Godawful time of night to be calling. What time is it?"

"No, I'm not drunk," Ben said. "I'm just happy. Really! I made up my mind. I'm going to Japan."

"You're not going right now are you?" Donald asked. "I mean, you're not getting on a plane or anything foolish, are you?"

"What is it, Donald?" Rose asked, stumbling sleepily against the gilt-edged mirror in the hall. "Is someone hurt?"

"Nothing, nothing. Now go back to bed, Rose. It's your brother. What did you say, Ben? That's Rose."

"I'm sorry, I woke you up but I had to tell you. I won't be leaving for a few months, but I—"

"Is he hurt?"

"What! Months! And you have to call now. You must be drunk."

"Oh, come off it, Donald. I'm not drunk."

"Is he drunk?"

"For God's sakes, Rose, will you let me speak to him!"

"Don't shout, Donald. You'll wake Tommy."

"I wanted you to know. I've made up my mind. Really, I've been thinking about it a long time."

"You speak to him. He's your brother. I'm going to bed."

"Ben, are you all right?"

"I'm going to Japan."

"You're all right?"

"...one thing about Japanese life that we might all remember is the respect children show their parents. The father is the head of the house in the realest sense, the most real sense, the father is really the head of the household in Japan. When he comes home from work, everything is prepared for his..."

"Tim!"

Raising his eyes from his beer glass to Ben Connell, Tim Toomey looked like a man whose private moment on the toilet had been invaded.

"I thought I might find you here. Oh! I thought you were alone."

"This is Hilda. Mic Connell."

"I'm just leaving now," the large, soft woman in the booth said. "You 'see I—"

"Oh don't, don't leave on my account."

"—I gotta get to work. In the morning. It was nice runnin' into you again, Tim."

"Huh?"

Ben watched Hilda gracelessly hurry away, pulling on her red rabbit-trimmed coat. He seated himself in the booth. "You doan come here."

"I just wanted to see you. I'm sorry I barged in. I didn't mean to— to barge in. Your friend left."

"She's slut."

"I'm sorry, Tim," Ben said, leaning toward the aisle. "I just wanted to tell you, I've decided to go to Japan."

"Why?"

"Well—I think there's a challenge there, a chance to help the people of Japan establish a democratic way of life, a chance to—"

"Bullshih."

"What do you mean?"

"Shoo 'em today, kiss 'em tommorrh."

"The war is over, Tim."

"Sez who. Thes bassarrs sneaky. Shoo you in the back —lice—ping ping-trus' 'em." Tim feebly shook his head once and slumped down, his forehead resting on the rim of his mug.

"...and they have beautiful pagodas and temples with shapes that curve and arch in and out until they become spires stretching up to the sky. They're painted yellow and green and red and they don't look like any building you've ever seen. The Japanese people visit them just as we visit our churches. And synagogues.

"And some of the pagodas look like a curved sandwich that keeps getting smaller at the top and has a sharp knotted toothpick sticking through. They..."

'Wat kind of talk is that?' Ms. Hulitt asked herself. 'It will take me a week, when we get to Japan, to undo the harm he's done. I'll see Mr. Milton. I won't even mention it to Mulloy. I'll see...'

"Marion? Marion?"

"Mmmmh."

"I've made up my mind. Are you awake?"

"Anmh."

"I'm going to Japan. Did you hear me?"

"Bahl."

"What?"

"Bahf—fet. Clean or buffet."

"Never mind. Christ, you don't even care."

Dawn came on unsteadily. Ben went in the bathroom and washed his face and hands. The excitement that had kept him awake all night was beginning to pale. He saw no reason to go to bed now. He would only have to get up in a few hours to go to work. But if he stayed around the house, the kids would be up soon and he'd have to take care of them, at least supervise breakfast. He was too tired for that. Maybe he'd have time to fix himself a little breakfast and get out before they woke up.

He drank a cup of tea with his eggs and toast. It was too much effort to fix a pot of coffee. He went without bacon because it took too long to cook. He wiped up the egg yolk with a piece of toast, then put the milk away, but left everything else on the table because he did not want to rattle around and wake everyone up.

Outside, he thought of taking his car for a drive around the city, or even out into the country, but he knew what the city looked like—gray, somber, hungover—and it was too far to real country. Besides, he would have to drive back. And there would be no one to go with him.

Pete will be going to work soon. But he'll be in a hurry. But he always starts his car and lets it warm up for five minutes. I should with mine. Especially in winter. I'll ruin the motor. I could tell him then. Hell, I can tell him in two minutes, I don't need five. He'll want to know about their politics. I'll tell him they've outlawed the Republican Party. In fact, they won't even receive Republican Congressmen. He'll love that.

Ben waited and thought and waited and planned until he had a whole routine sketched out in his mind.

Forty-five minutes later, the untold jokes were growing stale in his mind. No lights had appeared in Pete Langley's house.   Wondering if Pete had taken sick, Ben started back into his own house. He was stopped by an exact voice.

"Good morning, Mr. Connell," William Bradshaw said.

"Good morning, Mr. Bradshaw." Sometime if they lived next to each other for a hundred years, Ben expected that he and Mr. William Bradshaw would eventually come to be on a first-name basis. "Did you hear they outlawed the Republican Party in Japan?"

"Is that so?" Mr. Bradshaw said. He studied the orderly plants behind the wire fence on his lawn. "Interesting. Very interesting." He settled the brim of his hat firmly over his glasses and turned up his driveway toward his garage. It was obvious that he felt he had spared enough words in the cause of neighborliness.

"Yeah. That's why I'm going over there. All Democrats are welcome. We may lead a worldwide movement from Japan to abolish

Republicans everywhere."

"I see."

"Mr. Bradshaw, I'm going to Japan."

"Oh." Mr. Bradshaw stopped halfway up his driveway, touched his index finger to his lips, and came back down to Ben. "You're selling?"

"What?"

"You'll be selling your house."

"I guess so. I hadn't thought about it. Sure. I mean, I am going over there on a permanent basis, to stay. I hadn't thought about it."

"Yes. It sometimes does good to think about these things. You realize the struggle it has been to keep this neighborhood up to par."

Ben did not respond. He was remembering the cool reception the Bradshaws had given him and Catherine when they first moved there. The Bradshaws were polite enough when met in the street, but their eyes said young Catholic couples raised children and taxes and lowered property values. Now he was being enlisted as a member of the Old Guard to fight the New Barbarians. "There are always certain elements looking to purchase real estate in a neighborhood seemingly to find out how quickly they can destroy property values built up through years of effort. I don't need to point further then the end of our own street to illustrate my point. A few more families like those people and this neighborhood could easily degenerate into a slum. It does well to consider property transfers in that light."

"Yes, well I hadn't—"

"You might. I must be off or I'll miss my trolley." Every morning Mr. Bradshaw drove to the same parking lot and took the same subway train into Boston. Ben wondered if he parked his car in the same stall every day.

"I hope things work out better for you in Japan," Mr. Bradshaw said in parting.

It was the first time Ben realized that his neighbor considered him less than a success.

"...the Japanese are an industrious and clever people. For a long time, for centuries perhaps, they were considered a sleeping nation, but once the Western world intruded upon their sleep, they realized that to survive they should have to work hard and learn new skills. And learn they did, until they reached a point..."

"You're early, Mr. Connell."

Mr. Tsiatsios, the elderly druggist whose days were spent pulling sticky hands from comic books and candy bars, did not expect Ben Connell until nine o'clock. That was when Coughlin the postman stopped by before beginning his rounds. The three of them officially began their days by discussing any and all issues they could agree upon.

"Guess what."

Mr. Tsiatsios realized the need to say nothing.

"I'm going to Japan."

Dimly perceiving that this might affect his morning schedule, Mr. Tsiatsios felt that he was about to be cheated, but said nothing.

"I'm going to accept a job as superintendent of an entire district. They want me to set up their entire program. It's a tremendous opportunity."

Mr. Tsiatsios opened the cash register and carefully unwrapped a roll of nickels which he slid into the drawer. "The pay is good?"

"Oh yeah! A lot more than I'm making now, and they pay all my moving expenses and I'll have a large staff, American and Japanese. But it's the opportunity that interests me. It's a great challenge, trying to blend the best in education of two countries."

Hoping that his store did not burn down or that he was not robbed before he retired, Mr. Tsiatsios could not share Ben's excitement about new challenges.

"You don't like your things here anymore?"

"It's not that.Well it is that. Things could be a lot better, and I'm not sure they're going to get better if I stay. But more than that, Japan is an exciting place to be right now. They're trying to establish democracy and a new economy and educational programs and a way of life that will make them, really, a Western nation. I want to be part of it. I want—"

"So they can compete with the American businessman?"

"...and there are beautiful snow-capped mountains in Japan and the whole countryside has a pleasant appearance of order and harmony. Each house..."

"Hi, Ma."

"Don't hi me, Marion. What's this about that fool husband of yours?"

"Wait a minute, Ma. I left the stove on."

Marion found her cigarettes, matches, and an ash before returning to the phone. She was not eager to hear her mother's latest attack on Ben.

"How are you feeling, Ma?"

"Never mind that poppycock. What's your husband up to? Timothy didn't go to work today. He's home with a cold. I think it's his sinuses. Anyway, he said that he ran into your husband in the Square last night and your husband said something about Japan. What crazy scheme is he up to now?"

"I don't know what you're talking about, Ma. Ben hasn't said a thing to me."

"Don't lie to me, Marion. If you don't want to talk about it, just say 'I don't want to talk about it,' but—"

"I can't talk about something I don't know anything about!"

"—but don't lie to me. You know I hate little white lies. In God's View, a lie is a lie. I thought I taught you that. All this nonsense about venial sins. A sin is a sin and that's all there—"

"Ma! I don't know a damn thing about any scheme or Japan or anything!"

"Don't try to replace reason with vulgarity. It won't—"

"I'll call you later, Ma. Goodbye."

Marion wondered momentarily, before going upstairs to make the beds, if her mother was getting senile or if her brother was imagining things out of a bottle or if, possibly, as he had done before, her husband had somehow neglected to tell her something.

"...the Japanese are an artful people. Their beautiful silks and garments, their delicate paintings, even their beautiful   girls,   all

237

reflect a sense of grace, a sense of expression, of living..."

"We hate to lose you, Ben," Superintendent Milton said. "You know that." He wanted to shout for his secretary, slap her on the ass and chase her out to buy cigars for everyone, call his wife and tell her to tear up his diet, they were going out for oysters and French fries and beer, give everyone a half-day holiday, ride around in his car and throw bricks at school windows. But none of this was expected of him, so he paused, then wheeled around in his chair to gravely face Ben Connell. "But we all knew it was coming. We've been in this business, just an expression, we all know it's a profession, we've been in this business long enough to know that when you have an able young administrator, you either reward him or you can expect to lose him. And, the situation being what it is, we haven't been able to reward you with a promotion. We're not saying that one wouldn't eventually come, but youth must be served, and 'eventually' sounds like a long time. Of course—"

'Retire you old bastard!' flashed through Ben's mind but he dismissed it as unworthy of the moment.

"—when you've been in the game, and we feel free to use that term with you, when you've been in the game as long as we have you accept all this as business as usual. Good luck, Ben. If we can be of any assistance, let us know."

It was the shortest and most pleasant interview Ben had ever had with his boss. He returned to his office where he sat looking with pleasure at the shelf full of pamphlets and the file cabinet stuffed with papers that he would soon be able to throw away.

Burn them? I'll invite the whole office staff out to the front lawn for Ben's bonfire. All printed, mimeographed, and typewritten crap welcome. Throw in a few desks and chairs for show. I'd like to get ahold of Milton's files. Hot stuff. Pppshuu! Maybe I should start sorting this stuff now. I'll get a jump on myself. The day I leave everything will be wound up, finished, burned, buried or forgotten.

Ben spent the next half hour thumbing through, and occasionally reading, the papers in the top drawer of his file cabinet. He chose for elimination a cryptic, ten-year-old memo. With a sense of pride in accomplishment, he tore it into small pieces, throw it in his wastebasket, and left his office.

Helen Crowley, chief receptionist, whose desk was at the front of the secretarial pool, lifted her grayish-blue head to expose a sad face. Ben was amazed to see her face crumple and tears form in her eyes. "We'll miss you terribly, Mr. Connell. It won't be the same around here without you."

Ben reached for a clean handkerchief he did not have, then watched in puzzlement as Miss Crowley sniffed her way towards the ladies' room. It was not usual for Mr. Milton to divulge information. In fact, he made a practice of keeping everything from his employees until the last possible moment.

As soon as Miss Crowley was out of sight, the rest of the girls descended on Ben Connell.

"Congratulations, Mr. Connell."

"You're really leaving?"

"Your wife'll have to look out for those geisha girls."

Ben idled away the rest of the morning talking, at the water cooler and in the coffee room, with anyone who wanted to hear about Japan. At noon he called his colleague, Frank Molloy, and offered to treat him to lunch. Ben explained, while they ate their appetizers, the reason for the celebration. During the rest of the meal, he listened, believing not a word of it, as Molloy put forth his own plans for breaking with the system.

When he returned to the office, all the girls, except for Miss Crowley, smiled and waved and winked to establish their roles as assistant conspirators. In his own office Ben found James Johnson seated at his desk, riffling through a new textbook.

"Ben Connell!" Jimmy John said, leaping up and churning Ben's hand. "You sly dog! All this time you've been planning to run away from us and not a word, not one word about it! Congratulations! It sounds like a fabulous opportunity. Eminently fabulous!"

If he did not sense the relief a competitor feels when his opponent withdraws from the contest, Ben could have appreciated Jimmy John's enthusiasm more. "Thanks, Jimmy."

James Johnson's smile flicked off. Ben Connell, who never called him anything but "Jim," or "Mr. Johnson" in front of students, had come painfully close to using his hated nickname. Gradually, his face re-lit. "You will keep in touch with us peons when you reach the Orient, won't you? Perhaps you could dispatch some films that students might view. It would add an extra dimension to the teaching process if they knew that a local inhabitant had transmitted the material. And letters, can you imagine the impact letters would make?"

"I'll keep in close touch, Jim." The distance Ben had been striving to maintain lessened. Jimmy John and he had been through a lot together and his old colleague (friend?) had made a special trip to offer his congratulations. "In fact, I might need your help, Jim. It's going to be a big job."

"...we cannot and should not expect Japan to become another America overnight. Instead, we should hope to gradually fuse the best aspects of Japanese life with the best that America has to offer and hope for..."

Marion wanted to scream into the phone and puncture Rose's eardrum. Yet she knew whose fault it was.

"Yes, Rose," she said.

"Oh, we've had our differences. Little things. Nothing really. But I have to take my hat off to you, Marion. I'd be scared to start off brand new in a country I know nothing about. But Ben didn't seem worried at all, and I'm sure you're the reason for that. He sometimes, oh he never says anything right out, but you sometimes seem to sense that he's worried about your support in some of the things that he's done or wanted to do. But he wasn't worried one bit, and I'm sure I've got you to thank for that. Have you thought about the kids going to school over there?"

"Yes, Rose."

"What?"

"No. No, Rose. Nothing's been worked out yet."

"Welll, the transition may be rough on Tommy and Joe."

But not Sean and Margaret. "Yes, Rose."

"And if they got into a poor high school, it might hurt their chances to get into a good college. You have to think ahead to that. They will be coming back to the States for college, won't they? I mean, Ben isn't going to stay over there forever, is he?"

"I really have to go now, Rose. I have an awful lot of work to do."

"I'll bet you have, what with all the preparations and planning and—"

"I'll call you when I have something definite to tell you."

"I wish you would and—Marion."

"Yes, Rose."

"God bless you. Ben hasn't sounded this happy in years. I think you're doing a wonderful thing for him."

Joseph came downstairs as Marion was hanging up the phone. He had gotten out of the habit and necessity of obeying her by dealing with her only when she was in an ordinary or happy mood. Although he had intended to ask her to wash his athletic supporter, one look told him this was not the time. He went back upstairs quietly, two steps at a time.

Tommy came in from the backyard where he had been making irregular patterns in the bushes with a pair of rusty clippers. He tiptoed up behind Marion who, with arms folded, was staring, out the kitchen window, rocking from her heels to her toes. He tickled her ribs.

"GODDAMNIT!!" Marion jumped. Are you some kind of a nincompoop! Don't ever do that to me again."

"What are you so mad about? I was just fooling."

"Go up and clean the bathroom."

"Ohhh, Ma. I just got through cutting the bushes."

"You heard me. I don't want any backtalk."

"How come I have to do everything? Why doesn't Joey do something?"

"Go up and clean the bathroom and don't give me any of your shit!"

"Sure, sure. 'Tommy do this, Tommy do that.' How come Joey

241

never does anything. You afraid of him?"

"You son of a bitch!" Marion leaped to the stove and grabbed the pan by the handle as Tommy fled. She released it as soon as Tommy was out of sight.

Of all the goddamn rotten lousy shiteaten rotten tricks, this is it. I'm not gonna stand for anymore. If he thinks he can pull this on me I'll— Not one word. Not one goddamn lousy word. Everyone in the city knows about it but not one word to me. Who am I? Why the hell should he tell me? I'm just his goddamn stupid wife. I just have to pick up the pieces. I don't care. He can spend his money and play the great man with the world and ignore the kids and treat me like shit but he can't do this. I won't let him. I won't.

Marion could do little for the next few hours but fume. She banged cupboard doors and smoked cigarettes in the pantry. She started to wash the dishes, but remembered her husband's constant carping on the subject. She thought of being daring and pouring herself a drink but she remembered how she had picked at her husband the few times he had drunk in daytime. She quickly discarded the thought of packing up and going to a hotel. Who would get the kids supper?

Around four-thirty, Margaret came in from her novena. "Is supper ready?"

"No. Go out and play for awhile."

"Is supper ready?" Sean asked a few minutes later.

"No. Go out and play for a few minutes."

"I don't want to go out. Some kids chased me."

"Chased you?"

"Well, we were playing basketball and I gave this kid an elbow and his brother—"

"Are they out front? Is Margaret all right?"

"Oh yeah. It was over on Lee Street."

"Go up and clean your room."

Ten minutes later, Joseph called down: "Is supper ready yet?"

"No. Come down here a minute, Joey. I want to talk to you."

"I have to do my homework."

"Come on down. It's all right Joey. I'm not going to ask you to do anything. I'm not going to bite."

Joseph was suspicious at the use of his nickname. He was sure he was going to be asked to do something, but he grudgingly clumped down the stairs and stood in the kitchen doorway.

"Sit down."

"I have to do my homework."

"There's plenty of time for that. You can do it tonight."

"Tonight I have to—"

"Do you remember when you were a little boy your father bought that dog?"

"Yes?" Joseph looked at the stove where supper should have been cooking. "What about it?"

"He said to me, 'Marion. A boy should have a dog.' Donald must have told him that, or he read it somewhere."

"Didn't Uncle Donald get the dog?"

"Yes. That poor puppy. Your father put him down cellar and he'd go down there, whenever he thought about it, to feed him and train him. One day the poor animal'd get ten meals and the next day none. And the training sessions, they'd last about five minutes, and then your father would come stomping up the stairs, mad as hell, and tell me, 'Marion. That dog is stupid.' If Donald hadn't rescued the poor beast, he'd be down there still, shitting all over the place."

"Ma!"

Marion chuckled. "Remember the summer we had that tent in the backyard? Your father—"

"Yes. I—"

"—bought it for fifty dollars at an army and navy store. He said it was a steal and we were supposed to sleep in it every weekend so we'd be ready to go on great camping trips, Carlsbad Caverns, Niagara Falls, the Grand Canyon, but it took your father three weeks to set it up, and then it wasn't right, and he found out the first time it rained that his "steal" leaked buckets."

"Didn't we play in that?"

"Yes, you played with it for the rest of the summer, and beat the hell out of it, and Ben finally gave it to someone." Marion was smiling broadly.

"Ma, are you going to make supper? I have to go—"

"In a minute, in a minute. Do you remember the victory garden?"

"I think so."

"Ben wanted to raise all the vegetables we ate. He was so excited he leased two plots instead of one. I told him he had to prepare the soil, it was lousy, like hard crust, but he planted the seeds right away. He rent down there every night for about ten days. When nothing much happened, he decided he needed fertilizer so he bought about twenty bags and buried everything in fertilizer."

"Did it grow?"

"No, so he decided the fertilizer was no good. What he needed was "natural fertilizer." That's all he talked about for weeks. I got so tired of hearing about shit three meals a day. 'You'll see the difference natural fertilizer will make, Marion.' By this time, other people's plots were beginning to grow. Ben was furious. He bought a big metal washtub and drove up to New Hampshire to get his natural fertilizer. Some farmer charged him ten bucks for it and he had to shovel it himself and he was so mad and the stuff stunk up the car so much, he heaved the whole mess into the woods on his way home. He never went near the garden again, but I went down there one night and found a few skinny radishes and brought them home and made up a salad just so I could use them. Ben wouldn't eat them. He said they were terrible and told me never to buy any again from wherever I got them." Marion laughed. Joseph at first restrained himself but, infected by her continuing rising and falling laughter, soon joined her.

"...we can help point the Japanese people to a new future. We can help teach them all our skills and, in teaching them, we will also learn. We can..."

Ben Connell came home exhausted and exhilarated. He was still flushed with congratulatory words and the good feeling his decision had generated, but he came home purposely late to avoid the squabblings and bickerings that were sure to take place at the supper table while he tried to hear the news. Although he insisted that the family eat supper together, he was often tempted to take Marion's advice and have the kids eat early. And maybe she was right, a television might help. Tonight he wanted to eat in peace. He did not want to enforce table manners or warn Sean and Margaret about fooling at the table or listen to Tommy's babbling, or fend off Joe's requests for money. Instead, he wanted Marion to chase the kids away and sit down with him while he quietly told her his plans.

Sometime during the day, he had realized that she was sound asleep when he spoke to her. He thought of calling her but decided it would be best to tell her in person. She was very touchy about some things.

In the front hall, Ben was puzzled. There were no food smells coming from the kitchen and, judging by the noise, all the kids were upstairs or out. Usually they gulped their supper and then hung around the kitchen, interrupting his conversations with Marion.

He found his wife in the kitchen, opening a box of spaghetti over a large pan of boiling water. Ben figured that something had happened to delay supper this long. But it was not bad news, whatever it was. Marion was humming to herself.

He decided this would be the perfect time to tell her.

"Marion. I'm going to Japan."

"Oh, Ben," Marion laughed. She dropped the long, brittle strands into the hot water and laughed and laughed as they went soft.

"...and so, for these many reasons, we should look to Japan as our new neighbors in a world that grows increasingly small, should extend our hand to them as allies, we should give with no thought of..."

In his den, Ben Connell tried to recover from his wife's reaction. She had laughed in his face and then gone on to tell him how ridiculous she thought the idea was. He was too old to begin a new career. He had built up years of service in the Medlen system. Why throw that away? Tommy and Joseph and Sean and Margaret didn't want to leave their friends. They would have to all adjust to new schools. They didn't know the language. The house would have to be sold when they had invested so much in paying the mortgage. Did Ben really want to leave his relatives and friends behind to go off to a new place they knew nothing about (Did they have plumbing?) and start from scratch. She didn't. Didn't they have enough bills to pay without taking a wild trip to nowhere that they couldn't afford.

Dumbstruck, Ben had listened. Now he wondered why. His wife had not let him explain the situation or describe his new job. Why hadn't he hit her, or at least told her to shut up for a minute? He would have if she had yelled at him or griped or whined. But she had laughed. And then gone on to reason with him as if he were a child trying to move the ocean to his hole in the sand. And she had stressed the children, the difficulties it would create for them.

Ben paced his den, stopping to push a half-read book into line with the others or glance at one of many dusty sheets of paper on his cluttered desk. He had started to write several chapters of a guidebook for administrators but had never completed one. Whenever Marion pestered him about moving his books and papers up to the attic so they could use the den for a family room, he ranted about the necessity for a private place and wrote the introductory lines to a new chapter.

The thought occurred to him that he might not finish the book. It wasn't important. Something else was. What Marion said about the children was true. It would be difficult. But more than that, if he took the job in Japan, he would have even less time to spend with his children. Joseph and Tommy would be gone soon. Sean and Margaret were in the difficult years. He had not been the father he wanted to be.

A little after midnight, Marion woke up and walked across the hall to the den door.

"Ben?"

"What?"

"What are you doing in there?"

"I'm getting my things together. You can have the room." He would buy a television. It would be an educational experience for the children. They would watch together as a family.

"Come to bed, Ben. You have to get up in the morning." Marion walked softly away. Ben was sitting at his desk, charting a weekly schedule for private meetings with each of his children. Three hours on Saturday and three on Sunday were blocked out for family outings. He would begin the next day with Sean, who needed more attention than the others. But first, Ben needed a wider audience to speak to.

"...so if we begin today—" The mid-morning bell interrupted Ben's sentence. Behind him he heard Mrs. Hulitt getting up from her desk. "—if we begin today, we can look forward to a brighter tomorrow, a future in which Japan and America will be brothers, and the children, both you and the Japanese children, will learn today to live better lives in the international community together tomorrow. Thank you."

The children fled to recess.

17 | Night Call

"Detective Sergeant Kuchinski here, Mrs. Connell."

"My father! I wanta speak to my father."

"Is that Sean? Is something wrong? Is he hurt? Did he hurt himself?"

"PAAAAAAAAAA!"

"No, he's all right Ma'am. He was in an accident, but he didn't get hurt. He insists on speaking—"

"Paaa! Get on the phone, Paaa!"

"You can hear for yourself, Ma'am. Is Mr. Connell there?"

"What is it, Marion? Where's my cane?"

"You're sure he's all right? You're Positive? You wouldn't lie to me?"

"He's fine, Ma'am. Really. I wouldn't lie to you. He's drunk, but he's not hurt. Could you put—"

"Bullshit? Sober as a judge! Sober as judge."

"Give me the phone, Marion. And get out of the way."

Marion Connell yielded the telephone to her husband and stepped out of the circle of light cast by the table lamp.

"This is Ben Connell." Oh Christ, what did he do. "Who is this?"

"This is Detective Sergeant Kuchinski, Mr. Connell. I'm calling from Hampton, New Hampshire about your son—"

"Where?" What the Hell is he doing up there? "Hampton?"

"Yes, in New Hampshire. Your son—"

"Sean?"

"Yes, he—"

"Is he alright? Is he hurt? Let me speak to him. Can he talk?"

"Is that my father? Is that Daddy? Is that Puh-Puh-Puh-PAAAA! I wanta talk to you Pa. Got a lot to say, believe or not."

"Mr. Connell, could I talk to you for a minute before I put him on?"

"Sean's all right?

"He's fine. A little bump. He's fine. I don't know how he did it, but he's fine. He's drunker than—"

"What do you mean—'he's drunk'?" He's drunk. He's stinking drunk.

"DON'T BELIEVE A WORD! Don't believe a word, Daddy. Don't don't don't don."

"Mr. Connell, he's drunk. Take my word for it. He's been sitting here for an hour, falling asleep and waking up and trying to dial you directly like you had a local phone. Please. Believe me, Mr. Connell. The boy is drunk. I wanted to talk to you about what he's saying. He keeps talking about police brutality. No one, no one at all has put a hand on him. He did get one officer mad, but no one touched him."

"Put him on."

"Your father wants to speak to you."

"Pa? Is that you Pa. Pa?"

"Yes, it's me."

"Pa? It's all right, Pa, don't worry about a thing everything's gonna be under control, don't you worry, bay-bee, s'all right, I know what they're try to do, little whappo, rubber hose, no marks, whoo hoo hoo, don't fool me. They're tryin to lock me up, Pa—they're—"

"You're drunk."

"Shhhh! Don't say that. That's the rap. Trying to pin me. Police brutality remember that guy in the Square right to a lamppost chained handcuffed right there, rack, right in the ribs, gink, kidneys. Wait for the car, sure, with stick in the kidneys stick in the balls, right in the balls, smack, smack—"

"Shut up!"

"—smack in the balls, give it to him because he said be happy cop be sunshine I'm sunshine I can't shut up, gotta tell you it's all right not a scratch I showed 'em police brutal don fool me—"

"Put the officer back on.   I can't talk to you."

"—fool me. Hah. Don't wanta stay here, Pa. They're tryn lock me up throw away the key you get me Pa, you come and get me—"

"I can't come and get you tonight. I'll try and get you a lawyer. I can't—give me the officer."

"— don wanna stay here rubber hose don wanna—"

"Mr. Connell."

"What did you say your name was?"

"Kuchinski. Detective Sergeant Kuchinski."

"He sounds scared, Detective. He sounds awfully scared."

"He should be scared, Mr. Connell. He nearly killed himself. But no one touched him and I guarantee no one will."

"Are you sure?"

"Mr. Connell, I'm tired of talking about it. He's been talking about it for an hour. He wouldn't give us anything but his name, rank, and serial number for forty-five minutes. He wouldn't admit to owning his own wallet. If anyone deserves a dose of police brutality, he—he got one of the arresting officers so mad that we had to restrain him—"

"Don't believe it, don't believe anything you read in the papers! Dick Tracy. He's not Irish! KUCHINSKIIIIII!"

"I'm sorry, Detective."

"Sergeant. Sergeant's fine. Would you excuse me, Mr. Connell. If you don't want to speak to your boy anymore, I'm going to have one of the officers put him in a cell?"

"Could he stay in a hotel? If I paid for it?"

"A hotel? No, we'll have to lock him up. For his own good too."

"All right, Sergeant. You do what's best."

"Dolan, take him down to Cell Seven. And be careful."

"Come on, Ski. It was Fournier that was mad at him. Let's go, Connell."

"Where we going? Buy you a drink, just a little teeny one."

"Mr. Connell, do you know a Roger Littlefield?"

"I think so. I think   it's one of Sean's friends. Is he there?"

"No, but we found his registration in the car your son smashed up.

He—"

"Smashed up?"

"Yes. He sideswiped a parked truck, hit a speed sign on the other side of the street, and drove into a field. And he crashed into a barn. He was lucky."

"Oh my God! And he's not hurt?"

"No, a doctor checked him, but the car is close to totaled."

"What happens now?"

"He'll go to court in the morning and—"

"He can't go to court in the morning. He's drunk."

"He'll get about six hours sleep. We won't wake him until nine and let him wash up and he'll be all right. Do you want to get a lawyer up here or call a local one?"

Marion had heard enough. She went into the kitchen, fumbled in the broken teapot for cigarettes and sat down, crossed her legs, and smoked in the dark, flicking her ashes onto the floor. Her husband hang up the phone and sought her out.

"Marion?"

"I'm in here."

"What are you doing, sitting in the dark? I have to call O'Donnell and see if he can get me a lawyer who'll go up to Hampton."

"Why?"

"Because Sean has to go to court tomorrow morning, and he could lose his license for a year, and maybe go to jail if anyone presses charges for damage. It's going to cost a lot of money. Maybe I can borrow some money from Donald and get a loan and pay him back."

"Why should you?"

"Because if I call a Hampton lawyer, sure it'd be cheaper, but I wouldn't know who's a shyster and who isn't. O'Donnell can—"

"How do you know O'Donnell won't come up with a shyster?"

"What's the matter with you? Sean's in trouble and you sit—"

"Why should you do anything, Ben?"

"What! Are you crazy! Your own flesh and blood's in trouble and you can sit there and talk like that. Do you want me to sit on my hands?"

"Maybe. It might be better."

"I can't understand you anymore. I don't know what's come over you. You're not the same woman I married. Why don't you turn some lights on in here. Get up and move around instead of sitting there like a zombie. Next thing you'll be telling me I should disown my son because he's in trouble."

"I didn't say disown him."

"I'm going to call O'Donnell." Margaret locked up and now Sean, and Marion acting crazier than both of them.

Dinny O'Donnell coughed into the mouthpiece of his telephone before asking: "What is it?"

"It's me, Dinny, Ben Connell. I'm sorry to bother you—"

"You should be! This is one hell of an hour to be calling! Can't it wait til morning,? I'm a little old for these night games."

"Damn it, Dinny! I wouldn't call if it wasn't important. Sean's in trouble and if you—"

"Hold it, Ben. Don't go off the deep end now or say anything we'll both be sorry for. I'm just naturally grumpy when I'm woken up. Hell, I won't even talk to anyone before a decent hour in the morning for fear I'll snap their head off. I never forget a friend, you know that, and I remember clearly what you did for me with that McDonald thing. I'd be sittin' on my can now out in the cold if you hadn't told me what those back-stabbing bastards were up to. You calm down a second, and let me get my glasses."

You'll help me Dinny, and then it will be through. You won't owe me a thing. And when the School Board votes, you won't have to say a thing to them.

"I'll write a few things down here, Ben. What seems to be the problem?"

Marion Connell took her cigarette to the pantry sink, ran cold water on it, threw it in the trash bag and started upstairs. Ben interrupted his conversation, placed his hand over the phone, and whispered fiercely: "Where the Hell are you going?"

"I'm going to bed."

"That's grand. That's just grand. The rats desert the ship." Ben took his hand away from the mouthpiece. "I don't know if it was a private truck or a city truck, Dinny."

After his telephone conversation, Ben Connell went into his parlor and sank down into the easy chair. He closed his eyes and for a few seconds laid his head back against the chair. But his thoughts crowded together and clashed so he opened his eyes and shook his head.

"MARION."

"What."

Ben did not know how to phrase his request. After a few seconds, he said: "You can sleep down here tonight, if you want to. Did you hear me?"

"I heard you."

Damn you. Am I supposed to beg? "WELL?"

"I don't feel like doing anything."

"I didn't ask you to do anything. Do you think I feel like doing anything. I just said you could sleep down here if you wanted to. If— the phone rings you won't have to come all the way downstairs again."

"Who's going to call?"

"HOW THE HELL SHOULD I KNOW! Never mind. Never mind. Just forget it. I thought—" Ben did not finish his thought. He held his cane in the middle of the stem and lifted it and banged it and lifted it and banged it against the rug.

"All right."

"Don't do my any favors."

"Do you want me to come down or not."

"If you want to."

Ben was settled in his bed in the dining-room for several minutes before Marion came down, climbed into the bed, and turned on her side away from him. Ben turned to her and put his hand under her flannel nightgown.

"I told you Ben, I don't want to—"

"I'm not doing anything. Don't get excited. I just wanted to touch you."

"All right. But don't keep it up. I want to get some sleep."

You're not so touchable anymore, you know. Who else wants to touch you. You're getting old, old woman. Your breasts hang down and your stomach isn't smooth and your thighs are sloppy. And my legs are gone and Margaret and Sean are. The doctor said, I didn't tell you but I will, a nice little trip to the country would be in order. They're going to bury me in the country, Marion. Are you going to help them? It'll be good for me. The doctor said so. Not really a hospital, Mr. Connell, but I don't have to see him tomorrow. I've got an excuse. Margaret didn't really go to a hospital either.

Ben lit a cigarette and pulled his ashtray closer. "Do you have to smoke in bed, Ben? It's not good for you."

They're going to lay me to rot in the country, Marion. Will you bring flowers? Never mind. There will be plenty and they'll push my wheelchair out to blink at them and the sunshine and beg to get back to the cool shade in the ward, but it'll be for my or own good, it'll be healthy, turn him around Ralph, and over and upside down and inside out, it's for his own good, he's not done on the left side. Maybe if I wheeled out to the cemetery and dug my grave next to Catherine's, not to hurt you Marion, I'll save you a spot on the other side, if you're interested, and sat there they'd take the shovel back and take mercy and put a bullet through my head. No, it would have to be a needle.

Don't con me—You! I don't want to hear it—that garbage you've been feeding me all my life. Suicide. No. It would have to be done for me. Just making room. Shoot the old dogs. I'll stand still. Well maybe Judas was no fool. He knew he wouldn't be as weak in Your world. Damnation? Where is Joseph and Thomas and Sean and Margaret. And Marion? Where's your Christian charity. Catherine?

You have enough pups to play with. Die in peace. Quickly. Quickly. No more guilt, no lies, no promises. Without a priest? I don't need a fat cleric huffing and puffing, I never understood the Latin. No hand-holding into Hell. I think You're full of it anyways. What hell. You're a Softie. The Great Mushie One. Come off Your high horse. As you would be done unto. I'm done with the whole bloody kit and kaboodle. I've paid for my last privilege—lit my last candle—kissed my last ass, O Asseous One. Kill me.

"Are you asleep, Marion? Marion?"

"No."

"I don't think I'll see the doctor tomorrow. I want to get this mess straightened up."

"All right. Try and get some sleep, Ben. You'll be dead tired in the morning."

Lunging around the cell, trying not to look at the lidless toilet in the corner, as if not looking would decrease the intensity of the smell of his vomit splashed inside and outside the bowl, Sean tried to shake the dirty, itchy feeling from his skin and the mad thoughts clashing in his mind. For the first time he realized that suicides in jail cells were not all convenient accidents arranged by sadistic police.

He had made a fool of himself. More than that he had embarrassed and hurt and worried his father. It was turning light, a cold and empty and sickly light, outside the small high window across the corridor from his cell. In a few hours he would go before a judge, and what? Lie? He was guilty, Sergeant Kuchinski had not used that word, of hitting a truck and smashing a sign and wrecking the front end of a car against a barn. No one was with him they said. But he was haunted by the feeling that someone must have been hit. The lawyer would know. The lawyer his father was paying for. A hack who could lie him out of drunkenness and destruction?

Sheila. Was her name Sheila? How did she get home? Or was she going there. That was probably the worst thing he could do to her, take her wheels away. If the giant cockroaches and the slimy feeling went away, he could try to get some sleep. He couldn't go into court in this in-between state, moments of calm and lucidity alternating with the urge to scream to be set set free, to go and apologize and explain, he was not a criminal, a real criminal, was he? Sean forced himself to sit on the bunk which was attached to the wall by chains and covered with a mattress cover that had gone from cream to brown. Goile mor, the

Gaelic words goile mor, the big appetite, kept repeating themselves in his mind. Goile mor. His father never had the patience to read, preferring his own sporadic bursts of story-telling, unwilling to be limited even by the boundaries of fairy tales.

A policeman, Sean suddenly understood the meaning of "turnkey," woke him at eight-thirty when the lawyer arrived. After splashing water on his face and neck and behind his ears and rubbing his teeth with a soapy finger, Sean went out to meet a middle-aged, conservatively dressed man named Sullivan. Sean held out his hand let the lawyer shake it. What kind of lies could they devise?

"Your breath stinks," Mr. Sullivan said. "Here." He handed Sean a few loose mints from his pocket and a pack of gum. "Are you as guilty as you look?"

Marion answered the phone and hesitated before accepting reversed charges. She put the phone down immediately. A few minutes later Ben spoke. "Did the lawyer get there?"

"Hi, Pa. I'm sorry I—"

"Did the lawyer get there?"

"Yes, he's here."

"Well?"

"He says to plead nolo contendere and he'll point out to the court that I don't—make a habit of this."

"That's great. You need a lawyer to tell you you're guilty. Let me talk to him."

"No, there's no sense in that Pa. I just called to tell you that I—I really—I miss you." There was no response. "You there Pa?"

"I was just thinking about all the money I spent on law school, all the books I bought and studied. Right now I could be getting a fat fee and travel expenses to tell some dumb Irish mick to plead guilty. I guess I got in the wrong racket."

Sean's hangover and the accompanying nausea were pressing in on him. He hoped only that he could stop talking to his father soon and that the court appearance would be brief.

"And tell Roger," Ben said—Sean thought better of interrupting his

Robert Crotty

father to tell him that Roger was not there—"that the Red Sox are going to win it all next year. He can put money on it. Ben Connell predicts. Take care of yourself."

18 | The Barker

"Should we hire a dog, put a 'Woof' sign around his neck and pat him as a family when Gramps enters," Joseph said, lowering his chin and peering upward in imitation of his father's mock stern look which usually masked Ben's secret amusement. "We could stick a flashlight behind the false logs and sing 'Galway Bay' too."

Ben could not help smiling. Here his oldest son was taking the part of his stepmother, unusual enough since Joseph was known for his ability to disappear when emotions overcame logic and to reappear only when the type of climate he functioned best in had returned, and, he was using humor and parody to dispel the black mood. They must be teaching him something in college.

Seconds before, Ben had accused Marion of niggardliness: "You'd begrudge a sip of water to Christ on the Cross!" And Marion had retorted: "Oh, that's who's coming. I might have known you wouldn't spend the mortgage money on anyone else like just an unknown relative from Ireland who claims he's a relative so he can freeload."

Joseph spoke in time to keep Ben from expressing more vehemence than he felt. Ben wanted everything to be perfect, but Marion had a point. Who was this "old fellow" from County Cork who was coming to visit "for a time." His father's distant uncle or his grandfather's younger cousin? If only he had paid more attention, when his father was alive, to the family stories. His name was Connell and that made him a relative, one way or another. Rose's decision to call him "Gramps" connoted enough respect, while retaining a friendly ring, to satisfy Ben.

For weeks Ben had puzzled over the best welcoming possible for Gramps. He could take him to Charlestown, or was it Chelsea, anyway, by the bridge to see the Constitution. Or they could run down to Anchors Away for fried clams. But Rose would be hosting an elegant supper for the old boy that night. If he didn't have an appetite, it would be a disaster. Rose would be sure to have lobster and roast beef and to urge ladles of food on everyone, criticizing herself if the smallest tea spoon were out of place and terribly crushed if everyone didn't immediately, enthusiastically contradict her and swear that everything was perfect. And Donald would drive all over hell to find fresh corn-on-the-cob in mid-September.

Everything Ben thought of he had done recently or vividly enough to not want to repeat, having learned early as a teacher that he performed best when he had a genuine enthusiasm for the subject. He had insisted on meeting the old man's plane at eleven thirty in the morning and entertaining him until six-thirty so that Rose would not be a nervous wreck. Ben's only obligation was his annual speech to the young teachers—he could do that with his eyes closed—and the socializing that followed. If he cut that a little short, he'd easily make it to the airport on time.

Marion, amidst furious scurrying to clean the house for a person she was not sure merited it, suggested a quiet afternoon of talk in the parlor.

"He'll probably be tired, Ben, and you might find out which branch of the family tree he dropped out of."

"He can rest in the grove," Ben said. "He's coming to see America.. It's his first trip, and his last. There'll be plenty of time to sit around and chew the fat."

But what exactly to do had not occurred to Ben by the morning of Gramps' arrival. He was sure something would come to him as he drove to the high school auditorium to address the young teachers. Ben's original idea for a fall meeting of young teachers at the end of October had led to so much pressure for change and requests for improvements in the system that Superintendent Milton "modified the agenda," moved the meeting to mid-September when teachers were still groping to establish a routine, and replaced Ben as meeting moderator with Mrs. Marjorie Hulitt for, according to one of Mr. Milton's infrequent memos to Ben, "enhanced inter-teacher communication levels as has been your long-stated goal."

Mrs. Hulitt—she insisted that everyone call her "Marjie" including Superintendent Milton who thought it a "peppy" name and her "quite a girl"—had done the rest. Under Ben's direction, the end of October meeting consisted of informal individual presentations of successful methods or recurrent problems followed by small group discussions. The meeting lasted from 9 a.m. to 1 p.m. and then adjourned to Jake Wirth's in Boston for an afternoon of drinking and bitching, followed by a hearty supper and assorted impromptu evening activities. To give the devil his due, Ben had decided that Mr. Milton's decision to change the meeting was as much due to the "Hallowe'en Howl" that followed it as to other considerations.

Mrs. Hulitt, although she was very active in P.T.A. and vice president of her garden club, felt that she had few chances outside her sixth-grade classroom to display her brilliance with words and her fund of humor. Consequently, she expanded the mid-September meeting into a full day of activities, each of which starred Marjie Hulitt. "Coffee Chat" was at 7:45 a.m. with Marjie circulating her brightly-garbed bulk among all the sleepy, unresponsive groups, asking pointed questions about any teacher she did not see which obviated a forthright taking of attendance.

From eight to nine a.m. "Washroom Etiquette" was the subject. A training film, made in the 1930's, showed a cunning teacher's clever substitution of the word "washroom" for the words "toilet" and "bathroom." The high point of the film, as far as the teachers were concerned, came when their masterful screen counterpart, holding up his wrist and scrutinizing his watch, asked an angelic, freckle-faced child: "Which faucet are you going to use, Number One or Number Two?"

Throughout the film, Mrs. Hulitt stood by the screen holding a long wooden pointer. She was not a tall woman and had weight to spare. Every time she raised her arm, loose masses of flesh hung down. Her lips, often pursed, were painted in a large vermilion cupid's bow. Occasionally she poked the pointer into the screen teacher's nostril or eye and instructed her audience, "Notice the ease of his approach. See how he smiles," or "Notice his firmness. This is not a time for jollity."

A half-hour discussion followed the film. When questions were not forthcoming, Mrs. Hulitt produced a typewritten list of her own and asked them.

"Miss Heath, can you tell me what the best way to learn of constipation in a child is?"

"I guess, Mrs. Hulitt, if the child is fidgety and complains of stomach cramps or never raises his hand to go to the bathroom—"

"Washroom. Remember? And call me Marjie, Dear. We're all friends here. And why don't you stand up so we can all see how pretty you are."

"—and never raises his hand to go to the washroom, you might think—"

"That's not the best way, Dear. The best was is to have a note from the parents."

"Oh yeah, yes."

"But that was a good try. Sit down, Dear."

The veteran teachers had dubbed the session "piss-and-tell period." To most it was better than the next hour or so which was billed as "Just a few words before we hear from the man we all came to hear." Ben never had the heart, although he was scheduled to speak from nine forty-five to ten twenty, to make up for the time Marjie usurped. Even on occasions when he had something he considered important on his mind, he suppressed it or cut it short rather than force the teachers to race through their scheduled ten-minute "Bun Break." And it did no good to come early. Mrs. Hulitt had never finished before ten. She had collected her thoughts and was determined to share them. The fall meeting of young teachers was her annual benefit. If she could have, Ben was sure she would have charged admission.

"...Yes, you deserve the title of educators now," Mrs. Hulitt was saying as Ben let himself into the auditorium by the side door and walked softly toward the stage. "You've almost finished a year's campaign. I'll make the rest of my remarks brief because we all know whom we came to hear. And hear we shall," she promised, shooting Ben the same tight smile she used on her twelve-year-olds when they came in after the last bell. Ben bit his lower lip and twice formed the word "fall" to signal Mrs. Hulitt that she had slipped into her spring speech to freshman teachers. She merely shook her curly, peroxided head once as if shaking an irrelevant word out of her ear, filled her bepearled bosom with breath and cantered on. "It is not for us now to sit back and say, 'I am a veteran. I know all there is to know.' Oh, Nooo. That way lies danger. It is rather for us, the teachers, to say, 'This year's lessons shall not have been learned in vain; this year's...'"

Ben settled into his chair, fastened his eyes on Mrs. Hulitt's great, broad backside, made more impressive by her choice of a dress with red and yellow flowers printed on white, and eased into his considerations.

Joseph's a man. A young man, but a man. How did he get there? He's always been around but I've hardly ever seen him. Except to say hello and pass the mustard. He could be a father soon. My God, Tommy could be a father soon. And Sean, first chance he gets, will tell me to go to Hell and disappear. And Margaret, Margaret.

Ben did not want to think about Margaret, earnest Margaret, growing up and becoming a mother. It seemed indecent. So he switched back to his oldest son.

He'll want to know about raising a family. What will I tell him. It's too late for that, but, raising children. No scolding. Ridiculous waste of time. Answer all questions. Whatever they ask you, treat it seriously. Give them the best answer you can. Treat them like adults, they'll behave like adults. Will they? Probably. Is that good? Well, yes. Treat them like adults—but—let them enjoy their youth. I'll speak to Joseph about that.

Ben pictured lengthy story-telling sessions with his grandchildren sitting on the parlor rug surrounding his chair of magic and mirth. And in the first years, before the families grow, if they want to bring along some of their young playfellows to be enchanted also, that was fine. Hans Christian Connell, Good Father Goose would welcome them all, declaiming: 'Little Jack Hor-ner sat in a cor-ner—'

"...my pleasure to introduce our Assistant Superintendent of Education, Dr. Bernard Connell, who will speak to us now. Dr. Connell," Mrs. Hulitt said, yielding the floor graciously, smiling in the certain knowledge that any irrelevancies he might choose to add would not detract too much from the words she had so deeply inscribed on the young teachers' minds.

"Most of you," Ben said, nodding grim thanks to Mrs. Hulitt for using his hated name 'Bernard,' "have met me by now. I'm Ben Connell and I'm still working on that doctorate, Mrs. Hulitt. A few more courses and a dissertation. A few more courses, one of my professors swears, and I'll be able to teach the whole program," pausing until the titters stopped.

"If you can't get a job—teach." Ben held the lectern and bowed his head momentarily to let that much sink in, to let the young teachers compare that opening with the expected one. "That is a popular misconception of how teachers come to their profession, but there is enough of a grain of truth in it for me to urge anyone here who came to teaching for the supposedly short hours or the long summer vacations to get out now."

Ben allowed time for Mrs. Hulitt to adjust her creaky folding chair to a new position in order to study him more closely and for the teachers to exchange quizzical looks.

"Get out now or you will have the minds of hundreds and thousands of children on your conscience. Don't wait until you are sixty-five and can look back only on hours put in at a job. This is not what teaching means." Ben fought for control of his monitor. Is this you, Bull? Shut up. "Don't stand before a class and repeat exactly what is printed in the book because you can't be bothered to prepare. Better to get out now, because this is not what teaching means.

"Teaching means opening children's minds, not closing our own. Because, in the long run, it is not a child's IQ, or spelling ability, or neat papers and nice manners that count—what counts is the child's mind and what we have done to open it, populate it, beautify it. It is the children that count, and we are the children's servants..."

Half an hour later when Ben sat down, Mrs. Hulitt was upon him in all her fleshiness. 'Perhaps,' he reflected before being totally wrapped and submerged in her pink plumpness, 'I said too much about female devotion.' "That was the finest speech," Mrs. Hulitt cried, "I've heard in thirty years of teaching. I feel as if I've been," she bawled, breaking down totally, "in CHURCH! Oo-hhooo-hoo."

Ben slipped away during the coffee break that followed the speech. Mrs. Hulitt graciously expanded it to twenty minutes even though this threw her schedule out of kilter. Ben could have used the time, as he had before, to deal with immediate questions or size up a few problem teachers who would need help. He knew he would have to make up this time, fill the mental folders, but it wasn't every day that you got a visitor from Ireland.

On the drive to Revere Beach Ben cursed himself for inviting Winifred O'Leary. At the airport right after he had kicked Sean in the shins for tickling Margaret unmercifully, Ben had determined that he should whisk Gramps away to the cocktail lounge for the full-glass hospitality he had received on his long-ago trip to Ireland. Marion had not objected. She thought it crazy to invite Winifred and Jack O'Leary—it was bad enough to keep the kids together and quiet, worse to have to do it in front of others—but everything else about this visit seemed screwy to her. Why not let Ben get looped with the old man? At least Ben would be cheerful and not pick at the kids and try to get them to behave as they never had behaved yet.

"But he might be a Pioneer!" Winifred had insisted.

Ben did not know what a Pioneer was so he looked at Winifred as if he were engaged in deep thought, frowning and feeling his almost clean-shaven chin. He had never been fond of Winifred, she was too fidgety and much too aggressive for a woman, but he wanted her husband Jack along because—well, because Jack was a strange figure, a man who worked with his hands at the shipyard, who always looked incalculably sad, unable to overcome or begin to express that sadness, a working-man sure to get along famously with Gramps Connell, another working-man sure to have the sadness of Ireland stamped on him.

"You know, Ben," Winifred had lectured, "Pioneers take an oath at age twelve to never touch a drop. It would be an awful affront to the man to shove him into a bar and tempt him to break a life-long promise in the name of hospitality. You wouldn't want that, would you?"

She had him there. Ben shot a killing glance at Marion as if it had been her idea to invite Winifred, as if she had not argued against it, even insisted that it would be all right to invite Jack alone since Winifred usually had a million things to do. Ben argued persuasively against the rudeness of a single invitation, emphasizing how awkward it would be for him since Winifred did some substitute teaching and he would eventually bump into her at one of the schools.

Ben had first introduced Winifred into the Connell household after meeting her this way. She had been "dying to go" to an NEA convention in Washington to "keep up on the latest methods." Impressed that a substitute could be so dedicated to the profession, Ben volunteered Marion's services as baby-sitter for five-year-old Peter O'Leary. Her return from the convention marked the beginning of Winifred's good deeds for the Connells.

Usually after early Sunday Mass but also at other unannounced times, Winifred would drop by with "a little something" for the family or one of its members. Her Sunday offering was fresh tarts or fig squares or a pie from the bakery. She presented Margaret with a pink ribbon to match the dress for her first, and last, dancing class. Winifred noticed Sean carrying his sneakers and gym clothes in a brown grocery bag and came up with a blue gym zipbag for his first basketball game in the recreation league. And always there was money for Tommy and Joe to "get yourself something nice." Marion's protests were dismissed, waved away: "Don't be silly, it's nothing. Go on now, Boys. You've got a lovely family, Marion."

When she came visiting, Winifred either rapped loudly and longly with her knuckles or, if she were wearing gloves, tapped sharply with a key, rat-a-tat-tatting fiercely on the window pane of the front door as if trying to reach sanctuary. She danced around on the porch, shielding her eyes with her hand to peer through the glass, looking over her shoulder quickly, then tapping or rapping again.

Sweeping into the kitchen as soon as the door was opened, Marion following in her wake, Winifred would lay her package (the children greedily guessing its contents) conspicuously on the table and perch on the edge of a chair. She undid the top button of her coat and said right off: "I can't stay more than a minute, Marion." Since the Connells never hurried except when they were impossibly late, the rest of the family figured that this constant bustling of Winifred's caused Ben to say a quick hello and then disappear outside or down cellar. Marion admired Winifred tremendously. She also liked her, but found it very hard to relax around the woman.

Although Marion was a few years older, Winifred was always in command. Huge and ruggedly built as she was, Winifred looked somewhat ridiculous as she remained poised on the edge of a straight-backed wooden kitchen chair, her legs and feet turned in and her weight on her toes, a pigeon-toed sprinter listening for the gun. She wore institutional dresses, all olive or gray, with usually a cameo brooch at the neckline. Her hair, naturally straight, was always curled and sprayed to stay exactly in place. Instead of a feminine look, it gave the appearance of something unnaturally fluffed and stiffened, like spun lead.

Fifteen minutes after Winifred first sat down, Marion offered to hang up her coat for the second time. Winifred buttoned her one loose button, repeated how rushed she was for time and sat there for an hour or more, refusing all comfort but a cup of plain tea. After one of Winifred's departures, Ben had re-appeared to exclaim: "For Christ's sakes, Marion, will you tell that woman our toilet's working fine. She doesn't have to sit and wiggle half the day and then run off to use hers."

Marion laughed for a moment, caught herself in the act and immediately launched into a spiel about what a wonderful person Winifred was. She outdid herself in matching the intensity of her sermon to that of her initial laugh. Then she lapsed into a reverent wistfulness, probably asking God's forgiveness that she couldn't like Winifred more.

With Winifred's husband, Jack O'Leary, Ben Connell was different. He would never think of calling on Jack, but he made a special effort many evenings to be sitting on the front steps at dusk when Jack passed by on his way home from the shipyard. Ben always read the paper in the late afternoon immediately after it arrived, demanding silence on the porch at that time, but any evening he sat on the steps he would take the paper with him and be looking at it again in the dim light when Jack came striding along.

Jack's arms never swung when he walked. They hung limply by his thick thighs which threatened to burst the tight brown work pants he always wore. Often his right hand pressed a brown paper bag and its rectangular contents against his hip, the bag itself wrapped tightly around what was obviously a six-pack. With his grey work cap pulled down so that his eyes were always shaded and one fist clenched at his side, Jack looked ready to fight the world. He had a wide, flat nose, a mangled ear, and blotches of red and white skin. Jagged, red lines surrounded the pupils of his eyes. Often he looked as if he had just been crying or was about to.

"Ben."

"Oh! Hi, Jack," Ben Connell, feigning surprise, lowered his paper. "How have you been?"

"Pretty good. You?"

"Fine, Just fine. How's the work going?"

"Pretty rough. We got a new ship in today. Gonna take a lot of climbing."

"It's a beautiful day."

"It was," Jack said, shifting his weight onto his right foot so that his hip arched, and trying vainly to stuff his hand into his tight trouser pocket. Failing, he stood there, his hand dangling uselessly, his gaze on the cement sidewalk.

A silence was disturbed only by the sound of a passing automobile or the shouts of children playing relieve-ee-o at a nearby lamppost.

"Well, I don't want to keep you from your supper, Jack."

"Mmm. I better be getting on." Jack strode off, seemingly a little relieved, after the brief socializing, of an enormous weight he was carrying. Ben had his own ideas about the cause of Jack's sad reticence. Ben had a theory about Jack, that Jack had a burden, a dark spot that he was too much of a man to talk about.

Ben's theory seemed to be proving itself when Winifred rushed from the waiting area onto the field as the ground crew rolled the steps up to Gramps' plane. The gate guard moved over too late to stop Winifred but just in time to block Ben from following. "Ma'am," the guard called, "the rules call for you to wait here for debarking passengers." Winifred rushed back, reached around the guard and grabbed Ben's hand. "Fiddlesticks," she said. "This man came all the way from Ireland." Red-faced, brushing past the guard, Ben allowed himself to be dragged toward the plane. The guard turned his venom on Marion and Jack and the children and others standing near them. "Get back now. This isn't any joke. These are federal rules. That woman might find herself in court tomorrow morning." Jesus, Mary, and Joseph, Marion prayed, not that. On top of all the rest.

Winifred danced around the foot of the stairs, almost hugging a tall, sedate gentleman who sidestepped her indignantly. When a short sturdy old man, dressed in a long grey overcoat and grey working cap with white hair beneath and a long navy-blue scarf wrapped twice around his neck and trailing over his shoulder and down his back, uttered: "God Bless America," upon touching earth, Ben stepped forward, hand outstretched, to welcome Gramps Connell. Winifred beat him by half a step. She pumped Grumps' hand and bussed him on the cheek. "We're so glad you could come!"

"Rose darlin'," the old man said.

"No she's Winifred," Ben tried to explain as Winifred locked arms and marched Gramps Connell off.

"Winifred, to be sure," Gramps said, "and you must be Bernard."

"No. Yes! I'm Ben." But Winifred was on the fly with Gramps in tow, introducing him all around, tossing off, "Don't have a bird," to the gate guard, herding everyone to the parking lot and assigning them to cars. Jack, Marion, Joseph, Tommy, and Margaret were in the O'Learys' car with Marion driving, much as she hated to, because Jack had not renewed his license in two years. Sean, Winifred, and Gramps were in Ben's car, the lead car with Ben installed at the wheel—"You drive Ben"—as if by royal edict of Winifred O'Leary.

"How was your flight, sometimes it can be awful rough," Winifred said, leaning far forward from the back seat to plunk her arms on the front seat and rest her head on her hands. "When I went to Ireland two years ago—"

"You went to Ireland?" Ben asked, turning his head.

"Of course I did, didn't I tell you, better watch the road Ben, didn't Marion tell you, oh you know how she is, she'd forget her head if it wasn't glued on, I had two whole weeks in Ireland, first class, I traveled to the West and..."

Winifred detailed every landmark, castle, meal and rest stop as Ben seethed. He stomped on the accelerator, realizing too late that he had left Marion caught at a light but unable to stand the thought of pulling over and waiting for her to catch up. A movement on the seat next to him caught Ben's eye. Gramps had formed his hand to frame a glass and was tilting it back and forth.

"...and walking around those castles, you realize they were such small people, such—oh Gramps, that's so funny," Winifred interrupted herself, "here you are dying for a drink and we thought you were a Pioneer, hah, didn't we Ben? Well, we'll just fix that. Ben, you pull over to the first decent-looking cocktail lounge and we'll get Gramps a nice drink."

"Yeah, Pa," Sean spoke for the first time, startling Ben, "I'm dying for a shot of booze. Aaaahh, my throat's dry. I—haven't—had—my— daily ration-o'rum."

"Just cut that out, Young Man."

Oh, Ben," Winifred said.

Gramps Connell turned around slowly to study this specimen of American boyhood. "Mind your foolishness when you're talking to your father," he sharply admonished Sean. "Show a decent respect."

Stunned, red-faced, Sean withdrew into himself. Winifred took up his part. "He's just having a little fun. Sean's a good boy."

"There's fun and there's fun." Gramps said. "Bernard, would you ever do me a favor and stop by here. It looks as good a place as any."

Ben pulled over to the curb, his heart warmed that Gramps had picked a neighborhood tavern, a place far from decent-looking and perhaps rough enough to discourage Winifred from entering. But she was the first out of the car, opening Gramps' door and waving Sean out, "Come on, we'll get you a Coke." Gramps lingered on the sidewalk, fussing with his scarf until Ben caught up with him as Winifred and Sean went inside.

"Who is that woman?"

"Oh, she's just a casual friend of the family. I wanted you to meet her husband, Jack. I never should have invited—"

Gramps held up his hand. "Into every life—would you take it hard, Bernard, if I was to twirl my scarf round her throat."

Gramps and Ben entered laughing. Winifred greeted them with: "They've got Irish whiskey here. Isn't that wonderful."

"It's not unheard of," Gramps said.

"Here we are." Winifred passed around the drinks she had paid for, profoundly embarrassing Ben. "Welcome to America. Hurray for the Irish."

Gramps took off his cap, revealing a bald spot, and held up his glass: "God bless all here."

He did it with such natural dignity that Sean stopped sipping his Coke and straightened up momentarily. Winifred raced on, praising Ireland and the Irish and America and the American Irish. Ben had thrown down two shots and felt nothing, the liquid running off the cement sidewalks into the gutter of his stomach. As it churned, he asked himself why he had invited Winifred, why not someone sensible and decent like Pete Langley, why did his plans never turn out the way he envisaged them, why did he put up with this from almost a perfect stranger who acted like a kissing cousin. The door opened and Marion, looking for her husband, came in reluctantly.

"Ben! Excuse me—Gramps. I'll talk to you in a minute Winifred. Sean, what's that you're drinking? Oh. Ben, can I talk to you?" When Ben pointed out a booth away from the bar, Marion sat down gingerly, glanced right and left for lip-readers, and unloaded. "I got lost, Ben," she whispered fiercely. "Why didn't you wait? I've been driving around in circles, looking for the car. And I can't drive that car. I hate driving somebody else's car, you know that, and you're in here setting up the house and—"

"I haven't bought a stinking drop," Ben said, working up an anger. "Your friend there—Marion! You're an angel in disguise. That's it! Let her drive her own car. She's been driving me up a wall, acting as if Gramps was her own invention, buying rounds and making me look like a piker. Tell her you can't drive her car and that you're coming with us. Just—"

"I had a wonderful idea," Winifred said, charging the booth. "Marion, you and I will take the kids to the beach and the men can have a nice quiet talk together and meet us there, by the roller coaster, in half an hour, or they can leave half an hour after we do. Isn't that great? Wouldn't you like to have a man-to-man talk, Ben? Sure you would. Sean, finish up you're Coke. We're leaving."

While Winifred marshaled forces, Marion lingered a moment with Ben. "I hope Gramps can talk. Jack hasn't said a word since we left the airport. Ben, you won't get—"

"Come off it, Marion. We'll have one more drink and then we'll come along. I promise to put up the storm windows and install weather-stripping and fix all the locks if you'll get that woman away from me for ten minutes. I'll take you out to Le Bon Chapeau for frogs legs even, Lambie Pie."

Marion smiled and left with Winifred and Sean. A few seconds later Jack came into the bar. For the first time since Ben had known him, his face relaxed into a near smile. Ben ordered a round with a double for Jack to catch up.

"I usually drink beer, Ben," Jack said, looking sad again.

"This one time, Jack, won't kill you."

"Would it be all right with you," Jack asked slowly and quietly, causing Ben to lean forward to hear, "if I was to order a beer chaser?"

Ben laughed and threw a twenty-dollar bill on the bar. "Order anything you like and more of it."

Jack relaxed, threw down his double shot before the bartender returned to put Ben's change on the counter, and sipped his beer as Gramps waxed nostalgic.

"...The boy's only just past thirty and nothing will do but he's bound and determined to move a mile from the village with his new bride. And Edward, as you know, God bless him, has his own bed-and-breakfast trade down the road. He's up to buildin' on. That leaves only John."

"John's the youngest?"

"John's the eldest. And he's got notions of marryin'. Ah, Bernard, it isn't the same..."

Ben listened to Gramps intently, hoping for a name or scrap of information that would help to define their relationship, but he couldn't help noticing Jack throw down another double and order a re-fill. What kind of a scene would Winifred cause if he delivered her husband drunk? Did a "man-to-man talk" allow for early afternoon stupefaction? Winifred couldn't be the good sport all the time or Jack wouldn't be like he was. Gramps noticed Jack throwing down his third double, interrupted his own discourse on the terrible burden of taxes in Ireland, and leaned towards Ben.

"Is somethin' troublin' the lad?"

"No, he's fine," Ben said. "He's just quiet. He never—"

But Gramps moved around Ben to stand between him and Jack. "Is it all right with you, Mr. O'Leary?"

"I don't know how it is in Ireland," Jack said, his voice thickening, "but how would you like to live with a woman—"

Jack stopped and Ben was not sure he wanted him to start again. Teachers and colleagues were always telling Ben things, some of which he didn't really want to hear, but it was part of the job, an essential part. And those conversations took place in the late afternoon, sitting tired or mellow in an empty classroom or a teachers' lounge or a sparsely populated cocktail lounge or bar. Ben was not sure at all that he wanted a high noon confession from this sad, simple man whom he met frequently and barely knew.

"Maybe we better get along to the beach," Ben offered.

"Hold on now, Bernard. Let the man have his say. I know how it is to live with a woman. Was there more to it than that?"

Jack swallowed slowly, as if tasting all the gall of his years of marriage. "Do you know what it's like to live with a woman who when you come home from work with a little refreshment and you open the refrigerator door and you can't even fit it in because she's got it full of her laundry and you go to move it a little and she raises holy hell?"

Gramps looked at Ben, wondering if there were a deep significance to this tale that he had missed. Ben, wide-eyed, stared at Jack.

"It's true," Jack said. "She keeps her ironing in the refrigerator."

Gramps coughed and asked where the gents was. As he turned away from the bar, Jack clamped his shoulder. "But I fixed her, oh about five years ago I came home one night, after a couple of shots under my belt and she starts right in on me, 'Well, if it isn't the Lord Mayor of Dublin himself,' so I open the refrigerator and start throwing out those plastic bags full of wet stuff and she yells, 'What do you mean coming in here drunk and throwing things out of my refrigerator,' so I told her shut up or I'll start throwing more than GD shirts that shouldn't be in the refrigerator in the first place and I walked out and didn't come back until after last call. That fixed her wagon." Jack released Gramps and chugged his beer. "But she still does it...she still does..."

On the ride to the beach Jack slept in the back seat of the car as Ben told Gramps about the huge roller coaster, the reason he had chosen Revere, and asked the old man if he were game for a ride. "We'll have a go at it, Bernard." Ben mused about his new-found fondness for his given name, the way Gramps used it, as he pulled to the curb across from the roller coaster. Marion and the kids waited in front of the entrance as Jack stirred groggily and Winifred charged across the street. "It's closed!" she shouted, thrusting her head a second later through Ben's window and coming face to face with Jack who had almost gained an erect position.

"It's damp down here this time of year anyway," Winifred said, twitching her shoulders, "We might as well go back to the city. I'll take Jack and Margaret and Sean—"

"Hold on a minute, Winifred. We'll get something to eat," Ben smiled, covering his deep disappointment that the roller coaster was closed, "and a cup of coffee and maybe walk along the boardwalk and see if—well, there must be plenty of things open."

"The season's over, Ben. Anyway I have to visit Mrs. Moriarty this afternoon, I almost forgot, so we'll just run along. Can you fit seven of you in your car?"

"God speed," Gramps called after the departing O'Learys and to Ben added, "They're a grand couple and certainly deserving of each other."

The only stand open in that stretch of beach was selling frozen custard so Ben ordered a round for everyone except Joseph who had taken off down the sidewalk to find out what exactly was still open. Marion was smiling foolishly, "Ben, we're freezing to death and eating frozen—," when Joseph hurried back with the news, "The Dodgems are open."

"What might that be?" Gramps asked.

"Dodgems?" Joseph paused a second. "They're—cars—"

"Bangem, smashem cars," Sean said. "You hop in and whirl around and wham, you hit the guy—"

"I believe," Gramps said, not turning to look at Sean, "That Joseph was speaking."

Sean crushed his cone, threw it in the gutter, and stalked off in the direction of the Dodgems. Ben started after him. "Sean, you—" Gramps laid his hand on Ben's arm. "Go easy now, Bernard. The boy has a terrible temper and high spirits. He puts me in mind of your grandfather. Even in a wheelchair the old fella was a terror, a sight to behold, smashing his chair into the sideboard one day..."

They sauntered down the boardwalk as Ben eagerly listened to his family history, throwing a quick triumphant look at Marion when it finally came out that Gramps was his great-uncle. Marion retaliated a few minutes later, tugging at Ben's sleeve and nodding knowingly when he looked back, right after Gramps revealed that the family was "getting by" on 8,000 pounds from the combined incomes of the farm and the bed-and-breakfast boarding house and the jobs they held in Cork. And Ben had insisted that Gramps pay for nothing while he was in America. The old fella was a capitalist, directing a vast financial empire from the back of a donkey cart. Ben made a foolish face at Marion and she had to put her hand over her mouth to keep from laughing out loud.

Up ahead, Joseph and Tommy had caught up with Sean. As the three of them passed the entrance to a garishly painted concession which a barker out front was touting as the home of "the strangest sight you've ever seen," Joseph said, "Come on, don't even slow down. If Pa tries his farty stuff, ignore him or we'll never get to the Dodgems. Don't even look at the sign." Tommy didn't understand, but he obeyed. "What do you mean, Joey? What sign?" Sean slowed down and looked at the sign: "PREHISTORIC MONSTER IN CAPTIVITY."

Sean hesitated, then moved forward to rejoin Joe and Tommy as his father's voice boomed: "Boys! Boys, will you look at this. Come here a minute. Bless my soul if this isn't amazing. My good man, is that sign an highly accurate description?"

The barker stopped his weak, dreary "you won't believe your own eyes the most fantastic colossal stupendous creature in captivity" spiel to check out the rube in suit and tie and one tail of his white shirt sticking out, the only action on the beach but definitely a rube on the con.

"That's what it says, Mister."

"And what, Sir, might you charge for this mystically edifying cataclysmic experience, pray?"

"Twenty-five cents. One quarter. A-piece."

"Ben," Marion said, "Tommy and Joe have gone ahead and Sean—"

"Cheap at thrice the price. What do you say Gramps, we go in and absorb this spectacle of prehistory, this relic of the age of mastodons and pterodactyls." Gramps did not, for the first time since meeting his relatives, know what to say. Was he related to an absolute fool, a man who could have the wool pulled over his eyes in this fashion? He nodded.

"Sean," Ben called. "Come on." Sean turned back, affecting a bored, disinterested shuffle. "My good man?"

"Whuh?" the barker said. He definitely did not trust this one. Maybe the shirt tail covered a flask. One mad son-of-a-bitch could queer the act, put you out of business for days, and the summer had been bad enough. He needed all he could get. The ordinary ones screamed loud enough when they came out. You'd think they paid a hundred bucks for a command performance.

"Could you," Ben asked with a concerned frown, "ah— reassure me on one point?"

"Whatsa matter, you wanta go in or not. You got a quarter or a federal case?"

"Rest assured," Ben patted the barker's hand which he pulled away quickly. "I do have a quarter. Maybe ten. Perhaps 100. Not wishing to brag, but perhaps."

"So?"

"If I take members of my family in there, including our honored visitor from Ireland, can you guarantee their safety?"

"A dollar twenty-five," the barker said.

"There's a chill on," Gramps said, as they walked down the damp winding cement corridor to the dim interior. "A man could catch his death."

Ben surged ahead, thoroughly enjoying the faded, hastily sketched murals of dinosaurs and winged animal-birds on the thin walls. He stopped at the foot of the ramp and quickly took in the low round iron-railing fence in the far corner of the room and, suspended from a long overhead cord, a dull yellow bulb showing through ripped purple tissue paper. He threw out his arms, palms back, to halt the others. "He's gone! He's escaped. The monster is ravaging the beach, chewing up the roller coaster, rolling Dodgem cars like marbles into the sea, stomping through the roof of the frozen custard stand on his way north. Listen. Listen."

"Oh, Ben," Marion smiled briefly and glanced around to see where Margaret was.

"For Chrissakes, Pa," Sean said, stepping around Ben and walking toward the corner enclosure.

"Did the child say—" Gramps started to ask Marion who was not listening to him, but reaching for Margaret's hand.

Ben came up quickly behind Sean and shouted: "Look out! There he is, Sean. He's crouched to spring." Ben beat his chest and gave out his Tarzan yell: "Eeeeeyaaaoouwowingayaeee!," whipped a coin from his pocket and whizzed it past Sean who stood still, terror-stricken, trying to see what his father had seen. The penny flew through the iron railings, as Gramps leaped forward to pull Sean back from danger, and struck a slumbering crocodile sprawled on a dark green tarpaulin beside a plastic pool of murky water. The crocodile opened one eye and closed it, blending back into his surroundings.

On the way out Gramps put his hand on Sean's shoulder, "You're father's a terrible gas man. A terrible man entirely."

"An amazing sight," Ben reported to the barker, "ab-so-lute-ly terrifying."

"Yeh," said the barker. "You got a cigarette?"

"Do you always work the Beach?"

"Nah, I got hung up here with this goddam reptile cause my partner, my buddy, my best friend, got hung up with a broad and spent everything we made in Florida. We wuz gonna open our own animal farm, you know, for kids, with little deers and..."

Gramps and Sean walked down the boardwalk with Marion trailing them and calling back to Margaret to come along as Ben listened to the barker. "I'll wait for Daddy," Margaret called softly. "Suit yourself," Marion said. "But you'll freeze to death standing around like that." Margaret, not daring to interrupt, waited patiently for a chance to remind her father that they had a guest.

Ben spoke only to implore the barker to close up and join them for a whirl on the Dodgems. This put the barker on edge and it took Ben a few minutes to allay the man's suspicions and re-establish his own good intentions. Even Margaret grew impatient as her father encouraged the barker to push his front plate out to different positions and perform his whistling specialty. Finally she ran to catch up with the others.

www.ingramcontent.com/pod-product-compliance
Lightning Source LLC
Chambersburg PA
CBHW020416260626
47156CB00007B/2414